TUCKER'S WAY

BOOKS IN THE TUCKER SERIES

TUCKER'S WAY

David Johnson

LAKE UNION
PUBLISHING

Second edition

Text copyright © 2014 David Johnson

All rights reserved

Published by Lake Union Publishing, Seattle
www.apub.com

Amazon, the Amazon logo, and Lake Union Publishing are trademarks of Amazon.com, Inc., or its affiliates.

Cover design by Jason Blackburn

ISBN-13: 9781477827024
ISBN-10: 1477827021

Library of Congress Control Number: 2014943978

Printed in the United States of America.

I dedicate Tucker's Way *to all the people I have met in my counseling practice who have lived lives similar to Tucker's. People who, in spite of incredible odds, found a way to struggle forward, make a life for themselves, and not let their past define them. You have always been an inspiration to me.*

I.
WILDWOOD FLOWER

CHAPTER ONE

The screaming, spring-loaded hinges on Tucker's screen door announce to the world that she is coming outside. Her heavy work boots sound like a bass drum on the rough-hewn wooden planks of her porch as she marches toward one end and sits down in a weathered ladder-back chair. Reaching in the bib pocket of her overalls, she extracts a package of Red Man chewing tobacco and unfolds the pouch. Her thick fingers pinch a plug's worth of the moist tobacco leaves and insert it into her open mouth, where her tongue pushes it into her cheek.

The August sun has risen far enough that it has cleared the front eave of her roof, allowing her to look toward her barn without squinting or shading her eyes with her hand. Lying sixty yards away at the bottom of a small slope, the tired-looking barn is in stark contrast to the verdant green oaks on one side and the black-eyed Susans scattered around it. Tucker watches a mourning dove land in the loose dirt in front of the barn. Suddenly her peripheral vision detects movement at the back of the barn but not enough to be certain what it is. She watches closely, while at the same time enjoying the sweet taste of tobacco juice, her saliva having started breaking down the Red Man. Just before the mouthful of juice threatens to leak down her esophagus, Tucker turns her head to one side. Keeping her eyes on the back of the barn, she spits a brown stream off the edge of the porch.

Just then, her vigilance is rewarded as a chicken flies up in the air and travels twenty feet before dropping back to the ground.

That dadburn dog! If he don't leave them chickens alone, I'm gonna shoot him. Cupping her hands around her mouth, she yells, "Dog! Git up here t' th' house right now! Come on, I said now!"

Her call does not produce the bounding image of a handsome dog, his mouth open in a smile and his pink tongue out to the side. Instead, it brings a lanky coon dog slinking along the edge of the field toward the house, his drooping tail and ears nearly touching the ground. Instead of taking a direct route toward the house, he crosses the road farther down, then approaches the house from the side. He stops at the opposite end of the porch from where Tucker is sitting.

Tucker leans her chair back until it rests on the wall. "Dog, I know you're listenin' t' me an' I know you're standin' right there at th' corner of th' house. How many times have I done tol' you not t' bother m' chickens? Now come on up here an' take yore punishment."

Tucker's warnings and threats are met with a high-pitched whine. "Uh-huh, just like I thought. You tryin' t' hide from ol' Tucker like one of th' grandkids? Well they can't hide, an' neither can you." She claps her hands together twice. "That's yore last chance t' come on yore own before I come an' git y'."

Unable to resist his obedient, though imperfect, nature and the urging of his guilty conscience, Dog jumps up on the porch and slowly walks toward Tucker, finally belly-crawling the last six feet. When he reaches her boots, he rolls onto his back and slowly wags his tail in an act of penance.

Tucker ignores the entreaties for mercy and says in a harsh tone, "Y' been eatin' any eggs? I won't abide having a dirty, egg-suckin' dog 'round here. Like Johnny Cash sings, 'I'll stomp yore head in th' ground if y' don't stop eating m' eggs up, y' dirty ol' egg-suckin' hound.' That's one thing my ol' man never would stand fer. I seen him shoot a dog fer eatin' eggs. 'Course that don't mean nothin', 'cause I seen him kill animals just fer th' fun of killin'." Shaking her head slowly, she adds, "He was a wicked man. You're lucky it's 1974 an' I'm runnin' this place, not him."

Spitting another stream of tobacco juice, she lets her chair fall forward. The two front legs strike the porch floor with a bang and Dog, believing he's just been shot, cries out and scrambles to his feet, hoping to avoid being shot again.

Just as he is about to leap off the porch, Tucker grabs him by the collar and jerks him into a sitting position in front of her. Seeing his eyes squeezed shut in anticipation of a blow from her, she pauses. "Oh just get outta here an' mind yoreself. Next time y' might not catch me in a generous mood." She shoves him off the porch with her boot.

Dog scrambles underneath the porch, just in case Tucker changes her mind, and finds his favorite dug-out wallow where he can escape the heat of the northwest Tennessee summer by lying on the cool, moist dirt.

Standing up, Tucker turns to her left and walks to the other end of the porch and looks at the only other house within sight. The McDaniel place lies about fifty yards away. A deep gully, thick with twisting honeysuckle vines, briar-barbed blackberry vines, sweet gum saplings, and poison sumac, serves as a boundary to reinforce Tucker's solitary life.

She is just about to spit again before going back into the house when her movement is arrested by the sight of a green car appearing from around a far curve and pulling up to the front of the McDaniel house.

A tall, thin woman gets out and stands unsteadily, bracing herself with one hand on the roof of the car and the other on the open car door. After a few moments, she walks around to the back of the car and takes a couple boxes out of the trunk. Balancing one on top of the other, she makes her way to the front door of the house.

Tucker watches as the woman tries pinning the boxes between her body and the door facing while taking a key out of her pocket, but her balancing act fails and the boxes tumble, spilling their contents onto the porch.

Clumsy cow. How hard is it t' carry two boxes an' unlock a door? Besides, who is she an' what business does she have at th' McDaniel place? She better not be 'bout to move in! I knowed I shoulda snuck over there an' burned that place down when Pap McDaniel died. The fewer people they is in my life, the less chance they is of somebody takin' advantage of me.

CHAPTER TWO

Ella walks out of the bedroom of the McDaniel house and surveys the stacks of boxes on the floor. Some of them have yawning openings at the top with tongues of wrinkled newspaper used for packing dishes hanging down their sides. However, most of them are still taped shut. *I've got the rest of my life to unpack, so what's the hurry?*

She finds her CorningWare percolator and, after scrounging through some boxes, pulls out the package of Folger's coffee. After running some water into the pitcher, she spoons coffee into the basket and then sets it on one of the stove's eyes.

A sound like rumbling thunder catches her attention and she turns and looks out the front window as a school bus passes by. She walks to the window on the side of her kitchen to see the bus's destination. It slows to a stop in front of the only other house that's visible to her. The front door of the neighbor's house flies open and two boys and a small girl gallop and scamper toward the open door of the bus. The boys spring in through the door without breaking stride, but the girl has to stop and take the steps one at a time. And finally, a large person walks onto the porch and watches the bus drive off.

So you're Tucker. I've heard about you, or at least what the rumors in Dresden say about you; that you're our local Welfare Queen who dresses like a man and has a violent temper. She lets out a big sigh. *Well there's no sense in putting it off. You and I had just as well meet sooner than later, Tucker.*

Two hours later, Ella carries a warm apple pie with her and gets inside her green Ford Pinto. Looking in the rearview mirror, she adjusts her wig. She drives the short distance to Tucker's house and stops in front of it, uncertain exactly where she should park, since there are no clear signs that vehicles are ever present.

She stares in disbelief at the house. Time and weather have given it a tired, gray color. The tin roof adds varying shades of gray, tan, and brown to the palette because some of the pieces of tin are giving themselves over to the decay of rust. Tattered pieces of clear plastic held fast by staples decorate the edges of the windows, remnants of Tucker's efforts at keeping the cold out last winter.

It looks more like a house of cards than a house. She doesn't know how in the world it is standing up.

Hmm, I wonder if people think the same thing about me.

After getting out of her car with her pie in her hand, Ella walks to the front of the house and makes her way carefully up the three steps leading to the porch. She knocks twice and then takes a cautious step back.

A sound like Hessian soldiers marching in step comes from inside the house, first at a distance and then progressively louder. It dawns on Ella that it is the sound of Tucker thundering through the house, coming to answer the door. She takes in a breath and braces herself.

The door is jerked open so violently that Ella is afraid it will detach itself from its hinges. Though she has seen Tucker from a distance before, she is unprepared for the force of Tucker's presence. She is a woman, but there is nothing feminine about Tucker. She stands six feet tall, with a barrel chest, beefy arms, and large hands. Her small head seems out of place on such a large body. The thick eyeglasses that straddle her nose are so scratched up it is anyone's guess what color her eyes are or which direction she is looking. Her pants are pulled so high that the cuffs stop at her shins. Dingy, white socks stick their necks out the tops of the worn-out boots that anchor her to the floor. Her weathered face makes it difficult to be certain of her age, but Ella guesses her to be close to sixty years old, the same age as herself.

Even though Tucker hasn't uttered a word, Ella can feel that she's bristled like a porcupine ready for a fight.

"Hi, I'm Ella, your new neighbor," she says in her thin whisper of a voice. "I'm moving into the McDaniel house."

Tucker's face is a mask of indifference and she offers no reply, nor does she offer to invite Ella in.

Okay, so now what? Do we just stand here and stare at each other? Ella glances at the pie in her hand as if she's just noticed it. Giving a small laugh, she says, "I nearly forgot. This is for you. My mother used to say that good food shared makes for good neighbors." She extends the pie toward Tucker, who has remained so rigid that she seems like a statue to Ella.

Tucker does not take the offering.

Ella can't be certain, but it seems like Tucker is looking somewhere past the top of her head. Or, no: at her head. Of course. "Is it that obvious?" Ella says. She reaches up and tugs at her wig. "They told me it would look just like my real hair, but they lied. Besides, they never saw me with hair, so they don't know what I looked like."

For the first time, Tucker moves. It is a small move, just a shifting of her feet, but it encourages Ella to stay engaged in the moment with this unusual person.

"Whadda y' want?" Tucker barks.

The high-pitched tone of Tucker's voice is incongruent with the masculine image she projects. Ella is certain that most people would be rebuffed by such a harsh tone, but she doesn't shrink back. Instead she stretches her hands out again, offering the pie. Smiling, she says, "Here, I made this for you."

When Tucker again makes no move to take the pie, Ella's arms become fatigued. Seeing a chair by the side of the door, she sets the pie on the seat and says, "I'll just leave it here and you can do whatever you'd like with it."

Even in his sleep underneath the porch, Dog has gotten wind of the dessert. He jumps soundlessly onto the end of the porch and begins walking slowly toward the chair holding the pie.

Both Tucker and Ella are distracted by him, and they watch his approach.

When he gets within two feet of the chair, his tongue licks his chops. He pauses and looks up at Tucker.

"Do it and die," Tucker growls.

Recognizing the tone of voice, if not the message in the words, Dog slumps in disappointment, turns around, and heads off the porch to return to his resting place.

Ella and Tucker turn their attention back to each other and regard each other in silence.

Tucker folds her arms across her ample chest and says, "What's wrong with yore hair?"

Ella hesitates. Pride has kept her from being seen in public without her wig. *But if moving out here is to be about new beginnings and starting over, I may as well start right here with Tucker.* Reaching up, she grasps her wig and pulls it off.

For the first time since meeting Tucker, Ella sees her expression change.

Tucker's mouth drops open, and she says, "Y' ain't got no hair!"

Embarrassment turns Ella's face red, though she is certain Tucker meant nothing by her shocked exclamation. Rubbing her head from front to back, she says, "Bald as a billiard ball, that's me."

"Well I ain't never!" Tucker replies, and without another word, she shuts the door in Ella's face.

Before Ella can react, the door reopens. Tucker reaches for the pie on the chair and takes it inside.

CHAPTER THREE

Standing in the middle of her living room, holding the pie Ella just brought, Tucker stares at her closed front door. Her heart is beating rapidly and fear is peeking out from a distant corner of her mind.

I shoulda slammed th' door in 'er face as soon as she tol' me who she was. How was I t' know it was gonna be her? Th' onliest people who ever comes callin' on me is people causin' trouble, like th' law or th' welfare people. Who does this Ella person think she is comin' bargin' in like she did?

A wisp of memory comes floating into her consciousness. It is the memory of her mother. *I think what shook me up th' most is that she reminded me of my mama. Bein' tall, nearly as tall as me, an' her purty green eyes was just like Mama's. Mama was thin, too, but not as thin as Ella. Lord, she looked like she might be knocked down if Dog's waggin' tail hit 'er. 'Course, Mama was tanned in th' summer from workin' outside.*

Like pictures in a photo album, Tucker sees her mother hanging white sheets on the clothesline, two or three clothespins sticking out of her mouth waiting to be chosen for their assigned garments; then a picture of her mother laying out a row in their garden with a hoe; and another of her straightening up from being bent in half while picking peas, one hand on the small of her back.

I don't know nothin' 'bout Ella, but she for sure ain't never worked outside. She was nearly as pale as milk, an' I didn't see no calluses on 'er hands.

An' what's wrong with her that she ain't got no hair?! I ain't never seen a grown woman without no hair. I thought that only happened t' men. She's prob'ly got some kind of disease that's catchin'.

She looks down at the pie in her hand. *Why would she give me a pie? Th' onliest people that ever brings food t' me is them church people at Christmas, an' they're only tryin' to soothe their consciences fer not carin' 'bout poor folks th' other three hundred sixty-four days of th' year.*

Walking into her kitchen with its cardboard lined walls, Tucker sets the pie on her Formica dining table. Leaning back against the countertop, she stares absentmindedly at the pie. More memories, the ones she tries to keep locked away, are seeping out.

She is six years old and staring at her mama's freshly baked pie cooling in the open window over the kitchen sink. The smell of apples and cinnamon permeate the air. Her mother is busy washing the dishes when the back door swings open and her father walks in.

"What's that smell?!" he demands.

Tucker pretends to make herself very small in her mind and tries to stop breathing, hoping she won't be noticed.

Her startled mother turns away from the sink with suds on her hands. "It's an apple pie," she says meekly. "Is there something wrong? I thought you were going to plant corn today."

"Quit dripping suds everywhere! Don't be so stupid. You kill me sometimes. I thought I better make a surprise visit. I knew you was thinking I'd be in the field today, so I figured while the cat's away the mice might play. It appears I was right." Pointing at the pie, he asks, "So who's the pie for? Your newest boyfriend?"

Turning pale, Tucker's mother replies, "I made it for you. I don't have a boyfriend. How many times do I have to tell you that?"

As he walks toward his wife, he notices Tucker sitting in a chair at the table and slaps her on the back of the head. "You tell me what's going on, Tucker. Who's your mama expecting to come by this morning? Huh? Who's she been screwing?"

The memory of her father's visit to her bedroom last night is still raw and the pain between her legs almost unbearable. The last thing he said before leaving her bed was, "You tell anybody what happened and I'll kill and gut your mother in front of you, then I'll kill you and no one will ever find your body."

With immense effort, Tucker shakes herself loose from the scene and takes a deep breath in her kitchen.

Maybe I scared m'self with Ella, 'cause fer a second I thought 'bout askin' 'er t' come in. She didn't seem like she wanted nothin'. Sure didn't ask fer nothin'. But m' rule has always been, don't let nobody inside th' house unless'n they got court papers sayin' they can. People can't be trusted. They's all out t' git y' an' is only interested in themselves.

Turning around, she looks out her kitchen window toward the McDaniel house and sees Ella getting out of her car and going inside. *Who is she, an' where is she from?*

All of a sudden Tucker makes a decision. Going out the back door she walks around to the side of the house, where there are two large, tin-covered, hinged doors on the ground. She grabs the handle of one and pulls it open until it rests on the ground, then does the same with the other door. Carefully, she walks down the steps into the dark cellar.

After a few minutes, she steps back out into the sunshine with a half-full tow sack slung over her shoulder. She sets the sack down so she can close the doors, then picks the sack back up. She lumbers around her house, through the front yard, and onto the gravel road leading to Ella's.

On the way, she notices a bluebird sitting on a wooden fence post and hears a meadowlark's song. The bright "bob white" call of a quail comes from off in the distance. Occasionally a large summer grasshopper flies from the ditch on one side of the road to the ditch on the other side, perhaps trying to escape an approaching lizard or snake. A breeze rattles the dried leaves on corn stalks as she passes by.

By the time she is standing in the road staring at Ella's house, she is a little out of breath and has worked up a sweat. *I must be outta m' mind comin' down here. I don't know what I was thinkin'.*

Turning around she retreats a couple of steps toward her house, then stops and turns back around to look at Ella's house. *Y' done come this far, woman. What are y' afraid of? She ain't gonna bite y'.*

Slowly she steps toward the house. Once she's on the porch, she lifts her fist to knock on the door, but hesitates. Finally she takes the tow sack off her shoulder and drops it in front of the door. Then she turns and starts walking away.

She's barely gotten off the porch when she hears the front door open behind her.

Ella calls out, "Can I help you?"

Tucker slowly pivots and points to the tow sack by the door. "I brung y' some turnips."

Ella's eyes grow wide. "Well, thank you."

As they stand facing each other, Tucker's composed expression belies her racing heart. Every instinct tells her to run home to her safe castle.

"Do you want to come in?" Ella asks.

Tucker retreats a couple of steps. "Uh, no, no. I jes' wanted t' say thank y' fer th' pie." Without another word, she turns and walks away.

CHAPTER FOUR

Ella watches the retreating hulk of Tucker, but before she takes three steps into the yard Ella calls out, "Tucker, wait! Please."

Tucker stops and turns around to see what she wants.

"Won't you at least sit with me on the porch for a little bit? I'll fix us a glass of tea or a cup of coffee. I dread what's facing me inside, unpacking all those boxes, and really don't feel like doing it. Please, come join me."

Tucker blinks her eyes rapidly, trying to sort through the thoughts bombarding her and their opposing messages: *Look out! Quit being afraid! Don't trust! Take a chance!* After a moment, she says, "I guess I could sit fer a little spell. My chores'll wait."

"Wonderful," Ella says. "Let me drag a couple of chairs out on the porch for us." She disappears inside and grabs a dining chair, but when she tries to lift it, her knees buckle and she stumbles. *Oh good grief! This is pitiful! I'm so sick of being weak!* She straightens back up and, grabbing the chair by the top rail, begins dragging it across the floor toward the front door.

When she goes through the door, the chair legs bounce and bang their way across the threshold and onto the porch.

Seeing Ella's struggles with the chair, Tucker says, "Here, let me help y'." She grabs the chair, lifts it easily and deposits it on one side of the porch. "Where's y' other chair? I'll git it fer y'."

"Thank you. Just look anywhere inside. It doesn't matter which one you bring out. I'll have to buy some porch furniture later."

After Tucker returns with another chair, Ella asks, "What would you like to drink? Tea? Coffee? Water?"

"I'll take a glass of water."

Ella goes back inside the house and makes her way to the kitchen. She finds a couple of unmatched glasses, opens the freezer, and puts ice in them. As she pours water into the glasses, she thinks about her guest outside. She is struck by the realization that she has never had a poor person as a next-door neighbor. As a matter of fact, the only poor person she has ever truly known was Camellia, the black maid who worked for her parents for over fifty years. *And oh, did I love Camellia! But did I truly know her?* She never saw where Camellia lived or asked about her family. She supposes that, growing up, she'd been more interested in herself.

When she returns to the porch, she hands Tucker a glass. *My goodness! Her hands make that glass looks like a child's cup.*

Tucker turns up the glass and empties it in three gulps. The little bit of water that escapes her mouth she takes care of by swiping it with her sleeve. "Don't nothin' quench y' thirst like plain ol' water."

Ella takes a sip of her water and nods her head in agreement. She sifts through possible topics she could bring up to start a conversation with Tucker, but discards them all as inappropriate. A thought dawns on her and she is just about to speak when Tucker says, "How come y' ain't got no hair?"

Ella smiles. "I get the impression that you pretty much say whatever is on your mind."

"What's wrong with that?" Tucker says with a bit of an edge in her tone.

"Nothing, nothing. I didn't mean anything by it. It's just that most people are so careful about what they say that you sometimes can't be sure when they are being honest and when they aren't. Anyway, I lost my hair as a result of chemotherapy."

Tucker stares at her in stony silence, her face revealing nothing.

"Do you know what chemotherapy is?" Ella asks.

"I heared th' word b'fore."

"It's what they use now to treat cancer. It's sort of like putting poison in your body with the hopes it will kill the cancer but leave you alive, barely alive. One of the side effects is that all your hair usually falls out. I had breast cancer."

"You done had cancer? And you's still alive? I thought cancer killed folks."

"Oftentimes it does, but these new drugs are turning the tide in some cases. I'm alive today and that's all that matters."

Tucker looks at Ella's chest. Ella keeps her gaze on Tucker. "They had to remove both of them."

"You mean they cut 'em off? Well my lord . . ."

Ella feels the grind of trying to make conversation with Tucker exhausting.

Tucker points at Ella's bandaged index finger. "What'dja do t' yore finger?"

Ella looks down and says, "Oh it's nothing. I cut it last night when I was trying to cut open one of my boxes."

"Did y' put anything on it?"

"I would have, but I couldn't find the box with all my bathroom stuff. I'm pretty sure that's where I packed my antibiotic ointment. So I just put some tissue around it and put a piece of tape on it to hold it in place."

"Y' got any turpentine?"

"Turpentine?"

"Yeah, turpentine. Or coal oil or kerosene."

Confused, Ella says, "No I don't. But why—"

Suddenly Tucker stands up, leaves the porch and starts walking toward her house.

Ella shakes her head in bewilderment. *I give up. Let her go back home.* Maybe the woman is as crazy as everyone says she is.

Still not wanting to go back inside to the arduous task of unpacking, she watches Tucker disappear into her tired-looking house. In less than a minute, she comes back outside and begins walking toward Ella's. *What in the world?*

In a few minutes, Tucker, red faced and huffing and puffing, approaches Ella's front porch carrying something in her hand. Walking up to Ella, she says, "Here's wha'ch'y' need."

Ella takes the offered can and looks at the label. "Turpentine?"

Tucker takes the can back and grips Ella's hand. "Come over here t' th' side of th' porch so's we don't spill nothin' on th' floor."

Ella has thoughts of resisting Tucker's firm pull, but her curiosity overrules her reticence and she follows.

With no attempt at being gentle, and without asking permission, Tucker jerks the tape and bandage off.

Ella winces silently.

"Good thing y' let me look at it. It's one of them kind that can git real sore sometimes." Tucker shakes the liquid contents of the can. "That's what this here is good fer." Taking the cap off she begins bathing Ella's wound.

Ella winces and looks upward. *If only my mother could see me now. Dear Lord, I need a little mercy here. Please don't let me have won the battle over cancer only to be killed by this country woman's cure for a tiny cut.*

Apparently satisfied with her job, Tucker says, "Now then, that ought t' be better by mornin'."

The women resume their places on their chairs. Tucker looks at Ella expectantly, as if she is waiting for Ella to direct the conversation.

Feeling like she's the captain of a sailing vessel that has to keep tacking back and forth in order to catch an ever-shifting breeze, Ella decides to make one last effort at finding something that will sustain their conversation. "Didn't I see a school bus at your house this morning?"

"Yep," Tucker replies, but offers no elaboration.

"So you have children at home?"

"Lord, no. My daughter's kids live with me."

"Oh," Ella says thoughtfully.

"Yeah. I've had 'em most nearly all their lives. She pops 'em out, but they end up livin' with me."

"You're raising three young children? On your own? Oh my goodness, I can't imagine how hard that is. How do you do it?"

Tucker's eyes blink rapidly. She cocks her head a bit to one side and shrugs her shoulders. "I don't think nothin' 'bout it. I just do what I gotta do. That's the way I've always done."

Pleased that she has finally found something that Tucker seems willing to discuss, Ella keeps things rolling by saying, "I guess maybe they are a help to you, taking care of your animals."

"Them boys is pretty good at chores, if I stay after 'em. But little April . . ." Tucker's voice drifts off.

After a few moments of silence, Ella prompts Tucker. "April?"

Tucker answers thoughtfully, "She don't talk. Ain't never said a word. In six years I ain't never heard a peep outta her. Them teachers says she's retarded. But she ain't. I watch 'er close and can tell she's smart. I seen 'er readin' 'er brother's books, movin' 'er lips, an' callin' words to herself. No sir, she ain't retarded." Her voice cracks a bit and her eyes have reddened.

Ella is touched by this subtle crack in Tucker's turtle-shell facade. "You really love her, don't you?" she says softly.

A solitary tear slips from the corner of Tucker's eye and rolls down her rounded cheek.

Just then, the mail carrier turns into Ella's driveway and pulls up to the house.

"Hey Tucker," he calls out as he exits his vehicle.

Tucker clears her throat and wipes at her eyes. "Howdy, Ted."

With some letters in his hand, he approaches the porch. Looking at Ella, he says, "Mrs. McDade?"

"Yes, that's me," Ella says.

"Nice to meet you, ma'am. I was told you would be on my route now. I'll hand these to you today, but from now on you'll have to walk out to your mailbox to get your mail. I just wanted to say hi." Turning around, Ted returns to his car, and drives off.

Ella is looking at her mail and doesn't notice Tucker's reddening face.

"Yore name's McDade?" Tucker asks loudly.

Startled by Tucker's dramatic tone, she cautiously says, "Yes."

Tucker stands up. Her normally high-pitched voice hits another octave as she says, "Do you know Judge Jack McDade?!"

"Uh, yes, he's my husband. I mean—"

Before Ella can finish, Tucker grabs her glass from off the floor and throws it against the side of the house. The glass explodes, sending shards of glass and ice cubes across the porch. "That man is my swore enemy!"

Tucker stomps toward the steps, then pauses and turns around. Walking back toward the front door, she reaches down and picks up the tow sack she'd brought to Ella earlier. "Gimme my turnips back!"

And for the second time today, Ella finds herself staring in bewilderment as Tucker storms away from her house.

CHAPTER FIVE

Looking down at the gravel road, Tucker stomps so hard that her cheeks jiggle in rhythm to her heavy steps as she heads to her house. *The wife of Judge Jack McDade! I can't b'lieve I was s' stupid t' trust her an' talk t' her 'bout m'self. An' what business has she got movin' out here in th' first place? Prob'ly sent by Judge Jack t' spy on me, or somethin' like that. Who knows if her story 'bout cancer is even true, or if anything she said is true? I oughta go back an' punch 'er in th' face. But I ain't gonna waste th' time or th' effort t' turn 'round an' go back.*

When she finally begins slowing her pace, she looks up and notices a dark cloud coming from the southwest and hears a low rumbling in the distance. *Good, maybe a summer shower'll cool things off some, an' cool me off some, too. Ella McDade! I'll bet that pie she left me has somethin' in it that'll make me sick, maybe even got poison in it. I don't put nothin' past a McDade.*

A solitary drop of rain strikes her on the forehead. She stops and looks up. That lonely drop was apparently sent down to prime the air, because now Tucker can see it is thick with tiny drops of rain heading toward the summer-baked earth around her. In a matter of seconds her face is peppered with the stinging droplets.

The combination of her anger and the rain on her face opens the vault on a memory and Tucker is no longer in the present.

Lying on her back on the ground, rain stings Tucker's face as she looks up into the dark night sky. She is only vaguely aware of the tinny sound of the metal fasteners on her father's overalls as he loosens them. His rough hands push her legs apart. As he lowers his body onto hers, it becomes difficult for her to draw a breath. The smell of his whiskey-saturated breath is mixed with the smell of horses, cows, hogs, manure, hay, sweet feed, and mud.

She has the strange sensation of looking down at what is happening, like a spectator at a play in school.

The grunting of her father as he lies on top of her reminds her of their farm animals during breeding. She uses a trick she learned years ago and shuts off all feeling in her body. It's as if her body doesn't exist.

With her body disconnected from what's happening, she now lets her mind go someplace else and tries to remember the first time something like this happened. But she is unable to find a point in her memory when this wasn't a regular part of her life.

The routine is as familiar to her as breathing. After supper her father says, "Tucker, come with me to go check the animals."

Excuses that used to pour from her mouth when she was younger have long since fallen silent. They are but memories of the futile cries of a voice long forgotten.

One night, while helping her mother wash dishes, Tucker found the courage to tell her what was happening. "Mama, when Daddy makes me go with him to see 'bout th' animals after supper, that's not what he really means. He takes me an' does things to me, touches me in places he's not supposed to. And it hurts, Mama."

The suddenness and viciousness of her mother's response caught even Tucker's catlike reflexes off guard. She swung one of their dinner plates, shattering it against the side of Tucker's head. Shards scattered across the linoleum floor.

"You little tramp! You slut! If you ever say anything like that again, I'll pack your things and throw you out!"

Now as she waits for her father to finish his business with her, lightning flashes and Tucker sees something shiny lying on the ground to her right. She turns her head and blinks the rain from her eyes. She squints but in the pitch dark sees nothing.

Another finger of lightning jumps from the dark sky and seems to point directly to the shiny object. In the flash of light Tucker recognizes her father's hatchet. Usually reserved for cutting kindling or killing snakes, it has fallen from its worn scabbard. Her father is presently so preoccupied with wielding a different tool, the one that has severed Tucker's soul from her body, that he is unaware of the loss of his hatchet and of its new, potentially threatening position.

Hope, having been buried long ago by Tucker, awakens in the mausoleum of her heart, raises its head and sits up. *Is it possible that t'night, on m' sixteenth birthday, I will finally put an end t' this nightmare?* As slowly as a cat sneaking up on its prey, she frees her right arm from beneath her father. When there is no change in his rhythmic grunting, she reaches for the hatchet, but only manages to come up with a handful of mud.

A blaring horn jolts Tucker back into the present. She is standing in the middle of the gravel road, drenched from the pouring rain. She turns around to see the children's school bus stopped within fifteen feet of her. Through the windshield she can see children pointing at her and laughing, while the driver motions for her to get out of the way.

Tucker takes a few steps to the side of the road.

The bus's engine races and when the driver lets out on the clutch the yellow behemoth plows forward through the rain and the muddied road.

Tucker follows in the bus's wake, plodding deliberately toward her house and her soon-to-be-deposited grandchildren, August, March, and April. *I wonder what kind of trouble them kids have been into at school t'day.*

The bus is gone and the children are already inside as she walks up onto her porch and stomps her feet to remove the loose mud from her boots. Then she opens the screen door and goes inside. Stepping into the kitchen she sees the children sitting at the dining table and staring at Ella's apple pie lying untouched in the center of the table.

"You kids keep yore hands off'n that there pie, an' I mean it. I ain't so sure it ain't been poisoned."

They look at her wide-eyed, realizing they could have succumbed like Sleeping Beauty if they'd eaten any of the delicious-looking pie.

"How come you were standing in the middle of the road in the pouring rain?" August asks.

Tucker goes to the refrigerator and takes out a half-gallon carton of milk. "Whose business is it why I do what I do? If I want t' stand buck naked in th' pasture, that's my business."

March bursts into maniacal laughter. When he gets his breath, he howls, "Oh my gosh—buck naked?!"

August ignores his little brother. "Everybody on the bus was making fun of you and laughing at you. They said you're crazy. Then they point and laugh at us because we're kin."

Setting three glasses on the table, Tucker pours milk into each one and then hands them to the children. "That's 'cause people is cruel an' they like t' hurt other people. People make fun of us 'cause we're poor. An' they make fun of you, August, 'cause yore daddy is black, don't they?"

August sets his empty glass down and tries to lick the lingering white moustache off his upper lip. "Yes ma'am they do," he says with a sad tone.

Tucker points to the ceiling. "You kids hear that rain outside?"

They all look up, nodding.

"But do y' feel any rain on y' inside here?"

Looking at her, they shake their heads in unison.

"An' how come that is?"

"Because we got a roof?" March asks.

"For certain we do," Tucker replies, "but what's on top of that roof?"

"It's got tin nailed on top of it," August answers thoughtfully.

"Exactly, and that's what all ya'll have gotta do t' yore hearts. Y' gotta wrap yoreselves in armor so that nobody can't touch y' with their hurtful words. Y' gotta be hard an' tough like me. Y' think it bothers me what people say 'bout me? I wouldn't take th' time t' spit on 'em. That's th' kind of attitude y' gotta have t' git by in this harsh world. Take m' word fer it."

Their young minds try to sift through the truckload of Tucker's truth that has been dumped on them. The effort causes them to bump into other truths they can't make sense of.

March asks, "How come August's daddy was black and mine and April's wasn't?"

Sighing, Tucker sits down at the end of the table. "All ya'll have got different daddies. Th' answer t' th' why of that is simple. Ya'll's mama, Maisy, is a whore."

August claps his hands over his ears and says, "Stop saying that!"

"That's not true!" March exclaims.

April's eyes blink rapidly at the explosion from her brothers, but she remains silent.

"I'm sorry, but there ain't no other way t' say it. Yore mama uses men fer money an' men use her fer whatever they want. Why do ya'll think y' ended up livin' with me? 'Cause she's more interested in herself than in ya'll."

Jumping to his feet, March says, "She's just waiting until she has her own place so we can go live with her. She told us last time we saw her that she was going to get married and we'd have a big house, so big that we would all have our own room." As he finishes, tears of anger, defiance, and hurt begin to trickle down his cheeks.

Tucker looks at August. "You's the oldest. Have y' ever heard promises like that from yore mama before?"

Recognizing the trap his grandmother has laid for him, August sidesteps her question and says, "But this time it'll be different, I know it will. Mama's going to change. You wait and see."

"I give up on that a long time ago," Tucker says, "an' th' sooner ya'll give up on it, th' better off you'll be. But don't none of that matter at th' moment. What matters right now is that th' chores need t' be taken care of an' I need t' start cookin' supper. So ever'body git up an' git busy."

CHAPTER SIX

Fighting demons in her dreams, Tucker thrashes in her bed. She awakes with a jerk and throws off her sweat-soaked sheets. Her breathing and her heart rate have clasped hands with each other and are running out of control down a steep hill.

Tucker sits up and swings her legs over the side of her bed, trying to orient herself to time and place. Looking down at her trembling right hand, she is surprised to see it gripped tightly around the pistol she has slept with every night for over forty years. She slips it back under her pillow and, using the bedpost to steady herself, stands up.

Her calloused feet sound like sandpaper on the gritty floor as she shuffles into the kitchen. Holding on to the sink, she shakes her head, trying to dislodge the lingering memory of her dream.

After drinking some water, Tucker walks to the front door, which stands open during the hot summer nights. She pushes open the screen door, its spring complaining about being awakened from sleep, and walks over to the porch swing. Bending her knees, she lowers herself as far as she can and then falls the last eight inches, as gravity takes over. She lands in the swing with a loud "Oomph!" The chains of the swing clank against each other, then quiet.

Drawing in a fresh breath of the night air, she lets it out slowly. She identifies the sounds that reach her, one at a time: *Them's crickets all 'round in th' yard; that's a tree frog in the oak tree; there goes the chuck-will's-widow singing like there ain't gonna be a t'morrow; that ol' screech owl sounds like a woman screamin'; sounds like somebody's huntin' coons way off in th' bottoms somewhere, them coon dogs is really tellin' it.*

Then from inside the house, she hears the sounds of someone coming down the stairs. She listens closely to see if she can identify which one it is. The lightness of the steps convinces her it is April who is up. In a moment the sound of the back screen door slamming shut tells Tucker that April is headed to the outhouse.

A few minutes later, the soft footfalls return and April cautiously opens the front screen door. Her blonde hair is a mass of tangles that hangs in her eyes. She casts looks in every direction, though the darkness of night makes it difficult for her to tell the difference between an object and its more frightening shadow. Looking toward the swing, she freezes.

"Come here, child," Tucker says.

April pads across the porch and crawls into Tucker's ample lap. Facing Tucker, she lays her head on her chest.

"You're up mighty early. Bad dream?" Though Tucker doesn't expect an answer, that has never prevented her from talking to April. "I don't care what nobody says. You'll talk t' me whenever y' git ready to, when y' think y' got somethin' worth sayin'. I ain't worried 'bout it."

Tucker lays one hand on the side of April's head and begins swinging slow and easy.

Perhaps it's the effects from her earlier nightmares, both sleeping and waking, but Tucker's thoughts keep drifting backward in time. *I don't know how come I never spent no time like this with Maisy when she was little. Seemed like I was always too busy in the spring trying to put out a garden an' a crop. During the summer I had t' put up hay an' can vegetables fer winter. Come fall I had t' make sure there was enough firewood t' last us fer th' winter. An' during winter I had t' keep the animals fed an' watered.*

She shakes her head and sighs. April's head rises and falls with her chest, but she has already gone back to sleep.

Bein' a momma at sixteen years old an' not havin' nobody t' help me with her, it's a wonder I didn't kill 'er just out of ignorance. What did I know 'bout bein' a mama? I didn't know nothin'. I never got no raisin' so I just done th' best I could.

Maybe if I'd a done a better job of raisin' 'er, Maisy might've turned out completely different. I let 'er spend way too much time alone. I should've done like th' Indians used to an' strapped her t' my back an' taken 'er to th' field with me. I see that now, an' I hate m'self fer it.

She gently strokes April's hair and pats her on the back. Tightness squeezes her chest and a wave of sadness with an undertow of regret sweeps over her.

But damn it, that still ain't no excuse fer Maisy turnin' out like she has! Usin' th' past as an excuse fer actin' a fool is what you'd expect a child to do, not a grown woman. I ain't as good a person as I ought t' be, but I sure ain't as bad a person as I might have been, 'specially when y' look at how I was raised.

I don't even like t' be around her no more. I'm tired of her hurtin' these kids, tearin' their hearts out of 'em with her empty promises. One of these days she's gonna say th' wrong thing an' I'm gonna tie into her like she ain't never had nobody do. An' Lord help me when I do, 'cause there ain't no tellin' how far I'm liable t' go.

She rests her head on top of April's and after a few minutes the swing stops moving.

Later, just as the dark night sky begins giving way to the muted grays of dawn, something causes Tucker to wake up. She looks around and realizes it was the sound of a car on the gravel road.

Headlights of an approaching vehicle snap her to attention. The relaxed, private moment with April has dissolved.

The headlights zigzag across the road like the cane of a blind person. Tucker makes two quick assessments: the driver is drunk, and—as though beckoned by Tucker's own bitter thoughts of her before dozing off—the driver is her daughter, Maisy.

CHAPTER SEVEN

Headlights sweep the porch and blind Tucker as the car rolls to a stop in her yard.

Putting her hand in front of her eyes, Tucker sees the door open as the engine stops and the lights are extinguished.

Stepping from the Cadillac Deville, Maisy calls out, "Is that you, Mama?"

Tucker clenches her jaw and squeezes her fists, but remains silent. April stirs in her lap.

Maisy, dressed in tight pants and an even tighter stretch top, takes exaggerated and irregular steps through the litter-strewn yard, somehow avoiding old truck tires, a claw-foot bathtub, and a twelve-inch, single-bottom plow. She's a picture—wildly curvaceous, her thick, raven hair brushing her round shoulders. Even the sun hastens its ascent so it can peek over the horizon to get a better look at this dark-featured beauty.

At the first step of the porch Maisy stumbles, the effects of the alcohol finally catching up with her.

Just like her daddy used t' do.

Holding the rail to steady herself, Maisy squints in the early morning light and scans the porch. Upon seeing Tucker and April in the porch swing, she cries out, "My baby, April!" Her high heels hammer across the porch as she moves to the swing.

Sitting upright, April rubs her eyes.

Maisy snatches her up and swings her wildly around. "How's my April? Whacha been up to? Mama come to pay you a visit."

Maisy stops spinning and looks more closely at April. April shows no expression and makes no sound.

"Aren't you happy to see me?" Frowning, Maisy turns to Tucker. "Is she still not talking?"

As if discovering she's holding a container of spoiled milk, Maisy drops April to the porch. "She must be retarded, like the teachers say."

April crawls to the swing and takes hold of the thick calf of Tucker's leg.

Turning toward the front door, Maisy calls loudly through the screen, "Where are my other babies? Where's my boys? Wake up and come see your mama."

August and March come trotting down the stairs and scamper to the door. In chorus they cry, "Mama!"

Maisy opens the door and throws open her arms. In spite of not having seen her in three months, and having heard Tucker's warnings earlier, the boys embrace the false security their mother's arms offer. August hugs her neck and March wraps his arms around her waist.

Questions fall out of their mouths like water over a cliff, unstoppable.

"What did you bring me?"

"Where you been, Mama?"

"When are you gonna come live with us?"

"Are you gonna take us home with you?"

"Where do you live?"

Throwing back her head and laughing, Maisy appears unaffected by their pleading tones.

Though Tucker's agitation is rising, she is also helpless to stop another memory from stirring.

She came home from school one day and found her house empty. Though her father was seldom home during the daytime, her mother was always present.

Tucker went from living room to kitchen to her parents' bedroom looking for her mother before she noticed her mother's ever-present hairbrush was missing from the dresser. She opened the drawers slowly, and their emptiness mimicked the empty feeling growing within her.

Though only twelve, Tucker had already learned the lesson that tears were useless. She went outside and sat on the porch steps, hoping for her mother's return.

That evening when her father came home, he stated simply, "Your sorry mam has run off. It's up to you to take care of things around here now."

At first her mother would come around every few weeks. At each visit Tucker's heart would soar on wings of hope that her mother was coming home for good or that she would take Tucker away with her. Promises fell from her mother's lips as carelessly as a cigarette smoker flipping aside an extinguished butt. And they were just as useless.

Tucker turns her attention to the scene on her porch with Maisy and the children and anger begins boiling within her. *They ain't learned th' hard lesson that I learned, an' it's gonna break their heart when they do. I'm gittin' tired of sittin' by an' watchin' it happen.*

Maisy sits on the porch, resting her feet on the steps, with August and March on each side of her. "I'm going to come get you real soon," she says. "My boyfriend and I are going to get married.

34

He's got all kinds of money. We'll have a big ol' house filled with all kinds of toys for you boys. Don't that sound nice?"

Tucker stops the swing. "Quit promisin' thangs you ain't gonna do and gittin' these kids all stirred up! Why don't y' jes' tell 'em th' truth? You're a tramp an' a whore. An' no man's gonna marry you. Why should they, when they git what they want without a marriage license?"

Jumping to her feet, Maisy faces Tucker. The full light of dawn reveals her face twisted in rage.

April releases her grip on Tucker and scampers to her brothers. They all clutch each other as the inevitable storm erupts.

"And what do you give these kids?!" Maisy shoots back. "An outhouse, a front yard that looks like Pete's Junk Yard, and a house that looks like the next gust of wind is going to blow it down! They even smell bad! Don't you ever give them a bath?!"

Tucker thunders to her feet, leaving the porch swing dancing on its chains. She closes the distance between herself and Maisy in three steps, and they stand facing each other eye-to-eye.

Quickly as a snake striking its prey, Tucker slaps Maisy.

"You sorry piece of white trash." Tucker's tone drips with disgust as Maisy bends at the waist from the blow. "If'n you're such a good mama, then why did the state take yore kids from you and give 'em t' me? How sorry a mother do y' have t' be fer th' state to take yore kids away?"

Maisy recovers and swings for Tucker's head, but Tucker is expecting it and catches her hand.

August yells, "Stop! Stop! Don't hurt my mama!" He runs into the fray and pushes Tucker, knocking her off balance.

Refusing to release her grip on Maisy, Tucker falls to the porch floor, pulling Maisy down with her. She uses her weight advantage and pins Maisy facedown.

Profanity spews from Maisy like lava from a volcano.

35

Tucker puts her mouth an inch from Maisy's ear and says, "I should've kilt you when I could've. It would've saved the world a lot of grief."

Suddenly August and March are pulling at Tucker and yelling. "Stop it! Get up! You're hurting her!"

Tucker rolls off Maisy and they both get to their feet.

Maisy straightens her clothes and pushes her hair out of her face. "Old woman, you're crazy," she says to Tucker.

Opening her mouth to respond, Tucker sees April over Maisy's shoulder. Sitting alone, her face is wet with tears and her mouth is open, but no sound is heard.

Tucker pushes roughly past Maisy. Picking up April, she says, "You boys git t' yore chores. The school bus'll be 'ere in a bit."

To Maisy she says, "You've caused enough trouble. Now git!"

Tucker hands April to August as the boys go through the front door to get dressed.

As the door slaps shut behind them, Maisy looks intently at Tucker and says, "Why do you hate me?"

Tucker folds her arms across her chest and says nothing.

Maisy's eyes flash. "Answer me! Why do you hate me?! You've always hated me! Is it because my dad got you pregnant and then run off? And you had to raise me by yourself? Is that it? All I remember growing up is you and me. Nobody else."

Drawing a deep breath, Tucker says, "Shut up. You don't know nothin' 'bout it."

"I don't know nothing because you never told me nothing. Every time I tried to bring it up, you brushed me off. I don't even know who my daddy is!"

Through clenched teeth, Tucker replies, "And you never will."

Tucker turns and goes into the house without saying another word.

Shaking her dark locks, Maisy shouts through the screen door, "Old woman, you are impossible! What's the point?!" She makes her way off the porch and into her car.

Inside the house, Tucker listens as Maisy sprays gravel while speeding off.

She hollers, "You kids hurry up with them chores! Yore oatmeal'll be ready soon."

CHAPTER EIGHT

Two hours after her fight with Maisy, Tucker hears the approaching school bus. "All right, you kids," she hollers up the stairs, "ya'll's bus is comin'. Git down here now." She claps her hands twice for emphasis.

March scampers down the stairs and runs toward the front door.

"Hold it right there!" Tucker snaps.

March skids to a stop.

"Turn 'round here an' let me look atcha."

Stuffing his shirttail into his jeans as he turns, March furrows his brow and pooches out his bottom lip. After turning 360 degrees, he faces Tucker.

"Now that's more like it," she says. "All y' need t' do now is get that 'I'm mad at th' world' expression off'n yore face."

Slowly, March lets the muscles in his face relax, but he does not smile.

"Good enough," Tucker says. "Head on out t' th' road an' wait fer th' bus. Tell th' driver that August an' April is comin'."

March bursts through the screen door, jumps off the porch, and runs full tilt toward the road. Just as he gets there, the bus rolls to a stop in front of him.

Tucker turns her attention to the stairs again and is just about to holler another warning when August starts down the stairs holding April's hand.

"Come on you two," Tucker admonishes them. "That bus ain't gonna wait ferever."

August reaches down and carries April down the last few steps. When he sets her down, he grabs her hand and starts pulling her. "Run, April. You know you don't want to be late for the bus." He hastens through the screen door, halfway dragging April with him.

Tucker stands looking through the screen door until August and April get on the bus, then returns to her kitchen. Once again she notices Ella's apple pie sitting in the middle of her table, staring at her like the eye of a cyclops. *I don't know what in th' world I'm gonna do with that pie. If it is poison, I can't give it t' Dog t' get rid of it. I could bury it. But what if it ain't poison? That'd be a waste of a good pie.*

Walking to the sink, she looks through the window toward the McDaniel house. *What I can't figure out is why the wife of Judge Jack would be movin' into the McDaniel place. That don't make no sense. There's more t' Ella's story than she's tol', that's fer sure.*

She's about to plunge her hands into the soapy water where the breakfast dishes are lying when there are two hard raps on her front door.

Who in th' world?

She stomps toward the door. When she gets there, she finds Ella facing her from the other side of the screen. Tucker notices Ella's car behind her with the motor still running.

Tucker is about to issue a challenge when Ella says, "Ex-husband. That's what I should have said. Judge Jack is my ex-husband. I just wanted to get that fact set straight." Without waiting for a response from Tucker, she turns and heads down the stairs, back to her car.

Tucker puts her hand on the door and pauses. When Ella opens her car door, Tucker pushes her screen door open and calls out, "Y' mean ya'll's divorced?"

Ella stands in the opening of her car door and looks at Tucker. "Yes, we're divorced." She continues standing, waiting to see if Tucker has anything else to say. After a moment of silence, she sighs and starts to get inside her car.

Walking out onto her porch, Tucker says, "Now hold on a minute. Don't go rushin' off. Seems like I might've judged you wrong. Why don't you come on back up here an' tell me what happened?"

Smiling, Ella turns off the motor, shuts her car door, and makes her way back onto Tucker's porch.

Tucker shifts awkwardly, unsure how to proceed. "Uh, I guess y' could sit yonder in th' porch swing an' I could sit in th' chair so's you can tell me yore story."

Ella lowers herself into the swing and gives a push with her feet. "There's nothing more relaxing than a swing, is there?"

"I ain't never thought 'bout it," Tucker replies. Reaching inside her hip pocket she pulls out her package of chewing tobacco.

"You know that's a nasty habit, don't you?" Ella says.

"I don't recall askin' you what y' thought 'bout it."

Keeping her tone even, Ella says, "All the same, it's a nasty habit."

Tucker looks at the package and then holds it out toward Ella. "Here, I bet y' ain't never tried none b'fore. Y' might like it." The shocked and disgusted look on Ella's face pleases Tucker, but she keeps her smile to herself.

"Are you serious?" Ella asks, shuddering. "I wouldn't put any of that in my mouth if you paid me to!"

Tucker folds the package of Red Man closed and puts it back in her pocket without getting any tobacco out. *Why should I care what she thinks? Maybe I just changed m' mind 'bout wantin' a chew. I can change m' mind if 'n I wanta.*

"Do you have any coffee?" Ella asks.

"Too hot fer coffee," Tucker replies. She gets the sense that Ella is trying to do something, but Tucker is unsure what. Suddenly she gets up and disappears inside the house.

After a few minutes she reappears through the door carrying two pieces of pie on a pair of mismatched saucers. Offering one to Ella, she says, "Y' want some?"

Ella reaches for the gift. "Thank you. I'm surprised there's any left. I expected you and those hungry children would have eaten it up last night."

Oh sh—! Now what am I s'posed t' say? I was afraid t' eat it 'cause I thought you was tryin' t' kill us?! Rather than respond to Ella's suggestion, Tucker stuffs a large forkful of pie into her mouth. "Mmm, mmm" she moans and nods her head appreciatively. With half of the bite swallowed, she says, "That there is some kind of good pie."

After Ella chews and swallows her own bite, she says, "Thank you. It's my mother's recipe."

Tucker finishes her piece of pie with two more large bites, while Ella has more than half her piece remaining.

Tucker watches Ella for a bit and asks, "So what happened 'tween you an' Judge Jack that now ya'll's divorced?"

"Before I answer your question, can I ask you why you hate the judge so much?"

"That's 'cause he hates me," Tucker replies quickly.

"What makes you believe he hates you?"

"'Cause ever' time I come up before him in court, he always talks down t' me an' makes fun of me in front of ever'body. I know

I ain't got no learnin', but that ain't no excuse fer him t' make fun of me an' th' way I talk.

"He's th' one who called me a Welfare Queen one day, an' th' title has stuck ever since. Well if I'm a queen, I wish somebody'd show me where m' castle is, 'cause I'm tired of this'n.

"He's always threatenin' t' take th' kids away from me, too. Says I ain't fit t' take care of 'em. He tells me if I don't follow th' orders of his court, he's gonna give th' kids to th' state.

"B'sides that, he's president of th' board of directors of the bank that holds th' lien on m' farm. He's th' one behind all them threats th' banker makes t' take m' farm from me.

"Don't none of 'em listen t' me, 'cause they don't care what I think. Any time I try t' explain somethin'," Tucker stomps her foot, "Judge Jack hammers his gavel an' says I'm in contempt of court. Truth is, I ain't got no feelin's of contempt fer th' court. My feelin's of contempt are fer Judge Jack."

Ella closes her eyes and nods her head as Tucker finishes speaking. "That certainly sounds like Jack." When her eyes open, there is a twinkle in them. "Did you really punch the judge and give him a black eye? Jack told me he accidently ran into a door at work, but I heard rumors it was you."

There is the slightest upturn at the corners of Tucker's mouth. "I did indeed. We crossed paths one day outside th' courthouse right after he'd tol' th' sheriff t' handcuff me t' the chair during m' hearin'. He said he was afraid I might do somethin' stupid like assaultin' him. Well that just made me mad. When I bumped into him outside after court, I reacted without thinkin'. I said t' him, 'Here's yore assault, y' sorry excuse for a judge,' an' I punched 'im right in th' face. He fell back'ards like a schoolgirl an' covered himself up. I thought he was gonna cry fer a minute. I just walked away an' left him on th' sidewalk."

Ella claps her hands. "Oh my, I wish I could have seen that! You have no idea how many times I've wanted to do the same thing. How long did you have to be in jail for doing it?"

Shrugging, Tucker says, "Didn't go t' jail. Never charged fer it, never went t' court fer it. I b'lieve it's 'cause th' judge didn't want no one t' know it was me that give 'im that black eye. His pride couldn't take it."

Ella looks at Tucker thoughtfully. "I'll tell you something, Tucker. You may not be book smart, but you certainly know how to judge a person's character. You have Judge Jack pegged perfectly. I just wish I was as strong and brave as you."

Tucker blinks her eyes rapidly as she tries to figure out where to place Ella's words of admiration and how to respond to them. She squirms uncomfortably in her chair. "Y' know, you seem like a decent sort of person. How in th' world did you end up with a snake like Jack McDade?"

Ella drops her head. "That's a complicated story."

CHAPTER NINE

Ella gazes across Tucker's front yard. Her gaze is not crossing the dimensions of space and distance but the dimensions of time and memory. Without turning her attention to Tucker, she begins, "I met Jack when we were students at Ole Miss. I grew up in Mississippi and both my parents had attended there, so it was expected that I'd attend there, too. Jack was in his last year of law school and I was finishing up my degree in elementary education.

"I had never met anyone like Jack. He had boundless energy, but that was nothing in comparison to the amount of self-confidence he had. Jack knew what he wanted, and nothing was going to stand in the way of achieving it.

"However, his reputation on campus as a ladies' man was reason enough for me to keep him at arm's length for a time. Even my best friend, Kim, told me that Jack was egotistical and a hothead and told me to steer clear of him. But I couldn't see those things in him. In spite of my best efforts to keep a wall up, Jack's persistence wore me down.

"I had never dated someone who wanted to be with me all the time, like he did. He seemed to be attentive to everything about me, noticing what I liked and didn't like, buying me presents. His ambitious, fiery spirit was intoxicating. However, like a drunk person, I was blind to the truth."

Ella pauses and looks at Tucker, who is listening closely. Sighing, Ella says, "It started out as a whirlwind romance. We married three months after our first date. But the whirlwind soon evolved into a hurricane."

Tucker stands up and walks to the edge of her porch. Resting her forearm on one of the posts, she spits a stream of tobacco juice into the yard. "That's what I think of men. I ain't never had no use fer 'em an' ain't missed out on nothin' by not havin' one around."

Ella can feel hatred dripping from each of Tucker's terse words. She considers probing Tucker to learn the why behind her attitude, but decides that taking that step might be just a bit dangerous.

Tucker turns to face Ella and says, "When did y' figure out that you was in trouble bein' married t' him?"

"I guess it was the first time he hit me," Ella replies and notices Tucker's knuckles turning white, she is gripping the post so tightly. "We'd already started arguing before that. He constantly quizzed me about where I was at all times and wanted an accounting of who I spoke to and what we talked about. He was convinced I was seeing another man. I tried to reason with him, but it is impossible to win an argument with a lawyer, or at least it was for me.

"One night we were arguing about something and suddenly he hit me in the jaw with his fist. Lying on the floor, I felt shock and disbelief. I tried to rationalize it away by saying he didn't mean to hit me. He even apologized and said it was an accident."

All of a sudden, Tucker punches the porch post. The entire porch shudders.

Ella flinches as if the punch was directed at her.

"Like hell is was an accident!" Tucker says through clenched teeth. She stomps over to her chair and plops down. "I'm gittin' riled up, Ella!" She snorts air through her nostrils like a deer snorting at potential danger.

"I don't mean for my story to upset you."

"Don't you worry 'bout me. I'm just addin' t' my list of reasons why I hate Judge Jack. You go ahead with yore story, 'cause I wanta hear it all."

Taking a deep breath Ella continues. "When it got really bad was when I became pregnant. Jack was obsessed with the idea that I was carrying someone else's child. I tried to reason with him, but my words fell uselessly to the floor. When I was a little over eight months pregnant we were arguing again about whose baby I was carrying. I got so angry that I told him if he didn't stop badgering me about it, I was going to leave him."

Ella pales at the memory, and her voice gets smaller. "It was like my threat was a trigger that released something inside of Jack, something horrible. He started hitting me again, over and over. I ended up on the floor half-conscious and tasting blood. I looked up and Jack was standing over me with his face contorted in anger. I'm telling you, Tucker, at that moment I thought he was going to kill me.

"Suddenly though, I felt the baby shift inside me and a sharp, stabbing pain in my side made me gasp. I wrapped my arms around my swollen abdomen and cried out.

"Jack realized what was happening and rushed me to the hospital, apologizing all the way and promising he would never hurt me again. Mercifully our son, Cade, was born that night completely healthy and unharmed. But my relationship with Jack would be forever flawed.

"The marriage took on the specter of a predictable emotional roller coaster, with Satan himself at the control panel. Things would go well between us for a time, followed by a period of tension. Ultimately Jack would explode and be either verbally abusive, physically abusive, or both. Almost immediately he would become remorseful to the point of tears, promising never to do it again. Like a fool, I would accept his promise, believing his remorse to be sincere and his tears real. Then the ride would start all over again." Ella slowly shakes her head and falls silent.

Without warning, Tucker bolts out of her chair and marches into her house. In a matter of seconds, she returns to the porch carrying an axe handle in her hand.

Startled, her heart racing, Ella's eyes grow wide.

Picking up her chair, Tucker slams it down within two feet of Ella and the swing. Then she sits down, facing Ella. Tapping the axe handle that she has laid across her knees, Tucker says, "Y' see this here? Let me tell y' somethin' 'bout it. I don't know hardly nothin' 'bout you, but no woman deserves t' be treated like he treated you. An' I'm makin' you a promise. This here axe handle has the name of Judge Jack McDade wrote on it with my own hand. I don't know when an' I don't know how, but one of these days I'm gonna give him his axe handle an' he won't never fergit it when I do. You hear what I'm sayin'?"

Exhausted from the telling of her story and from the stress of trying to understand this complicated, unpredictable woman in front of her, Ella smiles weakly. "I do hear what you're saying and I think it is one of the most noble things anyone has said to me in a long time. But I don't want you to end up in jail for beating a snake like Judge Jack."

"What do y' mean, 'noble'?"

Ella scolds herself for using a word that might be unfamiliar to Tucker. She reaches out and places her hand on Tucker's. "I simply mean that your willingness to take up for me when you really don't know me is a very decent thing to do."

Tucker quickly pulls her hand out from under Ella's. Folding her arms across her chest, she blinks rapidly.

Ella again chastises herself. *I went too far! I should never have touched her. This is a woman who undoubtedly has suffered much.*

Suddenly Tucker gets up from her chair and again goes inside her house.

Unsure if Tucker has ended their conversation, Ella considers getting in her car and leaving. But just as she is about to get up, Tucker reappears, this time carrying a burlap feed bag. Before Ella can form an opinion about what is in the bag, Tucker drops it heavily on the porch in front of her.

"You can have th' turnips back," Tucker says.

CHAPTER TEN

After watching Ella swing her tow sack of turnips into the front seat of her car, Tucker returns to her kitchen to finish her dishes. She hears Ella start her car and drive away.

That thar is one interestin' lady. Who would've thought somebody could hate Judge Jack as much as me? Thinkin' 'bout him hittin' a pregnant woman makes m' blood boil. But he'll have his day, sure as my name is Tucker.

After she finishes the dishes, she goes into her bedroom to make her bed. She smoothes the threadbare bottom sheet on her sagging mattress, then unfurls the rumpled quilt and lets it float down onto her bed. The quilt's faded Irish chain pattern provides the only color in an otherwise drab room. Its frayed edges brush the floor, and cotton stuffing can be seen trying to escape the thread-cinched chambers in which they were placed generations ago. Tucker speaks to the quilt, as she often does: "You's the only thing Mama left behind when she run off an' left me an' m' pa. She used t' tell me that you was really old, that maybe you come from across th' ocean. I'll bet if you could talk, you'd really have some tales t' tell."

Grabbing a broom out of her closet Tucker sweeps the dust from her bedroom floor out into the living room, where she adds to the small pile of refuse by attacking the corners of the room and reaching under the furniture. With short, practiced strokes she chases all the dirt toward her front door. Then she opens the screen door, holding it open with her foot, and sweeps it all out onto the porch. After she sweeps the porch clean, she sits down in the swing. A thin layer of sweat makes her face shine and her breathing is a little labored. "Whew! I must be gittin' old."

At the sound of her voice, Dog appears from his dark hole under the porch and squints at the bright sunlight. He meanders up the steps of the porch and approaches Tucker cautiously.

Tucker pats her thigh. "Come on over here, y' good fer nothin' hound dog. I ain't sure why I let you hang 'round."

Dog lays his head on her thigh and Tucker scratches his ears. He leans into the massage and groans in appreciation.

Tucker strokes his smooth head. The soft texture of Dog's fur, coupled with her slow, rhythmic petting, relaxes Tucker. Her eyelids begin to droop and her facial muscles sag. In a moment, she's asleep.

Lying on the wooden floor of the doghouse, Tucker shivers violently. She glances out the door opening and sees snow falling in the early morning light. She crawls around in the dim space until she finds Suzy, her father's favorite hunting dog, curled up in a corner. "S-s-s-uzy," she says through her chattering teeth, "I'm f-f-f-freezing. Help me."

Suzy unfolds her stiff joints and stands up. Tucker slides onto the vacated warm spot on the floor and curls into a ball. Reaching up, she gets hold of Suzy's collar and pulls her down on top of her, using her like a blanket.

With the intuition her breed is known for, Suzy seems to understand Tucker's need and flattens herself onto Tucker. She points her warm muzzle toward Tucker's face so she can feel her warm exhalations.

Three days ago Tucker's father came home drunk and got mad at her because she dropped a glass while washing dishes. He grabbed her by the arm and dragged her outside. As they were going through the door, Tucker saw her mother standing in the kitchen looking impassively at the scene.

The sharp, winter night air penetrated the thin, cotton shift Tucker wore for bed. As her father dragged her through the yard, he yelled, "If you're so clumsy you can't even pick up a glass without dropping it, then maybe you need to live with the animals for a while!" He violently threw her into the dog pen and padlocked the gate shut.

Now, as the warmth of Suzy begins to slowly penetrate Tucker's body, her shivering gradually subsides. Sleep, the refuge of abandoned and hopeless souls, silently folds its arms around her, and she slips peacefully away.

Suddenly there is a loud bark close by. Tucker awakens startled, scared, and disoriented.

Standing a few feet away from her with his hackles up, Dog growls.

Tucker places her hand on her chest in an effort to calm her hammering heart. She swears at Dog. "Y' done give me a heart attack, y' stupid fool!"

Following his line of sight, she sees what has triggered Dog's alarm. Walking slowly toward them is her tortoiseshell cat, casually wrapping its lithe body around each porch post it comes to. In a continuous motion, it pulls the length of its body free from a post, making sure that each knobby protrusion on the cedar post scratches its itch. With its tail the only thing left wrapped around the post, it pauses to look at Dog's threatening stance.

Tucker says, "Will y' shut up, Dog? It ain't nobody but Cat. If you'll leave 'er alone, she won't bother you. When're y' gonna figure out that you're better off makin' peace, instead of always trying t' start somethin'?"

With an air of nonchalance that Dog finds infuriating, Cat pulls her tail free of the post and continues her slow, seductive dance toward him.

Unable to contain himself, Dog explodes into panicked barking and bounds toward her on stiffened legs.

Cat stands on her tiptoes and arches her back menacingly, uttering a lone meow.

Dog stops both his approach and his barking and casts a furtive look in Tucker's direction.

Smiling in amusement at the scene, Tucker offers a word of advice: "I ain't gonna tell y' what t' do, but if'n I was you, Dog, I'd be real careful 'bout now."

He lifts his flattened ears, and an uncertain whine escapes his closed mouth.

Cat's body returns to its more familiar, relaxed position and she takes a step closer to Dog. When his whine jumps an octave, she takes another step toward him.

Like a little boy trying to take a hot marshmallow off a roasting stick, Dog jerks his head back and forth as he leans down toward Cat. Caution and reason tell him to walk away and return to his simple life under the porch, but his adventurous and careless spirit tell him that maybe this time he can get the upper hand on his feline tormentor. Caught between the two, unable to make a commitment in either direction, he stands frozen on the worn boards of the porch.

Cat lifts her head as high as she can. Their noses touch for an instant.

The effect on Dog is the same as if he'd touched an electric fence. He jumps back and gives a wounded bark.

A smile seems to spread across Cat's face and her eyes dance in amusement. Ignoring Dog, she walks over to Tucker and weaves a figure eight between her legs.

Reaching down, Tucker lifts Cat onto her lap. "Is that ol' dog givin' you a hard time? Dontcha worry 'bout him. He's all hot air."

Cat turns her head toward Dog and gives him a withering look of superiority.

Realizing he's lost another battle with his cunning antagonist, Dog drops his head and slinks off the porch. In a final effort to have the last word, he hikes his leg and pees on the forsythia bush before disappearing into his dark retreat.

CHAPTER ELEVEN

As Dog makes his final exit and disappears beneath the porch, Tucker slaps her thighs and says, "I guess I better git busy cannin' them tomaters I picked yesterday." Rising from the swing she walks through the house and out the back door to a bushel basket full of ripe tomatoes sitting beside the steps. Tucker hefts the basket off the ground, takes it inside the kitchen, and sets it on the countertop beside her sink.

Two hours later, a cloud of steam hovers over Tucker's stove. On one of the back eyes sits a pot of steaming, quartered tomatoes. The other back eye is covered by a pot of quart jars sunk in hot water. The small eye on the front of the stove has a pan of hot water with lids for the jars in it, while the other front eye holds a large pot of boiling water.

Tucker's sweat-soaked shirt sticks to her back and her face is as red as the tomato peelings in the sink. Using a pair of tongs, she lifts an empty jar out of its hot water bath and sets it on the stove. She reaches into a small bowl perched on the back of the stove and brings out a pinch of salt that she sprinkles into the jar. With a long-handled ladle, she dips cooked tomatoes out of the pot and pours them into the waiting jar. Carefully she wipes the rim of the jar clean of any juice that may have splashed on it. With the tongs, she gets a lid out of the small pan of hot water and places it on top of the jar, then picks up a ring and spins it closed on the jar.

Potholders protect her hands as she lifts a basket containing jars full of tomato juice out of the large pot where they have been boiling. Looking out over the top of her fogged-up eyeglasses, she carries the basket to the kitchen counter, grabs a towel off her shoulder, and uses it to help her take hold of the individual jars and set them on the counter to join the other rows of jars of tomato juice. Just as she slides one of the jars into place, two of the first jars she'd completed earlier give her a flat, metallic *thock*, letting her know they have cooled enough to create a vacuum and sealing the contents securely inside.

Walking back to the stove, she lowers the basket back into the boiling water and picks up the jar of tomato juice on the stove and carefully lowers it into the pot. She continues filling jars with juice and placing them in the pot until it is full. Looking at the clock on the stove, Tucker makes a mental note of the time, retrieves her glass of iced lemonade off the table, and walks back out on the porch, fanning herself with the hand towel.

"Whew-eee! I don't care if'n it is in th' nineties out here, it's cooler than it is inside that hot kitchen." She lifts the glass to her lips and drains it. An explosive and appreciative "Aah!" is the chaser to her drink.

A rumbling sound down the road catches her attention. Turning to look, she sees the afternoon school bus headed toward her house. *I was hoping I'd git done with them tomaters b'fore they got home. Oh well.*

The brakes of the bus squeal as it comes to a stop. The bus door opens and March bounds off, grinning a devilish grin, and runs toward the house. August steps off next, a scowl on his face. There is a longer pause and April appears in the door, hair tussled and cheeks tear-stained. August picks her up and sets her on the ground. Holding her hand, they follow March's trail to the house.

Stepping off the porch, Tucker waves down the bus driver as he begins to pull away. He stops the bus and opens the big door. "Any trouble, Bailey?" she hollers at him.

"Hey, Tucker! Trouble? When is there not trouble with them young 'uns? There's just so much I can tolerate, Tucker. You're gonna have to do something about that March."

At each window of the bus there are faces peering at Tucker. Some point and laugh.

Ignoring the children on the bus, Tucker keeps her attention on Bailey. "It ain't my kids what's th' problem. It's them other kids pickin' on 'em what causes problems. Why dontcha do somethin' 'bout them?" Giving Bailey no chance to reply, she turns and joins August and April as they make their way to the house.

"What happened on th' bus, August?" Tucker asks.

"March was shooting paper wads again," August answers tersely. "I think he lives just so he can aggravate people. One of these days somebody's gonna really hurt him, and it just might be me who does it."

"Y' know y' don't mean that."

August kicks at a rock in front of him. "Yes I do! It's bad enough that people make fun of us for how we dress and where we live. But March just brings more attention on us and makes people hate us. If he would just leave people alone and behave, it'd be a lot better for all three of us."

"How come April's been cryin'?"

"Johnny Winters started making fun of her and calling her retarded. I pushed him down on the floor and pressed my foot on his hand until he apologized to her, but her feelings was already hurt."

"That Johnny sounds like he's just like his dad and his grand-dad was. Both of 'em act like they's better than ever'one else, when th' truth is they ain't much better off than we are. Some people y' just have t' learn t' ignore." Reaching down, she lifts April into her arms and continues walking. "That means you, too, April. You have t' learn t' not always take ever'thing people says to you t' heart. You kids need t' always believe in yoreself, even if nobody else does."

March suddenly comes out of the house and calls out, "Hey, somebody ate some of the apple pie. Can we eat the rest of it?"

April's eyes open wide and she smiles.

August looks expectantly at Tucker.

"Oh all right," she says. "Ya'll finish it up an' play fer a little while, then git busy on yore chores."

April wriggles out of Tucker's arms. August grabs her hand when she lands on the ground and they break into a run.

By the time Tucker reaches the front door, August and March are heading out. "Y' mean t' tell me ya'll done ate that pie?"

"Yes ma'am," they both say.

"Where y' headed now?"

"We're gonna play war down at the barn," March answers her.

"And I'm gonna win this time," August says.

They leap off the porch and race toward the barn.

"If somebody gits hurt," Tucker calls out, "don't come back here cryin' t' me 'bout it."

CHAPTER TWELVE

Returning from a visit to Ella's and walking through her front yard, Tucker passes the woodpile with its eighteen-inch logs of oak, maple, and hickory resting in a perfect stack, waiting until the chill of autumn prompts their march into the wood-burning stove inside Tucker's house. The axe Tucker used yesterday to split some logs is lying on its side on the chopping block. Its shiny, sharpened edge catches the sun's rays. The bright reflection seizes Tucker's attention. Suddenly she is sucked into the vortex of an old memory. Helpless in its grasp, Tucker is flung mercilessly backward in time.

The weight of her father on top of her makes it difficult to get her breath. Out of the night sky above her, the raindrops of heaven's grief-stricken heart drop onto her face and intermingle with Tucker's own tears. Her hand that was unable to reach her father's hatchet squeezes the mud in her grasp until it oozes out between her fingers.

The hatchet lies there, inert and mocking. But Tucker sees in its sharp, shiny edge a portent of escape from her prison of abuse. Fate has intervened and offered her a gift on her sixteenth birthday. Tucker decides to seize the gift and never again allow her father to use her to satisfy his degenerate desires.

As Tucker lies underneath her father in the mud, her anger, like magma in a volcano, begins rising from a place it has lain dormant for years. Images flash across her memory: the three days her father locked her in the dog pen when she was seven years old; the time her mother, insisting on living in denial, broke the plate against her head; her father's leering face during all the times he knelt between her legs before raping her.

With a Herculean effort Tucker throws her arm to the side to its full extension.

Her father growls, "Be still!"

Tucker's hand lands squarely on the handle of the hatchet. She grips it with adrenaline-enhanced strength and screams at the top of her lungs, "You be still!" Swinging the hatchet, she buries it in the back of her father's neck.

There is a two-beat pause where time stands still for Tucker, and then her father exhales one last time. His entire bulk sags on top of her.

Letting go of the hatchet that remains in her father's neck, Tucker puts both hands on her father's chest, lifts him, and slides out from underneath. Staggering to her feet, her dress covered in mud, she looks up into the night sky and yells, "Yes! Yes! Yes!"

As if Nature herself were celebrating the death of the Tormentor, a flash of lightning rips the belly of the dark sky and a torrent of rain escapes. A clap of thunder as loud as a cannon firing makes the ground tremble. With the heavy raindrops peppering her upturned face, Tucker smiles.

Looking down at the inert silhouette of her father lying in the mud, she says, "Anythin' else you want t' say?" The only sounds answering her are the splashing raindrops, the singing spring peepers, and the rolling thunder in the distance.

The smile slides off Tucker's face as the pieces of a plan for disposing of her father's body begin coming together. Turning, she heads toward the barn. Her footprints leave unmistakable impressions in the deepening mud.

When she arrives at the barn, Tucker swings wide the double doors and props them open with sticks. Once inside, she gathers an armload of harness, reins, and bridle out of the tack room and walks to the end of the barn's hallway. Opening the door to the stall of their horse, Betty, Tucker clucks softly to her. "I know it's th' middle of th' night an' it's wet an' messy, but I need yore help, 'ol girl."

Betty lowers her head as Tucker slips the bridle over her head and places the bit in her mouth. Next Tucker slides the bulky upside-down U-shaped collar over Betty's neck and shoulders. Tucker runs the chains back from the collar, one on each side of Betty, and connects them to the singletree, the baseball bat–size wooden bar for connecting the harness to various implements.

Tucker hums quietly. Betty blows her nose loudly and steps to the side to let Tucker pass. Their movements are like a choreographed dance evolved from hitching Betty up for working in the field countless times. The links in the chains of the leather harness bump against each other, making a musical, tinkling sound like a wind chime.

With Betty's head facing the stall door, Tucker pushes it open and then moves behind the horse. Picking up the reins off the ground and gathering them in her hand, Tucker clucks her tongue and says, "Let's go, girl."

Betty's joints make a snapping noise as she begins moving out of the stall into the hallway of the barn. Tucker steers her outside into the night rain. As they pass through the barn door, Tucker grabs a section of log chain from its place on a nail and drapes it over her shoulder.

Betty's heavy, shoed hooves obliterate Tucker's previous footprints as they return to the scene of Tucker's liberating moment. With deft tugs on the reins, Tucker has Betty make a complete turn around her father's remains until she is parallel with him. When they get even with the body, Tucker pulls on the reins and says, "Whoa."

Stepping over to the corpse, Tucker takes the log chain off her shoulder. She reaches down to lift her father's feet and loops the chain around his ankles, securing it with a half hitch. She then hooks the two ends of the chain onto the singletree behind Betty. Returning to her spot behind Betty, Tucker clucks and pops Betty on the rear with the reins. "To the barn," she says.

Betty quickly adjusts her body to the increased weight behind her and slogs methodically through the mud. Tucker walks to the side to avoid stepping on the body.

An elongated finger of lightning arcs from horizon to horizon and splinters into scores of jagged strings of light. Tucker sees her father's mud- and blood-streaked face staring up at the spectacle.

Startled, Betty rears up.

"Calm down!" Tucker scolds her and Betty dutifully obeys.

Thunder begins off in the distance and gradually rolls forward, becoming louder and louder.

When they finally reach the barn, Tucker coaxes Betty into the wide hallway. Tucker doesn't stop until her father's body is lying directly in the opening of the doorway. She removes the block and tackle from its wooden peg on the wall. Standing on her tiptoes, she attaches it to the top of the doorway above her father and slowly lowers the hook. After she reaches down and releases the ends of the log chain from the singletree, she unloops the chain from her father's ankles.

Betty shakes like a dog to rid herself of some of the weight of her rain-soaked coat and, perhaps, to rid herself of the memory of the carcass she's dragged through the mud.

Always mindful of the needs of the farm animals, Tucker removes Betty's gear and follows her into her stall. She gets a scoop of sweet feed and drops it in Betty's bucket. Betty nickers a thank-you.

After fastening Betty's stall door, Tucker returns to her father's body. She grabs the loosened log chain off the ground with her right hand, lifts his head with her left, and wraps the chain twice around his neck. She then slips the chain into the hook of the block and tackle. Grabbing the rope of the block and tackle Tucker begins pulling. The pulleys squeak and squeal in complaint as inch by inch the body rises. When her father's feet clear the ground, Tucker stops pulling and secures the position by tying the rope off.

The sudden sound of heavy machinery approaching acts like a knife, cutting the string that has had Tucker tied to her past. And like a taut fishing line recoiling after it snaps, she is hurtled into the present. She looks toward her road and sees the County Highway Department's road grader coming down the road, performing its maintenance work of smoothing out potholes and cleaning out the ditches.

Tucker looks down at the shiny axe that launched her into her past. Picking it up, she drives it into the chopping block, burying the brilliant edge deep within.

CHAPTER THIRTEEN

A week after moving into the McDaniel house, Ella walks slowly from room to room enjoying seeing everything finally put into place and no stacks of cardboard boxes waiting to be unpacked. She runs her hand over the stitched names on her mother's friendship quilt, which she uses as a bedspread. The faces of old family friends drift up from Ella's memory as she touches each name. *Oh mother, how blessed you were with so many friends. In the last two years I've come to realize how small my life has become because of my lack of close friends.*

"Judge Jack!" Her tone drips with loathing as she spits his name out. Because she let him use her as decoration for his political ambitions, everyone viewed her as a one-dimensional caricature. They believed her to be as shallow and vain as he was. What a fool she was!

Passing by the hallway mirror she sees her reflection out of the corner of her eye and turns to face it. Her bald head, tired expression, and sunken eyes with dark circles underneath reinforce her feelings of defeat. As if she were the witch in *Sleeping Beauty*, she speaks to the mirror, "So is this to be the end of my life? I win my battle against cancer only to lose the war with Jack and move into this tiny house, with Tucker as my only neighbor, to live my last days in complete isolation? Is this it?" She stares in anticipation of the mirror giving her the words that will make sense of her life and provide a view of her future. After a moment of silence, she turns away. "Even the magic in the mirror has deserted me."

She stops to look at a photograph hanging on the wall. It is of an older couple, both bent with age, standing arm in arm in front of a flat-roofed house, with a background of an even flatter terrain. Her parents. If they hadn't moved to Texas and given away all their money to that snake-oil television preacher who'd promised to heal her mother's Parkinson's, Ella might have had enough money to buy a nicer place. She kisses her fingertip and then touches each of their faces. "Forgive me for being selfish. It's just so hard to believe you've been gone for four years. I sure do miss you, but I know you're happy in heaven."

A few hours later, the setting sun has left the living room in shadows. Ella lies on her side, sleeping on the couch. On the floor are photographs that have fallen haphazardly, having slipped from Ella's sleeping hands. Her soft snoring is a tip-off to the deep slumber she has managed to find.

She doesn't hear the sound of the Volkswagen van pulling up to her house, its headlights off. The driver gets out and stealthily closes the door, making no sound. For a few moments he stands in the twilight, seeming uncertain how to proceed. Finally he makes his way to the front door and taps lightly.

Ella continues her sleep uninterrupted.

The driver knocks a bit harder on the door.

Ella's snoring stops. Alert now, she lies very still, not sure why she's awakened lying on her couch. Finally she recognizes the outline of the cardboard box on the coffee table in front of her and remembers her walk down memory lane. The sound of a distinct knock on her front door pulls her to a sitting position.

Standing up, she waits for a moment to be sure her legs and feet are not going to fail her, a problem she's had since the chemo. Once she feels sure that she can walk without falling, she tiptoes to the front door. Switching on the front porch light, she peeks through the window shade.

Her hand flies to her mouth in shocked surprise. She quickly unbolts the door and flings it open. Throwing open her arms, she exclaims, "Cade!"

"Turn off the light, Mother," he says as he ducks his head. Ignoring her open arms, he quickly scoots into her house, closing the door behind him.

"What's wrong, Cade?" Like air escaping from a balloon with a hole in it, the excitement has gone out of Ella's voice. There is both weariness and resignation in her tone.

She turns on a lamp. It is then she sees Cade's normally perfectly combed hair looking like each hair has lost its way, lying helter-skelter. His tie is askew and both pants and jacket are rumpled. Taking his face in her hands, she turns it toward the light to get a better look. His puffy bottom lip and bruised cheekbone raise alarm bells in her head.

When she sees his red-rimmed eyes etched with bloodshot lines and sniffs his breath, she drops her hands from his face and says, "Not again, Cade!"

"What do you mean by that?!"

"Well let me think," Ella begins. "I haven't seen you in four months and suddenly you show up at my house at nightfall. I don't get a 'Hi, Mother' or 'How have you been?' Plus you look like you've been run over by a team of horses. Call me suspicious, but I don't think this is a social call."

Ella's penetrating assessment knifes through Cade's air of arrogance. Collapsing into an armchair, he says, "I'm in trouble."

Ella sits on the couch across from him. "What is it this time, another DWI? Or has someone's husband finally caught you with his wife and beaten you within an inch of your life, like you deserve?"

Cade lowers his head. "It's worse than that. I was driving through Lake County last night, in a hurry to get back home, when the Highway Patrol pulled me over for speeding. They made me do the sobriety tests and gave me a DWI citation."

When he doesn't raise his head, Ella says, "There's more, isn't there?"

Cade nods. "Somebody framed me!" he blurts out. "The State Troopers made me open my trunk. I don't know how it got there, but there was forty pounds of marijuana in it."

"Forty pounds?!" Ella exclaims. "And you don't know how it got there? Cade, really!"

"I'm telling you the truth!" Cade's defensive air has returned, but he refuses to look his mother in the eye. He gets up and begins pacing. "This is serious, Mother. They've charged me with trafficking. That's a felony charge with a lot of prison time attached to it. If convicted I would lose my law license and be disbarred. My career would be ruined. I need your help."

"Cade," Ella says, "I did my best to raise you to make good choices, to be an honorable man when you grew up. But your father wanted you to be just like him, greedy and ambitious, to the point where other people didn't matter. Unfortunately, you chose to follow in his footsteps, much to my dismay. So why come to me now? I'm sure Jack will get you off the hook, just like he has dozens of times."

Cade returns to the armchair and looks at his mother. "Not this time. He can't."

"Why not?"

"Because Charlie Watts is the district attorney." Cade diverts his eyes from his mother's.

"Your dad and I have known Charlie and Linda Watts for years. So what's the problem?"

Shifting uncomfortably, Cade, in a half whisper, says, "Dad has been having an affair with Charlie's wife for the past couple of years."

All the blood drains from Ella's face and she sags back into the couch.

Moving to sit beside his mother, Cade says, "I'm sorry, Mother. I hate to be the one telling you this. Charlie found out about the affair about two months ago. He is livid and has a vendetta against Dad. He's promised to ruin him. And besides all that, Dad told me last week that he is through bailing me out of trouble."

Ella looks blankly at Cade. "Linda?" she whispers. "He had an affair with Linda?"

They sit in silence for a few moments, lost in the details of their separate traumas.

Cade is the first to speak. Taking his mother's hand, he says, "You're my only chance, Mother. I believe Charlie will listen to you. He'll be sympathetic to your position. You've got to call him."

Slowly the color returns to Ella's face until it reaches a deep red. With fists clenched, she stands up. "Your father is the sorriest S.O.B. that ever walked the face of the earth. While I was battling for my life with cancer, he was out screwing one of my friends! And Linda . . . I don't even know what to say about her, except don't trust your friends.

"As for you, I don't *have* to do anything. You've made this mess. As far as I'm concerned you'll have to fix it yourself." She strides out of the living room into the kitchen, leaving Cade speechless.

He searches his mind for a twist he can put on this that will hook his mother into relenting. He forces himself to begin to cry, a technique he's used effectively on many juries. As the tears begin dripping down his cheeks, he finds his mother in the kitchen.

Ella is looking out the window over her sink, toward Tucker's house.

With tears streaming down his face, Cade gets on his knees beside her. Taking one of her hands in his, he says, "I'm your only son. I know I have been a disappointment to you and I haven't been there for you when you needed me. But I promise all that is going to change. I'm through with my cavalier ways. If a person can't count on his mother, what is to become of him?"

Ella looks into the face of her only child. She feels a pull in her chest and a tightening in her throat. Stroking his hair with one hand, she whispers, "Cade, if only I could believe you."

Burying his face in her abdomen as he hugs her, Cade cries, "I really mean it. I'm going to change. But I have to have your help."

Ella pauses a moment and then says, "I'll see what I can do."

Cade leaps up and embraces his mother tightly. "Thank you. Thank you. I'll make you proud, Mother. You'll see." He pulls back from her and kisses her on the forehead. "But now, why don't you go back to bed and get some sleep. I'm sorry to have gotten you up for this. I've got to hurry along home."

Giving his mother another kiss, Cade turns and heads out the door. As he does, a sly smirk spreads across his face.

Trying to collect her wits after Cade's departure, Ella spies a lone box resting beside the couch. Sitting down, she sets the box beside her and opens the flaps on top. Scattered inside is a stack of photographs, turned at random angles. Ella reaches inside and takes out the top photograph. A small, blond-headed child standing beside a swimming pool smiles back at her. She turns the photograph over and reads, "Cade—age four." Flipping it back over, she says, "Oh Cade, you were such a beautiful boy. Truly the joy of my life."

She brings out another photographic treasure from the box. The boy is a few years older and his smile has become snaggletoothed. The backdrop is a wooden picnic table, a tent, and thick woods.

Kneeling beside the boy is a strikingly beautiful woman with long, flowing blonde hair. On the back of the photograph Ella finds the notation: "Cade—age eight, Land Between the Lakes." "Our camping trips together are some of my favorite memories," she says, "even when you caught that black snake and brought it proudly to me."

Her eyes fill with tears. "Oh Cade, what ever happened to that little boy I was so proud of?"

CHAPTER FOURTEEN

The wrestling match between her head and her heart having kept her awake all night, Ella is restless and uneasy the day after Cade's evening visit. At midmorning she is sitting at the kitchen table staring at her cup of coffee, now grown cold.

She knows beyond a doubt that Cade is a philanderer, a narcissist, and a pathological liar. She would be a fool to swallow all the words coming out of his mouth without first giving them a generous sprinkling of salt.

That's what my head tells me. She rubs her temples. *But my heart is another matter.* She knows people can change, can see the mistakes of their life and make a U-turn and become a new person. Maybe this time the trouble Cade has gotten into will finally get his attention. All of a sudden, the sound of tires in the gravel driveway jerks her out of her ruminating. Getting up she makes her way to the front window. A massive, white Lincoln Continental rolls to a stop. The door of the car opens and Judge Jack McDade steps out. Like the talons of an eagle, an old fear seizes Ella's heart.

Ella immediately notices the firm set of his lips and his jaw jutting out. *No doubt this visit is going to be about Cade. The two of them are going to use the good cop/bad cop routine on me.*

Noticing that her hands are shaking, she takes a deep breath and exhales slowly to steady herself. She moves to the front door and opens it before Jack makes it onto the porch.

The opening door catches Jack off guard, and he stops with his foot on the first step.

They stand silent for a moment, staring at each other.

Without blinking, Ella says, "Good morning, Jack."

Jack breaks off his stare to take in the humble house Ella is living in. He looks back to Ella and says, "We need to talk."

Closing the door behind her, Ella takes a couple steps toward Jack. "Really, Jack? Is that the best opening line you could come up with?" A derisive laugh escapes her. "I'd say you closed the door to talking when you decided to divorce me the moment I lost the one thing about me that you valued when I got cancer—my looks."

"Now, Ella, there's no need to—"

"Don't 'now, Ella' me!" she snaps. "You threw me onto the waste heap with the countless others you've treated the same way." Smiling, she says, "Did I ever thank you for that, Jack? If I haven't, consider yourself thanked now."

Judge Jack's face darkens. "I don't want to dig up old bones, Ella. That's all ancient history. I'm here to talk about Cade. There's been some trouble."

Ella raises her eyebrows. "Trouble? What kind of trouble? And let me add that that is ancient history to you only because you don't have to live with the consequences like I do."

Jack steps closer to Ella. Lowering his voice, he says, "Can we step inside to discuss this?"

Pleased with how strong she is feeling in this tête-à-tête, Ella nods assent to Jack's request. Opening the door, she steps aside to let him in.

When she follows him inside and shuts the door, she immediately knows she has made a mistake. Jack's calm facial features have coalesced into a mask of anger.

"When did you get so high and mighty?" he asks. "As long as you had money to spend, you didn't care what I was doing. I got tired of you bleeding me dry."

Ella feels the energy of Jack's anger, and an old but familiar feeling of fear creeps into her chest. She takes a couple steps backward. Feeling the armchair at the back of her legs, she walks behind it and places her hands on its back to steady herself.

"You said you are here about Cade? What's happened? Is he okay?"

Just as he is about to unleash a full-court press on Ella, her comment redirects his attention. "Yes, yes. That's right. Cade's in some trouble. He's okay as far as I know, but I can't find him. When is the last time you saw him?"

Ella's eyes unconsciously shift to the couch on which Cade sat a few hours ago. Looking back at Jack, she says, "What kind of trouble?"

Jack looks at the couch and then back at Ella. He intently scans her face and reads something. "What's going on here?"

Ella grips the chair a little tighter. *Just stay calm. He doesn't know anything. This is just a fishing expedition.* Working to keep her pounding heart from making her voice tremble, Ella replies, "I don't know what you're talking about, Jack. I don't know where Cade is."

Like a lawyer trying to elicit the answer he wants from a defendant, Judge Jack takes a step toward her. "That wasn't my question. I asked you when was the last time you saw Cade."

"I'll have to think about that."

In an ominous tone, Jack says, "You never were a good liar, Ella. He's been here, hasn't he?"

Suddenly, something inside Ella snaps. Moving out from behind the chair, she says, "Yes, he came to see me! He had to come see me this time because you can't keep your pants zipped when you are around women! Linda Watts?! I can't believe you. I don't care about myself, but how could you do that to Charlie? He was your friend!"

With the swiftness of a viper's strike, Jack slaps Ella across the face. She reels backward, stumbling.

Full-blown panic petrifies her. The adrenaline coursing through her can't make up its mind whether to make her run away or to fight, and instead paralyzes her.

Moving toward her, Jack snarls, "I think you've forgotten your place, woman." He grabs her arm and jerks her up to his face. "Living out here with all the other white trash has clouded your judgment." His spittle sprays her face and he gives her arm a rough shake.

Ella tries to twist away from his grip. "Stop! You're hurting me!"

Jack lets go of her. As she rebuttons some of the buttons on her blouse, he considers her. A smirk spreads across his face. "Why bother?" he says, looking directly at her chest. "You're only half a woman anyway."

His words have a concussive force, driving her back another step.

He closes the gap between them and with his two first fingers punches her directly where her left breast was. "Half a woman!" he snarls.

Searing pain shoots through Ella and she collapses on the floor.

Bending at the waist and standing over her, Jack sneers. "You're pitiful."

Without warning, the front door of Ella's house bursts open, crashing back against the wall. Jack turns his head to look over his shoulder and sees Tucker standing in the doorway, gripping an axe handle with both hands. His eyes widen and all the blood drains from his face.

Tucker covers the distance between her and Jack in three quick strides. In her high-pitched voice, she screams, "You son of a bitch!" Swinging the axe handle with the agility and force gained from a lifetime spent splitting wood, Tucker strikes Jack squarely in his ribcage. Even through his clothes the muffled sound of ribs shattering can be heard.

Like a wild animal that has received a fatal blow, Jack staggers to his feet and sways back and forth, his eyes unfocused.

Tucker slowly draws back her arm, holding the axe handle high over her shoulder. Taking careful aim, she swings her weapon.

Ella screams, "Tucker! No!"

The axe handle catches Jack squarely on the side of the face. His broken jaw twists his snarl into a comedic grin. He crumples to the floor in a heap.

Twenty minutes later, consciousness dawns in Jack slowly. He cracks open his eyes and realizes he is lying on his side. He tries to move but the pain in his ribs pins him to the floor.

Sitting on a ladder-back chair in front of him is Tucker, with the axe handle lying across her thighs. Behind her stands Ella.

"Tol'ja he wudn't dead," Tucker says. Reaching down, she grabs his shirt at the shoulder. With seemingly no effort, she jerks him to a sitting position and roughly pushes his back against the wall.

"Owww!" Jack yells.

A smile flickers across Tucker's face.

"All right, Judge," she says. "This is how it's gonna be. You're gonna go t' th' hospital an' tell 'em you fell down th' steps at th' courthouse. 'Cause if you decide t' go see th' sheriff 'bout what really happened, then I'm gonna brag t' ever'body I see how I done whupped yore ass agin. You got that?" A grin returns to Tucker's face and this time stays there. Looking over her shoulder at Ella, she sees her worried expression. "Quitcher worrin', woman. He's gonna be fine. Eventually."

She lifts the axe handle off her lap with one hand and taps Jack on the foot. "Have we got us an understandin'?"

There is a slight nod of Jack's head.

Tapping his foot harder, Tucker asks, "You sure?"

Jack gives a definite nod of assent.

"That's better," Tucker says.

CHAPTER FIFTEEN

Cade eases the hospital room door open and slowly sticks his head inside. As soon as he sees his father in the hospital bed, he steps inside the room and stares in disbelief. Judge Jack's head is wrapped in layers of gauze. One side of his face practically glows with purple and reddish bruising and his eye on that side is swollen shut. Instead of the usual hospital gown, Cade sees that his father's torso is heavily wrapped.

When the door clicks shut behind Cade, Judge Jack's good eye looks in his direction. He motions impatiently for Cade to come closer. The only sound Cade can hear coming from his dad is a moaning sound.

"Your secretary told me I needed to get over here quickly," Cade says, "but she didn't say what happened. My god, you look like you've been run over by a truck—a big truck! What in the world happened?"

When his dad starts writing on a legal pad lying in his lap rather than answering him, Cade looks confused. He watches as his father's hand jerks agitatedly across the page.

After a few moments, Judge Jack hands the legal pad to Cade.

Cade reads his dad's jagged handwriting with ever-widening eyes. "Tucker?! Tucker did this to you?" In his carelessness he lets a smile slip across his face but quickly wipes it off.

But not quickly enough, as Judge Jack gives a guttural roar and lunges for Cade. Unfortunately for the judge, he, too, is careless and has forgotten about his broken body. Pain explodes deep inside his chest cavity and what feels like a hot iron bores into the side of his head. He blacks out and collapses in a twisted pile on his bed.

Believing his father has had a massive heart attack and died, Cade runs panicking into the hallway. "Help! I need a nurse or a doctor down here quick!"

A nurse steps out of a nearby room as Cade's cry for help rings through the hallway. With quick steps she makes her way to him and follows him into the room. Looking at her crumpled patient, she says sardonically, "Not again. You've got to be kidding." She walks to the judge and pulls his shoulders to ease him back into a sitting position on the bed.

Turning to Cade, the nurse says, "He's not a very easy patient to manage. I've told him not to make any sudden movements and to buzz for help if he needs to get out of bed. This is the third time I've found him passed out and it's all because he's so hardheaded. Clearly his reputation is well deserved."

"What all is wrong with him?"

Squaring up to look at him, the nurse says, "You must be Cade. They told me you'd be coming by."

"Who told you?"

"That's not important. All I'm saying is that I was warned that you are just as dangerous as he is, maybe more so."

Cade is taken aback by this small woman's directness. "Are you going to tell me the extent of his injuries, or do I need to call the administrator?"

The nurse waves her hand dismissively. "Don't try to pull your high and mighty routine with me. I'm not from around here and I'm not afraid of either one of you. But I'll tell you his injuries anyway. He's got four fractured ribs and a broken jaw. His story is that he fell down the steps at the courthouse. I've got my doubts about the truthfulness of that, but it's really none of my business."

A moan from the bed draws their attention. As they look at Judge Jack, his one good eye slowly opens, though it remains unfocused for a few moments.

"He's going to be okay," the nurse says matter-of-factly, "except for the fact that he's going to be in serious pain for at least a month." Walking toward the door of the room, she says, "I'll leave you two to each other. I've got other patients to see about."

"Wait a minute," Cade says. "When can he leave the hospital?"

Pausing at the door, the nurse turns to face him. "The admitting doctor said he can leave anytime he wants to. There's really nothing else to do. He'll have to be seen by his regular doctor, who can decide when his jaw can be unwired. I'll tell you, though, there's a pretty good pool of money being collected in the hospital by people who'd like to see his mouth permanently wired shut." She exits before Cade can mount a rebuttal.

Turning back to his dad, Cade says, "I'm going to go see the sheriff and have a warrant sworn out against that Tucker woman for assault. She can't get away with this."

Judge Jack holds up his hand and gently shakes his throbbing head. He writes a message on the legal pad and then hands it Cade.

"I didn't think about that," Cade says. "You're right. The paper would love to make a spectacle of the whole incident. You'd end up the butt of jokes all over the county. So what are you going to do?"

The judge motions for Cade to give him the notepad.

Cade waits in silence as his dad writes. When his dad hands the pad back to him, Cade reads the message written in all caps:

AS GOD IS MY WITNESS, I'LL FIND A WAY TO DESTROY TUCKER!!!

CHAPTER SIXTEEN

Leaning her axe against the chopping block, Tucker straightens her back with a groan and surveys the pile of kindling she's produced. Red-faced, she unzips her jacket and peels it off. *October's th' month when y' can't never tell what t' wear. It's cool enough in th' mornin's t' have a fire, but by noon it's done warmed up enough fer short sleeves.* She hangs the jacket on the upright handle of the axe. As she bends over to pick up an armful of wood, a black Chevy Nova pulls into her yard. Tucker drops the wood and straightens back up.

The car door opens and a woman steps out. No more than five feet tall, she is nearly as round as her height. The head of a pen peeks out from the round pile of gray hair on top of her head. She grips the handle of her black briefcase and shuts the door. Not seeing Tucker at the woodpile, she moves in quick steps toward the house.

Standing as still as a statue, Tucker watches the woman carefully. When the visitor disappears from view onto the porch, Tucker grabs her axe and quickly moves to the corner of the house.

Tucker hears the woman knocking on the door and calling her name. After a few moments, the rat-a-tat of her wooden heels lets Tucker know the woman is leaving the porch. Then there is the sound of rustling leaves as the interloper heads toward the back of the house.

Tucker hurries around the back of the house and positions herself at the far corner, her back pressed to the wall. As the woman nears her, Tucker raises the axe above her head.

Just as the woman rounds the corner, Tucker jumps into her path brandishing the axe and yells, "Boo!"

The woman shrieks at the top of her lungs.

Tucker bursts out laughing.

"Tucker, you scared the pee out of me!" the woman says when she finally catches her breath.

"Mary Beth Chandler, you'd reach yore hand in a tree trunk fer honey an' never notice the bees!" Tucker exclaims, still laughing. "I was standin' right thar the whole time. Watched y' git outta yore car!"

"Go ahead and laugh," Mary Beth says, as she begins to laugh, too, "because one of these days I'm going to get you back. You haven't changed a bit since we were little girls. You were always pulling things on me."

"We did have us some good times, didn't we?" Tucker replies. "Goodness, that was a long time ago . . ."

"Do you remember that time you put a little garter snake in my lunch box?"

Laughter bubbles up again in Tucker. "Sure I do. Y' made me open that lunch box ever' day fer a month just 'cause you was afeared to open it yoreself."

They stand for a moment regarding each other, memories whirling through their minds like a runaway merry-go-round.

As her merry-go-round slows, Mary Beth's smile fades. "Tucker, we have to talk. I'm here on official business."

"Figgered as much," Tucker replies. "I didn't think th' welfare office'd let y' come out here fer a social visit. Wanta go inside?"

"Sure. That'll be fine."

Once inside, Tucker offers Mary Beth a chair at the kitchen table.

Mary Beth sets her briefcase on the table, unlatches it, and takes out a thick sheaf of papers and some manila folders. Clearing her throat, she looks at Tucker, and says, "How long have I been your caseworker, Tucker?"

"How long y' been workin' fer the welfare folks?" Tucker counters.

"Exactly," Mary Beth says. "You were my very first client, almost forty years ago. Did you ever wonder why I ended up working with you instead of any of the other social workers?"

"Never give it much thought. All I knowed was that I hated takin' charity."

Mary Beth shakes her head. "How many times have I told you it's not charity, if you deserve it? I knew for a fact that you'd always done what you could to raise and grow enough food for everyone in your house, Tucker. Nobody's a harder worker than you. Getting folks like you the staples you couldn't raise or afford to buy is why I took this job in the first place, and why I requested you to be my client. You and I grew up together, so I knew what kind of life you had lived. I figured I was the only one in that office who knew all about you."

"Truth be tol'," Tucker interjects, "you was the only person who knowed ever'thing 'cause you was the onliest person I ever trusted t' tell. Not even Mama Mattie knowed ever'thing."

"Mama Mattie," Mary Beth echoes softly, almost reverently. "Now there was an amazing woman. She was a social worker before they were called social workers. There's no telling how many babies she helped into this world or how many people she gave food to from her garden or sewed clothes for." Mary Beth slowly shakes her head at the memory, then refocuses her attention on Tucker. "I was afraid people wouldn't understand you, Tucker. Afraid that they'd judge you and not be fair with you. That's why I wanted you as my first client. And you're going to be my last one, too."

"Whadda y' mean b' that?"

"I'm fixing to retire. Forty years is long enough. But that's not why I'm here. I've come to talk to you about April."

Tucker stiffens a bit and leans forward, placing her forearms on the table.

Their smiles evaporate and their reminiscing screeches to a halt as tension fills the small room.

Mary Beth lays a piece of paper between them. Speaking in a matter-of-fact tone, she says, "This is a report put together by the school system. It notes that April is mute and is possibly mentally retarded."

Tucker's meaty hand slams on top of the paper. "There ain't nothin' wrong with that girl! It's them school folks that's retarded."

Unfazed by Tucker's volatile reaction, Mary Beth says in an even voice, "All your yelling and carrying on is not going to bother me, and more importantly, it's not going to change anything contained in these papers."

Tucker folds her arms across her chest. "Go ahead an' speak yore piece."

Picking up a thick folder, Mary Beth lays it on top of the letter. "These are all the results from the tests that have been done on April that support the school's position." She takes a deep breath and lays another piece of paper on the rising stack. Looking Tucker in the eye, she says, "And this is a letter from the school to my supervisor recommending that April be removed from your home and placed in the state's custody so that she can receive the special help she needs."

Tucker feels as if she has been struck in the chest by a sledge-hammer. All the air has left her body. Dropping her arms heavily to her side, she sinks back into her chair. "Not m' April," she whispers hoarsely.

Mary Beth hesitates and fiddles with the corner of a piece of paper, recognizing how stunned her old friend must be. "There's more," she says softly. Laying the piece of paper on the stack, she turns it around so Tucker can read it. "This is a court order signed by Judge Jack McDade giving us permission to remove April."

Tucker comes off her chair like she was shot from a cannon. Grabbing the stack of papers she flings them across the kitchen, where they float through the air like falling leaves. She seizes the kitchen table and flips it across the room as if it were doll furniture. Turning around, she grabs her wooden chair and slams it against the floor, shattering its rails. Breathing heavily, she faces Mary Beth, who has remained seated and unperturbed. "Mary Beth, I'm gonna kill that man. I swear by all that I am. I'm gonna kill 'im!"

Mary Beth looks up at the glowering specter of Tucker, and says, "Are you done? Because if you aren't, I'm going outside. I don't intend to sit here while you act like a fool. But if you are through with your tantrum, then we've got to have a serious talk. Besides, I heard Judge Jack had some kind of accident that nearly killed him. He wouldn't be any challenge for you to take on in a fight."

"Mary Beth, wouldja really take April away from me?"

"That isn't what I want to happen. If you weren't such a blunder-buss, you wouldn't have made such a mess in this kitchen and destroyed your chair. You see, I have a small candle of hope to shine in this dark tunnel."

"Whatcha talkin' 'bout?"

Mary Beth grabs the chair beside her and slides it across the floor until it is facing her. Motioning toward it, she says, "Sit down and listen."

Tucker sits, her eyes wide behind her thick glasses.

Mary Beth continues, "Here is what I was able to get everyone to agree to: they are going to wait until the children come back to school from Christmas vacation and then retest April. If nothing has changed, she will be remanded into state custody, which means you have a little over two months to make a miracle happen. Bottom line, if April is not retarded, like you insist she isn't, then you have to get her to talk."

CHAPTER SEVENTEEN

Tucker sets a box of crayons on the kitchen table. Turning to April, who is sitting beside her, she says, "Let's try this again. Show me th' red crayon."

April's hand darts to the box and she pulls out the red crayon. Laying it on the table, she looks expectantly at Tucker.

"That's a good girl," Tucker says. "You're right. That's th' red one." Picking up the crayon with her thick fingers Tucker holds it up between her and April and says, "Now, I want you to tell me what color this crayon is."

April looks at Tucker. She purses her lips and then sucks them back in tightly several times, like someone kneading dough.

"Come on," Tucker urges her, "you can do it. Just whisper it if'n y' want to."

Finally, April drops her head.

"Okay," Tucker says, "let's try it this way." She takes the piece of notebook paper in front of her and writes the word *blue*. Turning the paper so April can see it, she says, "Read that word an' then find me th' crayon that matches it."

April peers closely at the large block handwriting. Her lips move as she sounds out the word in her head. Her eyes brighten as recognition dawns. She reaches for the box of crayons and pulls out the blue crayon. Smiling, she holds it up between her and Tucker.

"Well ain't y' th' smart one!" Tucker exclaims. "There ain't nothin' wrong with yore brain. You's as smart as they come." She taps the paper. "Lookie here again, but this time I want y' t' read th' word out loud."

April takes the crayon and underlines the word twice, then looks at Tucker with a hopeful expression.

"Now April, that ain't gonna git it done. You've gotta say th' word." Tucker feels herself getting agitated and angry. *What am I gonna do?! There has t' be a way t' git her t' talk. I just gotta find th' key that'll unlock her.* She sighs. "We'll try again later, an' we'll keep tryin' until you decide t' talk. It's Saturday, go run along an' play."

Knowing she has disappointed her grandmother, April keeps her head bent low and slowly slides out of her chair. As she walks out of the kitchen, her body language reeks of dejection.

Tucker snatches the paper off the table and wads it up into a tiny ball. Standing up, she pulls at her shirt collar and exclaims, "Whew, it's hot in here!" She opens the back door and a warm breeze greets her. *It's nearly November an' it feels like summer. This warm front ain't natural. Trouble may be on its way.*

She begins walking through the house opening all the windows. When she finishes, she walks out to the porch swing. Sitting down, she reaches for the funeral fan resting on the table beside her and begins fanning herself.

Time has faded the picture of Leonardo da Vinci's *The Last Supper* on the front of the fan and broken its thin cardboard, causing it to flop as she swings it back and forth.

She pulls the top of her shirt away from her neck and tries to cool her chest by waving air toward her neck.

She watches April and August playing marbles in the front yard. She hasn't seen March for a while, which isn't a good sign.

Aint' no tellin' what he's into. Rising slowly from the swing she walks stiffly down the steps into the front yard and looks intently toward the northern sky. She frowns at the ominous, black clouds she sees building on the horizon. "You kids stay here while I walk down t' Ella's. I'll be back shortly."

"Yes, ma'am," August answers.

Tucker lumbers down the gravel road toward Ella's house. When she arrives, she casts a furtive look over her shoulder at the dark clouds, then steps up on the porch and knocks on the front door.

After a moment, Ella opens the door. "Why hello, Tucker. Come on in."

"No thanks," Tucker replies. "I'm busy with th' kids today. I just wanted y' t' know that there's a storm comin'. A bad 'un."

Stepping out onto her porch, Ella looks around. "It's a beautiful day, Tucker, even if it is a little warm. What makes you think there's a storm coming?"

"It's *too* warm," Tucker says seriously. "It ain't natural fer this time of year. See them dark clouds t' th' north?"

Ella follows Tucker's pointing hand. "Well, yes, now I do. Is that some sort of sign?"

"My knees tells me them clouds is bringin' a bad storm. Could be a tornady, and Pap McDaniel never did dig him a storm cellar."

"It could be a what? A tor-na-dy? Are you talking about a tornado?"

Exasperated, Tucker says, "Yes, that's what I said! A tornady. Now where's yore root cellar?"

"I don't have one," Ella replies. "But I'll be all right. Besides, I've never heard of a tornado in November."

"Well, I'll tell you right now that them's the worst kind," Tucker says solemnly. "Listen t' me. If th' wind starts pickin' up real strong, you better come up t' my place. We've gotta root cellar we use when storms come."

"Well thank you for your offer, " Ella says. "I'll remember it."

By midafternoon the dark clouds have rolled in, ushering in a premature twilight. The wind seems unable to make up its mind which direction to blow, creating frequent swirls. There are intermittent downpours. And the temperature is dropping.

Tucker and the children are gathered around the table eating supper.

As Tucker finishes her last bite, she says, "March, you close all th' windows in th' house. It's gittin' cold. August, you go down t' Miss Ella's an' bring 'er here. Don't take no fer an answer from her neither. Tell 'er I says t' come now."

The boys scoot back their chairs and set out on their assigned missions.

"April, you come with me an' let's be sure thar's coal oil in th' lanterns in th' root cellar."

April grabs two fingers of Tucker's beefy hand and follows her out the door.

Walking to the side of the house, Tucker reaches for the door on the ground. Lifting it with a grunt she fastens the handle to a post to keep it perched open.

Staring into the dark hole, April wraps her arms around Tucker's leg.

"Quit actin' like that," Tucker says gruffly. "Ain't nothin' in there gonna hurt y'."

Tucker and April descend slowly down the steps, into the inky blackness. A moist, earthy smell welcomes them, and April holds her nose.

Feeling around in the dark, Tucker's hands find a lantern on a shelf and a box of matches resting beside it. She strikes a match and lights the wick. The sudden brightness causes the darkness to retreat to the corners and to hide behind posts and boxes.

Tucker shakes the lantern gently and hears the coal oil sloshing inside. Holding it at arm's length in front of her, she says, "Now where's that can of coal oil?" After a moment she spies it resting in a corner.

Walking over to the can she hefts it a few inches off the ground with a grunt and lets it drop with a thud. "Good. We got plenty of fuel."

March appears at the opening into the cellar. "Tucker!" he hollers. "I got all the windows closed. What now?"

A bolt of lightning streaks across the sky. Everyone freezes. Off in the distance a low rumble of thunder sounds, lasting several seconds.

A sudden downpour chases March down the steps into the cellar. "Yeeha!" he shouts excitedly. "We got us a storm coming!" He makes a face and lunges at April. As she darts behind Tucker, he gives a ghoulish laugh. "Watch out for the boogeyman, April," he taunts.

Tucker takes a swing at March, but he is expecting it and darts out of the way. "Leave 'er alone," Tucker says. "You're more aggervatin' than a case of th' chiggers. Go look an' see if August is comin' with Miss Ella."

"But it's raining," March counters.

Looking around, Tucker spies a broom. Grabbing it, she starts for March. "I didn't ask y' fer a weather report. Git on up an' do what I said."

March is up the steps in a flash, aided by a swat on his bottom from the broom, and disappears into the driving rain.

A sudden rush of wind rattles the treetops. A careening piece of tin pauses at the opening to the cellar and then darts off, powerless against the wind.

The rain shuts off abruptly. Tucker puts her hand on April's shoulder. "You stay here while I git ever'body rounded up." Looking up at the darkened sky, Tucker starts up the steps.

As her shoulders clear the opening, she hears March's voice over the howling wind. "Hurry up!"

She turns to see August coming around the corner of the house with his arm around Ella, the wind tearing at her dress. As they arrive at the cellar, Tucker takes Ella's hand. "Take it easy and foller me," she yells into her ear.

They go down into the safety of the cellar, March and August on their heels.

Tucker goes back up the steps to lower the door. As she unfastens it from the post, a brilliant bolt of lightning brightens the entire yard. An immediate clap of thunder shakes the ground. In the distance there is a sound like an approaching train. Tucker blinks twice.

Backing slowly down the steps, she eases the cellar door above her down to the ground. She joins the circle of people gathered around the glowing lantern. Everyone's face shines from moisture left by the rain, except for April's.

Ella and the children look expectantly at Tucker.

Trying to be heard above the deafening din of the storm outside, Ella yells, "Is it a tornado?"

Tucker does not reply. There is a glazed expression on her face.

"Tucker!" Ella persists.

"She's doing that thing she does sometimes!" March yells.

"Yeah, you're right!" August shouts.

Ella looks from one boy to the other. "What are you two talking about?!"

"Sometimes when there's a bad thunderstorm, she just kinda leaves," August explains. "I mean, she's still there, but she ain't there."

"Then after a bit, she comes back," March adds.

The sound of the roaring train drowns out Ella's reply.

The storm slowly inhales, opening the cellar door overhead. With an explosion, the storm exhales, slamming the door shut and blowing out the lantern.

The cellar is plunged into blackness.

CHAPTER EIGHTEEN

Standing in the hallway of the barn, Tucker looks at the silhouette of her father's body hanging in the doorway, backlit by lightning from the retreating storm. Heavy drops dripping from the edge of the tin roof can be heard plopping into puddles below. The rest of nature has fallen silent, as if shocked at what it has witnessed this night.

"There ain't but one thing left t' do," Tucker says to the lifeless form, "an' that's t' get rid of you so's no one won't never find you." Turning around she walks the length of the hallway, and opens the door to a room. Switching on the light, she scans the walls. Hanging on them are the handsaws, butcher knives, filleting knives and various-size hooks used for slaughtering hogs, an annual event Tucker has participated in since childhood.

She selects a fillet knife and a saw. *These'll be all I need.* Turning out the light, she walks back to the other end of the hallway.

Her father's overalls and underwear hang in a wad around his ankles, the same position they were in for the last act of his violent life.

Tucker reaches with her left hand and roughly grabs the part of him that has violated her so often. "Y' won't be needin' this no more," she says. With the fillet knife in her right hand she slices it off and throws it to the ground.

She then cuts his boot strings and pulls the boots off. Without the bulky boots to stop them, his overalls and underwear, heavy from the rain and mud, slide over his feet and land in a pile in the mud. Tucker kicks them to one side. After slicing off his shirt, Tucker lays the knife and saw on a bench in the hallway and wipes sweat from her face with her sleeve.

Walking into the darkness of the barnyard, she trudges through the mud toward the shed where their truck stays parked.

Tucker uses the gas pedal and hand choke to coax the black '49 Chevy pickup into starting. In coughing spurts, its engine responds and finally idles smoothly. She is backing it out of the shed when a sudden thought makes her stop. Pulling on the emergency brake and leaving the motor running, she walks to the side of the shed, bends down, grabs the edge of a heavy canvas tarpaulin, and begins dragging it. Underneath it, a twelve-foot jon boat slowly appears. Grasping the handle at the bow, she drags the aluminum boat to the back of the truck and lifts the bow until it rests on the lowered tailgate. Then she walks to the other end of the boat, picks it up off the ground and shoves the boat into the bed of the truck.

She circles the shed and finds an assortment of concrete blocks stacked against the other side. She grips a block in each hand and places them in the bed of the boat. By the time she has carried a dozen of the blocks to the truck, sweat is again pouring from every pore of her body. Winded, she leans against the side of the truck to catch her breath.

Like wolves circling and nipping at a wounded deer, her conscience keeps pricking her. *I don't care what people say or how they judge me. They ain't lived th' life I've lived. It was either me kill him, or I was gonna kill myself. I couldn't take it no more.*

Tucker returns to the cab of the truck and backs the truck down to the barn, stopping just short of the hallway opening. Cutting off the engine, she gets out and retrieves the fillet knife from the bench.

Standing in front of her father's naked body, she takes a deep breath and, gripping the handle of the knife, slices into the joint where his hip and leg join. After cutting all the tendons, she takes the saw and removes his leg. Once it is free, she tosses it into the jon boat. She repeats the process on his other leg.

With the same efficiency and technique, she removes both her father's arms at the shoulders and adds them to the grisly heap in the boat.

Then, taking the tip of the fillet knife, Tucker carefully pierces his skin just below the sternum and slices meticulously downward to his pubic bone, being careful not to pierce any organs inside. Using both hands, she spreads apart the slit she has created. Gravity suddenly takes over and blood, fluid, and organs cascade from the opening, making a smacking sound as they land in the mud. Steam rises from the entrails, carrying with it the metallic smell of blood.

Tucker walks over to the side of the barn opening and unties the rope leading to the block and tackle. Inch by inch she lowers her father's empty torso to the ground and unties the chain from around his neck. Squatting down, she hefts the carcass off the ground and lifts it into the jon boat.

Walking over to the hog pen, she speaks to the three occupants as she opens the gate. "Come on, you sows. I need you t' help me clean up."

Not accustomed to being awakened at this hour, the three hogs grunt noisily as they pass through the gate. Tucker leads them to the pile of viscera at the barn opening. Fully awake now, the three ravenously attack their midnight snack.

Tucker reaches down and picks up her father's discarded clothing and boots. Along with a can of kerosene, she takes them to the middle of the barnyard. After dousing them with kerosene, she takes a Zippo lighter out of her pocket and sets them ablaze. Sitting down on the step of the pickup truck, Tucker rests. The flames dance in her dark eyes and cast ghostly shadows on the side of the barn.

As the flames begin to die down, having finished their job of devouring the bloody clothes, Tucker checks on the progress of the hogs. There is nothing remaining, though the hogs continue to root in the mud, hoping to find another tasty morsel. Convinced the hogs have done her bidding, she shoos them back into their pen.

She then returns to the truck and drives slowly out of the lot and onto the gravel road. As she drives, the clouded sky begins breaking up and gives way to a brilliant full moon.

Forty-five minutes later she pulls off the main road onto a dirt lane that parallels the north fork of the Obion River. Tucker has been here many times with her father, fishing the flooded bottomlands thick with lily pads and teeming with alligator gar.

She slows to a stop and gets out of her truck with a coil of rope in her hand. When she drags the boat out of the bed, it lands with a heavy thud.

In spite of the bright moon, Tucker is not concerned about being discovered. She hasn't seen another vehicle for the past twenty miles and hasn't seen a house in the last five.

Opening a pocketknife she cuts the rope into four-foot lengths. She ties one end of each rope to a body part and then threads the other end through two cinder blocks and ties a knot. She uses six cinder blocks for the torso.

Fastening her hands firmly to the bow of the boat, Tucker digs her heels in and leans back with all her might. Inch by inch she pulls the boat toward the wet grave awaiting her father's body. Once she is knee-deep in the water, she goes to the rear of the boat and gives it a running push into the water. As the boat clears the bank, Tucker jumps in.

Reaching in the bottom of the boat, she picks up the paddle. In very slow, even strokes she navigates the boat through the inky water and its overlay of shiny lily pads.

Over the next two hours Tucker distributes her cargo over a three-mile stretch of water. "I've seen what you gar can do to a chicken leg," she says aloud. "You've picked it clean when I was usin' it fer bait. Now I want ya'll to finish this job fer me. Don't leave nothin' but th' bones. That thick mud on the bottom will take care of *them*."

When she finally arrives back at home and drives the pickup truck into its shed, the sky is lightening in the east. Exhaling slowly, she lowers her forehead onto the steering wheel.

After a moment, her body begins shaking and teardrops fall onto her lap.

CHAPTER NINETEEN

The early morning light begins filtering through the cracks in the door to the root cellar. April silently watches as it inches across the earthen floor. The only sound is the deep breathing of her fellow refugees from last night's storm.

After a few minutes, she tugs at Tucker's shirt. Tucker jerks awake, shouting, "I don't know where he is!"

Ella, August, and March are roused by Tucker's shouting.

"What's happened?" August asks.

"Tucker, are you all right?" Ella cries out.

Tucker comes fully awake. "Is ever'body okay?"

Except for April, everyone responds affirmatively.

Standing, Tucker says, "Well let's go have us a look-see."

She walks up the steps, lifting the overhead door as she goes. Once outside, she says, "Ya'll come on up."

One by one, the others walk past her, squinting into the brilliant sun. Yesterday's warmth has been chased away by last night's cold front. They all grab at their collars to keep the cold at bay.

"Where's the outhouse?" March asks. "I gotta pee."

They all look to where the outhouse used to stand and see only the seat, with no signs of the walls or roof.

Sweeping his hand toward the end of the house, August says, "All that tin in the yard had to come from somewhere. Must've come from the house or the barn."

Tucker turns to look at the house. "It looks like the pieces of tree limbs, rocks, an' trash that was flyin' in th' air busted out some winders."

Ella notices April pointing and silently crying. Kneeling down beside her she asks, "What's the matter, April?" She looks in the direction of April's pointing finger and sees a giant tree has blown over.

August moves beside April and picks her up. To Ella he says, "That's where her swing was. That was her favorite thing to do, swing in that tree swing." Wiping April's tears with his hand, he says, "That's all right. I'll find you another tree and we'll get you a swing put up. Okay?"

April sniffs and nods her head.

Tucker heads toward the back door of the house. "Let's see what th' inside looks like."

The children hurry after her. Ella pauses at the door, suddenly realizing this will be the first time she has ever been inside Tucker's house.

Stepping inside, Ella gapes at what she sees: the kitchen table with four mismatched chairs, the unfinished wooden floor with a ragged piece of linoleum in front of the sink, the walls covered in cardboard. *I knew she was poor, but . . .*

After scouting out the bedrooms, the children assemble in the living room to report to Tucker. Ella joins them.

Looking at Ella, Tucker smiles and says, "Well, looks like we done all right. 'Sides them winders, that tree in back an' th' outhouse, we didn't have no other damage."

Still trying to process the abject poverty her friend lives in, Ella says, "That's wonderful, Tucker. I better go see how things are at my house."

"Yeah," Tucker agrees. "You head on down. I'll send th' kids in a bit t' help out. Then I'll be down in a little while t' see what happened."

As Ella approaches her house she sees that the tornado did more damage to her place than Tucker's. Three trees are down in front, and one of them has caved in the front porch. As she gets to her mailbox she sees a strange man coming from around the back of the house.

He sees her at the same time and meets her beside the upturned trees. He is wearing a tan shirt and work pants that don't appear to have crossed paths with detergent and water in months. The knees are nearly black and the shirt has multiple stains of unknown origin. His thin face makes her think of Laurel, the skinny half of Laurel and Hardy. But this Laurel's face hasn't been shaved in a week. When he grins at Ella, she counts a total of three teeth visible in his mouth.

As he takes off his cap and sticks out his hand, Ella notices a shock of faded red hair on his head.

"Ehwoh. Ah 'ame iss 'ady Gween. Ooo gotta 'ess 'ere. Ooo ahnt me 'elp?"

Ella's mouth drops open, uncertain whether to scream, run, or chase this scarecrow off.

Grinning, the stranger says, "Ah ood wookeh. Ooo ass 'uckeh. She tell ooo." He points in the direction of Tucker's house. Putting his fist in the air, he bends his arm at the elbow. "Eel iss. Ah shrong," he says as he pats his thin biceps.

Trying her best to understand what this man is saying and to determine if she should be afraid or amused, Ella asks, "You know Tucker?"

"Oh sewer. Bebberbobby know 'uckeh."

At that moment August, March, and April arrive at Ella's house.

"Shady Green!" March yells and breaks into a run.

Ella's newest acquaintance catches March, throws him into the air, and catches him just before he hits the ground.

August comes and puts his arm around the man's shoulders. "You okay, Shady? How's your place after this storm?"

"Ol' 'ady, he be oh-ay."

Ella interjects, "You boys know this man?"

"Sure we do," March says. "This is Shady Green. Everybody knows Shady."

Ella looks at August, who nods agreement. Leaning toward Ella, he whispers, "He just don't talk right. That's all that's wrong with him."

Shady kneels in front of April. Reaching into his pocket he brings out a harmonica. April smiles in anticipation.

After tapping it on his palm a couple of times, Shady breaks into a rousing rendition of *The Wabash Cannonball*. He jumps and dances around April, looking every bit the part of Mr. Bojangles.

Watching him flap his elbows in rhythm, Ella is concerned his feeble joints will disconnect.

March and August whoop and holler. Ella has never seen April's face so alive and animated. It warms her heart.

As Shady finishes the tune, Ella says to them, "You all come with me."

Stepping through the branches on her porch, Ella pays no attention to the broken-down front door and smashed front window. She squeezes past a limb and into her living room.

The others follow close behind, with Shady carrying April.

Ella barely notices that her back door is standing open, framing a scene of devastation as far as the eye can see. After leading the group into her bedroom, she gets down on her knees beside her bed and reaches under it. In a moment she pulls out a black case. Sitting on her bed, she places the case beside her.

Shady and the children gather around, wide-eyed, to see what mission Ella is on.

Clicking open the latches she lays back the top to reveal a stringed instrument.

"Ooo ay at?" Shady asks.

Ella picks it up out of the case and lays it in her lap.

"What is it?" August asks.

"It's called an Autoharp," Ella replies.

"Ahmma 'aybell ay un," Shady chimes in.

Finally understanding something Shady has said, Ella smiles warmly. "Yes, Momma Maybelle Carter played one of these." Picking up the picks from the case, Ella begins strumming.

The children are spellbound.

"Ah oh at un," Shady says and he pulls out his harmonica to join in with Ella. Ella nods approvingly toward him.

Tucker pauses on Ella's porch and cocks her head to one side, much like a dog would as he listens to a mole boring underground. Listening closely to the music coming from Ella's house, Tucker recognizes the tune. It is a song she remembers her mother humming to her as a child and the same one that Tucker used to hum to Maisy.

Pushing her way through the downed limbs, she eases inside the front door and walks quietly through the living room. As she does so, she hears Ella's voice singing above the instruments, "We've no less days to sing God's praise than when we've first begun."

Tucker peers around the corner into Ella's bedroom as the strains of the song die out. She sees April sitting beside Ella, smiling and holding onto her arm. April's expression is an arrow piercing Tucker's heart. *I ain't never seen her look so content an' peaceful. What's Ella got that I ain't got that can affect April so much? I wasn't no 'count as a mother t' Maisy, an' I ain't done these kids no good either.*

CHAPTER TWENTY

Ella looks up from her Autoharp and sees Tucker standing in the doorway. Smiling, she says, "We decided to have a little impromptu post-tornado hootenanny."

"Come in," August says to Tucker. "Look at this amazing instrument Ella can play. She's really good!"

"It's called an autoheart," March says to August. "Don't you know anything?"

Ella tousles March's hair. "Thank you for trying to help, March, but it's called an Autoharp."

"Is that what angels in heaven play?" March asks.

"Don't be stupid," August says. "Their harps don't look like this one, do they, Miss Ella?"

Working hard to not appear to be choosing sides in this sibling battle, Ella says, "I really don't know. I've never been to heaven."

Shady Green says something to Tucker that is unintelligible to Ella.

"Don't look like you doin' much work t' me," Tucker replies.

Unsure what has put the edge in Tucker's voice, Ella laughs, hoping to diffuse things. "Don't blame him, Tucker. I was the one who dragged everyone inside for our little concert. It was Mr. Green's harmonica playing that made me think of my mother's Autoharp. I couldn't resist playing with him."

Shady blushes.

Suddenly, a woman's distant cry comes drifting in through the broken windows of Ella's house. Everyone in the bedroom turns their attention to the sound.

"Isn't that coming from the direction of your house, Tucker?" Ella asks.

The woman's cry sounds again, but this time more distinctly. "Tucker! April! Boys! Where are you?!"

Tucker folds her arms across her chest and sticks her chin out. Through clenched teeth she says, "Maisy."

"It's Mama!" August and March say excitedly. They race out of Ella's bedroom, past Tucker, and scramble through the branches of the tree in Ella's living room.

Ella feels April's grip tighten on her arm.

Tucker turns and follows the boys.

Shady looks at Ella and says something she thinks is about cleaning up. Pulling a pair of leather work gloves from his back pocket he slips them onto his hands.

Ella notices that they are both left-handed gloves, but Shady has turned one of them backward so he can wear it on his right hand. She starts to say something to him but doesn't want to run the risk of embarrassing him again, so she lets him go about his business.

Ella looks down at April, expecting to see the same beatific smile she saw a few moments ago, when she and Shady were playing music, but there is a look of fear dancing around the edges of April's eyes. Ella resists furrowing her own brow while wondering what is bothering April. Instead she pats April on the cheek and says, "Let's me and you go outside and find your mother. I'll bet she's worried about you."

Holding April's hand, she has to gently tug to get her to slide off the bed and follow her. She leads the way through the barrier of limbs and leaves in the living room. Each step they take, April seems to grip her hand more tightly. As they emerge into the daylight, Ella sees the boys running up the gravel road with reckless abandon toward their house while Tucker lumbers behind them.

Ella takes a step toward the road but is stopped by the backward pull of April's hand. She turns around and asks, "What's the matter, April?"

April looks down at her feet and says nothing.

"Come on, let's go find your mother," Ella says and again takes a step toward Tucker's.

April acts as if her feet are anchored in concrete.

Ella looks down at April. "Don't you want to see your mother?"

April looks up quickly at Ella. Her lips twist and her tongue can be seen working inside her cheeks, but she doesn't make a sound. Slowly, she looks back down.

What is wrong here? What is she afraid of? Not trying to hide her concern this time, she squats in front of April. "Come on. I'll go with you. It'll be okay." She stands and pulls a little more firmly on April's hand, and she finally acquiesces and begins walking with her toward the scene at Tucker's house.

Even with April's small stride, she and Ella reach Tucker's yard at the same time Tucker does.

Ella sees the boys talking to a woman, animatedly detailing the events of the past twenty-four hours. *I can't believe my eyes!* This has to be Maisy, but she doesn't look anything like Ella expected. She searches for any similarities between Maisy and Tucker, glancing back and forth at the two, but can find none, save for their height. Maisy's flowing dark hair, full lips, beautiful eyes, makeup, and shapeliness, readily revealed by her tight-fitting clothes, make her the virtual antithesis of Tucker.

March is tugging on Maisy's arm and pointing toward the back of the house. "And it blowed our outhouse away!" he says.

Ella stays at the edge of the yard as Tucker walks toward her daughter. April latches on to Ella's leg.

When Maisy sees Tucker approaching, she says, "Tucker, are you all right? I was scared to death when I got here and nobody was around. I heard the storm last night, but it didn't do no damage in town. I came out here as quick as I could. It looks like you all was lucky. March says you lost your outhouse. Maybe now you'll get you some indoor plumbing. I mean, it's crazy for you all to be living like you do. This is the 1970s, you know. It's not like we're living in the Depression. And where is April? I ain't seen her. Where is she? She's not still acting like a retard, is she? I swear I don't know what I'm going to do with her. But look at these boys! Aren't they handsome?"

"Can you just shut yore mouth?" Tucker interjects. "Good lord, child! You spit out words faster then I spit out my tobacky juice."

Maisy rolls her eyes at Tucker, but says nothing.

Tucker looks back toward Ella. "Thar's April right there, standin' with Miss Ella."

"Miss Ella this. Miss Ella that," Maisy says. "Seems like every time I come out here all I here about is this Ella woman. I'll be glad to finally meet her."

Tucker squints at Maisy. "You best mind yore manners, 'specially yore tongue. Ella's a good woman."

Ella is amazed that the two of them are talking as if no one can hear their conversation, when the boys are standing right beside them and she and April are within easy earshot.

Maisy snorts at Tucker's pointed admonition and folds her arms across her chest. When she notices she has duplicated Tucker's pose, she quickly drops her arms.

Curious to get a closer look at Maisy, Ella pries April from her thigh and approaches the proceedings. When she and April get within a few feet of them, April lets go of Ella's hand and darts behind Tucker, wrapping her arms around Tucker's thigh.

Maisy says, "So you must be Ella."

Extending her hand, Ella says, "Yes. My name is Ella."

When Maisy doesn't immediately shake Ella's hand, Tucker spits toward the side of Maisy's foot.

Maisy reluctantly takes the cue and shakes Ella's hand. "Nice to meet you, Ella," she says sarcastically.

Ignoring Maisy's tone, Ella says to Tucker, "Do you think I should get back down to my house and keep an eye on Shady Green?"

"He'll do y' good work," Tucker replies. "An' y' can trust him not t' steal nothin'. He just tends t' be a little lazy, that's all."

Ella notices the children's lips have turned blue and their teeth are chattering from running around in the cold air while wearing yesterday's warm-weather clothes. "The children look like they might need to put on some warmer clothes, don't you think?"

Tucker looks at each of the children. "If'n you kids is cold, git in th' house and find y' some warm clothes t' put on. I'll come in an' make us some breakfast." Looking at Maisy, she says, "You stayin'?"

"I'd love to stay and visit with you kids some more," Maisy replies, "but I've got to get back to town. I have an appointment I have to keep. Ya'll give me hugs now. And wish me happy birthday. Today's your mama's birthday!"

As she throws open her arms, August and March eagerly step into her embrace and wish her happy birthday. April peeps from behind Tucker but holds fast to her leg.

Ignoring April, Maisy bounces off to her car, singing, "Happy Birthday to me. Happy Birthday to me. Happy Birthday, dear Maisy . . ." The closing car door cuts off the final phrase.

Tucker turns to the kids and says, "Now ya'll git on in th' house like I tol'ja. It feels like it could snow by nightfall."

As the kids scamper off, Tucker scans the horizon.

"What are you looking for?" Ella asks.

"Jes' seein' if there's a cloud bank comin' this way that could signal snow comin'." She then turns and watches Maisy drive off.

Ella notices as a shiver jolts Tucker.

"It sure feels like yore birthday," Ella hears Tucker mutter. "A day just like th' day you was born."

CHAPTER TWENTY-ONE

When Tucker walks into her house, she sniffs and says loudly, "I do b'lieve somebody is cookin' sausage."

April comes scampering out of the kitchen, grinning. Taking Tucker's hand, she pulls her to follow.

When they get to the doorway, Tucker sees August standing at the stove, spatula in hand, as he looks into the cast iron skillet resting on the eye. Meanwhile, March is pulling plates out of the cabinet. "So what's this here all 'bout?" Tucker asks.

August has been so focused on frying sausage, he has not noticed Tucker. At the sound of her voice he jumps and turns toward her. He breaks into a grin. "We decided we'd get breakfast started!"

Tucker walks over to him. "You think y' know what you're doin'?"

Before August can reply, March drops the plastic plates he's carrying. They clatter and rattle across the floor. He drops on his knees and starts grabbing them up. "And I'm setting the table!" he says proudly once he gathers them.

A smile darts around the edges of Tucker's lips. Folding her arms across her chest, she looks at April and says, "An' what are you doin' t' help, little miss?"

April shrugs her shoulders.

"Well, why don't y' drag a chair over to th' sink an' I'll teach you how t' crack eggs in a bowl."

April quickly pulls a chair across the floor until it bangs into the cabinet.

As Tucker gets the eggs out of the refrigerator, she says, "First thing t' do is wash yore hands real good."

April leans over the sink and turns on the faucet. Picking up the bar of soap resting on the back of the sink, she passes it under the water and puts it back. Then she lets the water run over her hands until Tucker arrives beside her, and she turns the faucet off.

Tucker sets a bowl in the sink and selects an egg. "Now watch real close," she says to April. She taps it once on the side of the sink and turns it over for April to see. "You see how I hit it hard enough t' crack it but not hard enough t' crush it?"

April's head bobs up and down.

"That's somethin' you'll have t' practice a bit t' git it right. Then y' place yore thumbs on th' cracked place and push in until it cracks open more, like this. Then hold it over th' bowl an' pull th' two halves apart an' let th' egg fall in th' bowl."

April looks at the dark yellow yolk floating in the sea of clear egg white. She looks up at Tucker.

"You wanta try one?" Tucker asks.

April nods.

"All right then, try away."

August and March have stopped paying attention to their jobs, keen on seeing how well their little sister does.

April picks up an egg and gently taps it on the side of the sink. When she turns it over to look at it, the shell is still intact. She looks up at Tucker.

"Looks t' me like you're gonna have t' tap it a little harder."

April tries again, but has the same results.

"Smack that thing!" March says. "You ain't gonna have no luck just tapping it like that."

At her brother's urging, April slams the egg against the side of the sink. Yolk and egg squirt into the air and hit March right on his forehead. Everyone stares in shocked disbelief at March. But when the yolk starts sliding down between his eyes and down the bridge of his nose, Tucker and August burst into laughter.

"Hey!" March exclaims. "It's not funny!" But he is distracted by something behind August. Pointing, he says, "Where's that smoke coming from?"

August whirls around. "The sausage is burning!" He starts to grab the skillet, but Tucker grabs him just in time.

"Don't touch that hot skillet without a potholder!" Taking the spatula out of August's hand, she slides the skillet off the eye.

"August burned the sausage! August burned the sausage!" March taunts his brother.

August starts to make a move toward his brother when Tucker says, "Both of y' hold it right there. Don't start nothin' that I'm gonna have t' finish. March, clean yore face up in th' sink there. April, you're gonna have t' wait til some other time fer me t' help y' learn t' fix eggs. August, you pour ever'body some milk. I'll finish up breakfast."

Once breakfast is finished the four of them spend the rest of the day cleaning up the aftermath of the tornado's destruction. Tucker and the boys cut cardboard from the stockpile that they normally use to line the inside of their exterior walls in winter and place the pieces over the windows that the storm blew out. Later they find the pieces of the outhouse, nail them back together and place the completed structure over the seat.

As evening approaches, the air turns even colder. Tucker stirs the pot of homemade soup she's fixed for supper. She walks into the living room, where the children are resting. "August, you make sure they's plenty of firewood in th' house. March, you get a fire goin' in th' stove. I believe snow is movin' in." Suddenly she slaps the side of her thigh. "I clean fergot 'bout Miss Ella! I gotta go make sure she's gonna stay warm t'night in that busted-up house of hers. Who knows if Shady Green got any work done t'day? I'll be back in a bit. Supper's on th' stove. If I ain't back by bedtime, tuck yoreselves in."

She grabs her faded denim jacket off a hook by the front door and slips it on. As she steps outside, the north wind slaps her on the side of her face and tries to tear open her jacket. Tucker zips her jacket up to her thick neck and plunges her hands into its pockets. Lowering her head, she takes off toward Ella's as quickly as her tired legs will carry her.

She arrives at Ella's breathing heavily. The pile of freshly cut wood in Ella's front yard assures Tucker that Shady Green actually did some work today. Stepping into the area that was Ella's porch, Tucker is confronted by a wall of black plastic and duct tape. She calls out, "Ella!"

She hears a muted reply from inside. "Is that you, Tucker?"

"Yes."

"You'll have to come around to the back door."

Tucker makes her way around the house where Ella is waiting with the door open. A rectangle of yellow light spills out of the house.

"Come in, Tucker. You're going to freeze out there."

Tucker eases inside, immediately thankful for the warmth. "Looks like ol' Shady sealed you up in here. And yore heat's a-workin'?"

Setting two cups of hot coffee on her kitchen table, Ella replies, "Sit down first and warm up. Yes, Shady worked all day cutting the branches off my porch and then putting that plastic up for temporary shelter. And, amazingly, my heat is keeping it warm in here. What brings you down here so late?"

"It's gonna get real cold t'night an' I thought maybe you wouldn't have no heat. I was gonna offer t' let y' come t' my house fer th' night."

Ella's eyes fill with tears. "Tucker, that's the nicest thing anyone has done for me in a long time. I really appreciate it. But I think I'll be okay here tonight."

Shifting uncomfortably under the force of Ella's praise, Tucker says, "It ain't nothin'. You'd done th' same fer me I expect."

They sit in silence for a few moments as they sip their coffee.

Ella breaks the silence. "Can I ask you a question?"

Looking at her coffee, Tucker replies, "Sure."

"Have you ever been married?"

Tucker's head snaps up and her voice takes on an edge. "What makes y' ask that?"

"I'm not trying to be nosy. I was just wondering about Maisy. Does she have her father's features?"

Tucker gets up so fast her chair topples over and her coffee spills onto the table. "That ain't none of yore damn business!" She glares at Ella for a moment and then turns and stomps out the door.

Ella runs to the door and calls into the darkness, "Tucker! Come back here! I'm sorry. I meant no harm."

Tucker trudges through the dark toward her house. *That's what happens when y' try an' make friends! They try t' get in yore business an' ask lots of questions. My business is my business. Who does Ella think she is, askin' me that kind of question?*

By the time Tucker gets to her house her teeth are chattering from the cold. Entering, she feels the welcoming warmth of the wood stove. It is dark inside, the children having already gone to bed.

Tucker pulls her rocker close to the stove and drops heavily into it. Her mind is in a whirl thinking of Maisy's birth on a cold night just like tonight and of Ella's attempt at probing into the most private area of her life. With these unsettling thoughts weighing heavy on her, Tucker's head begins to nod as the stove warms her. Soon she falls into a fitful sleep.

CHAPTER TWENTY-TWO

Tucker's labor contraction grips her like a vise. She holds her breath and tries to grit her teeth but can't because they are chattering from the cold. As the contraction slowly eases, the carbon dioxide building up in her lungs explodes out her mouth. Immediately she starts panting like a coon dog hot on the trail of its quarry, eagerly filling her lungs with fresh air.

She's known for six months that this was coming. Six months ago she stood naked and turned sideways in front of the mirror in her bedroom to look at the bulge that had slowly been growing in her abdomen. She'd tried to pretend it wasn't happening, that it couldn't be true, that she just needed to stop eating so much. But standing in front of the mirror, she finally admitted to herself that, three months after her sixteenth birthday, she was indeed pregnant.

Curse you! I ain't never gonna be free from you! Now what am I going to do?

Walking over to her dresser she slid open a drawer. Lying inside were various-size balls of yarn her mother used to use when knitting or crocheting scarves and afghans. In the front of the drawer, staring back at Tucker, were two small knitting needles and a large, ominous crochet hook. She picked up the crochet hook and let her finger run along its sleek length to the pointed tip of the hook. She'd heard stories of women using one to get rid of the unwanted baby they were carrying. But there were also tales of women bleeding to death from doing it.

I can't have a baby, especially not this baby. I don't know nothin' 'bout babies or having babies. With dread wrapped around her like a shawl, she walked downstairs and out to the outhouse behind the house. She sat down inside, pulled her panties down to her ankles and hiked her dress up around her waist. Her hand trembled as she lowered the crochet hook between her legs. When the cold steel touched her private area, she flinched and lost her grip on the crochet hook. It tumbled down into the hole of the outhouse.

Tucker stared in shocked disbelief. Then she closed her eyes as a wave of relief washed over her. *I guess I'm a bigger chicken than I thought I was.*

Suddenly a thought occurred to her. *Of course! Mama Mattie, she'll know what to do.*

She drove the old pickup the half mile to Mama Mattie's house. Its ramshackle appearance always reminded Tucker of her own house. As soon as she got out of the truck, the front door opened and a short, thin black woman stepped out.

Shielding her eyes from the sun, the black lady called out, "Is that you, Tucker?"

"Yeah, it's me, Mama Mattie."

"Come up here on th' porch an' sit with me, child."

As Tucker stepped up on the porch, Mattie offered her a ladder-back chair. They sat facing each other.

Tucker searched her heart and mind for the words to tell Mama Mattie, but nothing sounded like it made sense.

With a posture that made it look like she had all the time in the world, Mattie sat in silence.

Tucker focused her attention on an odd-shaped knothole in one of the planks in Mattie's porch. In a quiet voice she said, "I've knowed you my whole life, Mama Mattie."

"Yes, child, that's right. I helped yo' mama deliver you."

"I think I'm in trouble, Mama Mattie."

"You's pregnant, ain't you, child?"

Tucker jerked her head up and looked at Mattie. "How'd you know?"

"Girl, Mama Mattie's done delivered hundreds of babies. I can tells when someone be carryin'. How far along is you?"

With a sigh, Tucker answered, "It must be three months."

"Does you know who the daddy is?" Mattie asks.

"'Course I do!" Tucker snapped. "Ain't but one person ever had me."

"Has you told him you's pregnant?"

Tucker tried to return the searching look from Mattie's dark eyes, but she finally blinked and looked away. "He ain't around no more."

"Umm hmmm. Has you told you daddy about it?"

Tucker gripped the sides of her chair. "Nobody's seen my daddy fer three months. He musta run off just like my mama did."

"Ummm hmmm. I sees," Mattie replied slowly. "Even though you's by youself, you's better off without that man. He's as sorry a man as I's ever knowed. Now tells me what you wants Mama Mattie to do for you."

Looking down at the floor, Tucker located the knothole again. "Can you get rid of this baby for me?"

"Why you wants to do that, Tucker? What's you afraid of?"

"I'm afraid the baby won't be right. Something will be wrong with it."

"Hush, child. That's just plain foolish talk. Strong girl like you'll have a fine baby," Mattie reassured her.

With eyes full of tears, Tucker looked up at Mattie and said, "You don't understand. I just can't have this baby."

Mattie scooted her chair to close the distance between them. Taking Tucker's hands in hers, she said, "First of all, I thinks I do understand. An' that's all I'll say 'bout that. Second thing you gots to know is, Mama Mattie don't kill babies. I know people in town says I do, but it ain't true. Why don't you let me help you have this child?"

As another contraction begins its squeeze on her body, Tucker cries out, "Damn you, Mattie!"

Just then Mattie opens the bedroom door carrying a pan of steaming water and an armload of towels. "What's that you done say about me? You swearin' at me?"

"Yes I am!" Tucker yells at the height of the contraction. "Why'd I let you talk me into having this baby?"

Mattie chuckles. "Lots of womenfolk done cursed my name whiles they in labor."

"Why is it so cold in here?" Tucker asks.

"Mattie know babies does better if they's born in the cold. It's better for you, too. After that baby gets here, we'll let some heat in and warm you both."

The next hour passes with Tucker squeezing Mattie's hand through the duration of each contraction.

When Mattie takes a watch out of the pocket of her apron and looks at it, she gets out of her chair and walks to the foot of the bed. Lifting the sheet to look between Tucker's legs, Mattie says, "It's time, girl. Time for you to bear down 'an push fer all you's worth."

Grunting, Tucker pushes with all her might.

"You's doin' good," Mattie encourages her. "You's almost done."

Suddenly Tucker feels something pass between her legs and then an easing of the pressure. There is the sound of slapping flesh and a muted cry.

"Lord Almighty!" Mattie exclaims.

"What's wrong?" Tucker cries out. "Is it deformed? Is it all right?"

Mattie answers, "I believe this is the most beautiful baby girl I done ever delivered. She is amazing." After wrapping the baby in a ragged towel, Mattie brings her to Tucker's side. "Look what you done done, child. You done had a baby. Ain't she beautiful?"

Tucker reluctantly looks at her baby. Even though the baby is brand-new, Tucker sees the traits of her father in every inch of her.

"Ain't that a beautiful head of black hair?" Mattie asks. "Now open up your top and let the little one nurse a bit."

When Tucker hesitates, Mattie unbuttons Tucker's top and pushes the baby toward her breast. As the hungry mouth latches on to her nipple, Tucker feels a familiar sick feeling in the pit of her stomach and turns her head away.

Mattie notices and strokes Tucker's head. "Now you listen t' me, child. I know this ain't easy. This baby didn't ask to come into this world but come she has. Ain't nothin' her fault. You gotta do the right thing by her and take care of her. Make her your baby, not your daddy's. Now what you gonna call this baby? What's her name?"

Wearily Tucker says, "I really don't care. Why don't you name her?"

"Well sir, she's such an amazing baby," Mattie mused, "why don't you name her Amazing? Amazing Tucker!"

As Amazing Tucker nurses on her, Tucker says, "I want y' to do one more thing fer me, Mama Mattie."

"Well sure, honey. Tells me what you want."

"I want you to burn all my clothes. All of 'em. As long as I live, I ain't never wearin' female clothes again."

Mattie gives a silent gasp. Tears roll down her ebony cheeks as she strokes Tucker's hair. "Rest easy, child. If'n that's what you want, then Mama Mattie'll do just as you says."

CHAPTER TWENTY-THREE

On Saturday following the tornado, Tucker announces to the children, "We's gonna go scrap corn t'day. The Thomas boys has done gathered th' corn with their big ol' combine, but I'll guarantee y' there's plenty of ears still lying on th' ground. Them big machines is powerful, but they leave lots behind. We ought t' be able to gather up enough ears t' feed them hogs fer a while. Ya'll put on yore boots an' wear yore gloves. I done got th' wagon hitched to th' truck. Come on out when y' git ready."

When the door closes behind her, March looks at August and says, "Man, all we do around here is work. I'll bet there ain't no other kids that work as much as we do."

August hands him a pair of gloves he has retrieved from the box of kindling beside the wood-burning stove. "I can't disagree with you, but what are you going to do about it?"

"I'll tell you what I'm going to do. One of these days I'm going to run away. I know there has to be a better life out there somewhere."

August pushes him toward the front door. "You are not going to run away from home. You're too big a chicken. Besides, things could always be worse. You need to think about that."

"Worse than living here? I doubt that."

The sound of their sister coming down the stairs draws their attention. She is pulling on a pair of oversize cotton jersey gloves.

Smiling, August says, "Come on, girl, let's go scrap us a field of corn."

April takes his outstretched hand and the three of them go outside and join Tucker in the truck.

Tucker drives the half mile to the field of picked corn and pulls in through a gap in the fence. All four of the passengers get out.

Reaching into the bed of the pickup, Tucker pulls out a pair of five-gallon buckets and hands them to August and March. Then she holds up a small pail and turns with it to April. "What is this, April?"

April stares at her but makes no sound.

"Come on, April. You know what this is, so just tell me."

April blinks but makes no effort to speak.

Tucker reaches to the ground and picks up an ear of corn. Waving it at April, she says, "Tell me what this is."

April's face begins to redden.

Tucker grabs April's hand and shoves the ear of corn in it. "You have got t' tell me what this is, do you understand? You have t' start talkin' or somthin' bad is liable to happen!"

A lone tear escapes from April's right eye and slowly rolls down her cheek.

Though the tear is round, its poignancy fits it with a point. Tucker feels as if a spear has been thrust into her chest. In frustration, both with herself and with April, Tucker throws the pail toward August and March and says, "Go on an' help yore brothers! An' don't be lazy 'bout it neither."

April turns around and breaks into a run toward her brothers.

Oh my lord in heaven, what am I gonna do? We ain't got but six weeks left. She ain't never gonna talk fer me, an' Judge Jack McDade is gonna take 'er away from me. If only I was smarter, I might be able t' do somethin'. I believe she knows how t' talk, she just won't do it.

After grabbing another five-gallon bucket out of the truck, Tucker begins walking down a row of picked corn. She takes small, shuffling steps through the fodder, waiting until she feels a round ear of corn under her foot. Then she bends over, picks up the ear, and drops it in her bucket.

A few moments later, she stops abruptly and stares into the distance. *Of course! Why hadn't I already thought of that? If anybody can help April, it'd have t' be Ella McDade!* "We'll just do three or four rows today," she calls out to the kids. "I done thought of somethin' I need t' do."

Once she has dropped the kids off at the house and backed the truck and trailer into the barn, Tucker walks to Ella's house and knocks on her front door.

Ella opens the door and looks surprised. "Well, hello, Tucker. What brings you by here?"

"I need t' talk t' you."

Ella backs up into her house and swings the door wide. "Of course, come on in. Is something wrong?"

After she steps inside the house, Tucker looks around uncertainly.

"Won't you sit down?" Ella asks, waving her hand toward the couch.

Tucker looks at the couch and then down at her clothes and dirty boots. "I'm too dirty t' sit down on yore furniture. I think I ought t' stand."

Ella puts her hands on her hips. "Look, Tucker, we've been through this already. Quit worrying about how you are dressed and about getting my furniture dirty. Furniture is made to live on, not to be viewed like museum pieces. Anything that might rub off of you will certainly be able to be washed off, if necessary. Now sit down, please."

Tucker hesitates and then sits down on the edge of Ella's couch. After Ella sits down across from her, Tucker says, "I got me some trouble."

When Tucker doesn't continue, Ella asks, "What in the world is it?"

"It's m' April. They's gonna try an' take her from me. An' that fool Judge Jack is b'hind it."

Ella stares at Tucker, trying to comprehend. "Judge Jack is trying to take April away from you? That doesn't make sense, Tucker. I need you to start at the beginning and tell me what has happened."

Tucker tells Ella the details of Mary Beth's visit to her. Staring at her hands lying helplessly in her lap, she finishes her story by saying, "Th' upshot is, if'n April don't start talkin', I'm gonna lose 'er."

"Oh my, Tucker," Ella says. "This is serious, very serious. The school system, the welfare system, and the judicial system all lined up against you are a formidable force." She gets up and begins pacing back and forth.

"I been tryin' t' work with April," Tucker says, "but I ain't gettin' nowhere. All's that happens is I just git mad an' frustrated with 'er. That's when I say or do somethin' stupid an' hurt April's feelin's, which makes me even more angry and frustrated. I don't know what I'm gonna do." Tucker watches Ella's face closely, looking for a hopeful sign, but all she sees are frown lines creasing her new friend's forehead.

Tucker's normally stony heart begins filling with dread and fear. Pricked by that two-pronged fork, she steps across the moat she has surrounded herself with since she was sixteen years old. She closes her eyes. *All she can do is say no.*

Opening her eyes, she takes a deep breath and says, "In m' whole life I ain't never asked fer help but from two people, Mary Beth Chandler an' a woman called Mama Mattie."

The seriousness in Tucker's tone stops Ella from her pacing.

"But I'm askin' you now, Ella. I need yore help. You can't let 'em take April from me."

Ella moves beside Tucker on the couch and places her thin hands over Tucker's beefy hands. Looking intently into Tucker's thick glasses, she says, "I'll do everything and anything I possibly can to help. I'm just not sure where to start." Then she's up pacing again. "I think better when I'm moving. I have to think, think, think. There has to be someone who can point the way for us."

After a minute of watching Ella pace and talk under her breath to herself, Tucker quietly says, "I got an idea."

Ella slows to a stop and faces her.

"You could help 'er t' talk," Tucker says confidently.

Ella's mouth and eyes open wide. "Me?! Oh Tucker, I don't know anything about helping a child like April. I mean, I love April and would do anything for her, but this is going to require someone with specialized skill in helping a child with her specific problem. Certainly not me. A speech therapist, that's what we need to find."

Shaking her head, Tucker says, "T'ain't so. Don't need no outsider helpin'. Don't trust 'em anyway." Folding her arms across her chest, she says firmly, "No, you's the one, Ella."

"Where in the world would I even begin to help?"

"I don't know, but I'll bet you'll figger out somethin'. She could git off th' school bus at yore house ever'day after school. She could stay with y' as many hours as you see fit, then you can bring 'er home before or after supper. Ya'll might even do some work on th' weekends. Time's runnin' out for us."

Ella's mouth opens and closes several times but nothing comes out.

Tucker smiles broadly, "See there? You got th' same problem as April does. You got a head full of sense, but y' just can't put it into words sometimes. Ya'll is a perfect fit."

CHAPTER TWENTY-FOUR

Ella slowly closes her front door as Tucker steps off her porch. As she leans back against the door, thoughts whirl through her mind like ingredients in a blender. *What in the world have I gotten myself into? Why did I tell Tucker I would do this? I know nothing about helping a child to speak. And what if I'm not successful? Tucker will hate me.*

Her mind skids to a stop on this last thought. She picks it up and examines it more closely. *Why does it matter to me whether Tucker likes me or not?*

She pulls back the curtain from the window to look at Tucker striding toward her own humble dwelling. Unpretentious—*that is the perfect word for Tucker. After living so long in Jack McDade's world, where pretentiousness was the order of the day, I think that's what I find so refreshing about this odd woman. Hmmm . . . Maybe not* odd. *Maybe* unusual *is better. She is exactly what she appears to be. She says exactly what's on her mind and is sincere in every way.*

She laughs out loud, thinking it was true and that she wanted to be more like Tucker.

Turning away from the window, she walks into her kitchen, pours herself a cup of coffee, and sits at the table. Her focus turns to

April. While recognizing the deficit in Tucker's parenting skills, she also realizes how devastating it would be for this family to be broken up. The weight of the task before her seems impossible to carry. *I have to find a way to make this work, for everyone's sake.*

The next morning Ella drives into Dresden and parks in front of the small public library. She gives a quick look at her reflection in the rearview mirror of her car, adjusts her wig, and gets out. *I just hope that nosy Teresa Wilson is not working here today. If she is, Lord, just give me strength to control my tongue and temper.*

Opening the door to the library she eases inside, taking a moment for her eyes to adjust to the dimmer light.

"Ella McDade," a woman sitting behind the book desk says. "I haven't seen you in a coon's age. How are you?"

Ella spies the speaker and says, "Well hello, Teresa. I'm doing well, thank you. How are you?"

Teresa walks from behind her desk to meet Ella. Looking like a half can of hair spray has recently been enlisted to enforce order on any unruly hairs, her bluish-gray hair sits stiffly on top of her head. The thin face and buzzard's nose go perfectly with her buzzard's scavenging compulsion to pick through other people's tragedies, looking for morsels she can devour and then regurgitate into gossip.

She gets close to Ella and in a low whisper says, "I was so upset to hear about you and Judge Jack. Everyone thinks it's just awful what he did to you. And that other woman—what a tramp! She'll get what's coming to her one day. I don't think the judge could get elected now if he ran for dogcatcher."

"What's done is done," Ella replies simply. "I'm looking for—"

"And that's the best attitude to have," Teresa cuts in. "Nobody can change the past, can they? We have to keep moving forward. But look at you! You are looking remarkably well having been through everything you've been through. Someone told me that you were on your deathbed with cancer. Yet here you are, alive and in the flesh. And your wig looks just like your natural hair. I hardly even noticed it. It's amazing how lifelike they can make those things now. Is it hot to wear? I've heard they are really hot, like wearing a wool toboggan."

Ella grits her teeth behind her smile. *It's your turn, Lord. You better hurry and save me or I'm going to choke this woman!*

Just then the library door opens and a young mother carrying a baby comes in.

Ella looks up and breathes a silent prayer of thanks for the interruption. "Teresa, I'm looking for a copy of *The Miracle Worker* and of Helen Keller's autobiography. Do you have either of them?"

Teresa frowns at the young mother, who is strolling slowly along the shelves. "Let me go check," she says to Ella. Behind her desk, she checks the card catalog and the cards of checked-out books. "I believe they are both here. They should be on the shelf against the back wall."

Ella walks to the shelf and begins moving slowly, letting her finger glide across the spines of the books. She always thought books in the library looked like they are standing at attention, hoping someone will choose them as their companion for a few days. A smile brightens her face as she finds both books she's looking for on the same shelf.

When she walks back to the front and places the books on Teresa's desk, she notices the surprised expression on Teresa's face.

"Usually it is one of the kids from the high school who checks these out. You know, for required reading." She looks at Ella expectantly. Are these for yourself, or for someone else?"

"It's really none of your business," Ella says. Even she is shocked at herself for being so blunt.

"Well, I never!" Teresa huffs.

"If you'll just stamp the books with the return date," Ella says, "I'll be on my way."

Teresa opens the back cover of the first book, picks up her rubber stamp, and pushes it against the lined card glued in the back. She rocks the stamp a couple of times to be sure the date is clear. After repeating the process on the other book, she hands the books to Ella.

"Thank you for your help, Teresa," Ella says pleasantly.

Back in her car, she drives the twelve miles between Dresden and Martin and winds her way onto the campus of the University of Tennessee at Martin. After parking in the lot beside the student center, she checks her wig, then gets out and walks across the street to the campus library.

She spies the information desk and walks up to it. An attractive young woman, whom Ella suspects is a student, looks at her expectantly. "I'm looking to do some research on speech therapy and helping treat children with mutism," Ella says. "And I have no idea where to even begin. Can you help me?"

The woman's eyes brighten. "Sure, I'd be happy to. Follow me." She begins walking across the spacious foyer. "This is the exciting part of library work for me," she says to Ella, who is walking beside her. "It's like a grand safari, looking through the jungle of shelves for that special, coveted quarry."

"I never thought about it quite like that," Ella replies, "but I can see how it could feel that way. You must be majoring in library science."

The woman flashes a smile at Ella. "Yes. This is my senior year."

"Congratulations. I can tell you'll be very good at your job."

Two hours later, Ella walks out of the library carrying a stack of books she can barely see over. When she finally manages to get the car door open without dropping any books and sits down inside, she pulls her wig off and tosses it in the floorboard. Closing her eyes, she slowly rubs her temples, trying to calm the dull headache that is grinding on her.

By 10:00 p.m. Ella is asleep in the armchair in her living room. Scattered on the floor, couch, and coffee table are books lying open with pieces of paper marking a place. Even in her sleep, Ella clutches to her chest the copy of *The Miracle Worker*.

CHAPTER TWENTY-FIVE

Ella looks at the clock on the wall, then walks over to her front window and peers through the curtains. *It's time for the school bus to be here. What's taking so long?*

Walking into the kitchen, she opens the oven door. The smell of chocolate chip cookies wafts out and fills her nostrils. She has to swallow the sudden surge of excess saliva this triggers. She slides out the pan of cookies and sets it on the dining table.

Her ears perk up at the high-pitched squeal from outside that signals the arrival of the school bus, the yellow transporter of the hopes and dreams of parents everywhere. *Finally!* She walks quickly to the front door and opens it to watch April as she emerges.

April stands at the side of the road watching the bus drive on to let August and March off at Tucker's. Eventually she turns and faces Ella's house and begins walking slowly toward it.

What in the world must be going through your mind, child? You hardly even know me and now you're coming here so I can help you talk. Ella opens the screen door and walks toward her.

The two approach each other slowly, both with apprehension bubbling inside their hearts. When they are five feet apart, Ella stops and lowers herself onto one knee so that she is eye level with April.

April stops to watch her, unsure of Ella's intent and of what is expected of her.

Ella extends her hand toward April. "I'm so glad you've come to visit me. Let's go inside. I've baked some chocolate chip cookies for you and have just taken them out of the oven, so they'll be nice and warm. Does that sound good to you?"

April's pensive expression is replaced by an eager smile. She nods and reaches out to take hold of Ella's hand.

April's touch of trust and acceptance warms Ella's heart more than any oven could. She stands up. Gripping April's small hand, she says, "Then let's go inside and see how many of them we can eat!"

Once inside the house, Ella watches April's eyes dance when she sees the cookies on the table. Setting a glass of milk in front of her, she says, "Help yourself."

April makes quick work of two cookies and half of the glass of milk before she pauses to catch her breath. Her head slowly turns as she checks out Ella's house.

"I don't guess you've been here since the tornado and seen my house all put together, have you?" Ella asks.

April looks at Ella and shakes her head. She gets up and walks to the back door.

Ella watches her, curious as to what is on her mind.

April opens the door and looks outside. After a few moments, she eases the door shut. She returns to the table and stands beside Ella, looking intently at her face.

"Do you want something?" Ella asks.

April nods her head.

Just as she is about to start guessing what April wants, Ella remembers something from her research. She looks at April and says, "Then tell me what you want."

April quickly looks to the left and to the right.

"August and March are not here to help you. It's just you and me. If you want something, you're going to have to ask for it."

This throws April off and her cheeks redden. A frantic look suddenly appears and she grabs her crotch with both hands. She begins dancing back and forth on her tiptoes.

Realization dawns on Ella. "I don't have an outhouse. My bathroom is inside the house. Why don't you ask me where it is? I'll be glad to show you, if you'll ask."

April's face turns crimson and her dancing becomes frenetic. Suddenly she stops and looks down.

Ella watches as the crotch of April's pants turns dark and then pee begins puddling around her shoes.

April lifts her head. Her blue eyes are swimming in a pool of tears that has collected in her bottom lids.

Ella is flooded with feelings of sympathy and regret that wash her resolve to hold a firm boundary with April. She throws her arms around her. "I'm sorry, April. I didn't know you had to go so badly. I shouldn't have been so mean and harsh with you. Let me show you to the bathroom. We'll get you all cleaned up and I'll wash and dry your clothes."

Twenty minutes later, April is sitting on the couch practically lost in the folds of Ella's large white housecoat. Ella walks in and sits beside her. "I've got your clothes in the washer. It won't take them long and then I'll put them in the dryer. But I have to talk with you."

April searches Ella's features.

"I don't know what Tucker told you, but I think it's only fair that you know the truth. You're going to start spending your afternoons with me in the hope that I can get you to talk. Because here is what could happen if you don't: you could get taken away from Tucker and be moved away somewhere to live with strangers. All because you don't talk."

The expression on April's face changes to one of fear and her eyes move from Ella's lips to her eyes. They are so intense and penetrating that Ella feels like she is looking at the face of an adult rather than that of a small child. *So many things about you are adultlike. There is no telling what kind of life you've lived or the kinds of things you've been through in your short life. But I've got to learn to keep my feelings of sympathy in check or this will never work.* She returns April's even gaze and says, "Do you understand what I'm telling you?"

April nods slowly.

"Very good. Now let me tell you what I believe. I believe you are a very smart girl. There is nothing retarded about your mind. I think you don't talk because you don't want to and, more importantly, because you don't have to. Now, I can't make you want to talk, but I might make you have to. Therefore, this is the rule when you are at my house: I won't get you anything or do anything for you unless you ask me. Do you understand?"

The corners of April's mouth droop and her chin trembles.

"Whoa, whoa, now," Ella says, and wraps her arms around April. "There's no reason to cry. I'm not upset with you or mad at you. I only want to help and this is the only way I know how to do it." Unwrapping her arms from April, she takes her face in her hands and says, "Okay?"

April responds with a smile.

"Great! Let's go check on your clothes to see if they're ready to put in the dryer. And maybe we could eat another cookie, too."

CHAPTER TWENTY-SIX

Opening the door to her wood-burning stove, Tucker sticks a poker in and stirs the coals. The newly exposed burning embers that were hidden under the ashes glow red, and the dark living room comes alive with ghoulish shadows created from the stove's hellish glow. If a picture of the scene were in a storybook, Tucker might be mistaken for the wicked witch in Hansel and Gretel, stoking the fire in which she will place the young children.

Tucker places a few pieces of kindling on the coals, and almost immediately they begin smoking. She moves her face closer to the opening and blows. As if she were a fire-breathing dragon, flames spring up from the bottom of the kindling and dance hungrily up and down the sticks.

The white and yellow flames change the personality of the living room. The bright light reflects the true color of Tucker's complexion and bathes that end of the room in warm, welcoming tones.

Certain that the kindling is burning well, Tucker places a few small pieces of firewood in the stove and closes the door. When she does, darkness wrests control of the room once again. Tucker drags her rocking chair closer to the stove, sits down, and pulls the afghan on her shoulders closer to her thick neck. *If April don't start talkin' I ain't never gonna be able t' git no sleep. Ella's been workin' with 'er fer a week an' says she ain't made no progress at all. I can tell April don't mind goin' there, but she just ain't cooperatin' with Ella. Somethin' has t' change!*

As her thoughts spin faster, the speed of her rocking chair keeps pace. *If Judge Jack tries t' take April from me, it'll be over my dead body or his.*

Suddenly a new thought seizes her, a thought so dramatic it stops both her rocking and her breathing. A pain stabs her chest and tears spring up in her eyes. *Let April go live with Ella? Oh my lord, should I? Could I?!*

Throwing the afghan from her shoulders, she rises and then makes her way into the kitchen, pushing on her chest with the palm of her hand, in hopes of easing the pain and pressure. Familiarity makes turning on the light unnecessary, and she gets a glass from the cabinet and puts it under the faucet. Once it is full, she turns it up and guzzles it. An audible "Aah" escapes from her when she finishes drinking, followed by a deep inhale.

April living at Ella's. It makes sense t' do it, but I can't imagine not havin' m' little angel in the house no more. Knowing Ella, she's probably done had th' idea herself, but she don't want to appear pushy. I remember Mama Mattie tellin' me one time, "Child, when times is desperate, desperate people gots to do desperate things." An' if there was ever a desperate time, it surely is now. What's gotta be done has gotta be done.

She hears a rooster crow outside. Looking out the window, she sees the black sky turning gray in the east as it begins making room for the entrance of the sun.

Resolution of her dilemma has calmed Tucker's fearful heart and given her the resolve to face the future. She turns to the tasks immediately in her path and flips on the kitchen light. Grabbing the coffee pot off the stove she begins making breakfast.

An hour later, the school bus stops in front of Tucker's house. It is empty, as this is its first stop of each morning. "It's six thirty!" Tucker hollers up the stairs. "The bus is waitin'. Ya'll git down here now!"

March appears at the top of the stairs. He begins running down them, jumps over the last three steps, and lands on the floor with a bang. Like a bullet bouncing off a rock, he ricochets off the floor and out the door in one motion.

"You better mind today!" Tucker calls after him. "And do yore work, too!"

When she turns back to the steps, she sees August standing breathless. "April's moving as slow as molasses. I can't get her to hurry."

"You go on out to th' bus. I'll finish gettin' 'er ready. You just make sure th' bus driver waits on 'er."

"Yes, ma'am."

As August exits the house, Tucker starts walking up the stairs. On the third step she hears a noise and looks up. April is standing on the top step, her hair unbrushed, her shirt on wrong side out, and her shoes on the wrong feet. Tucker puts her hands on her hips and says, "Come on down here. What's got you movin' so slow this mornin'? You're gonna be late fer school."

Tucker goes back down the stairs and waits for April. She reaches in her pocket and pulls out a rubber band. When April gets in front of her, Tucker turns her around and pulls her hair back into a slightly off-center pony tail and secures it with the rubber band. "Hold yore arms up," she says. She slides April's shirt over her head, turns it right side out, and puts it back on her.

The bus driver signals his impatience by honking his horn.

"Oh hold yore horses!" Tucker yells. To April she says, "Go on an' git on th' bus, but tell yore brother August t' fix yore shoes. They's on th' wrong feet."

Once Tucker is sure April is on the bus, she takes her jacket off the hook by the door and starts walking to Ella's. When she gets there, she raps hard twice on the front door. After waiting only a few seconds, she bangs harder with her fist.

The curtains by the front window move, then the front door opens. Ella is pulling her housecoat around herself. Her face is marred by sleep lines and her eyes are puffy. She looks in astonishment at Tucker and says, "What in the world is wrong? Do you know what time it is?"

"This here is important," Tucker replies, ignoring her questions. "We gotta talk. It's about April." Without waiting for an invitation, Tucker pushes her way past Ella and walks into the living room.

Ella gives a broad sweep with her hand and says in an exaggerated voice, "Please, why don't you come in." The effect is lost on Tucker.

Tucker sits down on the couch and starts talking. "This mornin' I was sittin' in th' dark by th' stove when I remembered somethin' Mama Mattie told me a long time ago. She said, 'Child, when times is desperate, desperate people gots to do desperate things.' I think that sayin' of hers came t' my mind 'cause this situation with April is a desperate one. Don't you agree?"

Ella stares at Tucker blankly. She squeezes her eyes shut and then opens them again. "Okay, so this is not a dream of some kind. You really are in my living room before seven o'clock in the morning and you are talking more animatedly than I have ever heard you speak. Actually, I believe that's the longest stream of uninterrupted words I've ever heard you say. Even though I'm not fully awake, I think I'm keeping up with what you are saying, and yes, I'll agree with you that we are facing a desperate situation with April. I've done everything I know to do so far. I think it's just going to take some time."

"Exactly," Tucker agrees. "And time is something we got precious little of. So I've come to a decision. I think I know what it's gonna take fer April t' start talkin'."

Ella is completely awake now. Her voice trembles when she says, "What do you believe it's going to take?"

Tucker locks eyes with Ella. In a soft, quavering voice she says, "April needs t' come here an' live with you."

Ella's hand slowly rises to cover her mouth. From behind her hand, she says, "Live with me? You mean, like come and literally live in my house with me?"

Tucker nods. "Once th' idea come t' me an' I got over th' shock an' over thinkin' 'bout my feelin's, it made more an' more sense. Truth is, I think April'd like livin' with you. There's lotsa stuff you could teach 'er that I don't know nothin' 'bout, more stuff than just helpin' 'er talk. You know 'bout things, Ella. You've seen an' done things I ain't never seen an' done. Th' world I can teach April about is just what I know about livin' on that little hill over yonder. That's a mighty small world. She deserves better than what I can give 'er."

As Tucker is talking, Ella's eyes redden. When Tucker finishes, the tears begin rolling down Ella's cheeks. Pulling a tissue from the pocket of her housecoat she blows her nose. Her voice breaks as she says, "Oh Tucker . . . You . . . I . . . ." She clears her throat. "I hardly know what to say to you. I know this, though: I believe this is the most sincere expression of trust and hope I've ever been given. I would argue with you about the soundness of your plan, but I've learned that it's pointless to try and argue with you." She pauses to smile. She takes a deep breath. "I don't know how this plan will turn out, and I make no promises. But I'm willing to give it a try."

When Ella finishes, Tucker pulls a red bandanna out of her hip pocket and blows her nose. "It's all settled then. I'll talk t' April 'bout it this afternoon."

"No, don't do that," Ella says. "Let me tell you about something I've been thinking about doing. Next Thursday is Thanksgiving. Do you all have any plans for the day?"

"We gen'rally don't do nothin' special," Tucker replies. "Sometimes, if I got one, I'll get a ham outta th' smokehouse an' I'll slice it up. That's 'bout it."

"Well I'd like to invite all of you to my house for a Thanksgiving meal. You fix whatever you want to bring. I'll have a turkey and the trimmings. And April can stay with me after the rest of you leave. You could wait until that morning to tell her about our plan. That way she wouldn't have time to get worried and anxious about it."

Tucker looks at the floor. "I don't know, Ella. These kids don't know how t' act right sometimes. An' we ain't got no nice clothes fer some kinda fancy meal."

"Oh hush!" Ella says. "You quit worrying about those sorts of things." She folds her arms across her chest in her best Tucker impersonation. "It's settled. You all's comin' t' my house fer Thanksgiving."

They stand up and look at each other for a moment. Suddenly, Ella throws her arms around Tucker and embraces her.

Tucker doesn't move.

Feeling she has crossed a forbidden boundary, Ella quickly disengages from Tucker and takes a step back. "I'm sorry. I get emotional sometimes. I just felt like doing that. I hope I didn't offend you."

Reaching across the gap between them, Tucker places a hand on Ella's shoulder. "It's all right. You a good woman, Ella."

CHAPTER TWENTY-SEVEN

Lifting the large pot of boiling water from the kitchen stove, Tucker carries it into the living room and carefully pours it into the huge, half-filled washtub sitting beside the wood-burning stove. All three children are gathered close by.

Tucker pitches a bar of soap into the washtub. "Alright, now you git yoreselves cleaned up. You's gittin' too big to bathe in front of each other, so we'll all go in th' kitchen an' you'll come in here one at a time. Then when y' git done, head on upstairs."

"Why in the world are you makin' us take a bath in the middle of the week?" March whines. "This is supposed to be our Thanksgiving break."

"I done tol' y' why," Tucker says sharply. "We's going t' Miss Ella's fer Thanksgiving t'morrow. I ain't 'bout t' take ya'll down there with dirt rings 'round yore neck or behind yore ears, smellin' like a field hand. You're gonna scrub yoreselves until y' turn pink." She turns and heads toward the kitchen. "Now come in th' kitchen with me. August, you stay here an' go first since you's th' oldest. When y' finish, head on up t' bed."

Tucker waits in the kitchen with April until August and March finish their baths. Taking April by the hand, she says, "Now it's yore turn, purdy girl."

Standing beside the washtub, April begins taking off her clothes as Tucker kneels down and soaps a rag. "Step on in," she says.

Tucker slowly and gently washes April's arms and hands. Without stopping her washing, Tucker says, "I need t' tell you somethin'."

April holds up her chin as Tucker washes her neck. "I've decided I want you t' go stay with Miss Ella fer a while."

April looks at Tucker. There is a crease between her eyebrows and a frown on her face. The only sounds are the soapy water dripping off April into the tub and the crackling fire in the stove beside them.

Tucker puts her hands on April's shoulders and turns her around. Washing her back, she says, "I ain't mad at y' or nothin' like that. Y' ain't done nothin' wrong. It's just . . . Well, it's hard t' explain." She turns April back around and starts washing her chest and stomach. After a moment, she looks directly into April's eyes. "It's yore schoolin' what's the problem. I know it ain't because you can't do all th' work. Th' problem is you won't talk. An' because you won't talk, there's people that says you need t' be taken away from me an' yore brothers. Miss Ella's been trying t' help, but so far there ain't nothing changed. I ain't smart 'nuf t' help you." Moving down to wash April's legs and feet, she continues, "Miss Ella is one awful smart woman, an' I trust 'er. That's what made me decide on this plan."

She reaches for a plastic bowl beside the tub and begins dipping it into the tub and rinsing the soap off of April. "You like Miss Ella, don't you?" Without waiting for April to respond, she says, "I know y' do. An' y' ain't gonna be that far away. I'll be lookin' in on you. I really think you're gonna like bein' there."

Unfolding a ragged towel, Tucker says, "Step on out now an' let me dry y' off."

April doesn't move. Her chin is touching her chest.

Tucker puts a finger under April's chin and lifts her face.

Tears are streaming down April's cheeks.

"Oh m' baby April," Tucker gushes. She wraps the towel around April, lifts her out of the tub, and folds her into her arms. Pulling her close to her chest, she says, "Shush, shush, don't you cry. You gonna break this ol' woman's heart. I know y' can't understand all this, but you gonna have t' trust ol' Tucker."

She stands up, still clutching April. "Why don't I carry you upstairs an' tuck you in fer th' night?"

The next morning Tucker is in the kitchen with a butcher knife, slicing the ham she has brought in from the smokehouse. With a small knife, she trims the skin and some of the fat from each slice.

As the children come into the kitchen, August says, "Mmm, what's that smell?"

"That's sweet tater pie," Tucker says, smiling. She opens the oven to take a peek. "It's 'bout done, too. April, you go on an' gather th' eggs fer us while I talk t' yore brothers."

As soon as April goes out the back door, March says, "I didn't do it. It was August that—"

"I did not!" August counters quickly.

"Oh hush," Tucker cuts them off. "I gotta talk to you boys 'bout April."

August and March sit down at the table and give Tucker their full attention. "What's wrong?" August asks.

"Ya'll know she ain't doin' no good in school, mainly 'cause she won't talk. These lessons she's been doin' with Ella in the afternoon ain't workin' out so good. Somethin's gotta change or the state's gonna take 'er away from us."

The boys look at each other and then back at Tucker. "Take her?" March asks.

"What do you mean?" August asks.

"I mean jes' what I said. They'll take 'er from us an' place 'er with th' state, if she don't start talkin' and doin' better in school. That's why I've decided she's gonna go live with Miss Ella fer a while."

The boys sit in stunned silence.

"Now ya'll go in April's room and put all 'er belongin's in a piller case and tie a string 'round th' top of it. When you're done, fix y' some toast an' jelly fer breakfast. We'll be headin' down t' Ella's in a coupla hours. I gotta finish cookin' this ham."

The boys turn to leave the kitchen, but August stops and spins slowly around. "Are you gonna get rid of me and March, too?"

Tucker stops in midslice, drops the knife on the cutting board, and puts her hands on her hips. "Now listen here, both of you. I ain't gittin' rid of nobody—April or either of you. I jes' decided that Miss Ella might be able t' get yore sister t' talk, that's all."

Peeking around the taller August, March says, "What did Mama say about sending April to Ella's?"

Stretching to her full height, Tucker folds her arms across her chest. "First of all, it's 'Miss Ella' to you, young man. And second, yore mama ain't got no say-so in this. I been th' one what raised all three of you since y' was babies. Don't never fergit it. Now git an' do what I tol' y'."

The boys quickly leave and go about their assignment.

As Tucker returns to her ham, April comes in the back door carrying a basket of eggs. She pulls a chair to the sink and begins washing each egg and setting them on a towel to dry.

Looking over the top of her glasses, Tucker says, "April, you remember that t'day is Thanksgivin' an' we're goin' down t' Miss Ella's fer a big fine meal, right?"

April stops washing the eggs and stands still.

"An' after me an' yore brothers git through eatin' an' visitin', we're gonna come on back home an' you'll be staying with Ella, just like we talked 'bout last night. Okay?"

April nods slowly and starts washing the eggs again.

Tucker has been so intent on April that she didn't hear the car pull up in front of her house. The front door swings open suddenly and the loud voice of Maisy echoes through the house. "Happy Thanksgiving to everyone! I'm here. Everybody come see me!"

"Oh my lord," Tucker mutters.

April drops an egg on the floor.

CHAPTER TWENTY-EIGHT

Maisy dances into the kitchen wearing a tight-fitting, low-cut red sweater, black ski pants, and red high heels that play a rat-a-tat on the hard floor. Her lipstick is the same color as her sweater and her thick raven hair is woven into a tall beehive on top of her head. Cradling a full paper grocery bag in each arm causes her breasts to appear as if they may spill out the top of her sweater like two cantaloupes. She sniffs the air noisily. "You brought in a ham to cook because I was coming?!" she exclaims. "That's unusually thoughtful of you, Tucker. I brought a sack of apples and a sack of oranges. I thought the kids might enjoy fruit for a change. Where's the boys at, anyway?"

Setting the sacks on the dining table, she looks toward the sink and says, "Hi, April. How's my girl? Looks like you dropped an egg. Now you better clean it up." She turns around and walks to the doorway between the living room and the kitchen. "August! March! Where are you?" Walking back into the kitchen, she says, "Boy, am I starved! Ham sounds wonderful. Isn't anybody happy to see me? Why the pouty faces?"

Tucker straightens up from slicing the last pieces of ham and throws the large butcher knife into the chopping block with a loud *thock*. The heavy handle of the knife swings back and forth like an upside-down pendulum. Glaring at Maisy, she says, "What are you doin' here?"

"What am I doing here?! What do you mean by that? It's Thanksgiving and I came to eat a meal with my family. Is that so unusual? If you would ever get you a telephone, people might be able to let you know when they are coming over. When are you going to join the rest of the world, Tucker?"

"So you expect me t' b'lieve you've had plans fer a while t' come here? I ain't that big a fool. It's more likely y' got stood up by a man an' y' ain't got no other place t' go." Not waiting for Maisy to answer her accusation, Tucker turns her attention back to the skillet full of sizzling ham. Using a meat fork, she begins turning the pieces over.

"Tucker, I'm not wanting to get into it with you. Why is everything a battle with you? My gosh, can't we call a truce for today and just enjoy being together as a family? You know, we can sit around the table and eat together and then afterwards we can sit in the living room and sing some songs or play some games."

Tucker opens her mouth to respond, but stops when she hears August and March coming down the stairs.

"Mama!" March yells as he runs toward Maisy.

Maisy embraces him. "Look at you! It seems like you've grown a foot every time I see you."

Carrying the pillow case with April's things in it over his shoulder, August walks up to his mother. "What are you doing here, Mama?"

"Is that the question of the day from everybody, or what? Can't a mama come see her children and eat a meal with them? Give me a hug, you cinnamon-skinned handsome boy. I don't think I need to call you boy much longer. You're becoming a man, aren't you?"

Maisy hugs him.

August returns it halfheartedly.

Noticing the pillowcase, Maisy says, "What's that for? And why are you boys cleaned up with your hair combed and good clothes on?" Looking around, she continues, "And why does April have a clean dress on? What's going on here?"

The children turn to look at Tucker.

Tucker forks the ham, lifts the pieces from the skillet, and places them on a platter. "If'n it's any of yore business, an' I ain't sayin' it is, it just so happens we got us some plans t'day. We've had us an invite t' go eat somewhere else."

A look of astonishment spreads across Maisy's face. "You mean to tell me that someone has invited you to eat Thanksgiving dinner with them? Ha-ha, you've got to be kidding! Who in the world?"

"We're goin' t' Miss Ella's fer our Thanksgiving meal," Tucker replies.

March grabs his mother's hand and says excitedly, "Why don't you come with us, Mama? We can all go together. I'm sure Miss Ella won't mind."

"Don't this just beat it all," Maisy says. "I decide to come and eat a meal with my family and they up and run off to eat with a stranger rather than with me. It sometimes seems like you all don't love me anymore." She begins to weep. "I know I haven't been the best of mothers to you, but I'm really trying to do the best I can. I wish you all could understand that."

"Don't cry, Mama," March pleads. "You know we love you. Don't we, August? Don't we, April?"

There is a sudden, loud rattling as Tucker reels out a sheet of aluminum foil and begins wrapping it over the heaping platter of country ham. "Ya'll can do whatever y' want, as far as I'm con-cerned. But me an' April is headed to Ella's." Grabbing April's hand, Tucker walks toward the door, the meat platter secured in the crook of her arm and the sweet potato pie gripped tightly in her hand. She leaves the door open and heads down the steps of the porch.

August shifts the pillow case on his shoulder, looks at Maisy and March, and then follows Tucker out the door. Over his shoulder he says to them, "Ya'll quit standing there and come on. I ain't about to miss eating some of Tucker's fried country ham and sweet tater pie!"

Maisy wipes her eyes and smiles broadly. "This might be fun, mighten it? Come on March, let's go catch up so we can all walk together to Ella's. Tucker does know how to fix ham."

As March and Maisy catch up with the rest, Maisy calls out, "What in the world are you carrying in that pillow case, August? And why are you taking it to Ella's?"

The excited expressions on the faces of the children suddenly drop onto the gravel road beneath their feet. A pregnant silence hangs in the air. The only sound is of shoes crunching on the gravel road.

"What is wrong with everyone?" Maisy finally exclaims. "Does the cat have everyone's tongue? Every time I say or ask something it seems like nobody wants to talk. I think ya'll are hiding something from me."

Quickening her pace, Maisy passes Tucker and then wheels around to face her.

Tucker stops abruptly to keep from running into her daughter, almost losing her grip on the ham.

"Tell me what is going on, Tucker," Maisy demands.

"You make me spill this ham an' you'll wish you'd never showed yore face here t'day. I've tol' you all I intend t' tell you. Now git outta my way."

Maisy hesitates for only an instant and steps out of Tucker's path.

Tucker proceeds past with April at her side. August falls quickly in line and, after a momentary pause, so does March. Maisy is left standing in the road.

"Well I never," she finally says. She removes her red high heels and hurries barefooted to follow the parade to Ella McDade's.

CHAPTER TWENTY-NINE

Ella opens the oven door, reaches in, and carefully bastes the steaming, golden-skinned turkey. A smile of satisfaction spreads beneath her pink cheeks. Closing the oven, she lifts the lid on a skillet and stirs the apples bubbling inside. The scent of cinnamon filters through her nostrils.

She goes to her spare bedroom. She bends down and smoothes the Strawberry Shortcake comforter and fluffs the pillows with their matching pillow cases. Turning her attention to the vanity and mirror, she touches the combs and brushes she has arranged there.

Lord, I pray she likes her room. And please calm my nervous heart! Give me the strength and courage to meet this challenge.

Just then she hears a knock at the door. Taking a deep breath, she says aloud, "The time has arrived."

She hurries to the front door. Throwing it open wide, she says, "Happy Thanksgiving, everyone! Come in."

"I brung that ham I promised," Tucker says unceremoniously as she enters.

Ella reaches for the platter, but Tucker seems reluctant to relinquish it. "Better let me put it on th' table. It's sorta heavy."

"Sure," Ella says. "Go ahead and set it on the table over there."

As the children follow Tucker inside, Ella says, "Hello, children. How are you?"

April is careful to keep Tucker between her and Ella.

March darts in without a word.

Giving a quick look over his shoulder as he passes Ella, August says softly, "We brought a surprise with us."

Looking past August, Ella sees a tall, voluptuous, raven-haired woman slipping into red high heels and then purposefully striding toward the house. In the few seconds it takes for the woman to arrive at the front door, Ella recognizes her.

Reaching out her hand and smiling, Ella says, "Hello, Maisy."

Maisy responds to Ella's outstretched hand by gripping it firmly in hers. Returning the smile, she says, "Once again I meet the incredible Miss Ella." She strolls through the front door as Ella closes it behind her.

Tucker steps in between Ella and Maisy. "I hope it ain't no trouble fer her t' eat with us. I didn't know she was comin'. She just showed up at th' last minute."

"No, no, of course not. It's no trouble at all." Ella says. "We'll have more than enough food."

Maisy strolls into the living room. Turning in a circle, she says, "My, my, Ella, you do have nice taste. I've got a couch just like that in my apartment. And I saw end tables like those in a magazine one time. Aren't those Norman Rockwell plates on that wall?"

"Why yes, they are," Ella replies.

Continuing to survey the room, Maisy says, "Nice, nice, very nice. I like this."

Growing a bit embarrassed by Maisy's focus on her possessions, Ella says, "Why don't we all go ahead and sit at the table? I believe everything is ready."

Tucker notices March looking at a shelf of glass figurines. He reaches to pick one up. "March," Tucker says. "Keep yore hands t' yoreself. Them things is expensive, an' they'll break. Come sit down."

March dutifully obeys but keeps glancing back at the figurines. Ella brings in an extra plate and set of silverware for Maisy.

"I'll sit at the end of the table here, close to the kitchen," Ella says. "Tucker, you sit at the other end. March and August, you sit on one side and Maisy and April, you sit on the other side."

After everyone is seated, Ella looks at Tucker. "Do you want to say grace?"

Tucker looks surprised and blushes. Looking uncertainly at Ella, she says, "Grace?"

"She means to say the prayer," Maisy interjects. "Don't you know anything? You'll have to excuse her, Ella, she doesn't—"

"I know what she meant," Tucker snaps. "Bow yore head. Dear Lord," Tucker begins, "thank y' fer th' hog what give us this fine ham. An' thank y' fer all this other fine food Miss Ella done cooked up. An' 'specially, thank y' Lord fer Miss Ella. Amen."

Quick as a wink March stabs a piece of ham with his fork and plunks it on his plate. August grabs the bowl of mashed potatoes and plops a heaping spoonful on his plate. With one hand Tucker takes two rolls out of the basket in front of her. Maisy dives with equal zest into the bowl of green beans at her elbow.

Smiling, Ella looks with amazement at the speed with which bowls are passed and plates are filled.

Quiet quickly descends on the room as everyone is intent on eating. The only sounds are knives and forks clinking and ice tinkling in the tea glasses.

After a few minutes, Maisy speaks. "I noticed on your mailbox that your last name is McDade. I don't think Tucker ever mentioned that to me. I know some McDades. Are you kin to any of the ones around here?"

"Actually I'm not from around here," Ella replies. "McDade was my husband's last name."

"Oh, I'm sorry," Maisy says. "How long has he been dead?"

"Oh, he's not dead. We're divorced."

Pausing before she takes a drink, Maisy says, "I see. So who was your husband?"

"Judge Jack McDade," Ella says.

Maisy spews out her mouthful of tea and begins coughing. Eyes bulging, she says between coughs, "Did you say Judge Jack?"

"Lord have mercy, child!" Tucker exclaims. "What's th' matter with you? Did y' swaller somethin' th' wrong way?"

August and March burst into laughter.

"You looked like a whale blowing air out its blowhole," March says.

"You blowed tea plum across the table, Mama," August chimes in, still laughing.

Maisy grabs a napkin to her mouth and tries to compose herself. To Ella she says, "I'm sorry. I guess I choked. But did you say Judge Jack McDade is your ex-husband?"

Puzzled, Ella says, "Yes."

Maisy begins to laugh. "Seriously? Oh my, this is too, too funny." Her laugh gets louder and more hysterical. Every time she tries to stop, she looks at Tucker and Ella and bursts out laughing again.

"Well I b'lieve it's finally happened," Tucker says, looking in amazement at her. "You done gone crazy." To Ella, she says, "She's done slipped a cog or somethin'. I ain't never seen such."

As Maisy's hysteria subsides, Ella says, "I guess I don't understand what's so funny."

Wiping tears, Maisy says, "It's nothing. Really. I just got tickled."

"Tickled?!" Tucker exclaims. "You acted a fool is what y' did. Can we git back t' eatin' again?"

Still smiling, Maisy says, "Yes, yes, let's eat this delicious meal."

Standing at Ella's front door with the children around her, Tucker says, "Ella, that was th' best Thanksgivin' I done ever had. And I know th' kids enjoyed it, too." She thumps the boys on the back of their heads.

In unison they say, "Thank you, Miss Ella. It was really good."

Over Tucker's shoulder, Maisy adds, "And thank you for letting me barge in." With a smile, she adds, "It was a memorable event for me, too, in more ways than one."

"Well you all are just more than welcome," Ella says. "It was lovely having all of you here."

There is an uncomfortable pause. Tucker reaches behind her and puts her hand on April's shoulder. Guiding her toward Ella, she says, "Now, April, you be good fer Miss Ella and do what she tells y'."

"Bye, April," August says. "I'll be checking on you."

"Bye, April," March chimes in. "Have fun."

"What's going on here?" Maisy asks.

Ella squats down to look at April. Stretching her hand toward her, she says, "I am so excited to have you staying for a while. I've got your room all fixed up. Want to go take a look?"

April places her tiny hand in Ella's. Ella squeezes it gently and smiles. "We're going to have fun. You just wait and see."

Standing, Ella says to Tucker, "You all run along. We'll be fine."

As Ella closes the door, she hears Maisy say, "I demand to know what is going on with my child!"

When the door latches, April looks up at Ella.

"Come on, let me show you your room," Ella says. When they get to the room, Ella spies a stained and tired-looking pillow case, tied closed at the top with a piece of string, sitting on April's bed.

Pulling free from Ella's hand, April dashes to the bed. She makes quick work of untying the pillowcase and dumps the contents out.

Ella sits beside her and sorts through the items: one pair of panties, one pair of socks with holes in the heels, two stained shirts, one pair of jeans, and a small teddy bear that is missing an arm and one eye. April snatches the teddy bear and hugs it tight to her chest.

"Is this all of your things?" Ella asks. "Or are there more things still at your house?"

April looks at Ella.

"Well," Ella continues, "it doesn't matter. I see you have a teddy bear. I'll bet he is your best friend. I had a teddy bear when I was your age and I told him everything."

April looks from Ella to her teddy bear and back to Ella.

Chuckling, Ella says, "It's true. My teddy bear knew everything about me, even my secrets. Now, I've got to go finish doing the dishes in the kitchen. You make yourself at home. Check out the rest of your room. You're free to go anywhere you want to in the house. Come get me, if you need me."

April sits still as Ella retreats. When she can no longer hear her footsteps, she grabs her teddy bear and shakes it violently. As her face reddens, she puts it to her mouth and bites it multiple times. Tears begin to run down her cheeks. Finally she pulls the toy to her chest and gently rubs its back. She rocks back and forth for a few minutes and then lies down on the bed, closing her eyes.

CHAPTER THIRTY

Ella places the last washed glass on the shelf with all the others. *Whew! I didn't think about how big a job cleaning up by myself would be.* She turns around and leans against the counter. *I guess April must be enjoying playing with the things in her room. I can't believe she hasn't come out once. But I'll see if she's ready for her bath.*

The closer she gets to April's room the more quietly she moves, listening for any sounds coming from inside. When her ears are met with silence, she tiptoes the last few feet and peeks inside the doorway.

April is curled on the bed, her toy clutched to her chest, asleep.

Ella walks over and sits down on the edge of the bed. She pushes some loose strands of hair out of April's face.

April stirs and her eyelids open a slit. Suddenly she sits upright, a look of terror on her face.

"Everything's okay," Ella says gently. "You're in my house with me. You just fell asleep and woke up not remembering where you were. Are you ready to take a bath?"

April looks at her and frowns.

"I'll go start your water and let the tub fill up some before you get in. Before I do, there's one thing I want to remind you of and that is the rule I told you about before. When you are here I won't do anything for you unless you ask me to. The main reason you are living with me is to see if we can solve the puzzle of what has kept you from talking all these years. We're going to have lots of fun living together, but we have to be focused on the goal, too. Okay?"

April's blue eyes search Ella's face, then she nods her head.

"I'll be right back," Ella says. She walks into the bathroom, sits on the edge of the tub, and turns on the water. Once the temperature seems right, she unscrews the top from a bottle of bubble bath and pours the pink liquid under the streaming water. Immediately, mountains of white bubbles start forming across the sea of swirling bathwater.

A movement out of the corner of her eye catches Ella's attention. She looks at the doorway and sees half of April's face.

Like a deer wondering whether it's safe to walk out of the woods into an open field, April hides the rest of herself from Ella's view.

Ella smiles at her and holds out her hand. "Come on in. Just look at all these beautiful bubbles you can play in."

April inches her way into the bathroom. Frown lines crease her forehead and there is a furrow above the bridge of her nose. She looks at the bathtub Ella is perched on and peers over the edge at the white foam of bubbles. Her eyes grow wide in amazement.

Oh my goodness! She's never seen a real bathtub or had a bubble bath. "Look," Ella says, and she pats the mound of bubbles, making it bounce.

April smiles.

"Let's get your clothes off and I'll help you into the tub."

April peels off her clothes quickly.

Ella grasps her hand and says, "Step right in, but be careful not to slip."

April steps over the side. Chill bumps race across her skin as she sinks into the warm water. The white mountain of bubbles is as high as her chin and she strains her neck to keep her face away from them.

Ella laughs. "Don't be afraid of them. They won't burn your eyes if they get in them. Blow them really hard and see what happens."

April looks at Ella to make sure she isn't joking. Then she takes a deep breath and blows into the bubbles. They explode into the air and float down. Some of them land on Ella's nose.

Ella crosses her eyes to look at the plume of bubbles on her nose.

April's eye's close in delight. Her mouth pops open and her head tilts back.

Ella looks and listens closely. *There's a laugh about to come out of her, I just know it.* A brief sound like the whimper of a puppy comes from April's open mouth. She immediately looks at Ella then claps her hand over her mouth.

"So you can make sounds," Ella says.

Ella's comment has the effect of someone putting their hand on top of April's head and pushing down. She drops out of sight beneath the white cover of bubbles.

Ella waits.

After several moments, April springs up and stands in the tub. Her wet hair hanging down in her face and over her shoulders, coupled with the streams of white suds sliding down her skin, give her the appearance of a sea creature that has risen from the deep. Choking on water she has swallowed, she has a coughing fit, sending small sprays into the air.

Ella pats her sharply on the back. "Bless your heart, you're going to choke to death. Cough hard and clear your lungs."

When April's coughing subsides, Ella says, "I'm going to go get your bed ready and find you something to sleep in. Why don't you just enjoy relaxing and playing in the bubbles? I'll leave you alone to play for a while. There are some dolls perched on the back of the tub that you can play with if you want to. You could even give them a good washing."

Walking back into April's bedroom, Ella looks at the sad pile of faded and tattered clothes on the bed. *The first thing we're going to do is run to the Ben Franklin store tomorrow and buy this girl some clothes. I've never seen such an anemic collection of a child's worldly possessions. No child in the United States should have to live like this. It's disgraceful there's not more help for her and others like her.*

She snatches up a pair of panties and walks to her own bedroom, where she selects a pair of white cotton socks from a dresser drawer and takes a short-sleeved pajama top off its hanger in the closet.

As she approaches the bathroom, she hears water splashing. When she steps in the doorway, her hand goes to her mouth and her eyes widen. The entire floor of the bathroom has water on it. The rug by the tub is soaked. She looks at the tub just in time to see April slide herself across the length of it, causing a tide of water to crash ahead of her against the wall. The expression of pleasure and excitement on April's face tempers Ella's initial urge to scold her. *Don't overreact. She's never been in a tub before and has no idea how to behave.*

"April?"

So engrossed is April in playing that Ella's voice startles her. She looks like a puppy that is being housebroken expecting another spanking for peeing on the floor.

"Having fun?" Ella asks.

April's fearful expression remains unchanged. She begins noticing the water splashed on the walls and sees the puddles in the floor at Ella's feet. Her face begins turning red.

"Yes, we've got a mess here," Ella says, "but we'll get it cleaned up. I guess I should have told you to be careful about splashing water. You had no way to know it would splash out so easily."

The color in April's cheeks returns to normal and her face relaxes.

"Let's let the water out of the tub and get you dried off. Then we'll get some towels and get all this water dried up."

Twenty minutes later Ella is helping April into bed and pulling the covers up around her neck. Suddenly a thought occurs to Ella. "I just thought of something. I'll be right back."

After a minute or two she returns to April's room carrying her Autoharp.

April's eyes sparkle and she grins from ear to ear.

"I thought you might enjoy me singing you a bedtime song. Would you like that?"

April's head bobs excitedly.

Ella begins strumming her instrument, waiting for a song to come to mind. "I know, I'll sing "The Wildwood Flower" for you. It's an old, old song. One of the first I ever learned. You lie back on your pillow and just rest while I sing it for you."

April lies back and folds her arms under the back of her head as Ella begins singing.

Oh I'll twine with my mingles and waving black hair
With the roses so red and the lilies so fair
And the myrtles so bright with the emerald dew
The pale and the leader and eyes look like blue

I will dance I will sing and my laugh shall be gay
I will charm every heart in each crown I will sway
When I woke from my dreaming my idols were clay
All portion of love had all flown away.

Oh he taught me to love him and promised to love
And to cherish me over all others above

How my heart is now wondering no misery can tell
He's left me no warning no words of farewell

Oh he taught me to love him and call me his flower
That was blooming to cheer him through life's dreary hour
How I long to see him and regret the dark hour
He's gone and neglected his pale wildwood flower.

As she ends the song, a single tear escapes from each of Ella's eyes and travels down a familiar path across her cheeks. She's become lost in the song and memory, oblivious to present time or place. The touch of a small hand on her cheek brings her back to the room.

April looks at her with concern as she wipes the twin tears away.

CHAPTER THIRTY-ONE

On Monday morning, after getting the kitchen and bedrooms straightened, Ella gets in her car and drives over to Tucker's house. She climbs the steps to the porch and makes her way to the front door. After knocking once she steps back to wait. When Tucker doesn't answer, she knocks again a little harder.

"Over here!"

Ella turns at the sound of Tucker's voice behind her and spies her walking from the barn across the road. "Good morning!" Ella calls out.

"Mornin'!" Tucker answers back. As Tucker reaches the yard she picks up her pace. "Y' got news 'bout April? Have y' done had a breakthrough?"

"Oh goodness no, that's not why I'm here." Ella waits until Tucker reaches the porch before she continues. "We had a good weekend just doing things around the house. She's getting more accustomed to her room, and I think she's sleeping fine."

"I knowed she'd settle in without no problems. So what does bring y' out this mornin'?"

"I was wondering if you cared if I bought April some clothes."

"Clothes? But I sent all her clothes with 'er when we come last week. What happened t' them?"

Tread carefully, Ella, you don't want to hurt her feelings. Guide my tongue, Lord. "Nothing's happened to them, and I really appreciate you sending them. I was just thinking if I got her some new things, that that might make her feel even more like it was home. But I didn't want to do anything without asking you first. And I don't want to make August and March jealous of her."

Ella watches the muscles in Tucker's jaw flex as she chews on Ella's words. There is no other change in her expression. Ella finds herself holding her breath, expecting some sort of explosion to erupt at any moment.

Finally, Tucker says, "I s'pose it won't hurt nothin' t' buy her some new things. You probably know lots more 'bout how t' buy fer girls anyway."

Letting out the breath she's been holding, Ella smiles and says, "I'm happy you're going to let me do this."

"All I ask is that y' don't dress 'er up like some kind of doll in a shop window. I still want 'er t' look like m' pretty April."

"Oh, I agree one hundred percent," Ella replies. "That's why I want you to go shopping with me, so you can approve of what I pick out."

For the first time since she met Tucker, Ella sees what she takes to be a look of shock on her face. Her mouth opens in a soundless O, and color rises in her cheeks.

"You want me t' do what?" Tucker asks.

"Go shopping with me for April's clothes. Why, what's wrong with that?"

Tucker shakes her head. "I don't think that's such a good idea."

"Why not?"

"What store are y' gonna go to?"

164

"I thought we'd go to Ben Franklin's and maybe even check out what Reavis & Sons has."

"I might go with y' into Reavis's, but y' can fergit 'bout Ben Franklin's. Th' last time I was in there, years ago, that dried-up biddy Louise Hammer follered me 'round like a buzzard waitin' on a cow t' die. I bet she asked me twenty times if she could help me. I think she thought I was gonna steal somethin'. I finally tol' 'er t' go find 'er a perch in a dead tree somewhere with all th' other buzzards."

Ella gasps. "Tucker, you did not tell her that!"

"Sure I did. She deserved it. She acted like it hurt 'er feelin's, but she quit follerin' me an' that's all I wanted 'er t' do t' begin with. I don't like people hoverin' 'round me. Anyway, I ain't been back there since. Figured they'd run me off if'n I showed up."

It's Ella's turn to shake her head. "Tucker, Tucker, Tucker, don't you realize that you make it easy for people to tell outlandish tales about you? By the time that story got told around town I'll guarantee you that it made you out to be some kind of lunatic."

"So what? Why should I care what people think 'bout me?"

Ella studies Tucker for a moment. "You really mean that, don't you? You don't care what people think about you."

"I ain't got no control over what people say 'bout me. People talked 'bout me when I was growin' up, makin' fun of me. But they didn't know nothin' 'bout th' way I was bein' raised an' what kind of hell my life was. So they was judgin' me based only on what they saw, which was just a fraction of th' truth." She pauses and cocks her head at Ella. "Y' know, I'll bet people judged you an' tol' tales 'bout you, too, without knowin' th' truth 'bout what yore life with Judge Jack was really like."

Tucker's words sting Ella, causing her to put her hand on her chest. Her cheeks flush and tears fill her eyes. "I swear, Tucker," she says, "you have such an unflinching way of stating the truth so it can't be dodged or denied. In your hands, the truth is like an arrow shot by an expert archer; it always pins its prey to the ground. Yes, it is true that people judged me and spread unkind rumors about me. When I learned about them, I was cut to the quick. Listening to you now, I guess I always cared too much what people thought about me." She pauses, then adds, "I think I've realized something very important. I've always allowed other people to dictate how I felt about myself and put them in control of my self-esteem." She shakes her head. "How stupid of me."

Ella places her hand on Tucker's folded arms. "I know you think I'm smarter than you are, and in some ways that may be true, but what I'm finding out in my association with you is that there is much I can learn from you about how to live life and live it honestly. Thank you, Tucker."

Tucker shifts uncomfortably, "Thank me fer what?"

"For just being you, that's all."

Tucker's heart tries to tug the corners of her mouth upward into a smile, but after a few failed attempts gives up.

Pointing at Tucker's feet, Ella says, "Now go take off those muddy boots and put some others on. You're not going to ride in my car with those. Let's head to town and see what we can find for our pretty little April."

CHAPTER THIRTY-TWO

The timer on Ella's stove clicks and the buzzer goes off, startling Ella, who has gone to sleep in her chair in the living room. *My stars! I can't believe I fell asleep. I'll be glad when I get some of my stamina back.* Pushing on the arms of the chair to help her, she stands up and walks into the kitchen. She switches off the timer, opens the oven door, slides out a pan of sugar cookies, checks to see that the bottom edges of the cookies are just beginning to brown, and then turns the oven off and sets the hot pan on a trivet on the dining table.

She looks at the clock. *Perfect.* It's time for the school bus any minute now. She's as excited as Christmas morning, aching for April to like the things she bought for her. *I know she's never had clothes like these, but I'll bet she's seen girls at school wearing them and wished she had some like them.*

At last the rumble of the approaching bus reaches her ears and she walks into the living room to look out the front window. Seeing April step off the bus causes a smile to burst upon her face and a feeling of sunlight to warm her heart. *I haven't had feelings like this since Cade was a little boy. I know she's not mine, but I'll treat her as if she is. And maybe somehow we can help heal each other.*

When April reaches the front porch, Ella steps over and meets her at the door.

Upon seeing Ella, April's face brightens with a grin.

"Come on in here and give me a hug," Ella says. "I've missed you today."

April steps into Ella's embrace and wraps her arms around Ella's thighs. Breaking away, she turns her head up and sniffs the air like a hunting dog that has caught wind of its prey. She follows her nose into the kitchen and then to the dining table, where her eyes widen at the sight of the fresh-baked cookies. She looks at Ella with upraised eyebrows.

"Yes you may," Ella says, but immediately regrets it. *I can't believe I gave her permission when she didn't ask for it. This is going to be as hard on me as it is on her.* She has to make herself stop and think before she agrees to anything with April. *Consistent, that's what I have to be for this to work.*

She gets a couple of glasses and fills them with cherry Kool-Aid from the refrigerator. Sitting down with April, she picks up a cookie and takes a bite. "Did you have a good day at school today?"

April sets her glass down, revealing a red moustache, and nods her head.

"Well, I've got a big surprise for you. It's been hard for me to wait for you to get home I've been so eager to share it with you."

April stares at her, her cookie and Kool-Aid forgotten for the moment.

"When you're finished with your snack, I'll show it to you."

April drops her cookie on the table and stands up beside her chair, scanning the area to see if she might spy what the surprise is.

Ella smiles. "Are you sure you're finished with your snack? There's really no hurry."

April walks around the table and begins pulling on Ella's hand.

"Okay then, I guess I'll go ahead and show you. Let's go to your bedroom."

Unused to receiving pleasant surprises, part of April wants to run ahead to her room and another part of her wants to be close to Ella in case things don't turn out like she hopes. She tugs on Ella but walks closely beside her, too. When they reach the doorway of the bedroom and look inside, April freezes. Draped on her bed and dresser are all the clothes Ella bought earlier in the day.

Ella watches her closely, recognizing the shock and disbelief on her face. "These are for you, April. Tucker and I went shopping this morning. You want me to show them to you?"

April nods enthusiastically.

"Let's start over here at the dresser, then. Here are some socks, T-shirts, and panties."

April picks up a pair of the cotton socks and rubs them gently on her cheek. She grabs the panties and holds them up to her nose. Smiling, she returns them to the dresser.

"And here are some shoes," Ella says. "Shoes to play in, shoes for when you want to dress nicer, and some house shoes to wear inside to keep your feet warm and comfy."

April touches the blue Keds tag on the heel of the tennis shoes. Holding up the black patent leather shoes, she looks at her reflection and makes a face at herself.

"Now come over here to the bed," Ella says. "Let me tell you about all these clothes." Picking up a pair of purple pants, she says, "These are called gauchos. They come from a design in Argentina. This white ruffled shirt goes good with them. And then you can wear this matching purple crushed velvet-look jacket with the outfit."

The texture of the jacket draws April's hand to it. She rubs it in both directions with the front and back of her hand. She draws an *A* in the nap with her finger.

"I'll tell you that some of these colors and designs are too wild for me, but I'm assured they are very popular with girls. Like this plaid pantsuit. Do you like it? Because if you don't, I can take it back."

April takes in the horizontal and vertical lines of the large plaid pattern. She holds it up and swings it back and forth. Finally, she nods approval and places it back on the bed.

"These are called rib-knit sweaters. You've got a black one and a pastel green one. They'll be really warm this winter. And this long, orange pleated skirt goes with this blue pullover vest. I actually kind of like those two colors together."

A big nod of April's head indicates she agrees with Ella.

"When it comes to these two, I'm just not sure. This green blouse is supposed to be worn with this pair of gold pants. What do you think?"

April looks at Ella. After a minute she shakes her head no.

"That's not a problem. I don't blame you a bit." Laughing, she adds, "As a matter of fact, I'm relieved. I don't know if I could have stood to let you wear it out of the house."

Ella is almost certain she hears the same stifled laugh coming from April as she quickly turns away. She decides not to push the issue. "And that leaves us with these two blouses, the pastel blue one and the one with a paisley design. And of course you know that these are two pairs of jeans."

April walks back over to the dresser and looks at each piece of clothing, picking them up and smelling them. Then she returns to the display on her bed and holds some of the items up to herself to see what they might look like on her.

"Don't you think we need to let you try everything on to see how they fit?"

April's smile fills her face.

"First thing, then, you need to take a bath. You don't want to put clean clothes on a dirty body, especially your new panties."

April frowns.

"I realize you may not be used to taking a bath every day. But while you are here we're going to make it a habit. I'll start the water. You pick out a pair of panties and one of the T-shirts and bring them with you to put on after your bath. Then we'll try on this amazing new wardrobe you have."

As she lies on her back in bed later that night, tears escape from the corners of Ella's eyes and drain into her ears. They are the hot, bitter tears of regret. *How different things might have been for me if I'd never married Jack. And how different Cade would have turned out if I could have done a better job of shielding him from Jack. This journey of my life out to Tucker's hill has been such an enlightening experience. Finding April has been like discovering a diamond in a plowed field. Despite all that she's been through she shines as brightly as a full moon on a cloudless night. She's captured my heart, that's for sure.*

She rolls over and looks again at the hand-drawn picture lying on her bedside table. Illuminated by the low wattage lamp, the picture is of a little girl with yellow hair. Opposite the little girl is a tall woman in a dress, with no hair. The rest of the page is filled with hundreds of hearts of every size and dimension. April had brought it in and placed it on her bed while Ella was taking her shower.

Yes indeed, she has captured my heart.

CHAPTER THIRTY-THREE

The next morning, April walks into the kitchen wearing her new housecoat and house shoes.

Ella is setting two bowls of warm oatmeal on the dining table when she notices April. "Don't you look warm and toasty this morning? Do they feel good?"

April pulls the housecoat closer around her neck, smiles, and nods.

Sitting down to eat, Ella asks, "Have you decided what you're going to wear to school this morning? You've got lots of choices in there now."

Ella watches April's tongue and jaw moving inside her closed mouth. *Just say it! Come on, let it out.*

April turns to her bowl of oatmeal and begins eating.

"Well, it's up to you what you choose to wear. If you need any help with getting dressed, just come ask me. I'll be glad to help you."

When April finishes her oatmeal, she carries the bowl and puts it in the kitchen sink, then goes to her bedroom. Opening a dresser drawer, she takes out a pair of new socks and a T-shirt. From another drawer she pulls out the plaid pantsuit and the black rib-knit sweater. After removing her housecoat and pajamas, she slips the T-shirt on over her head and then pulls on the socks. Once she gets the plaid pants on, she looks down at the orange and black squares. She high-steps across the floor, watching how the pattern dances with her movements.

Grinning, she starts pulling on the sweater over her head but finds the tight-fitting garment a much tougher opponent that her T-shirt was. Finally her head pops through the neck hole. Her face is red from the struggle and most of her long strands of hair stay stuffed inside the sweater. What hair does make it to the outside has so much static electricity in it that it dances in the air around her face. Ignoring her hair, she slips on the matching plaid jacket and goes to her closet.

Inside, she picks up the black patent leather shoes and sits down on the floor to put them on. She inspects the strap designed to fit across her instep. Working with the tiny gold buckle on the side of the strap, she tries to unfasten it, but the stiff material proves uncooperative. The longer she is unsuccessful in her attempts, the more frustrated she becomes. Finally, she flings the shoe into the closet, bouncing it off the back wall.

Standing up, she reaches inside the closet and snatches the offending shoe off the floor and stomps into the kitchen, where Ella is cleaning up the breakfast dishes.

When Ella hears April entering the kitchen, she turns around. It takes every bit of self-control she can muster not to burst into laughter at the spectacle of April. Her pants are on backward. The tendrils of her electrically charged hair look like the tentacles of a sea anemone swaying in the ocean currents. The frown and red cheeks are sure signs there has been a struggle.

April shoves her hand gripping the shoe toward Ella.

Seeing that the buckle is still latched, Ella immediately recognizes the source of April's frustration. "Is there something you need?" she asks.

Astonished at Ella's question, April shakes the shoe at her and points at the buckle.

"Yes, I see there is a buckle there. Is there something you want me to do? If there is, all you have to do is ask."

April shakes her head and points to the buckle.

"I've got to finish these dishes, April, and you have to finish getting ready for school so you can catch the bus." Ella turns around and puts her hands into the dishwater. *She's either going to do it or not. I can't make her talk.* She hears April's pounding sock feet returning to her bedroom. Slamming drawers and doors add exclamation points to her anger.

Ella focuses on drying her dishes and putting them in the cabinet. Glancing at the clock, she calls out, "Better hurry, April, it's almost time for the bus to arrive."

Right on cue the door to April's bedroom flies open. She comes out wearing the same tired-looking clothes she wore to school yesterday. She gives Ella the best withering look she can muster and marches outside to wait for the bus.

I can't let her go to school dressed like that! It would seem almost criminal! But I can't go get her and end up breaking the rule, either. My goodness, she is one hardheaded child! Beneath that angelic face lies a little chunk of Tucker. This is turning into a real battle of wills. I just hope I've got the backbone and the heart to win.

For the rest of the week the morning scene repeats itself. It ends the same, with April walking out the door in her old clothes and Ella feeling more and more frustrated. However, by bedtime each night all rancor and aggravation have evaporated as Ella plays her

Autoharp and sings. The combination of her smooth, even strumming, her rich alto voice, and the old-timey lyrics act like a poultice on any emotional sores left over from the morning skirmish.

April always watches with keen interest how the fingers on Ella's left hand depress the damper buttons to change chords while her right hand rhythmically strums the strings with thumb and finger picks.

On Saturday, as Ella is busy sorting clothes in the laundry room, she hears the sound of music coming from somewhere in the house. She pushes in the button of the washing machine to stop its noisy agitation, and she listens closely. *Is that my Autoharp? But how in the world—?*

She moves silently toward her bedroom as the sound gets louder and more distinct. *Oh my gosh, April is playing my Autoharp! And not just playing at it—playing a song!* Ella stops at the edge of her doorway, fearful of breaking whatever magic spell is at work. *She is remarkable! She has a good feel for rhythm and her chord progressions are accurate. Where in the world did she inherit her gift from?*

More importantly, is this the key that Ella can use to unlock April's tongue? Is there a way to draw her out through music?

Then she hears another sound that stops her breathing and sets her heart hammering in her chest like the thundering hoofbeats of a runaway horse. *Dear God in heaven, she is humming!*

CHAPTER THIRTY-FOUR

I miss April." March's comment interrupts an otherwise silent evening meal at Tucker's house.

"Yeah, me, too." August looks up from stirring his bowl of homemade vegetable soup and asks Tucker, "How long is she going to live with Miss Ella?"

Tucker lifts her quart jar of iced tea to her mouth and takes a drink. Placing the jar back on the table, she looks at the boys. "I done tol' you boys why April's at Miss Ella's. Somethin' has t' change or we're gonna lose 'er forever. Is that what y' want, t' have 'er taken away from us fer good?"

"No ma'am," March answers.

"No ma'am," August echoes his brother.

Both boys look back down at their soup and idly push the vegetables around with their spoons.

Tucker eats a spoonful of soup and then takes a bite of buttered cornbread. After she washes it down with a gulp of tea, she starts to eat more soup when she drops her spoon noisily into the bowl. "Look here," she says to the boys, "this ain't easy fer me neither. I miss 'er, too, but what was I supposed t' do? Sometimes in life y' have t' make a hard choice so's you can get somethin' better in return. This here's one of those times. B'sides, it ain't like April's run away an' never comin' back, or like y' can't see 'er if'n y' want to. Miss Ella says we can visit any time we like."

"Have you been down to see her?" March asks.

"No," Tucker replies. She looks down at her soup and eats another spoonful.

"How come?" March presses her.

Tucker acts like she doesn't hear him. *How in th' world can I explain t' these boys how bad m' heart hurts, how fearful I am of losing April 'cause she'll like livin' with Ella better than livin' with me, how I don't think I can bear t' see her without bringin' her back home with me?*

With her head still tilted down toward her soup, she steals a look at the boys from beneath her eyebrows. Both of them sit with their arms folded on the table, looking at her.

Tucker lays her spoon down on the table. Taking a slow breath, she says, "This here's th' only way I know how t' explain it to you. Do you two love yore mother?"

The boys nod.

"An' do y' miss seein' her sometimes?"

Another nod from both boys.

"When do y' miss 'er th' most, the day after she has visited y', or when y' haven't seen 'er fer a month?"

March and August stare at her. They turn and look at each other.

August turns to Tucker and says, "I never thought about it, but I guess after I haven't seen her for weeks I get used to not seeing her and I don't miss her as much."

March listens closely to his older brother's explanation. He drops his head and says, "The day after she's visited us I hurt right here." He points to his chest. "And sometimes I cry."

This pure and simple truth from the normally taciturn March catches Tucker by surprise. *I wish there was somebody who could've made a movie of that so's I could show it to his mother. Curse her! One of these days, there's gonna be a reckoning for her careless and hurtful life.* She lays her hand on top of his folded arms. "An' what 'bout when y' ain't seen her fer weeks? Do y' miss 'er as much then?"

March shakes his head and then lays his cheek on Tucker's warm, weathered hand.

Moved by his gesture but uncomfortable with the emotions building in her chest, Tucker slides her hand out from under March's face. "Well that's sorta how I feel 'bout visitin' April. I'm afraid if I go see 'er it's gonna hurt me so bad that I won't be able t' stop m'self from bringin' 'er back home with me. So fer th' time bein' it's jes' best fer me t' keep m' distance."

All three of them stare blankly at the tabletop that has become piled high with their truth and emotional intimacy. Each of them sifts through layers of it, looking for meaning and gaining new insight into each other.

Swept up by this new openness from Tucker, August takes a step onto the thin ice of this newly discovered land and asks, "Have you ever lost anybody that didn't come back?"

Even though his question was delivered lightly, the weight and force of the truth that lay in the answer push Tucker back in her chair. She blinks rapidly as the sound of steel doors closing echoes in her head.

March pushes his bowl of soup out of the way, folds his hands on the table, and rests his chin on them in eager anticipation of his grandmother's answer to his brother's brave question.

Tucker says, "That really ain't none of yore business."

Without thinking, March says, "How come?" When he realizes what he's done he winces in expectation of a slap from Tucker.

But Tucker resists the urge to slap March and bring to a halt this uncomfortable conversation. In a distant corner of her mind a memory is stirred of a lanky black dog running toward her, his pink tongue hanging out of his mouth and his ears pinned back. With unfocused eyes, she says, "I had a dog once, named Suzy. She wasn't no special breed, but a mixture of huntin' dog and shepherd, most likely. Suzy was always there fer me. One winter she saved m' life when I had t' sleep in th' dog pen with 'er. I could talk t' Suzy an' tell 'er anythin'. She was always ready t' listen an' always acted like she was glad t' see me. Sometimes I even snuck 'er into m' bedroom at night an' let 'er sleep with me. Next t' Mary Beth Chandler, Suzy was th' closest thing I had to a friend.

"Suzy went ever'where with me, helped me feed, and went t' th' field with me, too. If ever a cow wasn't up t' th' barn in time fer milkin', I'd tell 'er t' go round her up an' off she'd go. After a bit you'd hear that cow a-bawlin' and soon you see it runnin' toward th' barn with Suzy at 'er heels. Or if a sow with a new litter of pigs give me any trouble, she'd back 'er into a corner while I checked her babies. Never was a dog any better than Suzy."

Tucker pauses as she sifts through her memories. Picking up the thread of her story, she continues, "But Suzy got herself into some trouble. She an' some other dogs killed a neighbor's chickens. Leastwise that's what they said. I never b'lieved it m'self. But m' daddy b'lieved it and that's all that mattered." Tucker's fists suddenly clench. "I seen him outside beatin' Suzy with a walkin' stick—not a switch, mind y', but a walkin' stick. Suzy was hollerin' somethin' terrible. I think 'er ribs was breakin'. I run outside an' grabbed m' daddy's arm holdin' th' stick an' tol' 'im to stop. 'You're killin' 'er!' I screamed.

"M' daddy flung me t' th' ground an' said, 'Killin' her? I'll show you what killin' looks like.' An' he pulled a pistol outta his pocket an' shot Suzy in th' head. It killed 'er dead as a hammer."

March's face is filled with an expression of terror, while August wipes a tear from his eye.

The room blurs for Tucker as her eyes fill with tears. She hits the table with her fist. "How come ya'll had t' make me remember that?!" Pulling her glasses off, she reaches for the bandana in her hip pocket and swipes at her eyes, then blows her nose.

August gets out of his chair and steps beside his grandmother. Putting his arm across the top of her broad shoulders, he says, "I'm sorry, Tucker. Your daddy was a mean, mean man."

March sits up and says, "You should've killed him. Anybody that would do that to a dog should be shot, just like he shot Suzy."

In spite of her emotional state, March's appraisal of the situation finds its way to Tucker's consciousness. She looks at him. *If you only knew, child . . . If you only knew.*

CHAPTER THIRTY-FIVE

On the night following her discovery of April playing the Autoharp and humming, Ella pulls her Autoharp out from under her bed for their nightly ritual of music at bedtime. But instead of going into April's bedroom as she normally does, she pauses in the doorway and says, "I want us to have our music time together in the living room tonight. Okay?"

April looks at her with questioning eyes but slips out of her covers and follows Ella into the living room.

Sitting down on the couch, Ella pats the cushion and says, "Come sit beside me."

When April walks by the coffee table, she eyes the Autoharp resting on it, then joins Ella on the couch.

Ella lifts the instrument off the table and places it in her lap. "I can tell that you really enjoy music, don't you?"

April smiles and nods.

"I thought you might be interested in me teaching you how to play my Autoharp. You're young but not too young to learn. As a matter of fact, I wasn't much older than you when I started learning to play." She sees the sparkle and delight in April's eyes. "Okay then, let's start with the basics. You've seen me play it two different ways, on my lap or holding it to my chest in the crook of my arm. Either way works, but for you, you will need to just hold it in your lap because it's pretty heavy. Scoot back and let me put it on your lap."

April wiggles backward until she is against the back of the couch.

Ella lays the Autoharp on April's skinny legs. It covers her thighs and part of her shins. "Is it too heavy?"

Shaking her head, April shifts her weight to get more comfortable.

Ella opens a small compartment in the Autoharp case and takes out a handful of picks. "There are many different styles of playing an Autoharp, and they all require using different kinds of picks. To start with we're just going to use this plastic teardrop pick. Hold it between your thumb and your first two fingers, like this." She shows April the proper position and then hands the pick to her.

Once April has gripped the pick, Ella selects a pick for herself and says, "Most of the time you are going to strum the strings in one direction, starting at the thicker strings and going toward the skinny ones." She drags her pick across the strings to demonstrate.

As if it is clearing its throat, the Autoharp awakens and sings a discordant sound.

"Doesn't sound very pretty, does it?" Ella asks. "That's because all of the strings played. It's these buttonlike things with letters on them that help make the nice-sounding chords. When you push one of them down, like this, it dampens or prevents certain strings from playing and allows only the notes in the chord to be heard. You push one of the buttons down and I'll strum, then you can hear the difference."

April pushes down a button with an *A* on it and Ella strums the strings.

Responding like an orchestra to the conductor's baton, the Autoharp leaps to life and allows only those strings playing A, C#, and E to vibrate, filling the living room with a rich A chord.

"Now that's more like it, isn't it?" Ella asks.

Her question falls to the floor, unheeded by April, who is gripping the Autoharp with both hands and pulling it more tightly to her. She turns her face to the side so she can peer more closely underneath the strings. She pushes a button down and watches how it contacts the strings with its felt dampening pads. Then she lightly drags her pick across the strings, producing a different chord. She strums again, with greater pressure on her pick. The Autoharp reacts by increasing its volume. April closes her eyes until the last, tiny note fades into silence.

Oh my, how this child loves music! Ella can see it touches her soul in a place that nothing else does or perhaps ever has, and remembers having that same feeling when she was growing up. *I'll bet anything someone in her family tree had the gift of music.*

Suddenly April opens her eyes and starts strumming with purpose and a definite rhythm while pushing down the G, C, and D buttons in an alternating pattern.

It's the same song Ella heard her playing earlier today. *I wonder what song it is.* Ella tries out several melodies in her head to see if they fit April's playing. After a few moments she claps her hands.

Ella's clapping startles April and she drops her pick.

"It's 'The Wildwood Flower,' isn't it?" Ella asks.

Once she sees Ella's happy expression and knows she's not in trouble, April nods her head and grins.

"Okay then," Ella says, "you play and I'll sing."

Excited, April sticks her pink tongue partway out of her mouth as she concentrates, not wanting to make a mistake.

As April begins playing, Ella begins singing. Partway through the song, she nods encouragingly at April and pats her on the back.

She keeps her palm on April's back to see if she can feel any vibrations of her humming along with her. *Yes she is humming, the little stinker! She's humming right along with me. Now how in the world do I get that hum to turn into words?* All of a sudden an idea pops into her head. *That's it! I'll give her what she wants when she gives me what I want.*

The next morning April comes shuffling into the kitchen, pulls out a chair, and sits at the table. Her hair, with a life and mind of its own, swirls around her even though her head is still.

Ella turns from the stove holding two bowls of warm oatmeal with spoons in them. Sitting down, she slides a bowl in front of April and begins eating from the other bowl. After a couple of bites, and seeing no movement out of April, she says, "Okay, sleepy head, you need to take a bite of your oatmeal and wake your body up. You don't want to be late for the bus."

Acting as if her spoon were as heavy as a shovel, April lifts a half spoonful of oatmeal to her mouth. Like the gates on an ancient castle, her mouth slowly opens and allows the oatmeal to pass through. The gate slams shut and April pulls the spoon out through her tight lips.

Trying to sound casual, Ella says, "You know, I was thinking last night and came up with an idea I think you might like."

April looks at Ella, though her head stays tilted toward her bowl.

Ella takes a bite of oatmeal and sips some coffee. "Yes, I was thinking about that closet full of new clothes that you haven't worn yet. It does seem like a shame to have all those clothes hanging there not being used. I've even thought about taking them back."

April's head comes up at this suggestion.

"I know, I know. You want to wear them. And I want you to wear them. I really do. You would look so cute in them. But we've got this problem of me wanting something from you. You remember what that is?"

April stares wide-eyed and unblinking at Ella.

"Right, I need you to start talking. Well I was thinking about that last night and about our time singing and playing last night and I thought maybe I could change what I want from you just a bit."

April blinks and lays her spoon on the table.

"What if each morning you pick out an outfit you want to wear, then you bring it to me to help you put it on. I will agree to do that for you, if you will first of all hum a song for me. Just hum it. You don't have to sing the words or open your mouth. Just hum it for me."

In a perfect imitation of a habit her grandmother Tucker has, April blinks rapidly. She looks Ella in the eye and then looks away. Her face begins to redden and her jaw muscles flex.

Trying to keep the air light and decrease the pressure April is feeling, Ella stands and begins gathering their bowls. "It is just an idea, maybe not even a good one, but I thought I would share it with you. You can think about it and do whatever you wish. Right now, though, you need to go brush your teeth and start getting ready." Turning her back on April, she carries the bowls to the kitchen and starts running warm water in the sink. She resists the urge to sneak a peek at April's expression and reaction. *I've put a bridge out there for her, but she's going to have to decide if she's willing to cross it. Dear Lord, touch her heart and help remove whatever stone is blocking her path.* Plunging her hands into the soapy water, she finds the washrag and begins washing dishes.

Ten minutes later, as Ella is drying and putting away the dishes, she feels a tug on the leg of her pants. Looking down, she sees April holding the plaid pantsuit. Ella's heart jumps into her throat, but she tries to keep her expression neutral. "That's what you want to wear to school this morning?"

April nods slowly.

"I'll be delighted to help you, but first let me hear you hum a song."

April looks down at the floor and hums so faintly that only a note ever so often can be heard.

"No, no, no," Ella says, "that won't do. I don't want to strain myself to hear the song. Hum it where I can hear you clearly."

A scowl has replaced April's normally pleasant features as she looks up at Ella. An obstinate look flits across her face, then dissipates as she considers her options. Taking a deep breath, she begins humming loudly enough to be heard clearly.

Relief floods Ella and she says a silent prayer of thanks. She smiles warmly as the song begins winding to an end. "'Darlin' Corey' is one of my favorite tunes. It always makes me smile. That was a great job! Now let's go to your room and get you dressed in your new outfit!"

CHAPTER THIRTY-SIX

By the time Friday arrives, April is humming a song each morning without hesitation. Her face is relaxed and smiling this morning, mirroring Ella's expression. Strains of "The Wabash Cannonball" vibrate inside her closed mouth and resonate out her nose.

Ella starts clapping in rhythm to the song and then buck dances across the floor.

April's eyes twinkle and laughter begins bubbling up inside her at the sight of Ella dancing. She tries to contain the laughter and continue humming, but the laughter wins out and rolls out of her in shrill peals.

Ella turns and grabs April's hands and pulls her into the middle of the kitchen floor. "Dance with me!"

April does her best to imitate the quick movements of Ella's feet.

Ella starts singing, "Listen to the jingle, the rumble and the roar as she glides along the woodlands, through the hills and by the shores. Hear the mighty rush of the engines and that lonesome hobo call. He's riding through the jungle on the Wabash Cannonball."

As Ella sings the last three words, April, swept up in the energy of the moment, sings them aloud with her.

They both jerk to a stop and stare at each other, wide-eyed with astonishment.

April jerks her hands out of Ella's grasp and claps them over her mouth.

"April? Do you realize what you just did? You sang the words! My gosh, you sang out loud with me!" Going to her knees, she pulls April into her arms, hugging her tightly. "It's amazing and wonderful and unbelievable and . . . I can't even think of all the right words, but you did it."

Letting go of April, she holds her at arm's length. Immediately she recognizes by April's expression that she doesn't share the same feelings of excitement.

April's eyebrows meet in an arch and slant downward toward each side of her face. Her eyes look uncertain and dart away when they meet Ella's gaze. Her normally pink lips are pursed so tightly they've turned white.

"What's wrong, April? You look almost scared."

April twists away from Ella. Like a rabbit trying to figure out which hole to run to, she glances all around the room. Finally, she points at the clock.

Ella looks in that direction and says, "Okay, it is past time to get ready for the bus. We can talk about this later. Let's go to your room and decide what you want to wear."

After she sends April out the door to get on the bus, Ella returns to the kitchen, pours herself a cup of coffee, and sits down. Cradling the cup between her hands, she takes a sip. *What is going on in that little girl's head?* For the life of her, Ella cannot figure her out. April acted almost petrified after she sang out loud, like something bad was going to happen. *But it can't be because she's ever gotten in trouble for speaking out loud because Tucker's told me April has never spoken a word.*

She takes another sip of coffee. *Maybe I'm making it too complicated, overthinking it. The answer may be right in front of me but I'm straining to look around it.* She decides she'll make herself busy straightening up the house and maybe the answer will come to her. Besides, Tucker will be here for her daily visit after a while and she's got to decide what to tell her, if anything, about what has happened.

A couple hours later, Ella hears the familiar sound of Tucker's heavy boots thudding on her porch. She pitches the last handful of wet clothes she's transferring from the washing machine into the dryer and starts the machine. She is halfway across the living room floor when there is a sound like a sledgehammer striking the front door. She sighs. *There's no mistaking Tucker's knock.*

Opening the door, Ella greets her neighbor, "Good morning, Tucker. Come on in."

"Mornin', Ella." Tucker walks past her and toward the kitchen.

Ella follows in Tucker's wide wake. As Tucker is settling into a chair at the table, Ella retrieves a cup from the cabinet and fills it with coffee. She sets it in front of Tucker and sits down across from her.

Tucker takes a noisy sip of coffee and says, "Is she talkin' yet?"

Ella looks at Tucker thoughtfully. She's already come to the decision not to tell Tucker about the humming and about what happened this morning. *It would just give her something more to worry me about, and besides, I don't know if what happened this morning will ever happen again.* Finally she says, "Tucker, you've been coming here every day since Thanksgiving and asking the same question each time. And my answer is always the same: I'm doing the best I know how to do."

"But if'n she don't start talkin' I'm gonna lose 'er."

"I realize that. Believe me, I realize that! You can't imagine how much pressure I feel. And you coming here every day and asking me if she's talking just makes it worse."

Folding her arms across her chest, Tucker says, "Well, I gotta know somethin'. I'm th' one what's responsible for her."

Ella exhales heavily. "What I'm about to say is probably going to make you mad, but here goes. I don't want you asking anymore about my progress with April. When my time with her is up in three weeks, either this experiment will have worked or it won't have."

Tucker puts her hands around her coffee cup and looks quietly into it.

Reaching across the table and putting her hand on Tucker's, Ella says, "I promise you to do the very best I can with April. That's all I know to tell you. You're just going to have to trust me."

Tucker doesn't flinch from the touch of Ella's hand as expected. Keeping her eyes on her coffee cup, Tucker says, "Trust. Trust ain't somethin' I done since I was a little girl. Trust means somethin' bad's gonna happen."

Sensing the fear and tension in Tucker's voice, Ella resists the urge to jerk back from the unintended barb of Tucker's words. Tucker continues, "Mary Beth Chandler and Mama Mattie are th' onliest two people in m' life what never betrayed me." Her voice becomes husky and she clears her throat. "But I'm in a tight spot here." Lifting her head and looking at Ella, she says, "I've gotta trust somebody. An' you ain't never done nothin' that'd make me believe you's out t' get me. So trust you I will. I'll not bother y' n'more 'bout it."

A pair of tears runs down parallel paths on either side of Ella's nose. When they reach her lip, she reflexively licks them with the tip of her tongue. "Tucker, I don't know all the story of your life and I don't have to. It doesn't matter. But I'll tell you honestly that you are one of the truest friends I've ever had. You're honest. There is not a shred of pretense about you. I find that very refreshing."

"Pretense?" Tucker says with a questioning look.

"It means someone who is hypocritical," Ella tries to explain. "Someone who puts on airs."

Laughing, Tucker says, "Oh, I see. Well th' onliest airs Tucker's got is when she ain't bathed or when she's ate pinto beans."

Ella bursts out laughing. "Oh, Tucker, you won't do! You just won't do!"

Tucker slides back her chair from the table. "I best be gettin' on back t' th' house." She grimaces as she stands.

Frowning, Ella says, "Tucker, are you hurt?"

Tucker waves off her concern. "I got kicked in th' shin this mornin' by our milk cow. It was that dadburn March's fault. Ever'body knows cows git used to y' milkin' 'em from th' same side ever' time. This mornin' March got it in his head that he wanted t' milk 'er from th' opposite side. I tol' 'im he was askin' fer trouble, but if'n that's what he wanted t' do, then go ahead. Well I was th' one what shoulda paid attention. I was standin' beside 'im makin' sure nothin' happened. Ever'thing was fine when he put his stool b'side 'er. But as soon as he tugged on her teat she kicked sideways an' caught me square on m' shin. Give me a knot th' size of a lemon."

"Had she ever kicked you before?" Ella asks.

"No siree. She's 'bout th' calmest milk cow I ever had."

"And yet she kicked you just because you changed sides?"

"Like I said, animals get used t' doin' things a certain way, like mountin' a horse from th' left side. People think y' have t' do it that way, but it ain't so. Don't really matter which side y' mount yore horse from just so y' do it th' same way ever' time. Animals don't like t' change their habits."

Ella follows Tucker to the door. "We'll be seeing each other again," she says as Tucker exits her house. "Put some ice on your shin. It'll help the swelling and soreness."

When Tucker limps off the porch Ella shuts the door. She turns around and stares blankly. *Could it really be that simple? Could it be that April is so used to never using her voice that it feels odd, or even frightening to suddenly hear it and to let others hear it? Hmmm . . . I wonder . . .*

CHAPTER THIRTY-SEVEN

Ella rubs the rim of the glass with her washrag, then hands it to April, who is standing in a chair beside her. April turns on the faucet and rinses the suds off the glass and places it in the dish drainer.

Pulling the stopper out of the drain, Ella watches the water begin to swirl as gravity pulls it out of the sink. "Do you want to spray it clean?" she asks April.

April nods and grasps the spray nozzle with two hands as she pulls it out of its resting place in the back of the sink. Taking careful aim, she sprays water into each corner of the sink, flushing out the remnants of suds and corralling them into the drain. Once they've disappeared, Ella says, "Good job. I believe we're all finished in here. Let's go in the bathroom and brush our teeth before we put our pajamas on."

They make their way to the bathroom and reach for the tooth-brushes standing at attention like good soldiers in their holder. Ella squeezes toothpaste onto her brush and then onto April's. Just as April is about to stick her toothbrush into her mouth, Ella says, "Wait a minute."

April halts with her mouth open and her brush halfway inside it.

"Let's try something, just for the fun of it. Let's try using our left hands to brush our teeth."

Frowning, April closes her mouth and rests her hand holding the toothbrush on the edge of the sink.

"I know it sounds silly, but I was thinking today about how many things I do the same way every time, and I've done them that way my entire life. I started wondering if I could do any of them a different way, like brushing my teeth with my left hand. I think it'll be fun just to see if either of us can do it." She swaps hands with her toothbrush and opens her mouth. As she awkwardly tries to put the brush in her mouth, she grazes her upper lip, leaving a glob of toothpaste resting on it.

Watching Ella, April laughs a tiny laugh at Ella's toothpaste-laden lip.

Ella laughs, too, and replenishes the toothpaste on her brush. "If you think it's so funny, let's see you try it," she says, while again trying to find her open mouth with her brush.

April turns her attention to her own brush and slowly raises it toward her mouth.

This time both of them land their aircraft squarely on the landing strips of their tongues. They close the hangar doors and begin trying to brush their teeth. Their movements are herky-jerky, and occasionally they unintentionally pull the brush completely out of their mouths. As they try to stick it back in, they hit their cheek or chin, leaving a trail of foam behind. Laughing at their awkward movements and toothpaste-covered faces only increases the foaming action of the toothpaste. As though they are two rabid dogs, foam overflows from their mouths and runs down their chins. April gets so tickled that foam starts coming out of her nose.

Finally, Ella lifts a hand towel off the towel bar and wipes her face. "All right," she says, laughing, "enough is enough." She pulls a Dixie cup from the dispenser hanging on the wall and hands it to

April. "Let's rinse our mouths out." She pulls another cup out for herself and follows her own instructions.

After they've both rinsed and spit several times Ella reaches for a washcloth. "I think we both need some help on the outside of our mouths, too." She washes off April's face and then her own. "Now that was an adventure, wasn't it?"

Smiling, April nods her head.

"And it was a lot harder than I expected. I really didn't think it would be that hard because it sounds like such a simple thing to do. Let's go sit in the living room for a minute."

After they walk into the living room, Ella takes a seat in her favorite armchair. Reaching for April, she says, "Get that afghan off the couch and come sit in my lap." When April arrives with the afghan draped over her shoulder and dragging on the floor behind her, Ella swaddles her with it and, grunting, lifts her onto her lap. "Goodness, you're getting to be such a big girl." She squeezes April, who smiles and snuggles into the warmth and softness of the afghan, and also into the welcoming heart of Ella.

"Always remember this, April. You're never too old to learn. I learned something today, and I learned it from Tucker. She explained to me how animals like to do things the same way every time and how hard it is for them to change. Our little experiment tonight in brushing our teeth shows me that we humans are no different from the animals in that way. It's just easier to keep doing things the way we've always done them. And all that brings me to the subject of you and why you are living with me."

Up until now April has had her eyes closed, enjoying listening to Ella's voice and relaxing. Now her eyes pop open and she looks up at Ella from the cocoon of the afghan.

"Everyone has always wondered, 'Why doesn't April talk?' Your teachers, Tucker, the social workers, and I have racked our brains looking for some kind of dark, mysterious explanation for your silence. Well, I decided today that the answer is neither dark nor mysterious. The answer is so simple that it has escaped us all. You don't talk simply because you've never talked. If you started talking now, it would feel as awkward to you as brushing your teeth with your left hand."

April slowly sits up and turns so she can look into Ella's face. Her penetrating gaze that seems to cut straight to Ella's soul, and the serious expression on her face, cause Ella's breath to catch in her throat.

They sit in silence, searching each other's face with their eyes, probing, looking for meaning and understanding, trying to find a place to connect.

When Ella finds her breath, she says in a whisper, "Do you think that's possible? That you don't talk because it feels strange to you to even think about talking?"

April puts her small hands on both side of Ella's face and moves her face within inches of Ella's. She says in a whisper, "Yes."

Tears spring up in Ella's eyes like the geysers in Yellowstone. Quickly overwhelming her lower lids, they cascade down her face like a waterfall. Each time she blinks, tears splash and land on April's arms. Her breathing becomes convulsive and she hugs April tightly to her chest. After several minutes she is finally able to say, "Oh April."

CHAPTER THIRTY-EIGHT

Opening the door to her wood-burning stove, Tucker thrusts the iron poker in, shifting the burning logs so they can get more air. She throws in an extra stick of wood, closes the door to the stove, and stands up. She glances at the frost-ringed window-panes in the front of her house, and sees blurred movement outside. Walking to the front door to get a better look, she sees Ella's car pulling to a stop in front of her porch and she sees April sitting in the passenger seat.

Tucker jerks the front door open. Ignoring the swirling snow and bitter wind, she steps onto the porch. Before anyone even opens a car door, she yells, "Is April okay?"

Ella leaves the car motor running and steps out of the car, at the same time trying to tie her headscarf under her chin. Her gloved hands fumble for a moment in their task, but finally she pulls the knot tight. Once the scarf is secure, she wraps her arms around herself as if fearing the wind will peel off her coat. Keeping her head bowed against the wind, she walks carefully on the light snow with its undercoat of sleet.

Taking another step toward the edge of her porch, Tucker repeats, "Is April okay?"

Just now noticing Tucker, Ella is startled. "Yes, everything is fine. But you're going to freeze out here!"

As Ella starts up the steps, Tucker extends her hand to help. "Careful. Them steps is slicker than lard."

Once she lands safely on the porch, Ella says, "Thank you. Gracious, this is a raw day!"

"Come on in where th' fire is," Tucker says.

Ella follows her inside.

August and March have heard the shouting and have come to see what the commotion is all about.

Rubbing his hands over the woodstove to warm them, August says, "Hey, Miss Ella. How's April doing?"

"I'll bet you're ready to get rid of her, ain't you?" March asks.

"Hello, boys," Ella replies. "April is fine, and no, I'm not ready to get rid of her. Are you two enjoying your Christmas break from school?"

"Yes, ma'am!" they exclaim simultaneously.

Turning to Tucker, Ella says, "I just wanted to stop by for a moment and see what you all had planned for Christmas Day." Smiling at the boys, she adds, "It's day after tomorrow, you know."

When the boys don't return her smile, Ella looks to Tucker.

"We don't do much fer Christmas 'round here," Tucker says. "Sometimes some of them hippercrits from a church in town'll come an' bring stuff fer th' kids. Maisy usually comes by fer a visit, too."

Not having expected this, Ella tries to regain her emotional footing. She joins the boys at the stove and goes through the motions of warming her hands, even though she was not exposed to the elements outside long enough to get cold. After a few moments she says, "Well why don't all of you come to my house for Christmas dinner like you did for Thanksgiving?"

"Yeah!" March yells. "Holy cow, yes!"

"Let's do it!" August chimes in. "Can we, Tucker? Can we?"

"Well . . . , " Tucker begins, "I ain't got another ham t' bring. I could kill a chicken 'r two, I guess."

"No, no," Ella says. "This time it's all on me. I'll take care of the meal. You all just show up. It'll be fun."

"Come on, Tucker," the boys plead.

Waving her hand dismissively at the boys, Tucker says, "You boys hush up." She turns to face Ella. "That's a mighty nice invite, Ella. We'll be pleased t' come."

"Wonderful!" Ella exclaims. "I can't wait to tell April. She'll be so excited! And who knows—it looks like we might have a white Christmas!" She walks to the front door to leave and pauses when she opens the door. "Oh, and bring Maisy with you, too."

Two days later, August and March are up at the crack of dawn. By the time Tucker gets up they have finished their chores and have already fired up the woodstove. The frost on the inside of the windows has begun to yield to the heat, water running down the panes and dripping onto the windowsills.

Coming into the kitchen, Tucker sees August at the stove with a skillet and March with his head in the refrigerator. "What th' devil are ya'll doin'?"

March appears out of the refrigerator with a glass of milk in hand and kicks the door closed. Setting it on the table, where there is already a plate and silverware, he says, "Me and August are fixing breakfast for you."

"Well ain't this a turn of events," Tucker says. "Whata ya'll been up to? Who's in trouble?"

"Nothing," August says with a smile. "It's Christmas Day and this is what we decided to give you."

Smiling in spite of herself, Tucker says, "I could git used t' this. Any chance it'll happen ever' mornin'?"

The boys laugh. "Not a chance," March says.

August walks to the table carrying the skillet. He tilts it beside Tucker's plate, like she always does for him and March, and waits for the eggs he's cooked to slide out. When the eggs don't cooperate, August frowns and pushes them out with the spatula. They break into pieces and the deep yellow yolk bleeds out from the rupture. March lays three pieces of limp, half-cooked bacon beside the eggs and places two pieces of burnt toast on the edge of her plate. Both boys sit down to wait for Tucker to dig into her breakfast.

Looking at the unappealing palette of white, yellow, brown, pink, and black on her plate, Tucker stalls by asking, "Where's ya'll's breakfast at?"

"We done ate," August answers.

The three sit in silence as Tucker slowly works her way through the meal. She uses the last corner of her toast to wipe the egg yolk off her plate, puts it in her mouth, and washes it down with a drink of coffee.

August asks, "Are you done?"

Before she can answer, March asks, "Can we go down to Miss Ella's now?"

"Whoa, whoa there, both of you. Now I see what's goin' on here. Ya'll just wanta git to Miss Ella's as soon as y' can, but we ain't goin' until noon. Besides, yore mama might show up an' go with us."

Downcast, both boys fold their hands on the table and rest their chins on the back of their hands.

"Now ya'll just as well quit yore mopin', 'cause it'll just make time pass slower. Git on 'bout your business." As the boys slowly retreat from the kitchen, Tucker adds, "I enjoyed m' breakfast. It was real good."

Smiling at each other, the boys head to their room.

As the noon hour approaches, August and March have taken up positions of readiness in the living room. Both keep their eyes on the clock.

"Five more minutes, Tucker," March calls out.

"Quit bugging her!" August says to March. "You're gonna make her mad and then we'll have the devil to pay."

"I can tell time," Tucker calls back in reply to March.

They listen to her heavy footsteps coming from her bedroom. When they hear her bedroom door open, they spring out of their chairs. Grabbing their coats, hats, and gloves, they put them on as quickly as their hands will let them.

Tucker comes into the room already having donned her heavy coat, hat, and gloves. "Okay, you two, let's git goin'."

As they open the door to dash out, they are halted by Maisy approaching up the steps.

"Now isn't that the nicest thing!" Maisy exclaims. "Rushing out to meet your mama on Christmas Day." Throwing open her arms she says, "Ya'll love your mama, don't you?"

August and March look back into the house and then step apart to let Tucker pass between them.

The matriarch strides to the top step and looks down at her daughter. "From th' time you was born yore timin' ain't never been good."

Folding her arms across her chest, Maisy says, "What's that supposed to mean? Can't you even be nice on Christmas Day?"

The boys shut the front door and join Tucker at the top step, standing on each side of her.

Maisy looks at the three of them. Suddenly something clicks. "Oh I know what's going on here. You're going to Miss Ella's, aren't you?" With a sarcastic tone she adds, "Miss Ella McDade's."

"As a matter of fact, we are," Tucker replies. "An' she done said you could come too, if'n you showed up here t'day."

"I knew she liked me," Maisy replies, smiling brightly. "I could tell I made a good impression on her. She can tell class when she sees it. I think it'll be fun going there. I can't wait to see her decorations. I'll bet they look really nice. Probably not as nice as my apartment, but nice. Oh, you should see my apartment. It looks like the North Pole. I bet Santa would be jealous of it."

"Will you just close yore mouth?" Tucker interrupts. "Between th' wind comin' outta yore mouth an' this here north wind, I'm liable t' catch pneumonia."

August and March guffaw.

"Honestly, Tucker!" Maisy sputters. "I told myself before I came out here today that I wasn't going to let you spoil my good mood, and I'm not. Now why don't all of you pile into my car and we'll ride down to Ella's together?"

Giving a whoop, the boys leap from the porch to the ground and race to the car. The slick footing makes stopping difficult but they grab a car door handle to brake to a stop.

Once Tucker joins Maisy in the front seat, Maisy backs her car out and heads to their rendezvous at Ella's.

CHAPTER THIRTY-NINE

Following the Christmas meal, Ella says, "If everyone's finished, let's all go into the living room."

Tucker and Maisy sit down beside each other on the couch and March and August form bookends for them. April sits on her knees beside Ella.

"Now that it's getting dark outside," Ella says, "August, why don't you plug in the Christmas tree lights, and March, you turn out the overhead light."

As if practiced and choreographed, March switches out the lights at the very instant August plugs in the lights of the tree. The effect is dramatic. Red, green, white, and blue lights send their beams across the ceiling and floor.

"Oh man . . ." August says softly as he turns his head around the room to follow the tails of the colored comets.

March is transfixed. After a moment, he slowly walks toward the tree and stands beside it.

Tucker whistles low.

"It looks just like the tree in my apartment," Maisy says. "Except that mine is—"

Tucker cuts Maisy off with an elbow to the ribs. Through her clenched teeth Tucker says, "This ain't 'bout you."

Rubbing her side, Maisy shoots a mean look at Tucker but says nothing.

Pulling a chair up to the side of the tree and sitting in it, Ella says, "August and March, you come sit on the floor by the tree."

The normally boisterous March moves cautiously to join his brother at the base of the tree.

Ella clears her throat and says, "Now, I've done something without asking permission, and I don't want anyone to get upset about it. I did it because it's what I wanted to do. It's what I enjoy doing."

Everyone's attention is glued on Ella.

"I've got some surprises for you," she continues. "Will you help me, April?"

Smiling, April stands.

Pointing to a present under the tree, Ella says to April, "Give that one to August and that red one to March."

"Presents!" March yells at the top of his lungs.

"Wow," August says quietly.

"Now just a minute—" Tucker begins, but Ella cuts her off.

"Shush right there, Tucker. I just got through saying that this is something I wanted to do and no one is stopping me."

Tucker exhales and eases back into the couch. "It's yore right t' do what y' wanta do, I guess."

August and March are sitting on their knees and looking at Ella, their unopened presents in front of them.

"Well what are you waiting for?" she asks. "Open them."

March jerks and tears at paper and bow like a Tasmanian devil. August unties the bow and then breaks the hold of the tape on the paper. Identical boxes are exposed underneath the colorful paper. They open the boxes simultaneously and pull out sheepskin denim jackets. With eyes as big as their open mouths, the boys are speechless.

"Oh my lordy," Tucker exclaims. "Put 'em on, boys, 'an let's see how y' look."

Standing up, the boys slide their arms into the sleeves and pull the jackets over their shoulders. August stands tall and looks down at himself. March spins around in front of everyone.

Maisy says, "Don't my boys look handsome?"

Handing two smaller presents to April, Ella says, "Take this one to Tucker and this one to Maisy."

With a wide grin, Maisy grabs her gift and opens it quickly. She pulls out a long scarf. "How pretty." Standing, she wraps it around her neck and prances across the floor. "Don't I look beautiful?"

Tucker opens her present slowly, her thick fingers fumbling with the paper and bow.

"What did you get, Tucker?" August asks.

"Give me a minute," Tucker says. Finally getting it open, she pulls out a pair of leather work gloves. She puts them on and admires her gloved hands. "Now them's some fine gloves right there. I ain't never had none this good. Thank y', Ella. Boys, whadda y' say?"

"Thank you, Miss Ella," March says.

August walks to Ella, puts his arms around her neck, and says, "Thank you, Miss Ella."

Tucker thumps Maisy's ankle with the edge of the sole of her boot. "Ouch," Maisy exclaims. "Watch where you're—"

Catching Tucker's eye, Maisy stops and says, "Thank you, Ella. This scarf is lovely."

Looking very pleased, Ella says, "Now, April, why don't you go get your Christmas present and put it on so everyone can see it?"

Smiling, April runs to her room.

Reaching behind the tree, Ella pulls out her Autoharp case and lays it on her lap. As she begins unbuckling it, August says, "I've seen that before. That's where you keep that thing you played when we were here after the tornado. What's it called?"

Opening the lid, Ella reaches inside. "It's an Autoharp." Lifting it out of the case, she says, "Move the case for me, will you March?"

March quickly obeys and Ella places the Autoharp on her lap. She pulls out a pick and strums it a few times. The notes float through the air like the seeds of a dandelion.

"How pretty," Maisy says softly.

"You just wait, Mama," March says. "She's really good at playing that thing."

"What about 'Jingle Bells'?" Ella asks her audience. "Anyone in the mood for 'Jingle Bells'?"

Clapping her hands, Maisy says, "Yes, yes. That'll be fun. We can all sing together."

"Okay then," Ella says. "Here we go."

She attacks her Autoharp with relish and begins singing with the same verve.

Maisy immediately joins in.

March and August gape at their mother and swap looks of amazement. Shrugging their shoulders, they join in as well.

As they head into the chorus the second time, Maisy says, "Come on, Tucker. Sing with us."

Looking embarrassed, Tucker smiles almost shyly.

"Yeah," August encourages her, "sing with us."

March darts over and begins dancing in front of her. "Sing, Tucker. Sing."

Softly at first, Tucker begins singing.

"We can't hear you!" Ella calls out excitedly. "Let 'er rip, Tucker!"

Finding a voice she hasn't used in decades, Tucker throws back her head and sings lustily with the others.

Maisy looks at her mother with wonder.

August moves to take his mother by the hand and pulls her off the couch. They dance in circles.

"Come on, Tucker," March says. "We can do better than them." He tugs on her with all his might.

Laughing, Tucker rises to her feet.

Soon the four of them are holding hands and dancing while Ella continues playing. When she stops playing, they turn to look at her.

Standing beside Ella is April dressed in a red dress, white tights, and red shoes. Her golden hair is pulled back and held in place by a red bow. Rhinestones on the front of her dress catch all the colors from the Christmas tree and reflect them into every part of the room. It's as if she is plugged in, too. She smiles broadly at her family.

Tucker, Maisy, August, and March continue holding hands, but seem too stunned to move.

"If you would," Ella says to them, "please sit on the couch together. April has a present she wants to give to all of you."

Still appearing shocked, the four step backward and squeeze onto the couch, March sitting on Tucker's lap.

Looking at April, Ella says, "Are you ready?"

April smiles and nods.

Ella looks down at her Autoharp and begins slowly strumming and picking.

The notes of the song touch a memory in Maisy. She looks at Tucker, who has had the same memory stirred. Whispering, Maisy says, "Isn't that what you used to hum to me when—"

"Shhh," Tucker says gently. "Yes it is."

They turn their attention back to Ella playing. As they look, April takes a deep breath, opens her mouth and, in a voice as clear as crystal, sings.

Amazing grace how sweet the sound
that saved a wretch like me.
I once was lost but now I'm found.
Was blind but now I see.

As April continues with the next verses, Maisy openly weeps and lays her head on Tucker's right shoulder.

August's bottom lip begins to tremble as he lays his head in Tucker's lap.

March leans back as Tucker tucks him under her right arm.

And Tucker? Tucker puts her right arm around Maisy's shoulder and hums along with April.

CHAPTER FORTY

Tucker and Ella ride in silence in Ella's car while April sits quietly in the backseat with Ella's Autoharp lying beside her in its case. "What time is it?" Tucker asks.

Ella glances at her watch. "It's ten minutes until ten o'clock." Gripping the steering wheel with both hands, she adds, "We'll be on time."

Tucker wipes her sweating palms on her pant legs. *M' heart's runnin' as fast as a feist dog chasin' a squirrel up a tree. I can't remember th' last time I was ever this nervous. But this here is gonna be th' moment of truth. If April don't talk fer these people, I'll prob'ly end up goin' t' jail in tryin' t' prevent 'em from takin' 'er away from me. I just wish I could carry m' axe handle into th' meetin' with me just in case Judge Jack smarts off.*

Ella turns on her blinker to make the turn toward the building that houses the Health Department. She, too, is lost in her own thoughts. *I don't think I could be more scared if I was about to face a grizzly bear!* Everything is riding on this meeting and April's willingness to cooperate. Ella knows April can do whatever they ask her to do, but she has that stubborn Tucker gene in her that turns her obstinate at times. If that happens, all bets are off.

As Ella pulls to a stop at the curb in front of the building, Tucker spies Mary Beth Chandler standing outside the front door clutching her coat tightly around her neck with one hand and checking the watch on her other wrist. "We're late, ain't we?" Tucker asks.

"No we're not," Ella replies. "I just think that Mary Beth is as anxious as we are."

Tucker looks at Ella. "Are you nervous?"

Ella looks in the rearview mirror at April, whose expression reveals nothing about her emotional state. "Yes, I'll have to say I'm nervous. But I'm not afraid, because I know April is going to do fine. Aren't you, April?"

April turns her head and looks out her window without responding.

Tucker twists around in her seat and is opening her mouth to say something to April when Ella puts her hand on Tucker's. Surprised, Tucker glances at Ella, who shakes her head. Taking the hint, Tucker turns back around. "Well then, let's git inside an' show these people how foolish they are. They's th' ones that's gonna look retarded by th' time April gets through with 'em."

Tucker and Ella open their doors simultaneously and get out. Ella lets April out of the backseat and grabs her Autoharp case. After she closes the door, she stands with her eyes closed.

"What're y' waitin' on?" Tucker asks.

Another moment passes and Ella opens her eyes. "Just saying a silent prayer. It sure can't hurt."

The three of them walk up the sidewalk toward the two-story red brick building. As they get close to the door Mary Beth stomps her feet and says, "Hurry up! I'm freezing out here!"

"What're y' doin' standin' outside?" Tucker asks. "Are y' in trouble already?"

"No, of course not. I just didn't like sitting in there waiting. It was feeling too stuffy." She turns her attention to April. Smiling warmly, she says, "Good morning, April. You really look nice."

April gives her a polite look, but says nothing.

Mary Beth sends furtive, questioning looks to Tucker and Ella. When neither says anything, she points to the case Ella is carrying. "What is that? And what's it for?"

Grinning broadly, Tucker cuts in, "You'll see what it's fer, you will fer certain."

"We're all here," Ella says matter-of-factly. "Let's go inside and get this meeting started."

"Before we do," Mary Beth says, "let me tell you who all is here, just so you won't be surprised. Carol Horner, the supervisor of special education services for the county; Jerry Raines, the super-intendent of education; Pamela Mortensen, the director of social services; and my boss. Plus a court reporter just so we can have a transcript of the meeting in case anyone wants to dispute what happens and what is said." She takes a breath and adds, "And Judge Jack McDade is present, too."

"That's good," Tucker says. "Ever'one that thinks they know more 'bout what's best fer m' April than I do is here. They'll all hear it an' see it fer themselves, an' that'll finally be an end t' all of it. Lead th' way, Mary Beth."

Mary Beth turns, opens the door, and walks inside. Ella follows directly behind her. April trails closely behind, and Tucker brings up the rear.

The lobby of the Health Department building has been arranged into a meeting room. Two long tables sit end to end. The team of officials sits solemnly on one side of the tables, and the court reporter sits on one end. Across from them, approximately fifteen feet away, sit three folding chairs.

Mary Beth motions for Tucker, Ella, and April to sit in the chairs, then she takes a seat with the others on the other side of the tables.

Tucker scans the people facing her. *Carol looks like she done went an' overslept. I'll bet she didn't see them sleep lines on the side of 'er face. She's th' one that thinks there's somethin' wrong with April. She's gonna find out diff'rent t'day.*

I ain't never met the superintendent. He looks like he b'lieves there's a giant icicle hangin' over his head an' it's 'bout to drop on him any minute.

That Miss Mortensen is th' one who thinks I can't take care of April. I'll say this 'bout 'er though: she's honest. She speaks 'er mind whether somebody likes it 'r not. I can deal with that. It's just that this time she happens t' be wrong, as she'll soon see.

When she looks at Judge Jack she has to swallow quickly to keep from spitting toward him. *I ain't never thought smugness was somethin' that could be smelled, but he stinks of it. He looks like th' cat that ate th' canary, smilin' like he's already won this contest. I've half a mind t'—*

Jerry Raines raps his knuckles on the table, interrupting Tucker's thoughts. "We are here this morning to reach a decision on whether or not April Tucker should be removed from her grandmother's home and sent to a place where she can receive the special services she needs to help her reach her full potential as a human being. We express our thanks to Pamela Mortensen for allowing us to use the lobby of their offices for this special Saturday meeting."

He turns to Carol Horner. "Carol, I believe you are to be the first one to speak."

Carol slips her glasses on her face and refers to her notes. "April Tucker was first brought to my attention when she entered kindergarten last year. The teacher informed me that she was not talking at all. When I questioned Tucker about this, she affirmed that April did not talk at home either. As a matter of fact she said she'd never heard a sound from her. The teacher and I formulated a plan that was designed to draw April out. This plan was ineffective. At the beginning of this school year we decided to have April seen by a psychologist, who would do some testing. His conclusion was rather nebulous, mainly because April would not engage with him. It is my opinion that in spite of the best efforts of April's grandmother, Tucker, she is not progressing, that she has serious mental deficits and needs specialized help in a therapeutic setting." She takes her glasses off, folds them up, and sets them on top of her notes, then folds her hands and rests them on the table. After a moment, she turns to look at the trio in the chairs.

"I wanta say somethin' 'bout all that," Tucker says and makes a motion to rise out of her chair.

Jerry Raines taps the table. "That will not be allowed at this time, Miss Tucker. We have a format we need to follow where everyone will be allowed to present their evidence, and you will be able to respond. I'll ask you to wait your turn, please."

Judge Jack coughs loudly and holds his hand over his mouth, but it doesn't disguise his delight.

Tucker grips the edges of her chair.

Ella leans over and whispers in her ear, "Don't you dare do anything that will upset April. If you do, I will hurt you."

Shocked, Tucker jerks her head toward Ella, but Ella has resumed a calm pose and is gazing at Jerry Raines.

"Thank you for that background information, Carol," the superintendent says. "That will take us to Pamela Mortensen, director of social services."

Sitting forward in her chair and speaking in a clipped voice, Pamela says, "On or about October fifth this year, I was contacted by Carol with a complaint of neglect against Miss Tucker, due to the fact that April Tucker was not receiving the kind of help she needed. During a staff meeting among the social workers at our agency, I made the proposal that we formally remove April from the home and place her in foster care. Mary Beth Chandler, who has been Miss Tucker's social worker for many years, proposed a compromise. It was her suggestion that we give Miss Tucker a chance to get April to start talking, but if she was unsuccessful, April would be removed. Our staff agreed with this compromise. Miss Tucker and I have had our run-ins in the past, so I anticipated that this proposal would not go over well. That is why I sought out Judge Jack McDade to sign an order that would enforce the proposal. Today is the deadline to learn if Miss Tucker has been successful."

Listening to Pamela's indictment of her, Tucker feels pressure building in her chest and working its way up her throat. The sense of powerlessness that spread like a canopy overhead when she walked into the meeting begins lowering itself onto her head and shoulders, threatening to smother the life out of her. Now, tiny pinpricks of light begin flashing in her peripheral vision. She sees the superintendent's mouth moving, but his voice sounds distant and indiscernible. When his mouth stops moving, everyone is looking at her.

Tucker blinks rapidly and the pinpricks of light fade out. Slowly, her hearing returns. She feels Ella's hand on her arm.

"You may speak now," Ella says.

Her knees still feeling a little weak, Tucker decides not to stand up. "I ain't go no idea what ya'll want me t' say. I've been judged all my life by people who don't know nothin' 'bout me. That might have bothered me a long time ago, but it don't no more. I learned I ain't got no control over what people think of me, so let 'em think what they want.

"But now I see it startin' all over again with m' grandchildren, 'specially little April. I tell th' kids t' ignore what people says. I tell 'em t' always be honest an' be true t' themselves, 'cause themselves is who they have to spend th' most time with. If'n you can't live with yoreself, you won't never be able t' get along with nobody."

Glancing over at April, Tucker puts her large hand on top of her small, blonde head. "This here little girl is smart as a whip. I've tol' this t' ever'body in this room." She pauses and looks at Judge Jack. "Ever'body but that wart."

Judge Jack's face turns crimson. Rising from his chair, he says, "Now you listen here, you—"

A smile plays with the corners of Tucker's mouth.

The superintendent slams his open palm on the table. "Stop right there, both of you! We're not going to make this personal. Judge, I'll respectfully ask you to sit down. And Tucker, we'll have no more of that."

The judge slowly lowers himself back into his chair. To Tucker he says, "My satisfaction will come at the end of this hearing." Turning to the superintendent, he says, "I apologize for my outburst."

"Mr. Superintendent," Tucker says, "I'm sorry I hurt the judge's feelin's. I guess nobody likes bein' talked 'bout."

Ignoring Tucker's dig, the superintendent says, "Miss Tucker, we are now at the critical moment. It's time to discover whether or not April can speak."

All of a sudden, Tucker feels a wave of warmth and calmness wash over her. "Just like I said t' ya'll, I believe a person has t' be honest with themselves. One thing I had t' be honest 'bout was that I wasn't smart enough t' help April t' talk. So I turned t' m' neighbor an' friend, Miss Ella McDade, an' asked fer her help. That's why she come this mornin', 'cause she was th' key that unlocked m' angel." Looking at April and Ella, she says, "Ya'll do yore thing."

Ella reaches down and unlatches her Autoharp case. Lifting the instrument from its cozy home, she lays it in her lap.

April looks at Ella.

"You ready?" Ella says, smiling.

April nods.

"Then stand up and let's give these folks something to smile about!" Immediately Ella attacks her Autoharp with her pick, playing at a frenetic pace.

Without hesitation April starts buck dancing and singing "Ol' Joe Clark," her blonde hair floating around her head and face like a halo.

The mouth of each person sitting at the table, including the court reporter, drops open. Expressions of shock are painted on their faces.

The first person to recover is Mary Beth. She smiles broadly and begins clapping in time with the song. The court reporter, having forgotten about his duties, is the first one to join with her. Pamela Mortensen, Mary Beth's boss, hesitates for a moment, then, smiling, claps with them. The two educators look at each other, shrug, and, turning to enjoy the performance, join the others in clapping in time.

Judge Jack's shocked expression, open mouth, and unblinking eyes, along with his pale complexion, the result of all the blood draining from his face, give him the appearance of a statue.

Tucker and Ella share a long look with each other. Without missing a beat, Ella nods toward April.

When Tucker gives her a questioning look, Ella repeats the gesture. Finally understanding Ella's meaning, Tucker breaks into a grin, jumps from her chair and begins buck dancing across the floor.

II.
FOR TUCKER

CHAPTER FORTY-ONE

Shading his eyes from the brilliant sun with one of his large hands, Smiley Carter enjoys the beauty of the cloudless, turquoise-colored February sky. His almond-colored palms complement the coffee-colored skin of his face. Ivory-colored teeth fill his broad, effervescent smile. White eyebrows sit like snow-capped mountains above his lively eyes.

He steers his Ford 801 tractor into Tucker's front yard. As it rolls to a stop, he reduces the throttle and cuts off the engine.

Raising a gloved hand, he hollers, "Hello, Tucker!"

The springs of the seat squeak as he lifts his heavy frame and steps to the ground.

Joining him, Tucker looks up and says, "How y' been, Smiley Carter? Ain't seen y' 'round in a while."

Carter takes off his cap, revealing close-cropped white hair. He slaps Tucker on the shoulder.

Tucker rocks a step from the blow.

"Ol' lady Tucker. Hows you been? You know ol' Smiley Carter is one busy man."

Recovering her balance, Tucker says, "One o' these days you're gonna call me that and I'm gonna knock them iv'ry teeth out, y' smilin' fool."

Carter bends double as a hearty laugh escapes him. "Now you knows you ain't gonna hurt ol' Smiley Carter. Cause if you do, who's gonna plow your garden for you?"

One corner of Tucker's mouth turns up imperceptibly and then retreats. "I ain't worried. I know yore granny, Mama Mattie, made y' promise to help me whenever I needed it."

Nodding somberly, Carter says, "'Tis so, 'tis so. An' if'n I don't, I'm afeered she'll come back and haunt me."

Tucker slaps him hard on the back, sending him stumbling forward. Smiling, she says, "So y'ain't got no way outta it. Foller me an' see what I need y' t' do."

Straightening up, Carter arches his back. As Tucker walks away he says, "Damn, woman. I think you done broke somethin' in my back."

Carter catches up with her halfway to her barn. As he comes even with her, she says, "I'm ready t' plant m' early garden."

"You always does that in Februrary, doesn't you?"

"That's 'cause there's always one week in th' month that th' ground gits dry enough to plow," Tucker replies. "Irish taters, green peas, an' carrots all does better th' earlier you can get 'em in th' ground."

"You plantin' in the same place as usual?"

"Naw. I moved th' hogs t' th' other side o' th' barn, into th' ol' garden spot. I wantcha t' plow up th' ol' pen area. It oughta be good an' rich."

Lifting the latch on the double barn doors, Tucker swings them wide. Sunlight cascades into the dark hallway. Sitting in a circle around a large tub are March, August, April, Maisy, and Ella. They turn toward the brilliant sun and the silhouetted pair in the doorway. Their faces look as if they've been hit with a spotlight.

Not until he speaks does anyone recognize Tucker's partner. "Hello, children," Carter calls out.

Jumping to his feet, March exclaims, "Smiley Carter!" and runs to greet him.

Carter catches the boy as he leaps toward him and swings him skyward. "My goodness, March! You have grown, boy."

August is on March's heels, but slows to a stop when he gets to Carter. "Hey, Smiley Carter," he says.

Dropping March to the ground, Carter turns his attention to August. He begins walking around him, shaking his head. "And who is this tall, strappin' boy? Tucker, you used to have a skinny kid hangin' 'round here. What happened to him?"

Unable to contain himself, August says, "It's me. I'm that boy."

Carter crouches into a boxer's stance and starts throwing air punches toward August. "Let's see if you is. The boy I remember had lightning-fast hands."

August mirrors his stance and, stepping toward him, throws five quick punches to Carter's midsection. Bouncing back, he thumbs his nose and blows air out of it.

Carter collapses to the ground howling. "Tucker! It's my liver! That boy done ruptured my liver!"

August rushes to Carter's side and falls to his knees. "I'm sorry. I didn't mean nothing by it! I just meant to be playing with you."

Quick as a flash, Carter bear hugs August and rolls across the ground, laughing loudly. He stops rolling and pins August on his back. "Don't you worry about ol' Smiley Carter. I can still manage to take care of myself against any young pup like you."

Smiling, Carter gets off the ground and offers a hand to August. August grabs the hand and Carter pulls him into a warm embrace.

Ella, April, and Maisy have gathered round to witness the commotion.

Spying April, Carter squats in front of her but still has to drop his head to look her in the eye. "And here's beautiful April, as pretty as the dogwoods in spring. Have you decided to talk to ol' Smiley Carter yet?"

April looks toward Ella. Ella nods. "Hi, Smiley," April says softly.

Carter's eyes and mouth open wide. As if shoved backward by April, he falls on his rear. Looking at Tucker, he says, "What is this?" and points toward April.

"They's been some changes 'round 'ere since you was last 'ere. April's been a-talkin' ever since Christmas."

Carter reaches slowly toward April. He touches her face, his large hand dwarfing her small features. "An' just like dogwoods bloom after a long winter, so has you, child. So has you."

Placing her hands on her hips, Maisy says, "Well aren't you even going to speak to me? What's a woman have to do to get noticed, anyway?"

Getting off the ground and brushing himself off, Carter turns to look at Maisy. He coughs and spits. He gives her a curt, "Hello."

Turning toward Ella, he says, "Don't believe I ever met you, ma'am."

"That there's Miss Ella," Tucker says. "She moved in t' th' McDaniel place a few months ago."

Flashing a broad smile, Carter bows to Ella and says, "Pleased to meet you, Miss Ella. People 'round here call me Smiley Carter."

Ella returns his smile. "Pleased to meet you, Smiley Carter."

Stomping the ground, Maisy turns and heads back to the barn, muttering under her breath, "Well I never! 'Pleased to meet you, Miss Ella.' You'd think she was the queen of England or something."

Clapping his hands, Carter says, "Okay, let's get busy plowin' and a-plantin'." He steps onto his tractor and fires up the hammering engine. He checks to be sure the twelve-inch two-bottom plow behind the tractor is off the ground and then follows Tucker's lead to the old hog pen.

"Which way you want the rows to run?" he hollers at Tucker over the sound of the engine.

"North and south," Tucker hollers back.

Carter backs the tractor into position, lowers the plow to the ground, shifts to first gear, and heads south. The points of the plow slide easily into the nutrient-rich dirt, folding over the dark topsoil in neat, humped rows behind the tractor. The smell of humus fills the air.

Looking at Carter's audience lined up along the fence, Tucker says, "Ya'll got them seed taters cut up and ready fer plantin'?"

CHAPTER FORTY-TWO

Making a sound like fabric tearing, the slicing of potatoes fills the silence in the barn hallway. The potato wedges fall one at a time into the waiting washtub. In order to avoid cutting a thumb or finger, everyone is focused on the task.

Tucker lifts her head as she hears Carter's tractor leaving the side of the barn and heading past the door.

Carter slows as he passes the entrance and calls out, "I'm going to get the disc. I'll be back in a bit."

Tucker waves without saying anything.

Maisy stands, pulls a rag from her back pocket, and wipes her hands. "Well I've got to be going."

"We ain't near done yet," Tucker growls.

"I know," Maisy says, "but I've got plans for the evening. I've got to get home and get cleaned up."

Tucker spits a stream of tobacco juice into the dirt floor of the barn. "Plans! I jes' wish I could live t' see th' day that you finish somethin' y' start. We've still gotta plant these taters. And I got some carrot seed, too."

Folding her arms across her chest, Maisy snaps, "I done more than my fair share when I was growin' up. You worked me like a dog when I was little—fetchin' water, choppin' kindling. It was never enough for you. Even when I said I was sick, I got the back of your hand and was told to get back to work."

Ella looks apprehensively toward Tucker.

Tucker slowly wipes her knife blade on her pants and stands up. In an even voice, she says, "You done?"

Maisy blinks and says, "Well, yes."

"Then git. Y' ain't no help 'ere anyways."

As Maisy retreats toward the house, Tucker says, "You kids help me lift this tub and take it to the garden." Pointing toward a door, she adds, "Ella, look in there an' bring a couple o' hoes an' a rake."

When they all get to the garden site, the sound of Carter's approaching tractor is heard in the distance. In a moment he comes rolling through the gate, drops the disc behind him, and begins churning the thick upturned soil into fine powder.

"That is beautiful," Ella says to no one in particular. Kneeling down, she sinks her hands into the womb of the earth. "I've never been this close to this kind of thing. It's about rebirth and rejuvenation. And look at all these earthworms!"

August and March look at each other and shrug their shoulders.

"Bring me a hoe," Tucker says to March. "Bring some taters, August."

Ella rises and walks toward Tucker.

Making his last pass over the garden spot, Carter lets the tractor roll to a stop and cuts off the engine. He gets stiffly off the tractor and joins everyone.

"Miss Ella," Carter says. "Did you wrap newspaper 'round those taters?"

Ella looks at the tub of potatoes and then to Tucker. "I . . . guess not. I just did like everyone else."

"Then how you expect to keep that dirt outta their eyes?"

There is a pause and suddenly everyone except Ella bursts into laughter. Realizing she's been the butt of a joke, Ella laughs, too.

"I remember when you got me on that one, Smiley Carter," August says.

"Don't think nothin' about it, Miss Ella," Carter says, laughing. "Smiley Carter's always pullin' somethin' on folks."

Ella smiles. "No offense taken."

Tucker digs into the soil with her hoe. "Ya'll quitcher carryin' on and drop a tater in this hole."

Moving quickly, August grabs a potato and drops it in. In three quick swipes with her hoe, Tucker buries the potato and tamps it. Without pausing, she moves one step and digs another hole. This time March drops a potato in.

"You're plantin' too deep," Carter says. "They'll never sprout."

Without looking up, Tucker says, "Th' day Smiley Carter can teach me somethin' 'bout growin' a garden is th' day . . . is th' day Maisy does an honest day's work."

Carter laughs. "You would say that when you has a hoe in your hand, if you get my meanin'."

Turning to Ella, he says, "Miss Ella, why don't you an' me shows them how to plant a garden?"

Knowing a covert message has just passed between Carter and Tucker, Ella is a bit hesitant how to proceed. "I've never planted a garden before," she finally says.

"Well you's about to learn from the king," Carter boasts. "Take off your hat an' roll up your sleeves, cause Smiley Carter don't take no prisoners. Bring me that other hoe, April."

As April begins dragging the hoe toward Carter, Ella puts her hand on her hat.

"Quit bossin' people around, Smiley Carter," Tucker snaps. "She don't have t' take off 'er hat if she don't wanta."

Carter stops and looks at Tucker, then to Ella. He notices Ella is blushing. "That is so, Miss Ella. It don't matter. Just grab a double handful of taters and drop 'em in while I dig the hole." In Tucker's direction he adds, "And not too deep a hole, either."

He ducks just in time to miss a well-aimed dirt clod thrown by Tucker. August and March laugh loudly.

Feigning hurt, Carter says, "See how they treat me 'round here, Miss Ella? It ain't Christian-like."

Soon they all settle into a steady rhythm of planting, August and March taking turns replenishing Ella's supply of potatoes.

After a few moments of quiet, Carter says to Ella, "You from around here? Don't believe I caught your last name."

Without glancing up, Ella says, "You might as well know, I'm the ex-wife of Judge Jack McDade. It sort of depends on how well a person knows him as to how a person feels about that. I think I'm prouder of being his ex than—"

She notices that Carter has dropped his hoe. Looking up, she sees him staring at her with his mouth agape.

"Did you say Judge Jack McDade?"

"Yes that's right. Like I was saying, I think—"

"An' you's done made friends with Tucker?"

"Well, yes. I think we have become friends. Why?"

"'Cause this is a day to remember. I've seen two miracles in the same day—April a-talkin' and Tucker having as a friend the ex-wife of Judge Jack McDade. Yes sir, this here's a day to remember."

CHAPTER FORTY-THREE

Sitting on the side of the bed, Maisy fumbles in the darkness for her cigarettes on the nightstand. She extracts a cigarette and places it between her lips. Her Zippo lighter clinks as she opens it and strikes a flame. Touching the flame to the end of her cigarette, she inhales deeply.

The flickering flame reveals smudged eye makeup. Her tangled dark hair gives her the semblance of Medusa.

She feels the bed move and hears a low groan. Smiling, she says, "Hey, Tiger. I thought you had gone into a coma. Was I too much for you?"

A male voice comes from under the covers. "Woman, you're killing me."

Moving across the bed, Maisy straddles her partner. Pulling the covers down, she enjoys the spreading smile on his face as he takes in her naked body.

"I still got it, don't I?" Maisy teases.

"What time is it?" he replies. "I've got to be going."

In a petulant voice, Maisy says, "'What time is it?' What kind of answer is that?! You wasn't in no hurry a while ago. I sometimes think you're just using me."

"Now, Maisy, don't get all stirred up. You know how it is with me."

Moving off her quarry, Maisy reaches for her T-shirt and pulls it over her head, shaking out her curls as she does so. "I'm about sick of that line." In a mocking tone she adds, "'You know how it is with me.'"

Sitting up, he reaches for the lamp and switches it on. They both squint as their eyes adjust.

His red hair catches the light and frames his face in amber hues. Fixing her with his clear, blue eyes he says, "You and I both know that I'm not the first guy you've danced with, so why should you think you've got sole possession of me?"

Maisy bursts into tears. "Are you calling me some kind of tramp or something? I've made mistakes in the past. I admit it. But it's different with you. I love you!" She moves beside him. Putting her head on his chest and slipping her hand under the covers she says, "You know you want me."

He grabs her arm and pulls it out from under the covers. "Look, I've got to get ready for work."

He reaches for his pants on the floor and, standing, slips them on.

Maisy's voice gets a little louder. "Oh, so you think you're too good for me. Is that what it is? You think you can do better?"

Without looking in her direction he says, "I never said that, Maisy."

He walks to the bathroom and begins brushing his teeth. As he lifts his head from the sink to look in the mirror, a glass ashtray whistles past his ear and crashes into the mirror. They both explode, sending shards of glass in a hundred directions.

Whirling around, he finds Maisy standing ten feet away with her fists clenched and eyes wide.

"Are you crazy, woman?! You could have killed me! What do you think you're doing?"

Maisy looks at him squarely. "You are not dumping me. Do you hear me? You are *not* dumping me."

Stepping carefully over the broken glass, he walks back into the room and picks up his shoes.

Maisy moves quickly to him. "Here, let me help you," she says sweetly. "I'm sorry. I didn't mean to scare you. I just lost my temper. Sit down. I'll put your shoes on you. Don't be mad at me."

Her hands tremble as she tries to slip his shoe on his foot.

Watching her sitting on her knees between his legs gives him pleasure.

"How long have we been seeing each other, Maisy?" he asks.

Maisy pauses. Thinking she hears a conciliatory tone, she slips closer to him. "It's been six years, three months, and five days. We're meant for each other." Taking his face in her hands, she purrs, "Let's go get in the shower."

"As much as I'd like to, I've got to go." He leans past her and steps into his other shoe.

"Fine!" Maisy snaps. "Go ahead and leave. I don't care."

Picking his keys off the table, he heads out the door. As the door closes, he hears Maisy call out, "I love you, Tiger!"

Moving to the window, Maisy watches him pull away from her apartment. Once he has driven out of sight, she goes to the phone. Dialing a number from memory, she waits for it to be answered.

In her cheeriest voice she says, "Hello, Tom. What have you been up to? I haven't heard from you in a while. Why don't you drop by this afternoon and let's get reacquainted."

Meanwhile, as he drives away from Maisy's apartment, he begins an internal dialogue. *What am I going to do with that woman? I'll lose my wife, my family, and my job if anyone finds out about us. Me and Tucker's daughter!* He laughs out loud at the implausibility of it. *How did I ever get involved with her?*

His mind turns back to his first encounter with her at the Elks Lodge. He spotted her dancing to Jerry Lee Lewis's "Chantilly Lace" playing on the jukebox. Her dark hair bounced in rhythm to the music as her body skipped lithely across the floor. Her ample breasts moved to their own rhythm.

After the song, she walked to the bar and stood beside him, humming "Don't the Girls All Get Prettier at Closing Time." She turned to him and smiled. Her iridescent blue eyes made his heart stop. He was spellbound.

Chuckling, she said, "Like what you see?"

That's when he realized he'd been staring. Quickly recovering, he said, "I sure do. Can I buy you a beer?"

"That'd be nice."

"What's your name?" he asked.

"Some people call me Amazing. But I'll let you decide for yourself if that's what you want to call me."

At that point he really didn't care what her name was or where she was from. He wanted her.

That night they drove the twenty miles to the Blue Bank motel, a quiet place beside Reelfoot Lake. Later, he told her she was well deserving of the name Amazing.

In the ensuing six years, their relationship has run hot and cold. He's tried to sever ties with her, but there is something about her that he finds irresistible. She's not the only woman he's seen through the years, but she is the one constant in his "stable."

Today's attempt to hit him with the ashtray has left him shaken. Her behavior is more extreme and desperate each time he leaves her.

Maybe it's time for me to end things with her once and for all.
But how?

231

CHAPTER FORTY-FOUR

Tucker, August, and March sit silently eating supper. The only sounds are their forks on their plates and the cold March wind whistling through the cracks around the doors and windows.

Without looking up from his plate, August speaks. "I miss April."

"Yeah, me, too," March adds. "When is she coming back home?"

Tucker takes a sip of coffee and puts a forkful of green beans in her mouth. "This 'ere's 'bout th' last of th' green beans we put up last summer. I'll sure miss 'em. Ain't nothin' any better 'n Kentucky Wonder pole beans. Another six weeks 'r so an' we'll be plantin' again."

Silence reclaims the congregation.

After a few moments, August says, "About the only time we get to see April is on the school bus."

March says, "She looks different than she used to. Have you noticed how many times she wears a dress to school?"

"Tucker," August ventures, "I thought you said she was just going to visit Miss Ella for a little while. It's like you've just given her away."

Tucker stops eating. The wind stops blowing. Electricity fills the air.

Slapping the table with the palms of her hands, Tucker makes the dishes rattle. With nostrils flared, she says, "'S'at what y' think? I give 'er away? That just shows how stupid y' both are.

"I'll tell y' what it's like when you're throwed away. M' daddy locked me in th' dog pen fer two weeks when I was a kid, no bigger'n you, March. I slept with th' dogs t' stay warm an' ate what they ate t' keep from bein' hungry. April ain't been throwed away!"

August and March stare wide-eyed at Tucker.

"Really, Tucker?" Augusts asks. "Did your dad really do that to you?"

"Man, that's sorry," March says.

"That's all right," Tucker says. "He got what he deserved in the end."

Turning toward Tucker, August says, "I've never heard you talk about your daddy. What do you mean 'he got what he deserved'?"

"I don't mean nothin'," Tucker replies. "He ain't deservin' of the breath it'd take t' tell it. Now you boys finish yore supper."

August and March drop their heads and pick at their food.

March mumbles something imperceptible.

"Y' got somethin' else t' say?" Tucker challenges him.

Looking at Tucker, March replies, "What's wrong with us? Mama don't want us and now April don't. Is it something we done?"

Tucker looks from one boy to the other. "If'n ya'll ain't th' whiniest coupl' o' little girls I ever listened to. Y' need t' grow up and quit feelin' sorry fer yoreself. I ain't raised neither one o' y' t' be some kind o' sissy. Supper's over. Git up 'an clean yore dishes."

Later that night, March and August are lying in their shared bed.

Out of the darkness, March says, "It's because of what we used to do with April. That's why she don't want to have nothing to do with us."

"Shut up," August hisses. "Just shut up."

"You know it's true," March insists.

"I don't know nothing and neither do you," August says. "Besides, we was just playing around. Nobody got hurt."

A silence fills the room that is thicker than the black of the night.

After a few minutes, March says, "I think that's why she never talked."

March feels August move and senses that he is on his elbow, looking in his direction.

August says, "I told you the last time it happened, that we'd never talk about it again." Seizing March around the neck and shaking him, he adds, "Now shut up!"

August flops back on his pillow and jerks the covers over himself.

Both boys lie motionless, lost in their thoughts.

In the stillness, March begins whimpering. After a moment, he bursts out in a broken voice, "August, you and me is going to burn in hell."

Meanwhile, under the naked light bulb hanging from the ceiling in her bedroom downstairs, Tucker sits on her bed. In her lap are a handful of photographs. One at a time she lays them side by side on her quilt.

The first photograph is a black-and-white of a smiling, dark-haired, handsome man in overalls. Beside him is a large woman in a plain dress with a scowl on her face. Standing in front of them is a small girl in a dress. The girl is expressionless. Her eyes look dead. In her arms is a small puppy.

The next photograph is a school photograph of a beautiful, dark-haired teenage girl. Her shimmering blue eyes have a seductive look about them.

Next is a photograph of a younger August, his kinked hair looking as if each strand has a mind of its own and refuses to be tamed.

Beside it she lays a photograph of a grinning March, with two of his front teeth missing and his dark hair sporting a crooked part down the side.

The last photograph is of April, her blonde hair unkempt and her lifeless eyes staring back at Tucker.

Tucker picks up the first photograph and holds it beside the one of April. She looks from one hollow-eyed girl to the other.

Clutching them to her chest, she begins to sob, "My baby, my baby. I ain't throwed you away. Sleep well this night and know that ol' Tucker loves you."

CHAPTER FORTY-FIVE

Turning in her car seat to look at her date, Maisy says, "I had a great time tonight, Tiger. I always like going up to Fast Eddie's. Lots of good food and good music."

"Glad you enjoyed yourself." Glancing toward her, he adds, "You know, I've got a name. You always call me Tiger."

Maisy laughs. "I like calling you Tiger. That's my personal nickname for you. I'm the only one who calls you that, aren't I?"

"You sure are."

"And you know why I named you Tiger, don't you?" She slips her hand between his thighs and grabs his crotch.

Jerking the steering wheel as he jumps, he swerves into the oncoming lane. He quickly yanks back into his lane. "Crazy woman! You could have killed us! You're just lucky it's late at night and there weren't any cars heading our way. Now keep your hands where they belong."

Pulling her thick hair back with both hands, Maisy giggles. "You should have seen your face. Your eyes were as big as half dollars."

He makes no comment, but keeps his hands firmly on the steering wheel.

"Okay," Maisy says, "I promise to behave myself." Smiling, she adds, "At least until we get to the Blue Bank."

They drive in silence for a while, the radio playing music from WLS-AM.

After an hour, he pulls the car into the parking area of the Blue Bank motel. As he approaches the check-in desk, he pulls his billfold out.

The overweight lady behind the desk looks up from reading a magazine. Winking, she says, "You back again, Mr. Smith? Haven't seen you in a few weeks. You want your regular room?"

"Yes," he says. "That'll be fine, Rose."

"How long you staying?"

"One night."

"That'll be thirty-five dollars," she tells him.

Opening his billfold, he takes out a fifty dollar bill, and slides it toward her. "Keep the change. And remember—"

"I never saw you," she finishes for him.

Taking the key from her, he says, "Exactly. You're as sweet as those Flippin Orchard peaches ya'll are famous for around here. Thanks, Rose."

He drives to the back of the motel. They get out of the car and disappear, hand in hand, into the dark motel room.

An hour later, they are lying side by side in bed.

Maisy says, "Hey, Tiger, I think you forgot something last month. I didn't get the usual deposit in my bank account. It must have slipped your mind."

Getting out of bed, he walks toward a chair. As he walks away from her, he says, "Maisy, we've got to talk."

Maisy's eyes widen and she takes a quick breath, but by the time he sits in the chair facing her, she's quelled the rising panic. She sits up cross-legged in bed and says with a lilt in her voice, "Talk about what?"

He is quiet, chewing the inside of his cheek. "Okay," he begins, "this is how it is. I'm not going to be able to continue to give you money every month."

The only indication Maisy has heard him is her eyes widening again.

When she doesn't explode, he feels bolder and continues. "You and I have had a great run, Maisy. And I think I've been more than fair with you the past seven years. You know the saying, 'All good things must come . . .'"

He stops speaking as Maisy slowly gets off the bed, never taking her eyes off him. Her fists are clenched. "Who is she? Who are you seeing? I heard talk that you've been out with your secretary, that Jane Simmons. How old is she? Twenty?"

Wiping his palms on the arm of the chair, he says, "Don't make this harder than it is, Maisy. It's not about another woman. It's just time for me to settle down and raise my family. I've got a career to think about."

Maisy laughs. "Don't try to tell me it's because of that cow of a wife you have. Your career, yes, I believe that. But don't try and give me that BS about your wife and family. You're way too narcissistic to care about anyone more than yourself."

"Believe what you want," he says. "But I'll never forget our time together. You are the best lay I've ever had."

She closes the distance between them in three quick steps and slaps him. Planting her hands on the arms of his chair, she leans into his face and hisses, "Now you listen to me. You are not getting rid of me that easy. You owe me! And you're going to continue to pay me. Go ahead and screw whoever you want, but you are going to continue making those deposits in my account. Do we understand each other?"

Pushing her aside, he gets out of his chair. "I've told you it's over and I mean it. Now get dressed so I can take you home."

Maisy takes his place in the chair, crosses her legs, and lights a cigarette. Nonchalantly tapping her fingernails on the table, she says, "You ever hear of something called a paternity suit?"

There is an imperceptible moment of motionlessness as he puts a leg in his pants. "I've read about scientists trying to find a test like that, but they've never been admissible in court. They're not reliable."

When Maisy doesn't respond, he slips his shirt on and says, "Why do you ask about that?"

Spinning her lighter on the table, Maisy says, "Oh nothing. I just read something a couple of weeks ago about it. Seems they've recently come up with something that's ninety percent accurate. I believe it's called HLA typing. Something like that. Some cases are now being resolved in court using the test."

He stops dressing and faces her. "What kind of game are you playing? And who is your unsuspecting target?"

"I've got my sights set on the father of my daughter, April," Maisy replies.

Shaking his head, he laughs. "That poor sucker. I pity him." He proceeds into the bathroom to comb his hair.

In the reflection of the mirror, he sees Maisy is now leaning against the bathroom doorframe.

"Is this some kind of act?" she asks. "Or are you really that stupid?"

Continuing to comb his hair, he replies, "What are you talk-ing—" He stops in midsentence and slowly turns to face her, his mouth hanging open.

Grabbing a fistful of his shirt, Maisy says, "Yeah, it's you, you idiot. You are April's father. So you can call it child support if you want, but the money is not going to stop."

His face flushes and his eyes bulge. He grips her wrist and twists it, tearing free of her grip on his shirt, then shoves her to the floor.

"Listen to me, bitch. I could produce a string of men you've slept with that would look like Macy's Thanksgiving Day Parade. Nobody will believe for one moment that I'm the father. Now get dressed!"

Maisy laughs. Getting up, she says, "You're scared, aren't you? Well that's good. You better be because I've already talked to a judge who will be glad to entertain a paternity suit using that new test I just told you about."

Turning her back to him and picking up her clothes, she adds, "And even if the case gets thrown out by a higher court, it should make sensational headlines in our local newspaper, don't you think? I'll give you a week to make a deposit. If you don't, I'm seeing the judge."

CHAPTER FORTY-SIX

A week later, on Valentine's Day, he drives his gray Oldsmobile Cutlass into the driveway of Maisy's apartment, extinguishes the headlights, and shuts off the engine.

He squeezes the steering wheel until his knuckles turn white. Eventually he jerks his hands free, as if the steering wheel shocked him. Letting out a slow breath, he leans back and puts his head on the headrest.

He pats the breast pocket of his sports jacket and feels the bulge of the plastic bag hidden inside an interior pocket. Making sure there is no passing traffic, he reaches for the door handle and exits the car.

After one knock on Maisy's door, the door slowly opens.

In the dim light he sees Maisy dressed in a tight-fitting green sweater, clearly with no bra underneath. It looks as if she was poured into her black jeans. The smell of White Shoulders fills his head.

"Hey, Tiger," Maisy says in a sultry voice. "Come on in."

As he steps in, she closes the door behind him.

When he turns to face her, she executes a slow, 360-degree turn on her bare feet and says, "How do I look?"

He opens his mouth to reply but only manages a dry cough. Trying again, he says, "Good enough to eat."

Walking to him, Maisy puts her arms around his middle, and pulls him close. Chuckling, she says, "I didn't aim to get you all choked up. Now, give me a kiss."

Plunging his hands into her thick, raven hair, he kisses her long and deep.

After a moment, Maisy pushes him back and gasps. "Wow, Tiger! A lady has to breathe, you know! I believe your motor was running before you got here. Slow down a little. Let's have something to drink."

"Sure," he says. "That's a good idea."

As she reaches for the Jack Daniels and glasses, she watches him glancing around her apartment. Taking the glasses and bottle with her to the couch, she says, "Come sit down and tell me why you decided you wanted to come to my place after all these years. You get tired of driving back and forth to the Blue Bank?"

Sitting beside her, he drains his drink. "I just thought it would be kind of exciting to meet you on your own ground, instead of sneaking off somewhere."

She pours him another drink and sips hers while she looks at him closely. "By the way," she says, "thanks for making that deposit. I thought you'd see things my way after you had time to think it through."

"Let's not talk about all that," he says. "I gave you what you wanted, that's all that matters." He shifts so that he is facing her. "I thought we might add a little spice to our evening by trying something new."

Maisy's eyes dance. "You know I'm always willing to try new things."

He reaches inside his jacket and pulls out a plastic bag full of capsules.

She frowns. "What are those?"

"They're called quaaludes," he replies. "My guy says that if you take some before having sex, the result is like nothing you've ever experienced. It's really popular in the big cities and on college campuses."

"I'm not so sure," Maisy says slowly. "Smoking pot with you is one thing, but I don't know about this. I've never heard of it. Have you used it before?"

"No," he says. "That's the whole point of my being here. I wanted my first time doing it to be with you."

An appreciative smile spreads across Maisy's face. "That's my Tiger. Okay, I'm game if you are."

He opens the bag and takes out two capsules. "Let's each take one and see what happens."

They slip the capsules in their mouths and wash them down with the whiskey.

"I better go to the little girl's room before we get started," Maisy says.

"Sure, go ahead," he says. "Let's get comfortable."

When she disappears into the bathroom, he takes out the bag of capsules and begins opening them and pouring the powdered contents into Maisy's glass. After the tenth one, he hears the doorknob on the bathroom door turn. After sweeping the remaining few capsules into the bag and slipping it back in his jacket, he pours them both a generous portion of Jack Daniels.

Maisy rejoins him on the couch by straddling him and kissing him.

After a few moments, he twists his face from hers. "Whoa girl. Remember, I've got to breathe, too. Let's finish our drinks."

He reaches for the two glasses and hands one to Maisy. "Here's to an unforgettable night."

Maisy clinks her glass against his, empties it, and says, "Unforgiveable." Laughing, she says, "I mean, unforgettable. I'm already feeling pretty loose, Tiger. Let's head to the bedroom."

He helps her off the couch. She tries to walk but sways clumsily. "Easy," he says as he catches her. "You don't want to fall and hurt yourself."

"I don't feel so good," Maisy says slowly. "Everything is spinning so fast."

"You're going to be fine," he says. "Just relax and enjoy the ride."

Maisy looks at him with unfocused eyes, blinks twice, and collapses on the floor.

CHAPTER FORTY-SEVEN

Kneeling down, he places two fingers on Maisy's jugular vein. He feels a faint pulse, stands up, and looks around the room. He steps over her, walks to the coffee table and picks up his glass. Taking out a handkerchief, he wipes the outside of the glass and sets it down, while still holding it with the handkerchief. He methodically repeats the process with the bottle of Jack Daniels.

He makes his way to the front door and wipes the inside doorknob, then opens the door and wipes the outside doorknob.

Closing the door, he walks back to Maisy, and again checks her pulse. Feeling nothing, he puts his ear to her chest. When he hears nothing, he smiles.

He pulls her to a sitting position and puts his shoulder to her midsection, letting her head and arms fall over his shoulder. He grabs her hips and, with a grunt, stands up.

Her weight is more than he calculated and he loses his balance. Sticking out his left hand, he finds a wall and steadies himself.

At the front door, he checks for activity on the street. Having seen no pedestrians or headlights, he uses his handkerchief to turn the doorknob, steps onto the porch, and closes the door behind him.

As he goes down the steps, he loses his balance again but grabs the handrail before falling.

He steps to the rear of his car, finds his keys, opens the trunk, and dumps Maisy's body inside. Easing the trunk lid down, he pushes it until it clicks shut.

Panting heavily, he quickly gets inside the driver's seat. His eardrums feeling like the bass drum in a marching band and his chest feeling as if it will explode any second, he slowly backs out of the driveway, his headlights off.

Passing through town, he makes his way around the court square and heads north toward Latham. At the last four-way stop before leaving town, a police car pulls in behind him and switches on its solitary, rotating red light.

The flashing red startles him. Looking in the rearview mirror, he sees the officer stepping out of his car. He rolls his window down as the officer approaches.

"Is there a problem, officer?" he asks.

The policeman switches on his flashlight. "Oh, it's you, sir," the policeman says. "Didn't realize who it was. Are you okay?"

Working to keep his voice calm, he says, "Sure, I'm okay, Lloyd. I was just visiting friends and family and heading home. Is there some kind of problem?"

"It's your headlights, sir. They aren't burning."

"Wow, thanks, Lloyd," he says, switching them on. "I guess I just forgot. Anything else?"

"That was all," Lloyd says. "I thought I was going to find a drunk driver. You be careful driving home."

"Sure will," he says. "Thanks again."

His hand trembles as he reaches for the gearshift and puts the car in drive. In five minutes the streetlights of the city are retreating in his mirror and the darkness of the cloud-filled country sky swallows him.

Twenty minutes later, he drives through the sleeping community of Latham. Once through, he slows, peering intently up ahead.

He crosses a bridge with wooden side rails. He slows and spies another bridge.

Just before crossing it, he brakes and pulls off the road onto a dirt path that leads to the Obion River and its backwater below. Though officially designated a river, the actual channel of the river is often no more than twenty feet wide.

Empty beer cans are scattered along the path, evidence that fishing isn't the only thing on the minds of those who use the path.

Seeing no other vehicles in the area, he rolls to a stop and turns off the engine. He pulls out a flashlight from the glove compartment and gets out of the car. Not as careful now, he switches on the flashlight, finds the bank of the river, and walks alongside it. After about fifty yards, his light discovers what he's been looking for—a Reelfoot boat fitted with an engine.

He sweeps his light across the length of the boat bottom and sees the concrete blocks and rope he'd placed there earlier. He unties the boat from the tree, pushes it into the water, and gets in. He finds the lawnmower engine sitting a third of the way from the rear of the boat, with its long shaft protruding over the back of the boat. The engine starts with the second pull of the rope.

Using his flashlight, he steers a course back to the bridge, pulls up on the bank and shuts off the engine. He makes his way to his car and opens the trunk. The dim trunk light falls on Maisy's ashen face. He thinks he sees her smirk and checks her pulse again before pulling her out, then shakes his head. He lifts her on his shoulder, walks to the boat, and then, leaning forward, lets her body fall into the boat.

Grunting, he pushes the heavy load into the stream and gets in. He cranks the engine and makes his way along the meandering path of the timber-lined Obion. Occasionally he switches on his flashlight to get his bearings, but mostly he travels in the dark.

He'd chosen a Reelfoot boat because of its ability to get past stumps and limbs that hover just beneath the surface of the water. The only sounds are the engine and the bottom of the boat bumping over downed limbs or submerged stumps.

After thirty minutes, he turns the boat out of the main stream and into a flooded open area thick with lily pads. As the boat slides through the lily pads, he cuts the engine off.

Squatting and keeping hold of both sides of the boat with both hands, he eases toward the middle of the boat, where Maisy lies. He sits on his knees and picks up a concrete block and a piece of rope. One end of the rope he ties to her ankle and the other to the block.

He continues until he's tied a block to each of her ankles, knees, and wrists. He wipes his perspiring face and takes a longer piece of rope and ties it around her waist, then attaches two concrete blocks to the other end. The final block he ties around her neck.

Looking at his handiwork, he says, "We said it was going to be an unforgettable night, didn't we, Maisy? Well, we were right."

He drops the blocks tied to her ankles over the side. Her body slides until her knees catch on the side. Lifting the next pair of blocks, he lets them splash into the water. The heavy blocks disappear and jerk Maisy's body after them. She would have disappeared then, but the blocks tied around her waist stop her progress.

Bending her like a pretzel, he takes the two blocks tied to her wrists and swings them over the side, quickly grabbing the one around her neck and casting it after them. The combined weight of Maisy's dead body and the concrete blocks jerks the side of the boat down so far that he loses his balance and is thrown head first into the inky water.

Maisy's body falls out on top of him, dragging him to the bottom and pinning him facedown in the mud ten feet below. Kicking and screaming, he frees himself from his own death trap and swims to the top of the water.

As the fresh air hits his face, he gasps, drawing in both air and water. Choking on the water, fighting to find enough air to stay alive, he treads water, trying to see above the giant lily pads and find his boat.

Something bumps the back of his head. Frantic, he yells in fright. Turning around, he sees it is his boat. He grabs the side rail and for some time just hangs on, catching his breath.

He swims to the rear of the boat, pulls himself in, and collapses in the bottom. As his body begins shivering, it dawns on him that, even though the air temperature is warm for February, hypothermia remains a threat. His hands are trembling so that he has difficulty grasping the rope to the boat motor. Finally, he starts it and finds his way back to the bridge and his car.

With wobbly knees he gets out of the boat. As he does the clouds break and the full moon forces the blackness of night to hide under the bridge. Opening the door to his car, he pauses and looks at the moon. His face is lit in its soft glow.

Sitting silently under the bridge on the other side of the river, a fishing pole in one hand and a bottle of bourbon in a paper bag in the other, is Smiley Carter.

CHAPTER FORTY-EIGHT

Standing in front of her mirror, April pulls the brush through her shiny, blonde hair. She sees her bed behind her, with its Strawberry Shortcake dolls arranged neatly on the pillow. Still looking in the mirror, she moves until she sees the poster of Big Bird.

Laying the brush down, she walks to her closet, and opens the door. She lets her fingertips graze each garment as she moves her hand over them. She kneels and matches and lines up all six pairs of her shoes.

She hears Ella taking her nightly shower, a habit April started imitating only recently.

Walking into the kitchen, she looks out the window over the sink toward Tucker's house. A faint light can be seen shining through Tucker's bedroom window. April can suddenly smell the familiar smoky interior mixed with the pungent body odor of Tucker and her brothers.

Having the sensation that they are in the room with her, she spins around. Standing in her bathrobe, with a towel around her head, is Ella.

"Thinking about Tucker and your brothers?"

"Kind of," April replies.

Ella takes her hand. "Let's go sit on the couch."

Sitting down, Ella takes April into her arms and pulls her onto her lap, facing her. "Do you miss them?"

April nods slowly and then shakes her head.

"Now that's not the way we do it, is it? We're supposed to use our words, right? Get them out of our head?" Ella prompts her. "What are you wanting to say?"

"Sometimes I miss them," April says. "And sometimes I don't. I ain't never—"

"You haven't ever," Ella corrects her.

"I haven't ever," April begins again, "had such nice clothes and things. And I for sure haven't ever been so clean."

Ella laughs. "I guess you must think I'm awfully silly sometimes. I just can't get out of my head the saying my mother had, 'Cleanliness is next to godliness.'"

"What is godliness?"

"Well let's see," Ella says. "How best to explain it . . . I guess it means you try to live in a godly way or to be like God."

Her blues eyes intent on Ella, April asks, "What is God?"

"You mean, who is God?" Ella replies. "Not what, but who."

"Who is God?"

Smiling, Ella says, "You certainly have your grandmother's trait of asking whatever is on your mind, don't you? I believe God created our world. He made the earth, sun, moon, and stars. And he made the first man and woman."

"Where is he?"

"He lives in a place called heaven," Ella replies.

"Where is heaven?"

"It's in a place that we can't see. I'm not sure exactly where."

April searches Ella's face.

Smiling, Ella folds her to her chest. "I love your little inquisitive mind. Asking questions is a good thing. It's how you learn. Now tell me what had you thinking about Tucker and your brothers."

Keeping her cheek resting against Ella, April asks, "Are you my family now?"

Ella's voice catches in her throat. She begins to cry.

April sits up quickly and looks at Ella with concern. "What's wrong? Did I do something wrong?"

Wiping her tears, Ella says, "No, no April. You rarely do anything wrong. In fact, most of the time you do everything just right. I just get emotional sometimes. You know," Ella continues, "I've told you I have a son named Cade. But I hardly ever see him. And of course I'm divorced. So it's sort of like I've lost my family. Having you live with me has made me very happy."

April lays her head back on Ella's chest. Speaking softly, she says, "And I have a mama, but she doesn't want me. She gave me to Tucker."

"It's been complicated for you, I know," Ella says. "But Tucker and your brothers love you, and they are your family. But maybe you and I can be a family, too."

April sits up. "I can have two families?"

"You can, if you want to," Ella tells her. "And you can love both families and you can miss them when you are away from them. Now, why don't we have us a glass of warm milk?"

Ella starts to get up but stops. "You'll have to walk. You're too big a girl for me to carry."

She finds a pot in the kitchen and places it on the stove. She gets the milk from the refrigerator, pours some into the pot, and turns on the eye.

April gets two glasses out of the cabinet and places them on the counter.

The creaking and pinging of the warming pot are the only sounds in the kitchen as April and Ella are lost in their thoughts.

Finally, Ella lifts the pot and pours some milk into each glass. She and April sit across from each other at the table.

Ella says, "I'll tell you what. You haven't been to Tucker's in a couple of weeks. Tomorrow is Saturday. Why don't we go to Tucker's and let you spend the day there, if you want to? Would you like that?"

Smiling, April says, "Yeah. I want to."

"Okay then," Ella says lightly. "Let's finish our milk and then off to bed."

April lifts her glass and empties it, leaving a white moustache on her lip. Ella laughs and says, "Okay, little kitten, you need to lick your lip."

April's pink tongue darts out and removes the white trimming.

After Ella takes their glasses and puts them in the sink, April takes Ella's hand and leads her into her bedroom. When Ella pulls back the Strawberry Shortcake comforter, April hops quickly into the bed.

Ella bends down and kisses April on the forehead. "Sleep tight, beautiful girl. Always remember, you are special."

Smiling, April closes her eyes.

Ella walks into her own bedroom, sits on the side of the bed, slips off her house shoes, and gets in.

Lying on her back, she lets out a long sigh. "Dear Lord, where is this incredible journey you have me on going to take me? You gave me the strength to escape my horrible marriage. You delivered me from cancer. Then you plop me into the middle of Tucker's life. And now you've given me the blessing of April. Help me to not be selfish in my attitude and feelings toward this little angel. Give me wisdom to know what to do and say with her. And protect us all. In Jesus's name, amen."

Rolling on her side, she closes her eyes and falls asleep.

CHAPTER FORTY-NINE

Walking to Tucker's the next morning, Ella says to April, "Look at that beautiful blooming dogwood at the edge of the woods."

"Which one is the dogwood?"

"The one with the white blooms," Ella replies. "And that purple one next to it is a redbud tree. I love how beautiful spring is out here in the country, don't you?"

After spying a clump of blooming daffodils in the ditch beside the road, April jumps in and picks a handful, then climbs back out of the ditch and stretches her handful of flowers toward Ella. "These are for you."

Smiling, Ella says, "Thank you. Why don't we take these to Tucker?"

"Tucker doesn't care about flowers," April responds. "She'll think it's silly to put flowers on a table like you do."

Keeping her voice light, Ella says, "That's okay. I'll carry them and be sure we take them back home after our visit. I think they're lovely, just like you."

April smiles and takes Ella's hand.

As they approach Tucker's house, they hear an engine in the direction of the barn. Looking in that direction, Ella sees Smiley

Carter and his tractor in the garden. Tucker is standing at one end of the garden. March and August are coming out of the barn.

"I wonder what's going on," Ella says.

April pulls on her hand and says excitedly, "Let's go see."

When they are fifty yards from the barn April calls out, "Tucker!" Smiley Carter's tractor drowns out April's tiny voice. Letting go of Ella's hand, she breaks into a run.

She darts past August and March as they carry hoes and rakes from the barn to the garden. They both holler after her sprinting figure, "April!"

Catching a movement out of the corner of her eye, Tucker turns. April is twenty feet away, running full speed toward her with open arms. Simultaneously they call each other's name. Bending down, Tucker catches April as she leaps into her strong arms.

Tucker stumbles a bit under the unexpected force of April's enthusiastic greeting. Her thick arms encircle April's small frame.

April buries her face in Tucker's neck and inhales through her nose, taking in the mixture of familiar odors—fried meat from breakfast, hogs from feeding, body odor from sweating, and the earthy smell of the garden. She whispers, "I missed you."

Tucker pulls April's arms from around her neck, sets her down, and says, "Y' come on a good day. We's plantin' crowder peas t'day. May's th' month fer plantin' peas, y' know."

Smiley Carter and his tractor reach them at the same time March and August arrive. Carter shuts off the engine and exclaims, "Well lookee here who has come to see ol' Smiley Carter. It's the princess April."

August and March stand a couple of feet away. "Hey, April," August says.

"Whacha been doin'?" March asks.

Looking at the boys, Tucker says, "What's th' matter with you two? Git on up 'ere an' see yore sister. Y' ack like strangers."

April positions her back against Tucker's thigh and faces her brothers.

Ignoring everyone, Carter strides toward April and says, "Well I'm no stranger to the princess." As April smiles at him, he picks her up and pitches her into the air, extracting a squeal of delight from her. He catches her and cradles her like a baby. "You are still as pretty as an angel!"

Ella edges quietly into the gathering.

August notices her first. "Hey, Miss Ella," he says.

Everyone turns.

"Hi, August. Hi, everyone," Ella says. "My grandfather used to throw me into the air just like that, Smiley Carter. I still remember feeling like my stomach was going to jump out of my mouth."

Tucker says, "Yeah, but Carter here's a broken down ol' man an' he's gonna drop her one o' these times."

Carter pushes his sleeves up, flexes his biceps, and says, "Does that look like a broken down ol' man? I can still work circles round men half my age."

"An' it's time w' all git busy an' plant these peas," Tucker says. Looking at Carter, she says, "Y' think y' got that ground worked up good enough?"

Waving his hand toward the area he has disked up, Carter says, "That garden is cut up as fine as coffee grounds. You's can probably just throw that seed at the ground and it'll sink in all's by itself."

"If'n hot air makes fer good ground," Tucker replies, "then it'll be th' best around after listenin' t' you. August, you an' March git the hoes an' start layin' off them rows. Me an' Ella'll plant th' seed."

August and March respond quickly and begin sliding their hoes through the soft soil, leaving a furrow in their wake. Tucker picks up a paper sack, reaches inside, and brings out a handful of small seeds. Ella watches closely and imitates Tucker's moves.

Watching August and March, Tucker calls to them, "You boys make 'em rows straight." Pointing to one row, she adds, "This 'un here's as crooked as a dog's hind leg."

She begins carefully dropping the seeds into the furrow. "You take that row beside mine, Ella."

Ella dutifully obeys and begins dropping seeds in.

Carter says, "I'll just grab me a rake and cover up them seeds." With a wink at Ella he adds, "But not too deep. Don't wanta smother 'em."

Catching his meaning, Tucker says, "You jes' look over at them taters an' tell me which plants look th' best, them y' planted shaller, 'r them what I planted right."

Shaking his head, Carter laughs and says to Ella, "Can you see what I have to put up with? This woman always thinks she's right. There ain't no point in tryin' to reason with her."

For the next few minutes, everyone works in silence.

Finally, Tucker says, "What brung you an' April over here, Ella?"

Keeping her focus on planting, Ella replies, "I think she was a little homesick last night. So I promised her we'd come visit today."

When Tucker gives no response, Ella continues, "I can't remember the last time she saw her mother."

Tucker spits and says, "She's better off not seein' 'er. B'sides, I can't 'member th' last time I seen Maisy, m'self. She didn't come see March 'r April fer their birthdays. As selfish as she is, that was at least one thing she always done."

She stops and cocks her head to one side, looking at the sky. "I guess I ain't seen 'er since th' end o' January. Hmmm. That is a long time, even fer Maisy."

Ella stops, too, and looks at Tucker. "Do you think she is okay?"

"How am I supposed t' know?" Tucker snaps. "She ain't never seen fit t' tell me nothin' 'bout what's goin' on with her."

Tucker looks at Carter, who is leaning on his rake and looking at her. "What're you lookin' at?"

"I's just waitin' for you two to get movin' again," Carter says. "I can't cover up a row that ain't got no seed in it."

Both women turn and start sowing the seed into the welcoming furrows.

After a few minutes, Ella says, "If you want to, Tucker, I can drive you to Maisy's place, just to be sure everything is all right."

"I ain't never knowed where she lives," Tucker replies. "She ain't never tol' me. All I got is a phone number she give me one time. I don' know why. I ain't never had no use fer phones."

"Well," Ella says, "there is a way I can use her phone number and get her address."

"You can if'n y' wanta," Tucker replies. "But I'll bet she's finally run off with some man. Ain't no tellin' where to."

CHAPTER FIFTY

Sitting on her couch the following Monday morning, Ella picks up the receiver on her phone and dials 411. After a moment she says, "Could I speak to Rebecca Wallace, please? Hello, Becky? This is Ella McDade . . . Fine, thanks. And you? That's great. Listen, I need to ask a favor of you. I have a phone number here that I want to find the address to."

She unfolds the paper Tucker gave her on Saturday and reads the number to Rebecca. There is a long pause.

"Really? And their bill hasn't been paid in how long? Give me that address one more time . . . Thanks a bunch, Becky." She hangs up the phone.

Staring at the address, Ella purses her lips and frowns. She stands up and slips the paper into her pocket and heads to her car.

Within a few moments she drives into Tucker's front yard. As she gets out of her car, she notices Tucker coming from behind the house.

Tucker sees her at the same time. "What's got you out early on a Monday mornin'?"

"I checked out that phone number Maisy gave you."

"What'dja learn?"

"Well the first thing they told me was that the phone number had been disconnected because the bill wasn't paid. The last payment they received was in January."

"Humph," Tucker grunts. "Don't surprise me none. Her sugar daddy o' th' month musta missed a payment."

"Maybe," Ella says, "but I've got an address we can go check out and see for ourselves what's going on."

Tucker shrugs. "I ain't got nothin' else t' do."

Ten minutes later, Ella turns onto Maple Street. "It's somewhere down this street. I'm just not sure which end of the street it is." Scanning the house numbers, she says, "We're looking for four seventeen." Tucker keeps her focus on the street.

"There it is!" Ella says and pulls slowly into the driveway. Dozens of newspapers, in varying shades of decaying yellow, lie scattered in the front yard and on the driveway.

As they get out of the car, Tucker says, "What's all them rolls of things in th' yard?"

"Looks like she was getting the daily newspaper," Ella answers. "But she hasn't picked them up in weeks. Sometimes people pay for their paper three months at a time, so I guess they've just kept on delivering them."

The two women slowly approach the steps to the front door.

"Isn't that her car?" Ella asks, pointing.

"It's th' last 'un I seen 'er in."

They arrive at the front door and look at each other. "Why don't you knock?" Ella suggests.

Tucker strikes the door twice with the bottom of her fist.

When nothing happens, Tucker grabs the doorknob and tries to turn it, but it doesn't yield.

Ella says, "Something doesn't feel right." Peering through the rectangular window of the door, she says, "I don't see any lights.

Let's walk around the apartment and see if we can see anything through the windows."

"I'm tellin' y', she done run off," Tucker says. "Jes' like m' mama done."

Looking at Tucker, Ella says, "What do you mean?"

Tucker waves her hand. "Nothin'. Never mind." Lumbering down the steps, she says, "We'll walk aroun' th' apartment an' check, like you said."

After making their way from window to window, Ella says, "Everything is still there—furniture, clothes, appliances. She wouldn't have left those behind if she was moving away. And the electric meter was pulled. I'll bet we'll hear the same story on that as we heard about the phone."

"So what're we gonna do now?"

"Let's go see Ron Harris," Ella says. "He'll know what to do."

"Y' mean th' sheriff?"

Walking toward her car, Ella says, "Sure. Come on."

When Tucker doesn't follow her, Ella turns around to face her. "What's the matter?"

"Me an' th' sheriff ain't always seen eye t' eye," Tucker says. "It might not be sech a good idee fer me t' go there."

"Oh come on," Ella urges her. "I've known Ron for years. It'll be fine."

A few minutes later, they pull up to the front of the sheriff's office. A deputy is coming out of the door when he spies Tucker getting out of the car. His eyes widen and he quickly ducks back into the office.

When Ella and Tucker stride into the office, Ella is startled to see four armed deputies lined up side by side along one wall. There is a hard look on each deputy's face. The tension in the air is thick.

Tucker folds her arms across her chest and returns their stares.

Ella sees Tucker's stance and steps between her and the deputies. "Hi, Frank. Hi, Eddie. How have you been, Kerry? How's your family, Roy?"

Each deputy gives a polite nod in Ella's direction but they keep their eyes on Tucker.

Ignoring everyone's posturing, Ella continues, "Is Ron in? We need to see him about something."

One of the deputies replies, "I told him who was coming."

At that moment a dark-complexioned, bald-headed man with black-rimmed glasses, wearing a white shirt, a black tie, and black pants, walks into the room. Stepping in front of the deputies, he extends his hand toward Ella. "Hello, Ella. It's been a while."

Shaking his hand, Ella smiles and replies, "Yes it has, Ron. How have you been?"

"Oh, just staying busy," the sheriff replies. "You know how it is."

He looks past Ella at Tucker, then back at Ella. "Are you two here together?"

"Yes we are, Ron," Ella says, "and we'd like a few moments of your time, if you can spare them."

"Okay," he replies. "Ya'll come on back to my office."

As he turns and walks away, Ella and Tucker follow him. The four deputies follow them in pairs.

Tucker smiles.

Glancing back at the sound of all the footsteps, Ella says, "Oh really, Ron. Is that necessary?"

Opening his office door for Ella, Ron says, "I think it's okay, boys. Ya'll go on about your business."

As the door closes behind him, Ron says, "Ya'll have a seat." He moves behind his desk and sits in his chair, accompanied by its complaining squeaks. "Now, what's on your all's minds?"

Ella explains to him Maisy's recent lack of contact with her children and what they've learned of her phone and electricity being cut off. "We went to her apartment and found it locked with her car parked in the driveway. Then we looked in the windows and saw that everything is in place as if she evaporated."

She waits for a response from Ron.

Thinking there must be something more, he says, "And your point is?"

"Honestly, Ron," Ella says, exasperated. "You need to investigate to see if she's all right."

Ron looks for a long moment at Tucker, then looks at Ella. "Listen, you may not know Maisy's history. She's not the most dependable or predictable person. I mean, I could give you a list of men you could call to see if she's with one of them. Now, Tucker," he quickly adds, "I don't mean no harm. But you know I'm telling the truth."

Tucker stands and says to Ella, "I tol'ja. This's been a waste o' time."

Ella looks at Ron incredulously. "You mean you aren't going to do a thing?"

Turning his palms upward, he says, "What do you want me to do?"

Ella's face reddens. "If I've got to tell you how to do your job, then maybe it's time we get us a new sheriff." She joins Tucker standing and says, "Let's go."

Before she closes the door behind her she turns and says, "I'm telling you right now, Ron Harris, that I've got a bad feeling about this. I think something's wrong."

He stands up and says, "Oh come on now, Ella, don't—"

The slamming door cuts off the rest of his reply.

CHAPTER FIFTY-ONE

With his head and one shoulder leaning out the driver's window, sixteen-year-old Gary Winslow watches the rear tire of his pickup truck as he backs toward the bank of the Obion River. The twelve-foot aluminum jon boat clangs in the bed of his truck.

Gary's companion and best friend, sixteen-year-old Ricky Fields, cracks his passenger door and watches the tire on that side as well.

Slowing, Gary says, "That looks good to me. What about your side?"

Ricky gets out of the truck, takes a few steps, and surveys the situation. "Yeah, looks good to me, too."

Gary sets the emergency brake and cuts the engine.

They untie the ropes that have held the boat in place, and, each grabbing a side, slide the boat backward until the rear drops to the ground. Then they push it into the water, leaving the bow on shore.

"Doesn't look like anyone else has been in here today," Gary says.

"We'll have it all to ourselves," Ricky says. "This is going to be a blast!"

"Whooo-weee!" Gary exclaims. "I can't wait."

They walk quickly back to the truck, lower the back of the front seat, and take out their bows and arrows.

"Lock your door," Gary says.

Ricky does, then reaches into the bed of the truck and lifts out a small cooler.

Gary grabs a cooler as well. "You get in the boat first and I'll push us in," he says.

Getting in, Ricky sets his and then Gary's bow and cooler in the middle of the boat. He takes a seat in the back of the boat, grabs a paddle, and says, "Push us off, matey!"

Gary grips the front of the boat and bends low, driving hard with his legs. With each step he gains speed, until suddenly the boat is freed and slides easily into the water. After leaping into the boat, Gary grabs the other paddle.

"Alligator gar, here we come!" Ricky shouts as they begin paddling. "Be prepared to surrender to the bow-fishing champions of the world!"

Gary bursts out laughing.

In a few moments they leave the brilliant June sun in the opening by the bridge and ease into the cool shade of the tree-lined channel. Both boys take in the quiet stillness.

"Don't forget," Gary says, "my dad says to be on the lookout for snakes hanging on branches. They love to drop in boats."

Brandishing a large hunting knife, Ricky says, "Just let 'em come. I'll cut their heads off!"

Gary laughs. "Sure you will. More than likely you'll jump out of the boat and let me fend for myself."

They row for a while in silence.

Suddenly Ricky says, "Up there on the left. That's what we're looking for."

Gary looks where Ricky is pointing. A large area, thick with lily pads, lies in the open sunlight.

"My granddaddy says those beds of lily pads are where gar like to stay," Ricky says. "He said it may look like there's no water there, but it's probably six to eight feet deep this time of year."

The boys paddle their way out of the shade. They grab their sunglasses as the dazzling sun blinds them.

Slipping off their white T-shirts, they reveal tan lines at their necks and upper arms. They grasp their bows. Each checks the reel on the front of the bow to be sure the fishing line will release freely. Then they tie the end of the line to an arrow.

"You want me to skull first, or you?" Gary asks.

"I'll go first."

Gary carefully stands up. Smiling, he says, "Let the games begin."

Keeping his paddle under water at the back of the boat, Ricky works it slowly back and forth, gliding the boat silently into the bed of lily pads.

After a few minutes, Gary whispers, "Easy. I see one."

Ricky keeps his paddle still.

Gary tenses. He slips the arrow onto the bowstring and slowly pulls it back to his cheek. The stretching bowstring emits a low hum in response to the tension.

Without warning, his fingers release the bowstring and the arrow flies invisibly, disappearing into the water with barely a splash, the fishing line spinning off the reel. He quickly grips the handle on the reel.

"Did you get him?" Ricky asks.

Keeping his eyes glued to the spot where his arrow disappeared, Gary replies, "I can't tell."

For a moment nothing happens.

Abruptly the line tightens and the bow is nearly jerked out of Gary's hand. "Oh I got him all right!" he yells.

The taut fishing line slices from left to right, the lily pads dancing out of the way of the thrashing fish below.

As if he were a marionette, Gary's arms are jerked first one way and then another.

"Hold him!" Ricky yells as Gary almost loses his grip on his bow.

Gary begins reeling in the fish with his right hand, while his left firmly grasps his bow.

Suddenly, the feathered end of Gary's arrow makes a dancing appearance among the lily pads.

Reaching toward the arrow shaft, Ricky says, "He's tiring. Just take it easy now."

Gary guides his prey toward the edge of the boat until Ricky is able to grab the arrow and lift the fish out of the water. The sun reflects off its thick, reddish-orange scales as he drops it in the bottom of the boat.

Gary sits down on his seat, lifts his feet to avoid the razor-sharp teeth of the thrashing fish, and says, "Oh my gosh, I'll bet it weighs ten pounds!"

"It looks like it's three feet long!" Ricky says as he picks up a hammer and delivers a killing blow to the gar's head. He grabs his bow. "Now it's my turn."

Two hours later, the bottom of their boat is littered with gar and their backs and shoulders are burned a bright red. Sitting in opposite ends of the boat, they both drink their Cokes and eat the remains of the sandwiches they brought.

"Man, I'm worn out," Ricky says. "We better start heading back to the truck."

"I know," Gary agrees. "But I want to take one last shot."

Grinning, Ricky says, "Okay. But just one."

Slowly Gary rises and begins looking in the lily pads. After a few minutes of Ricky skulling him through the water, he whispers, "Oh yeah, there's what I've been looking for. It looks like the granddaddy of them all lying there."

Ricky lets the boat drift on its own as Gary draws his bow.

Gary flinches and loses his grip. The arrow darts into the water. Slapping his neck, he says, "Stupid sweat bee! Just as I was getting set, the thing stung me. I know I missed the fish."

He lays his bow down, grabs the fishing line, and brings it in by hand. When the arrow appears, he seizes the shaft and begins lifting it.

"Something is on here," he says, "but it's not a fish."

As the end of the arrow comes out of the water, there is a wad of dark green on the arrowhead.

"Looks like a wad of moss," Ricky says.

When Gary grabs the green to remove it, he says, "I don't know what this is, but it isn't moss. And it feels like there's a rope or something here, too."

He hands it to Ricky, who pulls it toward him. A rope appears from the lily pads as he does so, its end disappearing in the murky water.

"What the heck?" Gary says.

Pulling with both hands, Ricky says, "Whatever it is, it's heavy. Help me pull."

Both boys clutch the slimy rope and begin pulling. In response to their efforts, the boat begins moving toward the point where the rope disappears in the lily pads.

"Maybe somebody hid a money chest down here, or something," Gary says.

Laughing, Ricky says, "If it is, we split it fifty-fifty."

They reach the point where the rope's descent is directly below them. Heaving with all their might, careful not to tip the boat, they begin lifting it toward the surface, peering into the water as they pull.

The lily pads abruptly part and the boys stare into the empty sockets of the bloated face of Maisy.

CHAPTER FIFTY-TWO

Leaning on her hoe, Tucker pulls a handkerchief from her hip pocket and swipes her sweating face. Stuffing the handkerchief back into its home, she surveys her morning's work.

The weeds and grass that had recently stood among her peas now lie limp between the rows, having surrendered to her sharp hoe. In the hot sun their deep green is already fading and the roots are turning brown.

Small clouds of dust surround Tucker's feet as she walks through her garden to the side of the barn. Squatting in the shade, she picks up a quart jar, unscrews the lid, and drinks deeply. Some of the refreshing water slips from the corners of her overanxious mouth and runs down her thick neck.

Pausing to catch her breath, Tucker leans her head forward and pours the rest of the water on the back of her neck.

She notices a sheriff's patrol car leaving Ella's house and heading toward her own. It pulls into her front yard. August and March come out on the front porch to meet the driver as he approaches the house.

Tucker watches as they point in her direction and sees the driver shield his eyes as he looks toward her.

The driver gets back in his car, turns around, and heads toward Tucker's barn. He coasts the last few yards, stops, and shuts off his engine. The door opens and Sheriff Ron Harris steps out. His sweat-soaked white shirt sticks to his chest and back.

Donning a tan Stetson hat, he calls out, "Tucker, you around here?"

Stepping out from the shade of the barn, Tucker says, "I am."

Sheriff Harris turns and spots her at the end of her garden. Walking slowly toward her, he says, "There you are. The boys said you was down here somewhere."

Tucker retreats from the heat of the sun by stepping back into the shade.

When he gets a few feet from her, the sheriff stops and uses his shirtsleeve to wipe the sweat off his upper lip. "It's gonna be a hot one today, isn't it?"

Tucker notices dried mud on the side of his face. "I spec' so," she replies.

Looking at her garden, he says, "My goodness, that's one of the best gardens I've seen anywhere around. What's your secret?"

"Hogs," Tucker replies.

"Huh?"

"Hogs. Y' asked m' what m' secret was an' I said, 'Hogs.' Can't y' keep up with th' conversation?"

Even though it is shadowed by his Stetson, Tucker sees the sheriff's dark face redden.

Taking off his hat, the sheriff says, "I came to see you for a reason."

"Figgered as much," Tucker replies. "Why dontcha git on with it?"

Shifting his weight, he says, "It's about Maisy."

"Figgered that, too."

"Two boys was out bow fishing for gar today and they found a body." He pauses, waiting for a reaction. When Tucker's stony face remains fixed, he adds, "Turns out it was Maisy."

"Appears Miss Ella was right, don't it?" Tucker says. "Maybe if'n you'd took 'er serious, Maisy might be alive now." She gives time for the weight of her accusation to settle on the sheriff's shoulders. Then she says, "Where'd y' find 'er?"

"You know that branch of the Obion north of Latham? She was about two miles from the bridge in a field of lily pads."

Tucker's head snaps up. "North o' Latham?"

"Yeah," he says, cocking his head. "Does that area mean something to you?"

Just as quickly as his story piqued her interest, Tucker resumes her dispassionate stance. "Nope. Don't mean nothin' t' me. How'd she die?"

"Well," the sheriff begins, "the exact cause of death will have to be determined by the state coroner's office in Memphis. But there's no doubt she was murdered."

"What makes y' say that?"

Slipping his hat back on, the sheriff shifts his weight. "I'm not sure you need to know those details."

With an edge in her voice, Tucker says, "I got a right t' know what happened t' my daughter."

After taking a deep breath, the sheriff says, "Somebody tied concrete blocks to her and threw her into that backwater. But she could have already been dead. That's what the coroner will have to decide."

In a faraway voice, Tucker says, "Concrete blocks . . ."

Again the sheriff cocks his head to one side, waiting for Tucker to say more. When she remains silent, he asks, "Do you know anyone who would have wanted to hurt Maisy?"

Tucker scoffs. "I 'magine you know more 'bout th' goin's on of Maisy than me. She didn't never talk t' me 'bout 'er life."

"Well, when was the last time you saw her?"

"I reckon it was sometime in Febr'ary," Tucker replies. "She didn' come see March 'r April fer their birthdays. That's sorta what got Ella thinkin' there might be somthin' wrong. You do remember us comin' t' see you, dontcha?"

"Look, Tucker," he says. "Ya'll were right. There was something wrong. But my guess is she was already dead by the time you came asking for help."

Fixing him with a stare, Tucker spits a stream of tobacco juice that just misses his mud-caked boots. Noticing he's clenched his hands into fists, she tightens her grip on her hoe.

The sheriff eases his right hand to the butt of his holstered pistol. "Now look, Tucker," he says, "let's not make things worse than they already are."

"All o' you, an' ever'one like you, ain't nothin' but a bunch of sorry—"

"Tucker." Ella's voice inserts a comma into the tension of the scene.

So focused had they been on each other, neither the sheriff nor Tucker had seen Ella walking toward them.

Stepping between them, Ella faces Tucker and says, "The sheriff stopped by my house on the way up here and told me what happened. I'm so very, very sorry."

Taking advantage of Ella's interference, the sheriff takes a couple steps back. "Listen, there's going to be a full investigation. We'll have to seal Maisy's apartment. So you won't be able to go over there without a deputy, at least not until we've finished. Until then, if you think of anything that might be helpful, give my office a call."

Both women ignore him.

When he realizes they are not going to reply, the sheriff says, "And one more thing. I'm afraid you'll have to go to the emergency room of the hospital to identify the body."

Tucker looks past Ella at the sheriff and says through gritted teeth, "To hell with you."

Placing her hand on Tucker's arm, Ella says, "We'll be in in a little while, Ron. Why don't you go on now."

CHAPTER FIFTY-THREE

Peering intently into Tucker's scratch-covered glasses after the sheriff has left them, Ella says, "I'm so sorry, Tucker. And I regret that my hunch something was wrong turned out to be right. It's just awful news."

Though Tucker's expression remains unchanged, Ella feels her arm begin to tremble. Suddenly Tucker locks one enormous hand around Ella's forearm. Ella resists the urge to wince at Tucker's iron grip.

Tucker gasps and holds her breath. She finally exhales, then gasps two quick breaths. Her body shudders.

Stepping closer to her, Ella says, "Can I hug you?"

Tucker relinquishes her grip on Ella and drops her hands to her side.

Ella lifts her arms slowly, places them around Tucker's neck, and says, "Poor Tucker."

Tucker unties a chain from her heart and lays her head on Ella's shoulder. Her breathing becomes ragged. A moan rises from deep within her.

Patting Tucker's back, Ella says, "Yes, let it go. Go ahead and cry."

Tucker raises her stiff arms and puts them around Ella's waist. Her moan grows into words, "Maisy, Maisy, Maisy . . ." Tears begin streaming down her tanned cheeks, leaving tracks in the dust left there from her work in the garden.

Feeling the damp warmth of Tucker's tears on her shoulder, Ella slowly sways left and right and touches Tucker's coarse, greasy hair. "Sometimes crying is the best thing for the soul."

All of a sudden, Tucker steps back from Ella. Clutching at her chest, she stumbles backward a few more steps.

"Tucker?"

As she bends at the waist, Tucker continues gripping her chest. Like a wounded animal, her knees buckle and she tumbles to the ground.

"Tucker!" Ella screams.

Hurrying to Tucker's side, Ella kneels and puts her face close to Tucker's. She begins unbuttoning the top buttons of Tucker's shirt. "What's happening?"

In a hoarse whisper, Tucker says, "It'll pass. I'm jes' havin' a spell. Help me get t' th' shade by th' barn."

Tucker gets to one knee. Ella puts Tucker's arm over her shoulder and does what she can to help her to her feet. Slowly, Tucker rises. With Ella's help, she walks unsteadily to the side of the barn and leans back against it. Ella joins her in the shade.

Breathing heavily, Ella says, "What kind of spells are you talking about? How long has this been going on?"

"It ain't nothin'," Tucker says. "It'll ease up in a minute."

Concern digs a furrow between Ella's eyes.

Tucker takes a long, deep breath. "Now that's better," she says. "Y' know, I've gotta tell th' kids 'bout their mama."

"Oh shit," Ella says. Her face immediately reddens. "I'm sorry. I didn't mean to say that. I meant to say, 'Oh shoot.'"

Through her dried tears, Tucker manages a half smile. "Woman, y' ain't gotta 'pologize t' me fer that."

Ella smiles briefly, then says, "The kids . . . Do you want me to go get April and bring her up here so you can tell all of them at the same time?"

"I reckon so," Tucker replies. "I'll meetcha up at th' house."

With a look of unease, Ella says, "Are you going to be okay to walk?"

Standing erect and breathing easily, Tucker says, "Sure, I'll be fine." She lumbers toward her house while Ella walks quickly to her own.

When they see Tucker coming into the yard, August and March come out of the house onto the porch.

"What did the sheriff want?" August calls out to the approaching Tucker.

"Yeah," March adds, "what's going on? I saw Ella come up there, too."

Tucker walks past the porch. "Ya'll come t' th' backyard. Let's sit under th' shade tree fer a bit."

August and March share puzzled expressions, raise their shoulders, and follow Tucker.

When they catch up with Tucker, March says, "The sheriff sure was hot and sweaty. Where had he been? Why did he come out here? Was he looking for somebody? Are we in trouble, or something? I promise I haven't been in trouble in school or on the bus either."

Under the welcoming shade of the giant oak tree, Tucker walks to the trunk, where a five-gallon bucket lies on its side. She turns it upside down, sits on the bottom, and leans back against the tree. "You boys jes' have a seat. Yore sister's comin', too."

March glances quickly at August. August scowls at him and motions for him to sit in the grass. They try to read Tucker's placid expression, but find nothing helpful there.

The sound of frantic cicadas, eager to enjoy their brief life in the sun, fills the summer air. August picks up a stick and idly digs a hole. March repeatedly tries to catch a tassel fly as it hovers close by.

In a few moments the three of them hear the sounds of approaching feet, then see Ella and April approaching hand in hand.

Frightened, April lets go of Ella's hand and runs to Tucker's side. "What's wrong?" April asks. "Ella wouldn't tell me."

Tucker puts her hand on April's head. "Why dontcha sit down with yore brothers. We gotta talk."

Sitting cross-legged in a semicircle, the three children look attentively at Tucker. Ella takes a seat on the ground behind them.

"I got somethin' t' tell y'," Tucker begins.

"Is it about the sheriff?" March interrupts.

August punches him on the shoulder. "Will you just shut up and let Tucker tell us?!"

Rubbing his shoulder, March looks aggrieved and returns his focus to Tucker.

"It's 'bout yore mama," Tucker says.

A quiet blankets the small group under the tree that is so suffocating, even the cicadas pause their incessant chatter to listen.

Coughing to clear her throat, Tucker takes her thick, scratched glasses off her face and holds them in her hand.

Ella is startled to realize she's never seen the color of Tucker's eyes and is amazed at their beautiful bright green hue.

Tucker looks into the distance and says, "The sheriff tol' us she's dead."

August's mouth drops open. March's eyes fill with tears. April's expression does not change. Ella's eyes redden.

Burying his face in his hands, March cries out, "Mama!"

In a voice that sounds detached from him, August says, "Mama's dead?"

Looking back at Ella, April's expression asks for permission to join her.

Ella moves close to the children on all fours and reaches her arms around them. "I'm so sorry children, so very sorry."

Ella's touch breaks the cord that had tethered August's tears to his heart. As he begins crying, he says, "What happened? I mean, how did she die?"

Ella winces when Tucker says, "The sheriff tol' us somebody kilt 'er."

Jumping to his feet with clenched fists, Augusts yells, "Who did it? I'll kill 'em! Nobody's gonna do that to my mama and get away with it. I'll kill 'em!"

Ella cuts in, "There's still lots that we don't know yet. The sheriff said there will be an investigation to figure out exactly what happened. So, we need to wait until we get more information before we can tell you all anything else. Why don't we go in the house and make us something to eat?"

She reaches for April's and August's hands. "Come on, let's go inside."

April readily takes her hand. August takes her other hand and reaches for March. "Come on, March," he says. March takes August's hand and stands.

Turning to Tucker, Ella sees her staring toward some faraway place. "What about you, Tucker? You want to join us?"

When Tucker doesn't acknowledge her, Ella says to the children, "You all come with me. Let's let Tucker rest out here for a while."

CHAPTER FIFTY-FOUR

Ella, wearing a black dress and hat, opens the back door of her car and April gets in. Ella reaches in and smoothes the wrinkles out of April's navy dress. "You look nice," she says.

Smiling, April says, "So do you."

They drive in silence the few hundred yards to Tucker's house. As they pull in the yard, March comes out of the house, his dark hair parted on one side and plastered to his head. August appears in the doorway. His normally unruly hair has been picked into a round Afro.

Rolling down her window, Ella calls out, "You boys come on and get in the backseat with your sister."

After the boys are loaded, Ella turns the car around and heads toward town.

"What's going to happen at this thing called a foorel?" March asks.

"I keep telling you," August chastises, "it's a few-ner-al, not a foorel."

Looking in her rearview mirror at the boys, Ella says, "It's just a chance to share some memories about a person who has died.

There'll be a preacher who will say a few words. And there will be some pretty music."

"Like Three Dog Night?" March laughs.

August punches him and says, "You really are a fool, you know it? Can't you be serious for Mama?"

March shoots August an angry look, but says nothing.

Ella says, "Let's just all ride quietly to the funeral home."

Though quiet on the outside, Ella is in a whirl on the inside, trying to process all that has happened and all she has learned in the last thirty-six hours.

It began when she asked Tucker if she wanted her to try and contact Maisy's father about her death.

"Ain't no need t' try that," Tucker replied. "He's done met his Maker a long time ago."

"I've never heard you talk about your father," Ella gently probed.

"M' father was a sorry son of a bitch. He abused me all m' life, up 'til th' day I kilt 'im."

Ella felt herself stagger in reaction to this bombshell. She had no time to recover before Tucker dropped an even bigger bomb.

"An' he was Maisy's father, too."

Ella stared at Tucker.

"It's a helluva note, ain't it?" Tucker said. "Don't nobody livin' know 'bout all that. You's th' onliest one."

"I . . . I don't know what to say," Ella said. "I figured you had a hard time growing up. But I never dreamed . . ." Her voice choked as tears welled up.

"It ain't nothing. 'Twas a long time ago."

"How come Tucker didn't come home last night?" August's question snaps Ella back to the present.

She glances at him in the rearview mirror. "She spent the night at the funeral home. That's what everybody did, years ago. Someone would stay all night with the body of their loved one."

"That's scary," April says.

Ella stops the car in front of the funeral home. "Okay now, everyone follow me and mind your manners."

The sound of taped organ music greets the four of them as they open the front door. Ella leads the way to the parlor room where the service will be held. The room is empty except for Tucker, Smiley Carter, Shady Green, Mary Beth Chandler, and the preacher.

Ella ushers the children into the empty chairs beside Tucker.

The music fades out and the preacher walks to the podium.

"After I moved here twenty years ago," he begins, "it wasn't long before I began hearing about Tucker and her daughter, Maisy. Most of what I heard was not worth listening to because it was nothing more than gossip. And gossip is a damnable sin."

Looking directly at Tucker, he says, "So I decided I would go see for myself what all the talk was about." Smiling, he says, "Do you remember my first visit to your place, Tucker?"

Tucker's stony expression is inscrutable.

"Well I do," the preacher says. "Tucker was shelling corn off the cob for her hogs. When I introduced myself and stuck out my hand to shake hers, she stuck an ear of corn in my hand and said, 'Git busy.'"

Shady Green cackles, "Tha' be her, aw'wight."

Smiley Carter concurs with a hearty, "Amen."

The preacher continues, "I've visited Tucker many times over the past twenty years, a fact I'm sure would shock my parishioners. I visited because I found Tucker refreshing. I never had to guess where I stood with Tucker."

Shifting his gaze to the small audience, he says, "Maisy was a different matter, though. She never seemed content. She was restless. And I'd say that restlessness was her undoing. For those of you left behind, it will be difficult for you to fit Maisy's violent death into your heart in a way that will make sense, for there's no sense to be made of it."

He pulls out a white handkerchief and wipes the sweat off his face. "To you children, I will say I am sorry that you didn't get to live long enough to experience the effects of the reformed life that I so badly wanted your mother to achieve. And to you, Tucker, I will say I regret that you have another sorrow to add to your difficult life. But this one thing I know—there is a better life awaiting us all. In that sweet bye and bye, all our burdens will be lifted and all our sorrows will be washed away. In heaven there'll be no weeping nor pining. May we all eagerly look forward to that day."

As the preacher leaves the podium, Smiley Carter rises, walks a few steps past the family, then turns to face them. All eyes are fixed on him.

The organ music begins playing again. After the introduction plays, Smiley Carter opens his mouth and, in a rich baritone voice that would make church pews vibrate and would reach to the rafters, sings,

> Well I'm tired and so weary, but I must go along;
> Till the Lord comes and calls me away, oh, yes;
> Well the morning is bright, and the Lamb is the Light;
> And the night, night is as fair as the day, oh, yes.
>
> There will be peace in the valley for me some day;
> There will be peace in the valley for me, O Lord, I pray;
> There'll be no sadness, no sorrow, no trouble I'll see;
> There will be peace in the valley for me.
>
> There the flowers will be blooming, and the grass will be green;
> And the skies will be clear and serene, oh, yes;
> Well the sun ever beams, in this valley of dreams;

And no clouds there will ever be seen, oh, yes.

There will be peace in the valley for me some day;
There will be peace in the valley for me, O Lord, I pray;
There'll be no sadness, no sorrow, no trouble I'll see;
There will be peace in the valley for me.

Well, the bear will be gentle, and the wolf will be tame;
And the lion shall lay down by the lamb, oh, yes;
Well the beast from the wild, shall be led by a little child;
And I'll be changed, changed from the creature that I am, oh, yes.

There will be peace in the valley for me some day;
There will be peace in the valley for me, O Lord, I pray;
There'll be no sadness, no sorrow, no trouble I'll see;
There will be peace in the valley for me.

As the last notes settle on the hearts of the audience, the only sound heard is sniffling. Everyone is wiping tears, except Tucker.

Her face a deep crimson, Tucker sits stiffly, her arms folded across her chest.

Ted Mays, the funeral director, comes into the room and announces, "This concludes the service for Maisy. Because her body is still at the coroner's in Memphis, there will not be an internment at this time. Thank you all for coming."

Outside, Tucker and the children pile into Ella's car. After speaking to the preacher, Shady Green, Smiley Carter, and Mary Beth, Ella gets in the driver's seat.

They ride in silence as they pass through town and head toward their houses. As they turn onto the road that will take them home, Tucker says, "Somebody's gonna pay fer what happened t' Maisy. Somebody's gonna pay."

CHAPTER FIFTY-FIVE

Two days after Maisy's funeral, Sheriff Ron Harris eases his police cruiser down the dirt lane to the banks of the Obion River. After parking beside the rescue squad's truck, he gets out and puts on his Stetson hat. He walks toward the river, passing several other patrol cars, and joins the group of officers and volunteers awaiting him.

A white-haired deputy, whose belly makes it impossible to know if his pants are held up by a belt, steps from the circle. "Come this way, Sheriff." He turns and leads the sheriff to a boat that is pulled up on the bank.

Pointing to two wet, mud-covered men, the deputy says, "Joey and Carl are the ones who found it."

The four men gather on either side of the boat. Peering in, the sheriff sees what has prompted the radio call for him to come out and inspect the discovery for himself—a whitened skull.

Looking at Joey and Carl, the sheriff asks, "And where did you find it?"

Joey and Carl look at each other and then Joey says, "It was in that patch of lily pads where Maisy's body was found. We were looking for any sort of evidence that might help us find out who murdered her, just like you ordered us to."

"We didn't know what it was at first," Carl adds. "It was covered in mud and moss."

Shifting his toothpick to the corner of his mouth, the sheriff asks, "What about any other bones? A skull doesn't just appear out of thin air and not have the rest of the skeleton attached. Did you look for more bones?"

Joey shifts his feet nervously. "That mud out there must be ten inches deep or more in places. Nearly anything on the bottom just disappears over time. It's a miracle we found that skull."

Fixing them with a hard stare, the sheriff says, "That didn't answer my question. Did you look for more bones?"

"We did for a little bit," Carl says. "But all we found were sticks that we thought might be bones."

To vouch for Carl and Joey, the deputy says, "You'd just about have to drain that slough and let it dry for a month before you could know exactly what's in there."

The sheriff steps into the boat and squats beside the skull to get a better look. Without taking his eyes from it, he says, "I guess you're right. You boys did a good job. I'd say this is definitely the skull of an adult. And I'd say it's been out here for a very long time."

Standing up, he makes a sweeping motion with his arm. "But what are the odds of finding evidence of two possible murders in the same place out here in the middle of nowhere? Pointing to the deputy, he says, "Jessie, bag that thing, put it in my car, and wait for me there." He calls out, "All you men gather around here for a minute."

Once the deputies and volunteer rescue workers are around him, the sheriff says, "Now I want every one of you to listen very closely to what I'm about to say. I don't want one word to leak out about this skull Carl and Joey found. I mean not one peep. And if something does leak out, somebody's going to have to answer to me. Everybody understand?"

There is a general murmur of agreement from the men.

"Good," the sheriff says. "All of you worked really hard the past several days. Good work. We're through out here now. Load everything up and head back to town. Jessie, you ride with me. Curt, you take his car back to the office."

In his squad car, the sheriff cranks the engine and turns the air conditioner on high. He and Jessie sit in silence as, one by one, the other emergency vehicles leave.

When the last one leaves, Jessie says, "What's on your mind, Sheriff?"

"How old are you, Jessie?"

Jessie laughs. "I'm as old as that mud Carl and Joey had smeared on them."

"No, I'm serious," the sheriff says.

"Well, this November I'll be seventy years old."

"That's about what I thought. And how long have you been in law enforcement?"

"Including my time in the military, it's been about fifty years."

The sheriff puts the car in gear, slowly pulls onto the highway, and heads toward town. Jessie lights a cigarette and lowers his window a bit to let the smoke escape.

After several minutes of silence, Jessie says, "I can hear your wheels turning, but I don't know what you're thinking."

"Okay," the sheriff begins, "let me ask you a question. What's this skull got to do with Maisy Tucker?"

"I don't know. Maybe something. Maybe nothing. It's hard to tell."

"Look," the sheriff snaps, "I'm not a lawyer trying to trap you. Just answer my question with a straight answer. What do you *think* it has to do with her?"

Flipping his cigarette out the window, Jessie says, "I remember when your granddaddy was sheriff. He always said there wasn't no such thing as coincidence."

"Exactly what I was thinking."

"So let me tell you a story," Jessie says. "Suppose there was this man who had a daughter. This man was known to be a very rough sort of feller, kept to himself—a real surly character. And let's suppose that anytime someone saw his daughter, she looked like a whipped pup. Maybe there was rumors going around that this man was abusing his daughter, and I don't mean just physically."

Jessie pauses to light another cigarette.

"Give me one of those," the sheriff says. "I swear, every time I try to quit smoking, something happens to set me off again."

Smiling, Jessie offers him the pack.

After they light up their cigarettes, Jessie continues. "Let's suppose that every man in the county would just like to have an excuse to get rid of this vermin of a man, but no one can ever unbottle the truth. And what if, when this little girl is about sixteen years old, suddenly nobody ever sees this man anymore. He don't come to town, never is seen in his field. I mean, it's like he vanished into thin air. Some people might say that the fellow ran off because he was afraid someone was going to find out what was going on between him and his girl."

The sheriff's eyes narrow as he listens intently to Jessie's story. The muscles in his jaw flex repeatedly. Glancing at Jessie, he says, "Are you saying somebody caught him out one night and did him in?"

"May have happened that way," Jessie says. "But suppose, just suppose, that this girl, who was not a little girl—in fact, she was quite a *big* girl, strong as an ox, even—finally got her fill of his evil ways. And maybe she decides this is something she can take care of herself."

The sheriff's eyes widen and he takes his foot off the accelerator. "And she dumps the body out here in the swamp! Do you mean Tucker killed—"

"I don't mean anything," Jessie cuts in. "I'm just speaking in suppositions. It's all speculation." He turns in the car seat until he is facing the sheriff. "But I'll tell you what your granddaddy said about this very story a long time ago. He said sometimes a person gets what they deserve, even if it is outside the law."

CHAPTER FIFTY-SIX

Sheriff Ron Harris pulls to a stop in front of Maisy's apartment. He walks past the Tennessee Bureau of Investigation car and another black sedan in the driveway. Opening the front door, he steps inside where one man is putting his camera away and two technicians are closing their briefcases.

District Attorney Whalen Kennedy, who played football with Ron in high school, is also present. Stepping toward the sheriff and sticking out a hand, he says, "Hey, Ron. How's it going? Sure is hot out there, isn't it?"

Shaking Whalen's hand, the sheriff says, "It's summertime in west Tennessee, that's what it is. H-H-H. Hot, hazy, and humid. What have they found in here?"

"They say it was definitely wiped down. There are two drink glasses, but only one has fingerprints on it—Maisy's. Even the bottle's been wiped down. You and your investigator had already concluded it must have been someone she knew, since there were no indications of a struggle. Nothing was taken, as far as we can tell. Fresh sheets were on the bed, so no chance of getting any evidence there."

Glancing around the apartment, the sheriff says, "It'd be nice if we had at least a sliver of something to go on."

The TBI agents line up to leave the apartment. One of them says, "This is our second sweep of the apartment, and we didn't find anything new. Sorry."

Whalen shakes his hand and says, "Thanks, fellows. We appreciate the extra effort."

As the agents walk out the door, the last man pauses, looking at the wall behind the door. Letting go of the door, he steps to the wall, putting his face inches from the surface. "Hey, Turner," he calls out. "Get back in here a second."

The sheriff and Whalen exchange a glance. "What it is it?" Whalen asks.

"Maybe nothing," the agent replies.

Turner comes back in and, seeing his fellow agent with his face against a wall, says, "Find something, Johnny?"

"Bring me the fingerprint kit."

Turner sits the black briefcase on the floor by Johnny. Without moving his face from the wall, Johnny says, "Hand me the brush. I don't want to take my eyes off this."

Turner fills the fine hairs of the brush with cyanoacrylate and hands it to him.

Johnny carefully spins the brush across an area on the wall and steps back. After waiting a couple of minutes, he places a black gelatin lifter over the area and then peels it off.

Holding it up to the overhead light, he says, "That's nice."

"What've you got?" the sheriff asks impatiently.

"Looks like someone put their hand against the wall," Johnny says. "And it's definitely larger than Maisy's hand."

The sheriff and Whalen exchange a look. "Might be something we can use, you think?" the sheriff asks.

"We'll take a look at it," Whalen says.

"So, how long before we know if there's a match anywhere?" the sheriff asks Johnny.

"Hard to tell," he answers. "Sometimes a week, sometimes a month. Since it's a murder case, it'll have top priority. We'll do our best."

"The only problem," the sheriff says, "is that lots of men have been in her apartment. So there's no telling when that print was made or who it will match."

Nodding, Whalen says, "That's for certain."

Outside the apartment, a gray Oldsmobile Cutlass pulls in behind the sheriff's car. The driver nervously licks his lips, then opens the door and gets out.

On legs that feel like Jell-O, he slowly walks past the TBI car and the car of his boss, the district attorney. Walking up the steps to the front door of the apartment, he is startled when Johnny opens the door and bustles past him.

Stepping into the living room, he says, "Hey, boss. Hey, Sheriff. What's the latest?"

Whalen says, "We may have finally gotten a break. They found a full handprint on the wall. And they're certain it isn't Maisy's."

The world tilts just a little bit.

The sheriff looks at him and says, "Are you okay? You look pale as a sheet."

With a wave of his hand, he replies, "Sure, sure, I'm all right. I've just had a touch of a stomach bug."

"Listen," Whalen says to him, "why don't you go with the TBI guys back to our office and help them clear out their stuff? They'll be heading back to Memphis."

"Sure thing boss," he says. Turning around unsteadily he makes his way back to his car.

Inside, he struggles to calm his breathing as he tries to retrace in his mind every step he made the night he was in Maisy's apartment. As he visualizes the events of the evening, he suddenly remembers staggering when he picked Maisy up off the floor and planting his hand on the wall to catch his balance.

His face flushes and he gasps. "Damn!" he says. "Oh my God, what am I going to do?!"

He loosens his tie and unbuttons the top button of his shirt, then slowly lowers his forehead to the steering wheel.

Inside the apartment, the sheriff nods toward the street. "How's that kid working out in your office?"

"Not too bad," Whalen replies. "His biggest problem is who his dad is. He has the same entitled attitude that grates on me. Thinks he knows everything when he really doesn't, if you know what I mean. Plus he has a roving eye for women."

"Sounds to me like he's a lot of trouble," the sheriff says.

As they walk outside, Whalen says, "He's got a sharp legal mind and a good eye for detail. And he's ambitious. I'm working to channel those traits and make good use of them."

They both look up and watch as the gray Cutlass pulls away from the curb and heads toward town.

"I'll probably see you tomorrow," Whalen says to the sheriff.

"Let me know the minute you learn something about the print."

"Will do."

"One more thing," the sheriff says. "Do you believe that sometimes a person gets what they deserve, even if it is outside the law?"

Cocking his head, Whalen says, "That's a curious thing for you to ask. What's going on?"

"You lawyers!" the sheriff says in exasperation. "Can't you just answer a question?!"

"Okay, okay. I didn't mean to rile you up."

The two men look at each other in silence for a long moment, and then Whalen says, "Just between me and you?"

"Yes," the sheriff says, "just between me and you."

"Then I'd have to say yes, it is true. Or at least, there's times I've hoped it is. Now, you've got to tell me what prompted all this."

Shaking his head, the sheriff replies, "It's nothing. I've just been chasing random thoughts lately. You have a good evening."

CHAPTER FIFTY-SEVEN

Tucker pushes the bushel basket ahead a few feet with her foot. Lifting the dark green leaves of the purple hull pea vines, she reaches for a handful of foot-long pea pods and pulls them from the plant, then pitches them into the bushel basket. She keeps this up, plant after plant, all while remaining bent at a ninety-degree angle.

Sweat drips from the end of her nose as she nears the end of the row. Once there, she slowly straightens and seeks shelter in the shade of a sassafras tree.

The sound of an engine draws her attention. Driving up her road is Smiley Carter on his Ford tractor.

She watches as he drives right up to her front porch, where the boys are shelling peas. They both answer an unheard question by pointing toward the garden. Carter waves a thank-you to them and heads toward her.

Carter stops when he gets to the garden gate, shuts off his tractor, and unfolds his large frame from the seat. After closing the gate behind him as he enters the garden area, he scans the garden until he catches sight of Tucker under the tree.

Waving one of his large hands in the air, he strides toward her.

As he gets close, he winks at Tucker and says, "Mmm-mmm, them is some fine-lookin' peas. Must'a had somethin' to do with how the ground was plowed."

Tucker does not reply.

Sensing her somber mood, Carter looks more closely at her. "You's got the sadness, Tucker. Yes you does. An' you got ever' right to the sadness. Losin' a child . . ." His voice drifts off.

Tucker turns her head away from him and spits tobacco juice. Looking at Carter, she says, "That was a kind thing y' done, singin' at Maisy's fun'ral. Thanks."

Shaking his head, Carter says, "'Tweren't nothin', Tucker. It was the least I could do."

"An' I didn' know y' had such a good singin' voice. Y' sounded like somethin' off th' radio."

Carter smiles. "Thank you, thank you. I do loves to sing."

Carter shifts from one foot to the other. He takes out his handkerchief and blows his nose. "Yes sir, them's some fine-lookin' peas."

"What'n th' world's wrong with you?" Tucker asks. "Y' act as nervous as a long-tail cat in a room full o' rockin' chairs. I know y' didn't come 'ere t' talk 'bout my peas. What's on yore mind?"

Before speaking, Carter licks his lips, then asks, "Has the sheriff got any leads yet on who killed Maisy?"

"None that 'e's shared w' me. It's been a week since th' fun'ral an' I ain't heared nothin' from 'im. You git t' town more 'n me. Whadda you hear?"

"Rumors," Carter replies. "Nothin' but rumors. There's for sure been no arrests. I seen a TBI car at Maisy's last week. Must be doing fingerprint stuff." Looking at her again, he adds, "How you holding up, Tucker?"

"If'n I can git m' hands on whoever murdered Maisy, I'll be jes' fine."

Just as Carter is about to speak, Tucker continues, "Look, I know what kinda person Maisy was. I ain't stupid. But not even a dog deserves t' have done what was done t' 'er." When Carter doesn't say anything, she says, "Dontcha agree w' me? Or do y' think she deserved what she got?"

Startled, Carter says, "No . . . Yes . . . I mean no. I mean nobody deserves what she got."

Tucker cocks her head to one side as she looks at Carter.

He sees her curiosity and unspoken question. "Okay, I gots something to tells you, Tucker. And it's something big, something important. But I's scared to tell, 'cause it may mean something and it may mean nothin'."

He feels her eyes piercing him from behind her nearly opaque glasses.

"Well here's how it is," he begins. "You know I likes to night fish, 'specially along the Obion. Well about four months ago I was fishing north of Latham." He swallows. "Fishing under the bridge. I was the only one there that night. I wasn't catching hardly nothing, but I was enjoying the quiet. About midnight I heard a car slowing down. The headlights swept down the road bank as it turned down the dirt lane where people unload their boats. The headlights was low to the ground, so I figured it was a car. 'Some kids come out here to go parking,' I said to myself.

"This fellar gets out of the car and shines a flashlight. I was under the bridge on the other side of the river. I didn't have no lantern burning, so he never knowed I was there. He starts walking along the bank, shining his flashlight like he's looking for something. He disappears into the timber and is gone about fifteen minutes, when I hear an engine start. Sounds like a lawnmower engine. So I figure it must be one of them Reelfoot boats. Sure enough, in a minute here he comes in that Reelfoot boat and runs it up on the bank behind his car.

"He opens the trunk of his car and gets something out, something real heavy, from the looks of it. He has it across his shoulder, like it's some kind of big feed sack or something."

Carter notices Tucker's breath becoming more rapid and her nostrils flaring. He glances away and continues. "Now you gotta remember, it was dark. Even though it was a full moon, the cloud cover kept everything mostly hidden. Shapes was easy to see, but details was hard. This man he dumps whatever it is into the boat, pushes out into the water, starts the motor, and heads back into the timber."

Carter feels his own breath quickening. His mouth feels like it has cotton in it. "Where's your water jar?" he asks.

Tucker points to a spot at the base of the tree. "Help yoreself."

After gulping several swallows, Carter continues. "This fella goes so far off that soon I can't hear the engine. He's gone for maybe an hour and I hear the engine coming back my way. He runs the boat up on the bank and gets out. He walks to his car and opens the door to get in. That's when there's a sudden break in the clouds. That full moon lights things up like it's midday.

"The man looks up at the moon and I get me a real good look at him. And I realize I've done seen him before, but I can't remember where. And I can't remember what his name is. Now remember, Tucker, this was nearly five months ago. I done forgot all about it until they found Maisy's body. And I started trying to remember who the fellow was that I saw. It was at Maisy's funeral that I suddenly remembered."

Carter pauses and looks directly at Tucker. "It was Judge Jack and Miss Ella's boy, Cade."

Tucker's mouth drops open. She sways back and forth. Her knees suddenly buckle and she crumples to the ground.

CHAPTER FIFTY-EIGHT

Kneeling beside Tucker's inert body, Smiley Carter frantically calls her name, "Tucker! Tucker! Lord almighty, Tucker, wake up!"

He looks in every direction in hopes of seeing someone he can call to. Seeing no one, he lifts her hand and begins patting it.

Tucker emits a low moan.

"That's it," Carter says. "Come on now, you's gonna be all right."

When Tucker stirs, he gets behind her and puts his hands under her arms. "Let me help you sit up."

Once in a sitting position, Tucker takes off her glasses and vigorously rubs her face. Giving her head an energetic shake, she says, "What happened?" She puts her glasses back on and looks at Carter. "Oh, now I 'member."

Sitting cross-legged in front of her, Carter says, "They just wasn't no easy way to tell you, Tucker. It was a shock to me, too, when I figured out who I seen that night."

"How come y' ain't tol' this t' the sheriff?"

"Well, this here's the problem," Carter replies. "That night the man was in such a hurry to leave that he left his boat on the bank of the river. I mean, he just drove off and left it. So I waited awhile to see if he'd come back. When he didn't, I took the boat for myself. I ain't never had a Reelfoot boat and you know I likes to fish. I ain't said nothing to nobody 'cause I was afraid they'd find out I took the boat and they'd arrest me."

Tucker's eyes open and close rapidly as she processes all that Carter has told her. "Judge Jack's boy," she says slowly. After a pause, she adds, "And Miss Ella's." She shakes her head. "Oh my lord, my lord . . ." She closes her eyes.

"Yes," Carter says solemnly. "As Mama Mattie would say, 'It sho' nuf is a mess.'" As they sit in contemplative silence, the singing of cicadas and field larks fills the void.

Reaching toward Carter, Tucker says, "Help me up."

With a grunt, Carter stands. Grasping Tucker's hand firmly in his, he pulls. They both groan with the effort until, finally, Tucker is standing.

"Sometimes," Tucker says, "I git tired o' fightin' against life. Seems like it's always somethin'."

Carter cocks his head to one side. "'Tis so, 'tis so, Tucker. But what're we gonna do?"

"Y' sound scared," Tucker says. "I ain't never knowed y' t' be scared o' nothin'. What's got in t' y'?"

"It's Judge Jack," Carter says. "That's what I'm worried about. He runs this county. What he says goes. He'll find a way to put me in prison afore he lets his boy get in trouble."

"Ain't but one thing t' do," Tucker says. "I gotta go see Ella. She'll know what's best."

As she begins walking toward the garden gate, Carter says, "Let me carry you on my tractor to her house. You don't needs to be walking after your faintin' spell."

When they get to his tractor, Tucker eyes it skeptically. "An' where am I supposed t' ride? There ain't but one seat."

Pointing to the rear axle, Carter says, "Climb up here and put your feet there. Then you can sit on the rear wheel fender. Gimme your hand and I'll help you."

Once Tucker is in place, Carter cranks the tractor, eases out on the clutch, and makes his way to Ella's. When they arrive, Carter helps Tucker off the tractor.

As Carter starts to remount the tractor, Tucker says, "Where y' think you're goin'? Git down off'n there. You're comin' in, too."

Leaving no room for discussion, she turns and strides toward Ella's front door. Reluctantly, Carter follows.

Tucker strikes Ella's door twice and waits.

When the door opens, Ella's face registers surprise. Before she can invite them in, Tucker walks past her.

"We come t' talk t' you," she says.

Carter takes his cap off and nods at Ella as he walks past.

Ella closes the door and turns to face them.

Tucker shifts from one foot to the other. Carter focuses his attention on the floor.

Finally, Tucker says, "Maybe we could sit 'round yore table an' talk."

"Sure we can," Ella says. She leads the way to her dining room. "Coffee or tea, either one of you?"

Pulling out a chair to sit, Carter looks at her and says, "Some iced tea sure would be nice. My throat's as dry as sand. And bring some for Tucker, too. She had a spell a bit ago and needs to drink something."

Something in Carter's expression causes Ella to halt on her way to the kitchen. She turns to look closely at Tucker. "A spell? What sort of spell?"

"I'm fine," Tucker replies. "We'll git t' all that in a minute."

A quizzical expression appears on Ella's face, but she refrains from asking more questions. In the kitchen, she fixes everyone some iced tea and brings it to the table.

Once she sits down, she looks expectantly toward Tucker.

Tucker takes a deep breath. "This here ain't gonna be easy. I ain't even sure you's th' one I oughta be talkin' to 'bout this. But I ain't got nobody else t' turn to."

Ella frowns. "Is this about April?"

Surprised, Tucker says, "Oh no. It ain't got nothin' t' do with her. It's 'bout Maisy."

Ella notices Carter squeezing his cap and he and Tucker exchanging furtive glances. "Have they found the killer?" she asks.

"I ain't heard it, if'n they did," Tucker replies. "This is 'bout somthin' Carter seen back in Febr'ary." She pauses and looks at Carter. "Why don't y' just tell 'er what y' tol' me."

Carter leans forward and holds his twisted cap between his legs. Sitting back up, he says, "Well here's what happened . . ."

When Ella finishes listening to Smiley Carter's tale about the fateful February night and his realization later of the identity of the person he saw, she stares toward him, but her eyes are unfocused. Her complexion is ashen. She mouths Cade's name but makes no sound.

Tucker eases her thick, rough hand across the table toward Ella. Ella looks down at it and then up at Tucker. A look of horror seizes her face. In a whisper, she says, "Oh no," and begins shaking her head.

Ignoring Tucker's hand, Ella gets up from the table and begins pacing. "No, no, no," she says. "There must be a mistake." Looking at Carter, she says, "You said yourself that it was dark that night. How can you be so certain it was Cade? And how well can a person see, even with the full moon, at such a distance?"

Dropping his head, Carter says, "I'm sorry, Miss Ella, but I know what I seen. And even though the rest of me is getting old, Doc White says I've got the eyesight of a twenty-year-old."

"But you don't know what he put in the boat," Ella says. "You didn't see what it was, did you?"

"No, ma'am. I didn't see that. Didn't really pay much 'ttention 'cause I figured it was somebody doing some fishing."

Ella begins pacing again. "But what would Cade be doing with Maisy? She was nothing but a—"

She stops midsentence and looks at Tucker. "Oh Tucker," she says in a pleading tone, "I'm sorry. I didn't mean to say anything hurtful. I'm just rambling. Please forgive me."

Folding her arms across her chest, Tucker says, "Y' ain't got nothin' t' 'pologize fer. I know what Maisy was. But nobody deserved what happened t' her."

Ella clasps both hands to her mouth. She rushes back to sit in her chair at the table and leans on her elbows toward Tucker. Her voice trembles as she says, "Tucker, please hear me. The biggest tragedy here is that your daughter, your only child, suffered an awful death. I sincerely and deeply regret that."

As she is speaking, Tucker's face begins to redden and tears well up.

"And now," Ella continues, "I've learned there is a possibility that my only child may have been responsible for the murder. But why?" Tears begin streaming down her cheeks.

Tucker unfolds her arms and places her hands over Ella's, dwarfing them. She begins to cry and lowers her head onto her forearms.

Ella mirrors Tucker's movements and washes her own forearms in tears.

The tops of their heads touch in the middle of the table.

Carter, also moved, places a hand on each woman's head and says softly, "The Lord is my shepherd, I shall not want. He maketh me to lie down in green pastures. He leadeth me beside the still waters. He restoreth my soul . . ."

CHAPTER FIFTY-NINE

Throwing his head back, Cade McDade punctuates the air with a hearty laugh. The other men at the table join him in laughter. "That's the best one yet," Cade says to the man on his right. "Where do you find all your jokes?"

Before the man can answer, Cade yells to a passing waitress, "Hey, sweet thing, bring another round of drinks for us, won't you?"

The waitress flashes a white smile and winks. "Anything for you, Cade."

This prompts a chorus of whistles and catcalls from the group of men. "You better get you some of that," one of them says to Cade.

"Who says he hasn't already?" another one says, laughing.

Another round of laughter erupts.

Shaking his head, Cade says, "No, no, boys. Not anymore. I'm reformed. It's time for me to settle down. All of your all's lies about me through the years have given me a reputation that's hard to live up to and hard to live down."

The group is silent for a moment until, as if on cue, they simultaneously burst out laughing.

"That's a good one, Cade," one of them says.

"Reformed, my ass," another one scoffs.

Suddenly everyone's attention swings toward the figure of the approaching waitress with her tray of drinks. As she sets the tray on their table, Cade hands her a twenty dollar bill. Pressing it slowly into her cleavage, she says to Cade, "Anything else?"

"No thanks, Tiffany," Cade says. "We'll be fine."

Looking back at the faces of his friends at the table, Cade reads the skepticism in their expressions. He takes a big gulp of his drink, stands, and waves a dismissive hand toward them. "You guys go ahead and believe what you want. I'm going home to my wife."

As he walks away, the covert accusations of his friends, wearing the disguise of teases, echo across the room and through the door as he steps outside. He opens the door of his Cutlass and slides inside.

Driving past the courthouse on his way home, he recognizes the car of Whalen Kennedy sitting under the streetlight. He looks to the third floor and sees lights on in their suite of offices.

He decides to circle the square. On the opposite side of the courthouse he sees the patrol car of Sheriff Ron Harris and beside it a car with a TBI logo on the door.

Cade's hands clench and unclench the steering wheel. He glances in the rearview mirror and then proceeds to his house, trying to force himself to breathe slowly.

Walking in the back door, he calls out, "I'm home, Julie."

From deeper within the house, a woman's voice answers, "Hi, Cade. I'm in here. You need to call Whalen. He called earlier and asked me to have you call him as soon as you got home."

Keeping his voice light, he says, "Did he say what it was about?"

"No. He just said it was important."

Lifting the receiver off the wall phone, Cade dials the number from memory.

After the first ring, his boss answers, "Kennedy here."

"Hey Whalen, this is Cade. Julie asked me to call you. What's up?"

"It's the Maisy Tucker case. The TBI found a match on some prints. Can you come to the office?"

"Uh, you mean tonight? Now?"

"That's exactly what I mean," Whalen snaps.

Whalen's tone is so sharp that Cade jerks the receiver from his ear. Slowly bringing it back to his face, he says, "Well, sure I can. No problem. I'll be there in a couple of minutes."

When he hangs up the phone, he is startled by Julie's voice beside him. "Is something wrong?" she asks. "You're white as a sheet. And why are you so jumpy?"

"No, nothing's wrong," he replies. "It's just that you snuck up on me. I've got to go to the office. There's been a break in one of our cases."

As Cade walks up the marble stairs inside the courthouse, his leather-soled shoes echo throughout the empty building. His damp palm squeaks as he slides it up the handrail. He quickly wipes both palms on his pants.

Arriving at the third floor, he turns down the darkened hallway to a door with light sneaking out at the bottom. Taking a deep breath, he opens the door and steps inside.

The electricity in the air makes the hair on the back of his neck stand at attention. The three men in the room turn to look at him: Whalen is standing by the window behind his desk; Sheriff Harris is sitting at one end of the desk and putting out his cigarette; the third man, sitting at the opposite end of the desk, Cade does not recognize.

Cade flashes a smile. "So, we finally caught a break in the Maisy case? That's great news!"

His excitement crashes into a wall of silence.

Pointing to the third man, Whalen says, "Cade, I want you to meet Special Agent Bowlin. The TBI has assigned him to this case."

Cade offers his hand to the unsmiling agent, and they shake.

Whalen nods toward a chair between agent Bowlin and Sheriff Harris. "Sit down, Cade."

As Cade moves to the chair, Whalen turns his back to the room and looks out the window through the blinds. The ticking of the ancient clock on the wall fills the room.

"Why the somber mood?" Cade asks. "I figured I'd find everyone excited."

Whalen turns from the window and sits in the chair behind his desk. "Remember that handprint on the wall at Maisy's apartment?"

"Sure." Cade feels his stomach twist.

"The TBI got a definite match," Whalen continues. "Remember that trouble you had a while back for having a trunkload of marijuana? You were booked and fingerprinted. I'd forgotten all about it until I got a call from Agent Bowlin. The handprint in Maisy's apartment is yours."

In spite of Cade's calm demeanor, his face reddens. He snickers and says, "Well yeah, I've seen Maisy. But, my gosh, what man around here hasn't?"

Sheriff Harris looks at him. His eyes darken and his expression is grim. Through clenched teeth he says, "I ain't."

Cade looks from the sheriff to Whalen to Special Agent Bowlin. "Whoa there, fellas. Are you thinking I killed Maisy? Because if you are, you're crazy. Why would I want to kill her?"

Special Agent Bowlin crosses his legs and says, "That crime scene was wiped down by someone who knew what they were doing. In spite of all the traffic that the sheriff tells me probably went through that apartment, there was only one print found that wasn't the victim's. That was yours."

"How do you explain that?" Whalen adds.

"And why," the sheriff asks, "would there be a full handprint of yours on a wall? I'll bet you couldn't find a full handprint of mine on any wall in my house."

Looking at the sheriff, Cade says, "I really can't explain that. And unless I'm being charged, I don't believe I have to. What I do in my private life is my business."

"How often did you see Maisy?" Whalen asks.

"Before I answer that question, do I need to consult a lawyer?"

Whalen looks to Special Agent Bowlin. "Mr. McDade," the agent begins, "we are not in a position to make any charges at this time. We are still gathering information. If you would like to help us in that process, it would certainly be appreciated."

"And," the sheriff chimes in, "we might be able to keep in this room the fact that you've been screwing around on your wife."

Cade glances at the ceiling and then back at Whalen. "I had a thing with Maisy several years ago and we saw each other pretty regularly. But I probably haven't seen her in at least two years."

The other three men exchange glances.

Sheriff Harris says, "Agent Bowlin, is it possible for a print to stay that long?"

"There's no valid test for proving how long a print has existed. I have no way to prove it was made last week or two years ago."

CHAPTER SIXTY

Ella and Tucker ride in silence in Ella's small Ford Pinto. In the backseat Smiley Carter's knees stick up higher than the back of the front seat. The low roof forces him to sit bent over, placing his chin within inches of his knees. His bulk makes it impossible for Ella to see out her rearview mirror.

"I hope you all knows what you're doin'," Carter says.

Staring straight ahead, Tucker says, "Miss Ella says it's the only way, an' that's good enough fer me."

"You both know," Ella says, "that we cannot keep this information to ourselves. The authorities have to know. And I think Sheriff Ron Harris is the best place to start. I believe him to be an honest man."

"I s'pose," Carter says. "But what about that boat I stole? What's he gonna say about that? Smiley Carter's too old to be going to jail."

"This ain't 'bout you," Tucker snaps. "It's 'bout m' girl, Maisy. You're just like all men. Y' think th' sun sets an' rises cause o' you." Her voice begins to rattle with agitation. "God forbid anything bad happen t' you. While m' girl was killed an' dumped like an animal into that nasty backwater in the bottom. Jesus!"

Carter's head drops a notch lower.

Ella uses her left hand to swipe tears off her cheeks. The movement catches Tucker's eye. Turning to look, she sees that Carter wasn't the only person stung by her words.

In a softer tone, Tucker says, "Ella, I didn' mean no harm."

"I know," Ella responds. "You only spoke the truth. That's the trouble with the truth sometimes. It may set you free, but first it will make you miserable."

Nodding his bowed head, Carter says softly, "That's so."

Ella turns on her blinker. "Well, here we are. We'll soon know if this was the right thing to do."

The little car leans first to its left and then to its right as Tucker and Carter exit on opposite sides. The three of them stand beside the car as if waiting for a valet, when the door of the Sheriff's Department opens and Deputy Jessie Wilson appears. Pulling at his sagging pants, he says, "Ya'll come on in. Sheriff Harris is expecting you."

Ella leads the parade, followed by Tucker. As Carter passes Jessie, Jessie sticks out his hand, "Hey, Smiley. How you been?"

Carter shakes the deputy's hand and says, "Doin' all right, I guess. When in the world is you gonna retire?"

"They wouldn't know how to run this county without me," Jessie says with a smile, then steps in front to lead them to the sheriff's office.

At the sheriff's office, Jessie knocks twice and opens the door. "Your company's here, Sheriff."

Sheriff Harris's voice carries from inside the room, "Bring them in."

As they enter the room the sheriff nods at each one and calls them by name, then motions toward three chairs lined up in front of his desk. "Ya'll have a seat."

"If ya'll don't care," he adds, "I'd like Jessie to stay. Sometimes it's better to have two sets of ears."

Ella looks at Tucker.

"Jessie ain't never done nothin' t' me," Tucker says. "Let 'im stay."

Ella then looks at Carter, who shifts in his chair.

Glancing from the sheriff to Jessie, Carter wipes his large hand across his brow and lets out a big breath. "Okay." Pointing to the office door, he adds, "But shut that door."

Sheriff Harris nods at Jessie, who closes the door and then takes a chair behind the three guests.

Turning his attention to the three, the sheriff says, "Before we start, let me say something." Handing a key to Tucker, he says, "We're all through with Maisy's apartment. You're free to get her things whenever you want to." After Tucker takes the key, he says, "Okay, this is your all's show. What's on your mind?"

"Ron," Ella begins, "this might have something to do with Maisy. Or it might not. Carter saw something back in February that he just told me and Tucker about recently. I think you need to hear his story."

Sheriff Harris raises his eyebrows and turns his attention to Carter.

Carter licks his dry lips and says, "Well, here's what happened . . ."

When Carter finishes his story, Sheriff Harris's mouth is agape. He glances at his deputy, who mirrors his shocked expression. He opens and closes several desk drawers until he produces a mashed cigarette package. Fishing out a bent cigarette, he places it in his mouth, and lights it.

Blowing smoke out his nose, he says, "Why in the hell haven't you said something before now?"

Ella clears her throat. "Well Ron, there's a small issue that might cause a problem for Carter. That's why he was so reluctant. It's the matter of the boat."

Looking blank, the sheriff says, "The boat?"

"It's that Reelfoot boat," Carter says. "It's at my house in the shed."

"Are you telling me it was your boat that was used?" the sheriff asks.

Eyes widening, Carter says, "No! No sir! What I'm sayin' is that he drove off and left it at the river. I waited a couple of hours and he never come back. So—"

Understanding dawning, the sheriff says, "You took it."

"I took it," Carter says and drops his head.

His eyes closed, the sheriff rubs his temples. "Okay, okay," he says without opening his eyes. "We'll get to that later." He looks at Carter. "We need to pin down the exact night this happened. Can you do that?"

Carter raises his head. "The exact date?"

"Yes!" the sheriff explodes. "I need the date the murder took place. I can't piece this puzzle together until I have a starting place."

"Well," Carter begins, "I know it was in February." Looking at Tucker, he says, "It was a week or so after we worked up your garden." Suddenly he smiles. "I remember! It was February fourteenth. Well, late that night and on into the wee hours of the next day. The Farmer's Almanac said it would be a good day to fish. Yes sir, it was the wee hours of February fifteenth that I seen what I seen."

Sheriff Harris glances at his deputy in the back of the room and then looks at Carter. "Are you positive?"

"Yep, no doubt."

Standing up, the sheriff says, "That's all I need from you all right now. I really appreciate you coming in and telling me about all this."

"What're y' gonna do now?" Tucker asks.

"We've got to check some things out," the sheriff answers. "Just let us do our job. We'll be in touch."

Deputy Wilson coughs and opens the office door. The three visitors stand and begin filing out. As Tucker is about to step through the door, the sheriff says, "Tucker, can I speak to you privately for just a second?"

Tucker turns to face the sheriff and steps back inside his office.

"Shut the door, Jessie," he says. "But I want you to stay in here for this."

Once the door is shut, the sheriff says to Tucker, "You're familiar with the area where Maisy's body was found, aren't you?"

Folding her arms over her chest, Tucker blinks rapidly. "Might be. Might not."

Harris cocks his head to one side and says, "Let me put it this way. Some of our boys were in the bottom looking for clues to help us find Maisy's murderer. While searching through all that mud, they thought they found something important, maybe the remains of someone else's body that had been there a long, long time."

He pauses to let Tucker comment.

As if her features are set in stone, Tucker shows no emotion. The lock on her lips remains sealed.

The sheriff continues. "It turns out that what they found had nothing to do with Maisy. As a matter of fact, I'm not even sure what happened to the bones they found." Shifting his feet uncomfortably, he adds, "I guess I thought it was something you'd like to know. There's nothing left in those bottoms that has anything to do with Maisy or with you. Do you understand what I'm saying?"

Tucker looks from the sheriff to Jessie and back to the sheriff. "Is that all ya'll got t' say?" she asks.

"One other thing," the sheriff says. "This week I learned of something my grandfather once said. He said, 'Sometimes a person gets what's coming to them, even if it is outside the law.' I think my grandfather was right."

He motions at Jessie to open the door. When he does, Tucker strides past and heads to the waiting car outside.

Turning to the sheriff, Jessie gives a slight smile and says, "Good job, Sheriff. Your granddaddy would be proud of you."

"I hope so," the sheriff replies. "Now, you go pick up Cade McDade and bring him here to my office. I'm going to find Whalen and fill him in. I don't care how you do it, but you keep Cade here until I come back with Whalen."

CHAPTER SIXTY-ONE

Sitting in Sheriff Harris's office, Cade McDade looks at Jessie and asks again what this is all about.

Showing no emotion, Jessie says, "Can't say. I was told to find you, bring you here, and keep you here until the sheriff gets back."

Cade crosses and recrosses his legs. "Well this is ridiculous. I've got work I'm supposed to be doing for Whalen Kennedy, you know. Who's going to explain this to him?"

His question is met with a look of nonchalance by Jessie.

Just then the door to the office opens and Sheriff Harris strides in.

Immediately, Cade is on his feet. "I demand to know what the hell is going on here, Sheriff! Who's going to explain this to. . ." His voice trails off and his eyes widen as he sees Whalen enter the room.

Taking a more conciliatory tone, Cade extends his hand toward Whalen and says, "Am I glad to see you, Whalen. I was beginning to feel like a hostage."

When Whalen does not shake his hand, Cade backs up a step. Looking from Whalen to the sheriff, he says, "Is this about Maisy?"

"What makes you say that?" the sheriff asks.

"The last time I had to meet with both of you, that was the topic du jour. So tell me, what is going on?"

"Let's all sit down," Whalen says.

Once they are seated, Whalen asks, "Do you own a Reelfoot boat, Cade?"

Cade feels as if a sledgehammer has hit him in the chest. He laughs nervously. "A what?"

"You heard me," Whalen replies.

Cade licks his lips and says, "Actually I do own a Reelfoot boat, but I haven't seen it in months. Someone must have stolen it."

"Jessie," the sheriff says without looking away from Cade, "have you had any reports made on a stolen Reelfoot boat?"

Speaking matter-of-factly, Jessie says, "Not to my knowledge, sir."

The sheriff raises his eyebrows.

"No, I didn't report it," Cade volunteers. "It was only worth a couple of hundred dollars. And I never used it that much anyway."

"When was the last time you used it?" Whalen asks.

Cade looks at Whalen and blinks. "Huh?"

"I want to know when was the last time you used your Reelfoot boat."

"Uh, I guess last fall or maybe in December," Cade says.

Whalen and the sheriff exchange a glance.

"Tell me this," the sheriff says. "Where were you the night of February fourteenth?"

Cade's head snaps toward the sheriff. "Huh?"

"Boy, have you got hearing problems?" the sheriff says. "February fourteenth, and early into the morning of the fifteenth. Where were you?"

Standing up, Cade says, "Look, I don't know what's going on. I feel like I'm being questioned like a suspect. Do I need to have a lawyer here? Am I being charged with something?"

"At this point," Whalen says, "we are simply looking for answers to questions."

"Well maybe if you filled me in on what you are looking into, I could be more helpful."

"I suppose that's fair enough," Whalen says. "Cade, we have a witness who places you in the Latham bottom early in the morning on February fifteenth, near the site where Maisy Tucker's body was found."

Throwing his head back, Cade laughs loudly. "That's impossible! You're both crazy! Besides, why in the world would I kill Maisy? This feels like nothing more than a fishing expedition and I'm tired of it. Unless you are going to charge me with something, I'm leaving."

"So," Whalen says, "if you were not in the bottoms on the night of February fourteenth and the morning of the fifteenth, can you tell us where you were?"

Cade jerks on his tie to loosen it and walks to the door. Yanking it open, he turns to the men in the office and says, "If you must know, I was at my mother's house treating her with a Valentine's present." He slams the door behind him as he leaves.

Whalen looks at Sheriff Harris and Jessie. "What do you two think?"

"I believe he's lying," the sheriff says.

Nodding, Jessie says, "Absolutely. He started panicking when you told him about the eyewitness."

"This is as twisted up as honeysuckle on a woven wire fence," Whalen says. "And he's using his mother as his alibi. So you believe Smiley Carter's story over Cade's?"

"Yes I do," the sheriff says. "Smiley's got no reason to lie, especially since he incriminated himself by admitting to stealing the boat. He could have told the story lots of ways and left that part out."

"But he didn't actually see what Cade got out of the trunk and placed in the boat, did he?"

"No, he didn't," the sheriff replies. "We need to get the TBI boys back up here to go through the trunk of his car looking for evidence."

"We better get that boat as well," Jessie adds.

"Good idea," Whalen agrees. "But we'll need to go through another judge besides Judge Jack to obtain a search warrant."

"What's got me stumped," the sheriff says, "is why? What's his motive for killing her? You reckon she was going to tell his wife?"

Nodding, Whalen says, "Maybe, but if she did tell, it would be killing her own golden goose. Maybe when we get the coroner's report on the cause of death, it will give us some more clues."

"We should get that any day now, don't you think?" the sheriff asks.

"Why don't I give them a quick phone call," Whalen says. "They may have the results already but haven't yet typed them up. Sometimes, if I can get through to the right person, they'll go ahead and tell me."

The sheriff turns the phone on his desk so that it faces Whalen. "Help yourself."

Whalen dials the seven digit number. After a few moments of silence, he says, "Yes, this is Whalen Kennedy, district attorney. Is this Martha?" After a pause, he says, "I thought so. Listen, I need some help. You all have a body down there that I need a cause of death for—Maisy Tucker. I thought your people might have completed the autopsy and the report was just waiting to be typed up . . . Sure, I'll hold." He covers the mouthpiece and winks at Sheriff Harris.

In a moment he says, "Interesting. Thanks a bunch, Martha. I'll take you out to eat at the Peabody sometime. Take care. Bye."

Placing the receiver in the cradle, he looks at the sheriff and says, "Maisy's body was full of this new street drug called Quaalude. Enough in her to possibly kill her. But that's not how she died. She died of drowning. Her lungs were full of water."

A low whistle comes from Jessie.

"So," the sheriff reasons, "the charge will definitely be murder, not just illegal disposing of a dead body, because he could have used that defense. You know, 'She overdosed, I panicked and dumped her body.'"

"Exactly," Whalen agrees. "But motive, that's the hitch pin in this case. If we can't find a motive, it's never going to fly past the grand jury."

CHAPTER SIXTY-TWO

Ella stops at the four-way stop sign beside the courthouse. There is no traffic coming or waiting behind her, so there is no need to hurry.

In the silence of the hesitation, Tucker says, "Will ya'll go with me t' Maisy's?"

"Now?" Ella asks.

"Now," Tucker says.

Peering at Smiley Carter in the rearview mirror, Ella raises her eyebrows in an unasked question.

"Sure," he says. "I'll go with you two, if you wants."

After checking the traffic again, Ella says, "Then it's to Maisy's we go."

Tucker unlocks the front door with the key Sheriff Harris gave her and cautiously opens it. The air inside hasn't moved since the electricity was disconnected months ago.

The three explorers stand inside, waiting for their eyes to adjust to the dimness.

Ella looks to Tucker for a cue on how she wants to proceed. When she sees Tucker assume her closed stance with arms folded across her chest, she says, "Do you know what you'd like to do or where you'd like to begin?"

When Tucker doesn't respond, Ella gestures at Carter. "Let's open the curtains and windows."

Thankful to have something to do, Carter moves toward a window. "Yes, ma'am. That's a good idea."

As fresh air and natural light drift in, Tucker unfolds her arms. "I don't know what I'm supposed t' be doin'. I don't know th' person who used t' live here. She died t' me a long time ago. It's like I'm a burglar 'r somethin'."

Looking around the apartment, Ella says, "Maybe you will find some things here that you'd like to keep for yourself or give to the children. What about her dishes and things? Would you like to have those?"

"I s'pose," Tucker says reluctantly, looking toward the kitchen. "Carter, why dontcha stack all of 'em on th' table. We'll git some boxes later an' take 'em t' th' house."

"Good idea," Carter says. He reaches into the cabinets and begins pulling out the plates.

"There might be some pretty hair things that April would like to have," Ella says.

"Go ahead," Tucker replies. "Help yoreself t' whatever y' find. You might like t' have some o' her fancy clothes, too."

Glancing down at her breastless chest, Ella smiles wryly and says, "I don't think Maisy's clothes will fit me."

"Reckon you're right," Tucker agrees. She slowly walks from room to room while Ella and Carter go about their missions.

In a few minutes, Tucker calls out to them, "Y' know, there's one thing I'd like t' have. When she left home I give 'er th' only thing I ever had that b'longed to m' mother. It was a family Bible with fancy pictures in it. If'n ya'll see it, let m' know."

His hands full of glasses, Carter calls back, "Will do."

"We'll both help you look for it," Ella adds and waves Carter to join her.

For the next fifteen minutes, there is an intense search for the family Bible. Each newly discovered cubbyhole turns out to be an empty promise.

Finally they all assemble in the living room, hands on hips. They scan again, looking for any overlooked hiding places.

"I went through every book in that bookcase," Ella says, "but I didn't reach on the top of it. Could it be up there?"

Carter walks to the bookcase, reaches to his full height, and says, "Let ol' Smiley Carter see what he can find."

His hand pats across the top. Suddenly he stops and his eyes brighten. "I found something. It's big."

With a grunt, he grips and lifts the object he has found. Once it clears the edge of the bookcase, it is obvious it is the family Bible.

"Lordy!" Tucker exclaims.

"You found it," Ella cries out.

As Carter lowers it for all to see, an envelope escapes and flutters to the floor. All eyes follow its descent. In bold, three-inch letters are printed the words, FOR TUCKER.

Forgetting about the Bible, Ella and Carter watch Tucker as she slowly bends and picks up the envelope.

As if there were a need to clarify the clear inscription, Tucker reads aloud, "For Tucker."

Bending for a closer look, Ella says, "There's something written on the back, too."

Tucker turns the envelope over and reads, "To be opened upon my death."

Ella gasps.

"Jesus Christ!" Carter says and takes a step back.

"What's this mean?" Tucker asks no one in particular.

"Why didn't the investigators find this?" Ella asks. Answering her own question, she surmises, "I guess they just didn't think about looking way up there."

"What's this mean?" Tucker says again while looking at Ella.

Ella says, "Evidently Maisy wrote this before she died, sealed it up, and intended it to be read by you only, just in case she died before you."

"This here's a bad sign," Carter says, concern edging his voice. Shaking his head, he adds, "I gots me a bad feeling about this."

"Let's just sit down for a minute," Ella says.

Carter chooses the loveseat, Ella an armchair, and Tucker the recliner. Everyone sits on the front edge of their resting place. Apprehension tinges the air.

Tucker slowly rotates the envelope in endless loops. Staring at the envelope, she says, "You mean m' Maisy thought someone was a'goin' t' kill 'er? That's why she done wrote this 'ere letter?"

"That's what it sounds like to me," Ella answers. "Maybe the letter will provide answers to all the questions surrounding her murder."

Handing the envelope to Ella, Tucker says, "Here, you read it out loud. I can't do it. Besides, I ain't much of a reader."

Furrows crease Ella's forehead. Shaking her head, she says, "Oh no, Tucker. This is for you. It's written to you. It may be very personal. Please don't ask me to do this."

In a tone of voice only heard by April in quiet moments, Tucker says, "Ella, please, you have to do this for me."

As if reaching for a poison dart, Ella takes the envelope between her thumb and index finger. Holding it up toward the window, she spies the position of the letter inside, then tears off the opposite end and pulls out a sheet of paper.

CHAPTER SIXTY-THREE

Ella slides the letter out and lets the envelope fall to the floor. As she unfolds it, it is apparent that it was handwritten on yellow sheets of paper from a legal pad. At first glance, Ella is amazed at the beauty and style of the penmanship.

She finds no salutation as an opening. Clearing her throat, she begins reading:

> *Since you are reading this, it means it finally happened. I'm dead like you've wanted me to be since I was born. I hope you are happy now.*
>
> *All I ever wanted from you was a kind word. I gave up trying to please you a long time ago.*

Ella refolds the letter. "Tucker, I don't think I should be reading this. It is a very private letter."

"She ain't gonna say nothin' I ain't heared afore," Tucker replies. "It ain't no skin off my nose if you hear it, too."

"Very well then," Ella says. She opens the letter again and continues reading.

I know you never have been proud of me and the way I've lived my life, but I did the best I could. At least I never lived off of welfare like you.

I will give you credit for taking care of my kids. I know they love me and that's all that matters to me. I was planning on getting all of them back real soon. But if you are reading this letter, then it looks like they are yours for good.

I think my kids deserve to know who their daddies are. I was going to tell them eventually, but now I guess that's up to you.

All three men would probably deny the child was theirs, but I know what I know. There ain't no doubt.

August's daddy is Smiley Carter.

"What the—?!" Carter bolts out of his chair.

Ella repeats her plea, "I am very uncomfortable reading this letter."

"Th' cork's done been popped now," Tucker says. "Ain't no sense in stopping. Sit down, Carter."

Smiley Carter slowly sits back down, his eyes wide and reddening.

Ella returns her attention to the letter.

August's daddy is Smiley Carter. I was only with him one time. We had a few drinks together and one thing led to another. You know how it is. The thing I don't understand is that ever since he had sex with me, it's seemed like he hated me.

Carter mumbles something unintelligible. Ella glances at him, but continues reading.

March's daddy was with the carnival that came through town in June, the summer before March was born. I think his name was Scotty. He was really cute. He promised me he would take me with him when the carnival left town. But he skipped out on me and I never heard from him again. Well, that's his loss.

April's father was the only man I really loved. He took care of me like no one ever did. He made me feel alive and wanted. I always thought we would marry. His name is—

Ella's hand flies to her mouth. A muffled "No" escapes through the closed door her hand tried to place on her mouth.

Slowly withdrawing her hand from her mouth, she begins reading in a whisper.

His name is Cade McDade. Yes, Judge Jack's son. Crazy, isn't it? The children of two people who hate each other end up screwing each other. I got a laugh out of it quite often.

I decided to blackmail Cade, but I think I may have played my hand wrong. I didn't count on him being as crazy as I am. I think he's going to try to kill me. That's why I decided to write this letter.

I'll probably see him in hell.

The one and only Amazing!

The silence that fills the room acts like a vacuum, removing all the air. The three visitors look shell-shocked.

Ella's complexion is as pasty as it was the day she moved into the McDaniel place beside Tucker.

Smiley Carter sags heavily into the loveseat, his eyes unfocused.

Her mouth agape, Tucker reaches to her face with a trembling hand and slowly removes her glasses.

Finally, Carter speaks. "It just don't seem possible August is my boy."

His comment jerks Tucker and Ella out of their individual mental and emotional maelstrom triggered by the letter.

Ella sees Tucker's fists tighten and her cheeks flush.

"Smiley Carter." Tucker spits his name out like a stream of her tobacco juice. "After all these years of bein' friends, you and Maisy . . ." Tucker lurches to her feet and bolts toward Carter. "You sorry S.O.B.!"

Carter's mouth and eyes gape at the approaching Tucker. He throws up his arms in self-defense as she crashes into him. Tucker's momentum flips the loveseat onto its back, spilling them both to the floor.

"Tucker!" Ella screams. She jumps up and races to where the two are grappling on the floor.

Tucker's hands grip Carter's throat. He seizes her wrists and tries to pry her loose.

Grabbing Tucker's shirt, Ella yells, "Stop it, Tucker! Stop! Get off of him and calm down."

Carter rolls in order to pin Tucker underneath him. The movement catches Ella's legs and she collapses into an end table like a felled tree. The lamp clatters to the floor and Ella cries out in pain.

Her sharp cry knifes through Tucker's adrenaline-filled brain. Releasing her grip on Carter, she barks, "Git off'n me! Ella's hurt!"

Carter quickly obeys and they turn their attention to Ella, who has pushed herself into a seated position.

Taking Ella's hand in his, Carter asks, "Miss Ella, are you all right?"

Tucker sits beside her and puts her arm around her shoulders. "I'm sorry, Ella. I lost m' head. It's my fault. You okay?"

Rubbing her knee, Ella says, "Yes I'm okay. I just banged my knee on that coffee table. Help me up."

Carter and Tucker each grab an arm and help Ella to her feet. Carter slowly lifts the loveseat back in place. They return to their seats.

Tucker picks up the letter and says, "Y' think we better show this t' th' sheriff?"

There is a pause as each of them considers the implications of such a move.

"I don't think we have a choice," Ella replies.

"Seems to me it's the only thing we can do," Carter agrees.

A look of astonishment spreads across Ella's face. "Do you know what I just realized? If what this letter says is true, April is my granddaughter, too."

CHAPTER SIXTY-FOUR

Sitting in the leather chair in front of his father's desk, Cade McDade lifts the glass to his lips. He gulps the alcohol, hoping the burning effect will dull the power of the verbal tsunami that is about to inundate him.

Judge Jack McDade slams his open palm on the desk. The report sounds like a gunshot. His face is crimson.

Looking at Cade with disgust, Judge Jack roars, "Maisy Tucker! You and Maisy Tucker! I cannot believe my ears. You could have your choice of any woman in the county and you choose a low-class, two-bit whore. Someone who's spread her legs more times than I've spread mustard on a sandwich.

"What in the world were you thinking about?! No, don't answer that question. It's pretty obvious what you were thinking about."

The judge pauses to pour himself another drink. After draining it and wiping his lips with the back of his hand, he bellows, "You fool!" He hurls the empty glass at Cade's head.

The glass sails just wide of the mark, missing a stunned Cade by inches, and shatters against the wall behind him. Looking pale, he stands up. "Good god, Dad, calm down! Are you trying to kill me?"

"That's not a bad idea," Judge Jack snaps. "You know, something else I don't understand is why you decided to kill her just because she was going to tell your wife you'd been sleeping with her. I'm confident Julie knows all about your indiscretions. But she's too enamored with her comfortable life to kick you out."

Cade's face begins to redden. He avoids eye contact with his dad. "I guess I just got nervous. Maisy had a vicious mouth. I didn't know how much trouble she might stir up. And I was afraid Whalen might fire me, if he heard about it."

Cautiously taking his seat again, he continues. "There's no way they can pin this on me. All they have is one handprint on a wall in her apartment. But I get this feeling that Whalen and the sheriff are dead set on accusing me of the murder anyway."

The judge runs his hands through his hair. "All right, so let me be sure I've got this straight. Maisy actually died of an overdose of that drug, right?"

"Exactly," Cade replies. "I put enough in her drink to knock out an elephant. It should look like she died at her own hands."

"Okay," the judge says, "but what about Smiley Carter's statement about seeing you in the bottoms with a boat and something bundled up?"

A derisive laugh erupts from Cade. "The word of a nigger about something he saw? At night? We both know that will never stand up under any kind of vigorous cross-examination."

Judge Jack's expression does not mirror Cade's sudden light-heartedness. "What I'm guessing you don't know," the judge says, "is that Smiley Carter is a highly decorated veteran of World War Two. He was a sniper. Everyone knows his eyesight is keener than anyone's around."

The smile slides off Cade's face like melting wax down the side of a candle. "Oh," he says weakly.

He eases to the edge of his seat and, placing his fists on his father's desk, says, "All we have to do is go see Mother and convince her to give me an alibi for that night. I'm sure they will talk to her. Once she backs up my alibi, they'll have no case."

"And even if she doesn't," the judge muses, "they don't have a motive for the murder, do they? Is there anything else you're not telling me?"

Pouring another drink, Cade replies, "Absolutely not. They can fish all day and they won't find a motive for me murdering Maisy."

"Nonetheless," the judge says, "we need to have all bases covered. We'll go see your mother first thing in the morning. I'll pick you up at eight."

Sitting in Shorty's Diner, Whalen Kennedy listens intently as Sheriff Ron Harris tells him about the letter to Tucker that was found in Maisy's apartment.

Incredulous, Whalen asks, "You've seen the letter yourself?"

"With my own two eyes," the sheriff replies. "Tucker and Ella brought it to the jail. First of all I couldn't believe we or the TBI hadn't found it during our search of Maisy's apartment. We turned that place upside down. And when I read the letter I felt like an explosion took place in my head."

"How many more twists is this case going to have?" Whalen asks.

"I know what you mean," the sheriff says. "Think about it: one of Tucker's grandchildren is also the grandchild of Judge Jack McDade. I don't know what word to use to describe that."

"Our old high school English teacher, Miss Perry, would say it is a perfect example of irony," Whalen says. "Where is the letter now?"

"I locked it up in the safe in my office."

Deep in thought with the implications of this new evidence, they fall silent while diving into their hamburgers and drinks.

Breaking the silence, Whalen says, "This certainly explains all the magazine articles we found in Maisy's apartment on DNA testing and paternity tests. Especially that most recent one on HLA typing."

"HLA typing? What's that?" Sheriff Harris asks.

"It's the latest test for proving paternity. It's actually very accurate and is even admissible in court. The first of its kind."

The sheriff whistles. "I'll bet you anything that she threatened him with a paternity suit."

Nodding, Whalen says, "I'd say we've discovered our motive for murder."

"But what about his alibi for the night of February fourteenth? How could he have been out at Ella McDade's and be in the bottoms at the same time?"

Whalen's shoulders sag. "I forgot about that. But if he lied to us about everything else, who's to say he wouldn't lie about that, too?"

"Sure he could. But he would have to know that we would check out his alibi."

"Unless," Whalen says, "he panicked and made up his alibi on the spot, right when we questioned him."

"Which means he'll be heading out to his mother's very shortly to talk her into helping him."

Whalen pulls back the cuff of his shirt to look at his watch and says, "Wow, it's nearly ten o'clock. I don't want to go out there and wake her up. Let's go in the morning. I'll pick you up at nine."

"I'll be waiting," the sheriff replies.

CHAPTER SIXTY-FIVE

As she places the last rinsed plate in the dish drainer, Ella cocks her head at the sound of a car door closing. She pulls the drain plug in the sink to let the dirty dishwater run out, wipes her hands on her apron, and starts for the front window.

Before she arrives at the window, there is a polite knock on the front door. Opening it, she finds her Cade, smiling broadly.

"Hello, Mother," he says. Taking a step inside, he says, "Can we come in?"

A frown slaps itself on her face, chasing away the relaxed expression that had been there only moments before. The *we* has triggered her adrenal system. Every fiber in her body is on alert.

Not waiting for her to respond to the question, Cade and Judge Jack walk past her.

She recognizes Judge Jack's furrowed brow as a sign of concern that stands in direct contrast to Cade's lighthearted air.

After she shuts the door and turns to face them, Cade embraces her and kisses her forehead.

"How have you been, Mother? I've been so busy with the family I haven't been out to see you like I should have. But you look great!" Moving to the couch, he says, "Can we sit down?"

With a wary eye, Ella joins Cade on the couch, while Judge Jack sits in an armchair across from them.

"So what's wrong?" Ella asks.

"Wrong?" Cade says. A wounded expression replaces his smile. "Why do you ask that? Can't a son come visit his mother without there being something wrong?"

"Of course he can," Ella replies coolly, "but not *my* son. My son only comes by when he's in trouble or when he wants something."

Cade is unable to withstand her piercing, unflinching gaze. He turns to his father with a pleading look, but Ella surprises him by grabbing his chin between her thumb and fingers and jerking his head to face her. "Look at *me*. *You* came to see *me*. For once in your life, be a man and quit expecting others to bail you out."

Seeing the color in Ella's cheeks, Judge Jack says gently, "Now Ella—"

Extending her other arm in her ex-husband's direction, with her open palm toward him, she says curtly, "And *you* stay out of this."

Relinquishing her hold on Cade, she says, "Now, tell me why you are here."

"Honestly," Cade begins, "there is no real trouble. It's more like imagined trouble. It's about what someone thinks I did. The sheriff and Whalen have it in their head that I had something to do with Maisy's murder."

Feigning surprise, Ella says, "You and Maisy? Why would anyone think that you ever had anything to do with that woman? Everyone knows her reputation, and that it is well deserved."

Hanging his head, Cade comes out with it. "Uh, well, you are right about that, but I have to be honest and admit that I was involved with Maisy some time ago for a very brief time."

Slowly turning her head toward Judge Jack, Ella says in an icy tone, "Well the apple surely doesn't fall far from the tree in this family, does it? You boys just can't seem to keep your pants zipped up, can you?"

"Now look, Ella," Judge Jack says, "there's no use in talking like that."

Ella's eyes throw a dagger at Judge Jack that seems to immobilize him. "Really?" she asks. "There's no need in telling the truth? Is that what bothers you, Jack? Listening to the truth and hearing what kind of example you've set for your son?"

"Let me tell you what's going on, Mother," Cade says, attempting to defuse the situation. "The TBI found my handprint in Maisy's apartment. But that only tells them I was there at some point in time. It can't be dated. That's what made them turn their attention to me in the first place.

"But what really set them on my trail is some story concocted by Smiley Carter. He told them that he saw me in the bottoms one night in February while he was night fishing. He said I put something in a boat and went up the river. When I returned, supposedly there was nothing in the boat. He said he could positively identify me as the person he saw. Can you hear how this is all a bunch of conjecture?"

"That's an interesting story," Ella replies. "But why in the world would you supposedly want to murder Maisy?"

"Exactly!" Cade responds. "There is no motive. That's where it all falls apart."

Judge Jack clears his throat, looks at Ella, and asks, "May I say something?"

"Certainly," she says.

"What really brings us here," he says, "is that in his statement Smiley Carter gives a specific date that he saw Cade, and thereby a specific date for when the murder might have taken place."

Eyes widening, Ella says, "Oh really? What date is it?"

"The night of February fourteenth," Cade answers.

An uneasy silence falls on the group. Ella sees that both men are looking at her expectantly. She looks from one to the other, trying to discern their hidden motives.

"Well?" she says.

"Well what?" Cade replies.

"Well, where were you on February fourteeth? Tell them where you were and that will clear all this up, won't it? If you weren't where he said you were and if you don't have a motive for murder, then that shuts down their investigation of you. Right?"

Cade blushes. "And that's where the problem is. You see, if I reveal where I was on the fourteenth, it's going to compromise someone else. And I really don't want to do that."

Ella laughs.

Both men look at her with shocked expressions.

"I don't think this is a laughing matter," Judge Jack says.

Regaining her composure, Ella says, "I'm laughing because both of you are laughable. You've come here to ask me to give you an alibi for that night. Am I right?"

Tearing up, Cade says, "I was hoping that I could count on you to help me. You're the only place I can turn."

Like a striking snake, Ella slaps Cade. "Do not patronize me. Do not try to play me like one of your pitiful whores."

Judge Jack springs out of his chair and yells, "Now hold on just a minute. Who the hell do you think you are?"

Ella stands up and says, "I'm the woman who knows—"

The sudden sound of two car doors closing has the effect of closing Ella's mouth before she completes her thought.

CHAPTER SIXTY-SIX

The sound of the car doors has taken everyone's attention and sent it scurrying outside, wondering who the muffled voices approaching the house belong to.

Ella voices the question that's on everyone's tongue: "Who in the world could that be?"

As if the question releases a tension spring, there is a knock on the door. And though the knock is expected, everyone jumps.

As Ella walks past Judge Jack to answer the door, he grabs her arm and jerks her around to face him. "Whoever it is, send them on their way. We've got business to settle here."

A muted cry of pain escapes from Ella as she wrenches free of him. She straightens her clothes, walks to the door, and opens it.

His Stetson hat set squarely on his head and his face grim, Sheriff Ron Harris says, "Good morning, Ella."

Backing up and opening the door wide, Ella says, "Please come in." Seeing Whalen Kennedy behind the sheriff, she adds, "Hi, Whalen. I didn't see you at first. Both of you, please come in."

Recognizing the sheriff's voice, Judge Jack positions himself beside Cade to face the two new visitors. "Hello, Sheriff. Hello,

Whalen," he greets them. "Surprised to see you two boys out this early."

The sheriff gives an almost imperceptible nod. "Morning, Judge. Cade."

With a relaxed manner, Whalen says, "And I'm not surprised to see you here, Judge. Not at all. And good morning to you, too, Cade."

Moving past her newest guests, Ella says, "Let me get a couple of straight-back chairs from the kitchen so that everyone will have a place to sit."

Reluctantly taking his eyes off Cade, the sheriff says, "Let me help you, Ella," and follows her. He brings two chairs back from the kitchen and offers one to Whalen.

"Let's all have a seat," Whalen says.

Cade and Judge Jack sit on the couch. Whalen and the sheriff sit side by side facing the couch. Ella sits in an armchair where she can easily see both sets of men.

Looking at Cade, Whalen asks, "Did we interrupt something? I thought I heard loud voices when we got out of the car."

Smiling, Cade replies, "Not a thing. This is just a family get-together."

"Let's cut all the BS," Judge Jack says. "Why are you two out here?"

Before Whalen can answer, Ella speaks up. "This is my house. Who is here or who isn't here is no concern of yours. That's my business. Maybe I invited Whalen and Ron over for coffee this morning."

Judge Jack's cheeks turn crimson. His jaw juts out. "My apologies, Ella. Of course, you are right."

A slight look of satisfaction flits across Ella's features. Looking toward Whalen and the sheriff, she says, "So what brings you two out here on this pretty morning?"

"Originally," Whalen begins, "we wanted to ask you a few questions. But since Cade is here, I think I'd like to ask him some questions."

"That's fine," Ella says. Turning to Cade she says, "I'm sure Cade wouldn't mind, would you?"

Looking defiant, Cade says, "I've got nothing to hide."

"That's encouraging," Whalen says. "How long ago did you first start seeing Maisy?"

"Huh?"

"It's a simple question," the sheriff chimes in.

Looking uncertain, Cade says, "I'm not sure. I'd have to think about it."

Crossing his legs and leaning back in his chair, Whalen says, "I'm in no hurry. We'll give you all the time you need."

Confusion deepens the wrinkles around Judge Jack's eyes as he looks at Cade. "Just tell the man what he wants to know. What's your problem?"

Cade flinches at his father's bark. "Okay, okay. I'd say it was probably seven or so years ago."

The sheriff and Whalen look at each other.

"That would fit," the sheriff says.

"Fit what?" Judge Jack asks.

Uncrossing his legs and leaning forward in his chair, Whalen says, "You both know that the biggest concern in murder cases is motive. That's where we were stumped in Maisy's case. Why would someone murder her? And then out of the blue we got our first lucky break when Smiley Carter revealed his story."

A brief, scoffing laugh escapes Judge Jack. "You both know that that man's story will never stand up in court."

Ignoring the judge, Whalen keeps his eyes fastened on Cade. "And yesterday we got our second break. It gave us the motive we'd been looking for."

A pause as pregnant as a woman at full term holds everyone's attention hostage.

A thin sheen of sweat has popped out on Cade's forehead and above his upper lip.

"It was the darnedest thing," Whalen continues. "All our investigators missed it when they went through Maisy's apartment."

Whalen's eyes bore into Cade's. "How many people know that Maisy's daughter, April, is your child?"

Cade slumps back into the couch, his face ashen.

Judge Jack's eyes bulge in disbelief. "What?!" he roars. He leaps to his feet. "That's the most preposterous thing I've ever heard. You're just making things up now. I thought better of you, Whalen."

Without warning, the front door explodes into the living room, sending splinters of wood into the air. Ripped from its hinges, the door lands heavily and slides into an armchair.

Holding her axe handle cocked like a baseball bat, Tucker steps through the open doorway.

CHAPTER SIXTY-SEVEN

Like a bull charging a matador, Tucker lumbers across the floor toward Judge Jack.

Jumping from her chair, Ella screams, "Tucker, no!"

Judge Jack's eyes fill with terror and he collapses on the couch beside his stricken son.

Sheriff Harris pushes past Whalen and steps in front of Tucker. "Halt right there, Tucker," he says firmly.

Her view of Judge Jack blocked by the sheriff, Tucker stops suddenly. Her eyes refocus on the sheriff.

When he sees he has her attention, he says calmly, "Everything is under control here. There's no need for any violence. Okay?"

Slowly lowering the axe handle, Tucker blinks rapidly. She looks at Ella. "You okay?"

Nodding, Ella says, "Yes, I'm fine."

Looking at the broken door, Tucker says, "I'm sorry. I can fix th' door fer y'. I heared shoutin' an' thought there was trouble."

Ella inhales deeply and says to Tucker, "Go get a chair from the kitchen and join us."

By the time Tucker comes back with a chair, the color has returned to the faces of both Cade and Judge Jack.

Scooting forward, Cade says, "Where in the world did you get the idea that April is my child?"

Whalen holds up a piece of paper and says, "In this letter that Maisy wrote. Tucker found it when she went through Maisy's things at the apartment yesterday. In it, she says very plainly that, beyond a shadow of a doubt, you are April's father."

Waving his hand dismissively, Judge Jack says, "How do you know Tucker didn't write it herself and make up the story?"

"Because," Ella speaks up, "I was there when the letter was found."

Through clenched teeth, Judge Jack says to her, "You knew about this? And didn't say anything to either of us? What kind of game are you trying to play?"

Deflecting the attention from Ella, Sheriff Harris interjects, "So Cade, if you started seeing Maisy around seven years ago, that'd make April just about the right age, wouldn't it? When did she first tell you about April?"

"You don't have to answer that," Judge Jack cautions.

"That's true," Whalen agrees. "You don't have to answer anything. So far you haven't been charged with anything. However, I'm convinced we have the motive in hand." He turns to face Ella. "The only thing we have to establish is whether Cade has a legitimate alibi. He has told us that he was with you on the night of the murder. February fourteenth, to be exact."

All eyes turn to Ella.

Judge Jack stands up. "Ella, may I talk to you in private for a moment?"

Tapping her axe handle on the wooden floor, Tucker says, "Th' onliest person you're gonna have a private talk with is me an' my axe handle. I've laid wood t' y' once before, an' I'll do it agin."

Rubbing his jaw, the judge looks to the sheriff for help.

"Don't look at me," the sheriff says. "I've come between you once this morning, but I don't think I'll do it a second time. You're on your own. You just do what you think best."

The corners of Tucker's mouth turn up in a smile.

Sitting down, the judge looks at Ella and says, "Then I'll say to you what I would have preferred to say in private. These men are about to arrest your son and charge him for murder in the first degree. If convicted, he could receive the death sentence. All you need to do is tell them the truth. Tell them that he came out here on the fourteenth to celebrate Valentine's Day with you, just like he told them he did. Nobody will doubt your word."

Holding his hands out toward her, he adds, "It's all up to you."

An electric silence falls on the room as everyone looks at Ella.

Ella bows her head and smoothes the wrinkles out of her apron. When she raises her head, there are tears in her eyes. Clearing her throat she looks at Cade, and says, "When you were a child, my world seemed perfect. The future was bright. I thought I had everything I wanted.

"But the older you got, the more you came under the influence and spell of your father. And that," she glances at Judge Jack, "proved to be your undoing. Your entitled attitude, narcissism, and manipulative ways have made you as dangerous a person as him." A tear slips from the cradle of her lower eyelid and rolls down her cheek. "And that saddens me.

"The double blow of getting cancer and being divorced felt like my personal tolling of the bell. When I moved out here, I thought my life was over. And when I learned my only neighbor was the infamous Tucker, I decided life could get no worse. Death would have been a blessing."

She reaches toward Tucker's lap, holds Tucker's thick fingers, and squeezes, then looks at each of her visitors in turn. "Let me tell you all about this woman. I believe her to be the most incredible example of determination I have ever witnessed. She's rough and she's crude. And because of that she's judged harshly. But that's because no one knows all the incredible odds she's had to overcome."

The tears will not be held back any longer. They begin streaming down Ella's face. She looks at Tucker and sees her lip quivering. A solitary tear finds its way down Tucker's cheek and hangs tenaciously to her chin.

Turning back to the men listening, her voice rising, Ella says, "Tucker has become the truest friend I've ever had. Cade, you and your father expect me to turn my back on her and lie for you? The hell I will! For Tucker's sake, I will tell the truth."

She looks at Sheriff Harris and says, "Cade never came to my house on February fourteenth. As a matter of fact, tonight's the first time I've seen him since Christmas."

Standing, she turns a scathing look on Cade. "May God have mercy on your soul."

Taking his cue, the sheriff stands. "Cade McDade, you are under arrest for the murder of Maisy Tucker."

As the sheriff reads Cade his rights, Ella feels a tug on her elbow. Turning, she sees Tucker, cheeks wet with tears, standing with her arms held open.

As the two women embrace, Tucker says into her friend's ear, "I love you, Ella."

ACKNOWLEDGMENTS

Many people deserve a bow of thanks for helping me bring Tucker's story to the world.

The girls in The Gang (Brenda, Joan, Judy, and Tenia), who were the first ones to read Tucker's story and made me believe it was worthy of sharing with the public.

Danielle Marshall, my editor at Amazon Publishing. Thank you for finding me and taking a chance on me!

David Downing, my developmental editor. A man with a sharp eye for detail, who made helpful suggestions.

The members of the Women's Fiction Crit Group on Authonomy, who gave my original manuscript a thorough reaming out and taught me to see how to be a better writer.

But most importantly, all thanks to God, who has blessed me far beyond measure, giving me talents I didn't know I had until I stumbled upon them.

ABOUT THE AUTHOR

David Johnson has worked in the helping professions for over thirty-five years. He is a licensed marriage and family therapist with a master's degree in social work and over a decade of experience as a minister. In addition to the four novels comprising the Tucker series, he has authored several nonfiction books, including *Navigating the Passages of Marriage* and *Real People, Real Problems,* and has published numerous articles in national and local media. David also maintains an active blog at www.thefrontwindow.wordpress.com. When he's not writing, he is likely making music as the conductor of the David Johnson Chorus.

Made in the USA
Monee, IL
21 July 2024